THE MONSTER WAR

A TALE OF THE KINGS' BLADES

THE MONSTER WAR

A TALE OF THE KINGS' BLADES

DAVE DUNCAN

OPEN ROAD

INTEGRATED MEDIA

NEW YORK

Contains three previously published titles:
Sir Stalwart Copyright © 1999 by Dave Duncan
The Crooked House Copyright © 2000 by Dave Duncan
Silvercloak Copyright © 2001 by Dave Duncan

978-1-4976-4046-7

This edition published in 2014 by Open Road Integrated Media, Inc.
345 Hudson Street
New York, NY 10014
www.openroadmedia.com

To Anne McCaffrey:

Because you write wonderful stories,
Because you are a wonderful person,
And because when I was offered the chance
to write this book and asked your advice,
you told me to go for it.

The Minstrel Boy to the war is gone,
* In the ranks of death you'll find him;*
His father's sword he has girded on,
* And his wild harp slung behind him.*

—THOMAS MOORE

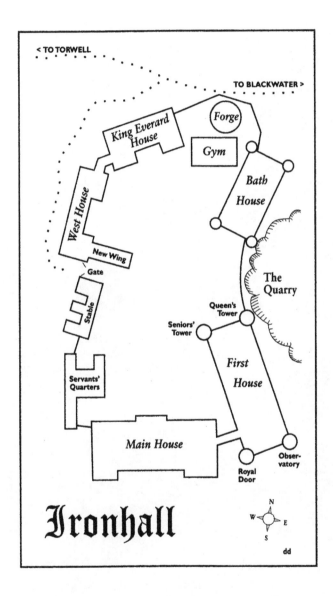

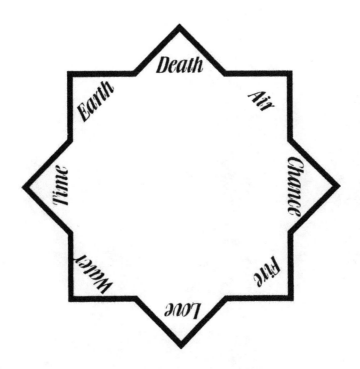

THE MONSTER WAR

A TALE OF THE KINGS' BLADES

BOOK ONE

SIR STALWART

1

Rude Awakening

ABOUT AN HOUR BEFORE DAWN SOME IDIOT
BLEW a deafening blast on a bugle right under the
dormitory window. Nine boys lurched up out of deep sleep
with yells of alarm, then registered the clattering of iron-
clad hooves on the cobbles of the courtyard. Nine blankets
flew off, eighteen bare feet hit the boards at almost the same
instant, nine bodies dived for the window.

Stalwart prided himself on being the fastest man in the
senior class, but he was also the smallest. He did reach the
window first, only to be hurled aside by a flying wedge of
superior muscle. No matter! It was still too dark outside
to see much, and he could guess what was happening—the
King had come to Ironhall. Judging by the racket, he was
being escorted by the entire Royal Guard, a hundred strong.

"When did the King ever travel by night before?" someone
cried, probably Rufus.

"Never!" That was Orvil, who was Prime, meaning he
had been in Ironhall longer than anyone. "And he used to
bring a dozen Blades with him, no more."

Eighteen eyes shone wide in the gloom as the senior class
thought about King Ambrose skulking around by night and
needing so many bodyguards. Nine naked or near-naked

youngsters shivered in the predawn chill. The unheralded royal visit was a chilling reminder of the Monster War. For the last eight months or so—starting with the terrible Night of Dogs—unknown sorcerers had repeatedly tried to kill the King of Chivial, killing many of the Blades in his Guard in the process. The only reason he ever came to Ironhall was to enlist new Blades, who would be chosen from the senior class—the very nine present in that dormitory. How many would he take this time? Tonight at midnight he would strike a sword through their hearts in a magical ritual to bind them to absolute loyalty, companions in the Loyal and Ancient Order of the King's Blades.

How many of them?

"Well, don't all stand there with your tongues hanging out!" yelled Panther. "Get dressed! Your King wants you!"

Eight seniors sprang into motion, quickly followed by Panther himself as he realized he wasn't wearing anything either. Someone struck a flint. Spark on tinder, flame on candle, many candle flames...With nervy haste the nine seniors rummaged in hampers to find their best and cleanest—breeches, hose, shirts, doublets, jerkins. Cloaks and boots and hats. Comb hair. Those who needed to shave began doing so—painfully, because no one dared run and fetch hot water lest he be absent when the summons came. There was some angry jostling around the candles and tiny mirrors.

Shaving was not yet one of Stalwart's problems. He sat on the edge of his bed and hugged himself, miserably uncertain whether the knot in his innards was wild excitement or just terror. He *wanted* to be chosen this time! Of course he wanted to be chosen! Why else had he spent the last four years working his heart out here in Ironhall if not to become a Blade? True, he was the youngest of the seniors, but he ranked fifth in seniority, and candidates always left Ironhall in the order in which they had come. He was worthy! Day in and day out he was the best on the fencing ground. And yet...Until the Night of Dogs a career in the Royal Guard had been a sinecure, easy pickings, ten years of lounging around the court charming beautiful ladies. Now it was as dangerous as lion wrestling. Two dozen members of the Order had died in the last half year. Ironhall was rushing boys through training faster than it had in centuries. None of the current seniors, even Prime, had been in the school for the standard five years.

"There's no great hurry," Orvil said squeakily, although he had been moving as fast as anyone. "First the King talks with Grand Master and tells him how many of us he wants. Then Grand Master sends the Brat to fetch us." Everyone knew this, because he had told them at least a dozen times. He had been present the last time, two months ago. "They always send for one more than they are going to bind, so he can—"

The door flew open. Two shavers cut themselves and screamed in fury. In walked Sir Dreadnought, Deputy Commander of the Guard.

"How many?" everyone yelled in unison.

Dreadnought closed the door and folded his arms. He surveyed the room in the dim light, smiling grimly. "As many of you as Grand Master can bear to part with. I just came to make sure none of you goes sneaking down to the kitchens. A whole day's fasting before a binding, remember."

The discomfort inside Stalwart, which had been worry, instantly became ravening hunger instead. Out in the corridor a mob of chattering, jabbering juniors headed for the stairs—so-pranos and beansprouts. The seniors clustered closer around Dreadnought, most of them still soaped for shaving.

"Have there been more attacks on the King?" Orvil asked.

"State secret. I'm not allowed to tell you that until you're bound." Dreadnought was a good man, a superb swordsman. He had won the King's Cup for the second time that summer, which meant he was probably the finest fencer in the entire world at the moment. On his jerkin he sported a four-pointed diamond-studded badge to show he was a member of the White Star, the highest order of chivalry in the country. Very few Blades had ever been admitted to the Star, but he had turned up wearing this wonderful thing two months ago. He'd conceded only that he had won it "killing something," but the other men in the Guard had added blood-curdling details of a shambling half-human monstrosity that had gone after the King when he was out hunting. Its fangs and talons had disposed of two other Blades and a horse before Dreadnought slew it. An excellent man!

A bit lacking in humor, maybe. You could tell a lot about a Blade by the name he gave his sword, and his was called *Honor.* Dull!

"And you *still* don't know who's doing this?" Orvil persisted.

"If the Guard knew that, sonny, blood would be shed and balefires lit. No matter how good their sorcery is."

Stalwart asked, "How many swords have you brought back this time?"

Dreadnought gave him a long, thoughtful look. Then he said softly, "Keep it to yourselves—eight."

The seniors exchanged shocked glances. When a Blade died his sword was returned to Ironhall to hang for evermore among the thousands of others in the great sky of swords. Elderly, retired Blades—the knights in the Order—died off all the time, but not at that rate, not eight in only two months!

"Well?" Dreadnought said mockingly. "Anyone want to chicken out? If you're going to turn yellow, you'd better do it now, while the going is good—run for the hills!"

Nobody moved.

"No cowards here!" Orvil said proudly.

2

Rejected

A S THE SUN ROSE OVER THE BARREN HILLS OF Starkmoor, Grand Master sent for the five most senior candidates. That meant only four would be bound, which was what Stalwart had dreaded.

The Flea Room was a small, bleak chamber that most boys saw only twice in all their years in Ironhall. Each newcomer met Grand Master there, and usually had to listen while whoever had brought him explained what a useless and ungrateful brat he was, and how nobody could do anything with him. Grand Master would hear the story, then talk with the boy in private and test his agility by throwing coins for him to catch. In most cases, he sent the boy and his guardian away and that was the end of it.

But if the boy had spirit and was nimble, Grand Master would accept him as a candidate. He was encouraged to take a new name and make a new person of himself. Whatever he had done in the past was forgotten. He would not see the Flea Room again unless he were set to clean it as a punishment. That was far from the worst that could happen to him, for Ironhall discipline was hard.

Time changed boys into young men. Ironhall's expert training plus a dash or two of magic turned the unwanted rebel into one of the finest swordsmen in the world. After five years or so, when the transformation was complete, the King would either accept him into the Royal Guard or assign him as bodyguard to someone else. It was back in the Flea Room that he learned his fate and met his future ward.

A companion in the Order was addressed as "Sir," although that was only a politeness, so tomorrow *Sir* Orvil, *Sir* Panther, *Sir* Dragon, *Sir* Rufus, but still only *Candidate* Stalwart...*sigh*!

At the door, Dreadnought took away their swords, because only a bound Blade could go armed into the King's presence. He sent them in by seniority: Orvil striding ahead, Panther close on his heels. Dragon and Rufus followed eagerly, like puppies wanting to romp. The reject trailed along behind, keeping his face blank to hide his disappointment.

There was no shame in being young, but why did it have to go on so long?

An icy wind blew off the moor, in one unglazed window and out the other. The five lined up facing Grand Master, who stood hunched in front of the inner door, clutching his cloak around him against the chill. With nine persons present, the room was crowded. The one staying out of sight at their backs would be Commander Bandit. The huge man in the corner was King Ambrose, but they must pretend not to notice him until they were instructed otherwise. He had set his hands on his hips and was grinning like a stuffed shark. His fingers glittered with jewels.

Orvil spoke the traditional words: "You sent for us, Grand Master?" He said them very loudly, so perhaps he was less calm than he was managing to appear.

"I did summon you, Prime. His Majesty has need of a Blade. Are you ready to serve?" Grand Master's beady eyes were set in a craggy, gloomy face. His name, although nobody used it, was Saxon. He was a distant, coldhearted man, inclined to lose his temper and lash out with harsh punishments, even expelling boys without fair warning. Since expulsion meant the culprit walked away over the moors with nothing but the clothes on his back—and usually no home or family to go to—it might easily be a death sentence. Even some of the elderly knights who dawdled away their final years at Ironhall would shake their heads at times and mutter that the Order had known better Grand Masters than Sir Saxon.

"I am ready, Grand Master," Orvil said quickly.

Grand Master turned and bowed. "Your Majesty, I have the honor of presenting Prime Candidate Orvil."

Now everyone could take notice of the King. Speed being more important than brawn to a swordsman, Master of Rituals used sorcery to prevent any boy growing too big. That rule did not apply to kings, though, and Ambrose IV, King of Chivial, was tall, wide, and portly. Between the calves bulging in his silk hose and the ostrich plume in his floppy hat, everything he wore seemed to be pleated and padded as if intended to make him appear even larger— knee breeches, doublet, jerkin, and fur-trimmed cloak. He loomed like a cheerful storm cloud and his voice thundered in the little room.

"Welcome to our Guard, Prime! Grand Master speaks highly of your skills."

Then Grand Master was lying. Stalwart could beat Orvil every time with rapiers and usually with sabers. Orvil would always win at broad-swords, of course, because a broadsword needed more muscle than Stalwart's body had yet gotten around to providing.

Orvil bowed low, then went forward to kneel before the King and kiss his hand. As he rose to return to his place in line, Grand Master turned to Panther.

"Second, His Majesty has need of a Blade. Are you ready to serve?"

And so on. Panther was a decent man and good with steel. After him it was Dragon's turn. Dragon was only a month older than Stalwart, but looked at least eighteen. What hurt was that he fenced like a crippled cow. Master of Sabers had told him in public that he needed two more years' tuition. Deputy Master of Rapiers muttered under his breath that he ought to chop wood for a living. Yet he was going to be bound and Stalwart wasn't. No justice…!

"Candidate Rufus…"

Rufus was all right. His fencing was competent, although he was horribly predictable. Being predictable would not matter in a real fight against opponents who did not know his quirks. Besides, Rufus was nineteen and sported a beard like a gorse bush. Rufus would look convincing in Guard livery. Even Dragon would. But Stalwart…*sigh*! That was the trouble—not age, not competence, just looks.

Tonight at midnight there would be sorcery in the Forge. Spirits of all eight elements would be conjured. Each of the four candidates would swear his oath and—unless the magic went wrong, which it almost never did—the sword wound would heal instantly, no harm done. Then he would be a Blade.

Not only would Stalwart have to share the day-long fast and the cold baths that began the ritual, he would also have to assist in the ceremony. That was adding insult to injury. When it was over and the lucky four rode off to court, he would remain behind as Prime, and that was adding *injury* to injury. Prime's job was to mother all the other boys and keep them from pestering the masters. Being Prime was always described as an honor, but it was an honor nobody ever wanted, communal nose drying and butt wiping.

"Finally, sire," Grand Master bleated, "I have the honor of presenting Candidate Stalwart, who will henceforth serve Your Majesty as Prime, here in Ironhall."

Rejected!

He had been told not to approach; he bowed where he stood.

"Stalwart the musician," the King said.

Feeling his face flame scarlet, Stalwart stared in dismay at the royal grin. King Ambrose was known to have very strong likes and dislikes. Did he disapprove of swordsmen playing lutes?

"I do play the lute a little, Your Majesty…."

"So do I," Ambrose said heartily. "Nothing wrong with lute playing. Maybe next time we can make music together."

Chuckling, he swung around in a swirl of velvet and brocade and fur. "Carry on, Grand Master."

Grand Master hastily opened the inner door and stepped aside as the King swept by him, ignoring all the bows directed at his back. Dreadnought crossed the room to follow him. Orvil led the candidates back the way they had come, although his stupid grin was so broad that it seemed unlikely to pass through the doorway.

Maybe next time, the King had said. That might be a hint that he intended to foist Stalwart off as a private Blade guarding some minister or lord. Bindings were permanent. A man had only one chance at the Guard.

"Stalwart!" said Grand Master. "Wait. I want a word with you."

3

Mysterious Alternative

THE DOORS WERE CLOSED. STALWART REMAINED, with only Grand Master and Commander Bandit for company. Lacking its normal shabby furniture, the Flea Room seemed even bleaker than it had been on that dread day four years ago when Sir Vincent had brought him here and thrown him on Grand Master's mercy. It was smaller than he remembered.

"My commiserations, Candidate," Grand Master said with a mawkish smile. He glanced briefly at Commander Bandit, who was staying back, out of the conversation. Then he pouted at Stalwart. Obviously he was in one of his crabbiest moods. "Had I put the question to you, how would you have answered? Would you be willing to serve?"

"Of course, Grand Master!" Why would he be there if he did not intend to become a Blade? Why would he be putting up with constant sneers and browbeating from Grand Master? Four years...

"It is unfortunate that you chose the name you did. You are not yet convincingly *stalwart*."

"It is not for lack of wishing, Grand Master."

"You have *dimples*!" Grand Master's face was spotted

with ugly brown blotches. Was being young more shameful than being old?

The school would not let a candidate sacrifice speed by growing too large, but it also required that he grow to man's strength. Time and again, Stalwart had begged Master of Rituals to perform a growth sorcery on him, but every time he was refused with much the same words: "It's not size that's your problem, candidate, it's just timing. If you're still on the small side when you've got a beard to shave, then we can do something about it."

"So you are willing to serve." Grand Master gave him a look that seemed to contain equal parts contempt and pity. "How willing? Would you tell lies to serve His Majesty?"

Now what? Puzzled, Stalwart said, "After I am bound I will do absolutely anything to defend him, naturally."

"That was not what I asked. I said *serve*, not *defend*. And I am not talking about *when you are bound*. I mean now. Would you lie to a friend if the King ordered you to do so?" Why was he so cantankerous this morning? Why take it out on Stalwart?

"I can't believe King Ambrose would ever give me such an order, sir."

"Can't you? Oh, grow up, boy! Suppose I tell you that you could best serve His Majesty by kicking up dust...jumping the hill...disappearing.... Does your loyalty extend that far?"

In this game to show anger was to lose points. A man could never win when Grand Master chose to pick on him like this, but he could play to a draw by remaining calm and courteous. That was rarely easy.

"With all respect, sir, I should not believe you."

"I assure you that this is His Majesty's wish." Grand Master's smile came very close to being a sneer. "And if you are going to call me a liar, the Commander will confirm what I say."

Dismayed, Stalwart looked to Sir Bandit, who shrugged.

"What Grand Master says is true, Candidate, but he is not telling you the whole story."

Grand Master sniffed. "The story's your business. I don't

know it and I don't want to know. Stalwart, I was told to tell you that the Commander speaks with the King's knowledge and approval. That's all."

He strode over to the inner door and shut it behind him with a thump that was very close to a slam. Bandit did not comment, but he rolled his eyes just enough to convey his opinion of that show of temper. Stalwart was duly grateful.

Bandit himself could hardly have been a more different person. Not in looks, of course. In appearance he was a typical Blade—graceful, athletic, neither tall nor short. His only remarkable feature was the way his eyebrows joined to make a single dark hedge across his face. He wore neither beard nor mustache. According to rumor, the Commander was one of the worst fencers in the entire Guard. There had been widespread surprise last Firstmoon when the King chose him to replace the legendary Sir Durendal, but he had proved to be an excellent choice. He had infinite patience. He spoke to the greenest recruit in exactly the same tone and manner he used to the King. His sword was named *Suasion*.

He walked over to the nearer window and stared out at the moor. "This is to be in confidence, every word."

"Yes, Commander."

"You were surprised that the King knew about your lute playing."

"Surprised that it interested him. I suppose Grand Master described all the seniors to him this morning?"

Bandit turned to share a smile. "He did not have to. He sends me detailed reports on all of you every week. I pass them on when the King wants to see them. He has been following your progress ever since you were promoted from fuzzy, last Thirdmoon."

"Oh!"

"He knows you've been here not quite four years and you won't be seventeen till Tenthmoon. He has seen Grand Master's reports describing you as lazy, insubordinate, and disliked by both the masters and the other boys."

Stunned, Stalwart said nothing.

Bandit continued: "Over the last two months he has become increasingly critical. He describes your fencing as very bad, virtually hopeless."

That was too much! "*Sir*! I suggest you ask the others. Master of Rapiers—"

"Says you can beat him nine times out of ten." The Commander was smiling again. "Not half an hour ago, Grand Master assured the King to his face that you are diligent, courteous, and industrious. He said no one was better liked, and no one showed more promise or ability at fencing. Does that make you feel better?"

"I hope that's closer to the truth, sir." Not at all bad, either! *No one better liked! Wow!*

"You can't possibly have had enough spare time here to learn how to play a lute. You must have brought it with you?"

"I was almost hanged for stealing it."

The Commander's long eyebrow arched in surprise, then he smiled. "Your past is your business. It's your present and future that interest me. You've turned out to be a late bloomer. It's no fault of yours and normally wouldn't matter. You'll get there in time; we all do. But, as Grand Master says, your chosen name does tend to draw attention to your current lack of stature." On Grand Master's lips the comment had been a sneer. When Sir Bandit said it, it was sympathy.

"Yes, sir. *Puny* would have been a better choice."

"I don't think the King would ever admit a *Sir Puny* to his Guard." The Commander eyed him thoughtfully for a moment. "Don't worry! It will come. And 'stalwart' doesn't just mean 'big and strong.' It also means 'brave and reliable.' That's the stalwart I need."

The man in question drew a deep breath to soothe the sudden turmoil in his insides. "*Yes*, Commander?"

"You won't know this, but this Grand Master has been forbidden to expel anyone else without the King's permission—no one wants Ironhall-trained men running around the country with chips on their shoulders. In his written reports, he has twice asked leave to…in my day we called it *puke* you. Throw you out, I mean."

Aware that the Commander was waiting for his reaction, Stalwart took a moment to think. Why should Grand Master write nonsense to Sir Bandit and the King, then turn around and tell them the truth in person? "He was *ordered* to write that trash about me? Who else reads it? Spies?"

"Well done! Yes, spies. Maybe spies—we're not sure. You know the evil we are up against—"

"Not exactly, sir."

The Commander turned and began to pace. "I mean you know about as much as we do. Counting the Night of Dogs there have been four attempts on the King's life in the last eight months, yes?"

"Yes, sir."

"No. There have been ten, four in the last month. That number is a state secret, Stalwart. No one outside the Guard knows that total, not even King Ambrose himself. You won't repeat it to anyone!"

"No, Commander." Stalwart thought his voice sounded a little thinner than usual.

"Obviously we don't know who the conspirators are or we'd hack their hearts out. Obviously they include some powerful sorcerers, and the attacks began when the King asked Parliament to levy taxes on the elementaries and conjuring orders. He saw no reason why wealthy organizations like those shouldn't pay their share like everyone else. Some of them disagreed. Now he's formed the Court of Conjury to investigate the uses of magic in his kingdom and it's turning up horrible evils. This is open war, Candidate—*and we don't know who the enemy is*!" Bandit returned to the window and stared out, probably seeing nothing. The King's safety rested on his shoulders.

"We aren't certain that the villains have eyes and ears at court, but it's a reasonable guess that they do. The only people we Blades trust are ourselves. Our binding keeps us loyal. We can deal with anything mortal, whether it's human or a monster created by magic. We have tasters for the King's food—and two of them have died. When it comes to secret sorcery we must rely on the White Sisters to sniff it out for us." The Commander swung around to stare at Stalwart. "I'll let you into another secret—just last week one of the Sisters detected something suspicious in the royal laundry. We burned the whole lot of it. Another smelled sorcery in the stables and tracked it to the King's favorite saddle. So you see that the evil extends right inside Greymere Palace."

For a moment, Bandit looked old and worried. Then he smiled and was young again. "Don't worry—Ambrose knows how you use a sword and he does want you in his Guard. Of course in normal times you'd have a dozen seniors still ahead of you, so you may not be quite as blazing good as you think you are. No matter, you are very good. The trouble is this absurd rule about taking men in order of seniority. There are good men coming along behind you, men like Badger and Marlon. I need those men. Forgive me, but I just can't see you in a Guard uniform yet."

Sigh! again. "I'd look about fourteen, wouldn't I?" Courtiers would make jokes about make-believe and children's pageants.

Bandit shrugged.

"Twelve?"

The Commander laughed, but not unkindly. "Not quite that bad! I'm glad you understand. Six months ought to do it. In the meantime I've got another job that you can do for the King, an important job. A risky job. He's given me authority to swear you into the Guard without binding you. Are you willing to serve?"

But the rules said…Stalwart realized that he was standing there like a lummox with his mouth open. "*Yes, sir!*"

"Are you certain?" Bandit asked quietly. "This is where I need that brave-and-reliable Stalwart. It will be dangerous. A Blade never needs to worry about courage, because his binding makes him brave." His eyes seemed to go out of focus. "On the Night of Dogs…some of those monsters were big as horses. They climbed three stories up the outside of the palace and came in the windows at us. They chewed through steel bars. They fought until they were hacked to pieces—*and so did the Blades*! I saw men with an arm bitten off pick up their swords in their other hand and go on fighting. A Blade defending his ward is more than human." He blinked and came back to the present. "I hope you won't have to face anything so bad, but you won't have that motivation."

Stalwart had been shown some of the gigantic teeth that Blades had kept as souvenirs. He shivered. "No, sir."

"And here's another secret. Some of the knights...well, let's just say they did not live up to the traditions of the Order. Not being bound any longer, they had to rely on raw human courage, and one or two of them didn't quite measure up."

Blades running away? Stalwart was speechless.

"That night was just the start of it," Bandit said. "There have been other horrors since. Twenty-four Blades have died so far—eight knights and sixteen companions. A score have been badly injured, and I've lost count of civilian casualties. We're not calling this the Monster War for nothing. Are you stalwart enough, Candidate Stalwart? Can you take on a dangerous job without being bound?"

He hadn't yet said what the job was. Apparently the planning had been going on for months and the King himself had authorized it. It must be important. Stalwart's heart thundered in his throat.

"I'll try my best, sir."

"I can't ask for more. Come with me."

4

Coward

BANDIT LED THE WAY DOWNSTAIRS, UPSTAIRS, through the maze of corridors. First House was the oldest building in Ironhall, much of it dating back centuries. Now Stalwart had time to have some second thoughts—and a few third thoughts, too. What exactly had he been flattered into accepting? Was it necessarily better than being assigned to guard the Lord High Admiral or the Master of the King's Chicken Farms? That was what happened to the dregs; only the best were allowed into the Guard.

So he looked too young to appear in Blade livery—why did that stop his being bound with the others? They could take him to court and dress him like a page if they wanted. What he was being offered instead was a major breach of the rules—and if the King had approved it, then why wasn't the King saying so? A binding ritual could not begin before midnight, so Ambrose had all day to kill. It had to be the royal hand on the sword that bound a Blade, but was Stalwart so much less than the others that he couldn't be spared a few minutes? Or did the King not want to be involved?

Bandit strode into the Records Office without knocking. Master of Archives stood at his writing desk under the window, surrounded by his usual wilderness of clutter. Heaps of scrolls and piles of great leather books filled the shelves, the chairs, and the floor, leaving nowhere to sit and precious little room to stand. He was stooped and perpetually untidy, with hair mussed and eyeglasses settled on the very tip of his nose. Even this day when everyone was spruced up for the King's visit, he seemed ink stained, shabby, and dog-eared. Yet the cat's-eye sword dangling at his side showed he was still a knight in the Order.

"Good chance, Lester!" the Commander said cheerily. Stalwart had never known, or even wondered, what the archivist's name was. "Need you to witness and record something." He fished a thin roll out of his jerkin and separated it into two sheets of paper. "File this. It's a warrant promoting Candidate Stalwart to companion, no binding required."

Master of Archives peered at it, holding it almost at the end of his nose. "I never heard of such a thing! In three hundred years there has never—"

"There is now," Bandit said cheerfully. "That's the royal signet. Fat Man is head of the Order and this matter is within the royal prerogative. You going to argue with him?" He handed the other paper to Stalwart. "Close the door, lad. Read that out."

The text was very brief, closely matching the oath sworn when a Blade was bound to the King:

> *Upon my soul, I, Stalwart, companion in the Loyal and Ancient Order of the King's Blades, do irrevocably swear in the presence of the undersigned, my brethren, that I will evermore defend His Majesty King Ambrose IV, his heirs and successors, against all foes, setting my own life as nothing to shield him from peril. Done this fifth day of Eighthmoon, in the three hundred and sixty-eighth year of the House of Ranulf.*

"Now sign it. May he borrow your quill, Lester? Add 'companion' after your name. Congratulations, Sir Stalwart!"

Master of Archives was making spluttering sounds like an annoyed goose. "That is absolutely outrageous!"

"We live in strange times." Bandit took the pen to write "Witnessed Bandit, Commander," under Stalwart's admittedly shaky signature, then handed it to Master of Archives. "Now you, Lester. File it somewhere very secure, and enter Sir Stalwart's name in the rolls."

"B-b-but…"

"The records must be correct, because there will be false stories spread." Bandit turned to regard Stalwart, compressing his long eyebrow in a frown. "Your sword's ready, of course, but you can't have it today. We'll try to get it to you. What's her name to be?"

Things were happening too fast. "Sleight, sir." Stalwart had said it before he realized that—*if* all this was for real, and *if* he didn't come out of it alive—the sword Sleight might be hung in the sky of swords before he had ever seen her or laid hands on her. "Not 'slight.' 'Sleight,' like sleight of hand."

The Commander chuckled. "Good one! I'll have Master Armorer inscribe it. Write that in your book also, Lester. Well, that's all, *Sir* Stalwart! Welcome to the Royal Guard." He offered a handshake.

"Th-thank you, er, Leader." Stalwart was miserably aware that his own palm was sweaty. He dearly wanted to ask why he wasn't being bound, but he feared he would not like the answer.

"Glad to have you. Here are your first orders. Go straight to your quarters. Gather up whatever you own, including that lute of yours, and then go."

"Go, sir?"

"Out. What was it Grand Master said—kick up dust? Must have been catchy talk fifty years ago. Walk out the gate. Take the Lomouth road and keep going. Someone'll be waiting for you at Broom Tarn."

The Commander's steady stare was a challenge to steady the new recruit's fluttering insides. Not just butterflies in the stomach—he had bats in the belly. A Blade could not refuse an order, but it was very obvious that he might have fallen into some sort of elaborate trap. Suppose there *wasn't* someone waiting for him on the road? Where would he go, what could he do?

"Yes, sir."

Bandit smiled to acknowledge what those two little words had cost. "I'll be at the gate to see you get past the Blades there."

"Thank you, sir!" He was to be given no breakfast?

"But if anyone asks you where you're going, you will not answer."

"*Sir?*"

The Commander shrugged. "Has to be, Stalwart. Despite what Grand Master said, I won't ask you to lie to your friends. I hope you can't, because it's not an ability to be proud of. And you mustn't tell the truth. If there truly are spies back at court, they'll assume you got puked because you're a lousy fencer. People here in Iron-hall will know better than that, but they'll assume the old man lost his temper with you. Or you annoyed the King, or something."

No, they would assume he'd lost his nerve and run away. He was going to be branded a coward.

Bandit did not say that, though. "Believe me, this is *very* important! We can't protect you where you're going, you see. If one careless word lets the enemy suspect that you matter, then you're as good as dead. So today you refuse to talk. Understand?"

"I'll obey orders, sir," Stalwart said hoarsely.

"Good man!" The Commander forestalled his questions with a head shake. "Don't ask. The man at Broom Tarn will explain. I don't dare tell you more now. Officially you've been expelled."

"Yes, Leader." Stalwart turned and went.

The instant the door closed behind him, Master of Archives said, "Well you can dare tell me! What is all this nonsense? What's going on?"

Bandit had his eyes closed. He let out a long, long breath, as if he'd been holding it for a week. "No, I can't tell you."

"I don't like this!"

"Neither do I."

"Spirits, Leader, that boy's only a...a...a *child*! Did you see how his chin trembled?"

The Commander opened his eyes and scowled. "Yes, I did. Did you see how he obeyed orders in spite of it?"

"You're sending a child into mortal danger!" Master of Archives yelled. "You're bound. You've forgotten what fear is like. I tell you, the week after I was dubbed knight and unbound I got into a fight and suddenly my hand was shaking so—"

The Commander's fist flashed out and grabbed the older man's jerkin. His eyes blazed. "Don't push too far, Lester! I've told you I don't like it. And you will not breathe one word of this to anyone, you hear? *Nobody*! Give me your oath on it."

"I swear, Leader."

"I'll hold you to it." Bandit released him.

Sir Lester restored his dignity by straightening his jerkin, like a chicken rearranging its feathers. "Is this Snake's doing? Is that who's he going to meet—Snake?"

"Snake or one of his men."

"You really think that...that *boy*...is going to do any good?"

The Commander turned and picked his way across the littered floor. "I can't tell you. I don't know what's going on either. Snake and the King dreamed it up. Maybe Durendal was in on it—I don't know. I do know that we've lost far too many men and Ambrose's luck can't last forever." With his hand on the latch he looked back. "I'm desperate, Lester. I'll try anything."

"Because all you're risking is one boy with no father to complain and no mother to mourn!"

"That's all," Bandit said harshly. "One starry-eyed boy. Lots more where he came from."

5

A Fateful Scream

TWO DAYS LATER, A STAGECOACH CAME RUMbling through Tyton, a town in eastern Chivial. It stopped at the Gatehouse, the entry to Oakendown, headquarters of the Companionship of the White Sisters, who were commonly known as *sniffers*, because they were trained to detect magic.

If the Monster War had put the King's Blades into a state of simmering alert, it had brought the Sisters to a wild boil. In normal times about twenty-five of them lived at court, assisting the Royal Guard in its duties. Another two hundred or so worked for nobles or rich merchants, and the rest were mostly teachers at Oakendown. Now the Blades were demanding the services of every Sister they could get. So were the nobles and merchants. Hundreds more people who had never given a thought to the dangers of evil magic had been alarmed by the Night of Dogs and were howling for Sisters to protect them. Probably few of them realized that a Sister could do no more than detect the presence of magic. Even other sorcerers could rarely defend against it.

At the best of times there were never enough Sisters. Only girls who were naturally sensitive and compassionate were accepted. They were taught courtly manners and given an excellent education—which was unusual in Chivial, where very few women knew even the rudiments of reading. Suitors pursued the Sisters like bees after blossoms. More than half of them were married within two years of taking their oaths. In the Monster War emergency, Mother Superior had appealed to all former Sisters to return to service. Many had done so, but there were still not nearly enough to satisfy the demand. Every prioress in the country was hunting for suitable recruits.

The stagecoach had brought six. They were met at the gatehouse by a young woman in the sparkling white robes and tall conical hat of a White Sister. She told them her name was Emerald and she would be their guide in their first few months at Oakendown. She did not mention that she had been a mere deaconess until the previous day. As she had not been due to take her vows for another three months and had been given only an hour's notice of her promotion, she had not yet quite adjusted to her new status. She was also still convinced that the hennin was about to fall off her head at any moment, but she didn't mention that either.

"Your names I do not want to know," she added, and smiled at their surprise. "Later I'll explain why. Meanwhile, I am sure you are tired and probably hungry. Which need do you want to satisfy first?" The vote was unanimous. She led them to the refectory to eat.

In the great hall under the high rafters, they gazed around with wide eyes while stuffing themselves with roast venison and rich fruit pudding. Especially they stared at passing Sisters.

"When do we get to wear the funny hats?" asked one, braver than the rest.

"When you finish your training. In about four years." It might be nearer three, Emerald suspected, if the present demand continued. She pointed out postulants like themselves, also novices, and deaconesses. "This is where we touch the world," she said. "On that side lies Tyton, and through this door, across the bridge, is the real Oakendown. We come to the gatehouse to eat sometimes, but not always.

It is a busy place, as you can see. Merchants come here to sell things to us. Persons who wish to contract for our services come here. If members of your family come to visit you, then you will meet them here. Outsiders are not allowed to cross the stream. See those people with hair on their faces? They are called 'men'!" The girls all laughed, of course. "Take a good look, because you won't see any of those on the other side of Oakenburn." The reasons for that involved one of the virtual elements and a lecture she would save for another day.

Meanwhile, her young charges seemed to be accepting her. Half a dozen scared, excited twelve- or thirteen-year-olds were quite a handful for someone only four years older, but she was an earth person and well able to cope. By the time the six were so full that they could not stuff in one more mouthful between them, she had won their trust. She took them to Wardrobe and saw them outfitted in postulants' brown robes. She explained that their own clothes would be given away to the poor.

"Suppose we want to go home?" wailed one of the air children.

"You can always go home, and we shall give you clothes to wear. Do you think we would put you in the coach naked?"

They laughed nervously. She had them classified now— one earth, one water, one fire, and three air. Every person's disposition contained all four of the manifest elements, of course, but one of the four was always dominant. Similarly, one of the four virtual elements would prevail: time, chance, love, or death. Those were a little harder to distinguish. Being an earth-time person, Emerald was solid, methodical, and patient. She was also heavy boned, destined for plumpness within very few years, and her broad features would never inspire poets to sonnets. "Comely" would be the most charitable epithet ever applied to them. Oakendown had taught her to accept what the spirits had brought her and not to fret. Her six nestlings were seeing her as trustworthy and motherly, which was undoubtedly why she had been assigned as a guide.

The sun was close to setting when she led her charges through the gate and over the footbridge that spanned the Oakenburn. She was always happy to leave the world's unfamiliar turmoil and return to the peace of the forest. Some Sisters remained in Oakendown all their lives, and she might turn out to be one of them if she did a good job guiding these six. It would not be so terrible a fate.

"Oakendown is very big, and I will need several days to show you all of it."

"Why do you live in trees?" squeaked one of the air types.

"Do we get to live up there?" another cried excitedly.

"Do we *have* to?" moaned the earth child.

They all peered up at the cabins nestling in the branches, the long bridges slung from tree to tree.

"Shush!" Emerald said gently. "You must *never* shout in Oakendown!" Time enough tomorrow to explain that postulants should rarely speak at all. "Yes, tonight you will sleep up in a tree. It is a very cozy, pleasant cabin, I promise you, and it doesn't sway at all. Later you will live in other places. There are lakes with many little islands and houseboats. There are caves—"

"*Caves?*" wailed the three air and one fire. The earth and water children smiled excitedly.

"Yes, caves. You have to learn to recognize the flow of the spirits. All your lives you have been in contact with earth elementals. Up in a tree, you are removed from them. In a cave, you are away from air—as far as you can be without suffocating. And also from fire, although we don't make you freeze to death. Gradually you come to sense the presence or absence of the various spirits. It isn't as difficult as it sounds."

It was a slow process, though, and not without hardship. Spending days underground was taxing for an air person; only a fire child could enjoy standing for hours under a blazing sun.

As they walked deeper into the forest, she mentioned that oaks were the only trees that extended their limbs horizontally. She pointed out how cunningly the aerial platforms were braced on those great boughs. When they reached their home tree she showed them the inconspicuous number written on the first riser of the wooden stair twining upward around the great trunk. This was Tree 65 of First Grove. Then she told them to go and explore. The three air girls went racing up ahead.

The earth child stuck close to Emerald. *Bounty* might be a good name for her. Her dominant virtual was almost certainly love, and with that combination her destiny was to marry young and produce children by the dozen.

Sixty-five was a juvenile tree by Oakendown standards. Its boughs held only a dormitory for the postulants, a private room higher up for their guide, a few meditation nests in the upper branches, and the necessary toilet facilities. No bridges connected it to other trees.

"Postulants are not allowed candles in the tree houses," Emerald explained, "so you get ready for bed now and then we'll talk." She watched to see how they settled the distribution of the pallets—who argued, who acquiesced.

Fire spirits had faded with the day, but the night was hot. She opened all the dormitory windows, sensing the air elementals rustling the leaves of the forest canopy. Then she gathered her little brood together in the deepening gloom as if she were going to tell them all a bedtime story, which in a sense she was. With all seven of them sitting cross-legged in a circle, she bade them hold hands, remembering her own first night in Oakendown and Sister Cloud doing this.

"Now you are among friends, in a very safe place. You can sleep soundly. Do not chatter in bed, because that is unkind to others. Dawn comes soon and the birds will rouse you, but I promised to answer any—"

Two of the air children tried to speak and the fire child drowned them out. "Why wouldn't you let us tell you our names?"

It was the question she had expected to come first. "Because in a day or two we are going to choose new names for each of you. I want you to try and forget your old names. I address each of you as 'Postulant,' and I want you to speak to one another that way, too. We won't force you to accept a name you don't like. When I came here I was given the name of Emerald and I soon realized that it was a much better name for me than the one my mother gave me. How could she know when I was born what sort of person I would turn out to be? No, Postulant, I will *not* tell you what it was, and you should not interrupt when I am speaking."

It had been *Lucy Pillow*, and she was still trying to forget it.

"If you later decide that the name we have chosen for you is wrong, then you may ask to change it. Names are words and words have power. It is with words that sorcerers bind the elementals, and some people are bound by their own names. We must find you names that express your true natures so they do not restrict you, that is all. What else?"

"What does magic smell like?" That query came from the little air child Emerald was already thinking of as *Wren*, although of course the Mistress of Postulants would have to approve her choices. The water child would probably be something like *Snowflake*. Water people were diverse and notoriously changeable, but this one already had an astonishing beauty, bright and cold. If her dominant virtual was death, as Emerald suspected, then she was going to shatter men's hearts like icicles. No matter how well-meaning death people might be, they were destructive to others and often to themselves as well.

She laughed. "I can't tell you. You have to experience it, and every Sister seems to experience it differently. It isn't really a smell. Often it's more a sound or a feeling." But it could be a smell, especially when air elementals were much involved. She sniffed...

Oh, nonsense! Just talking about it was making her imagine...There were places in Oakendown where sorceries were performed, of course. Once the novices had learned to recognize the natural flow of the spirits, they had to be taught the distorted forms produced by magic. But never in the groves.

And yet she could almost swear...

"Tell us about the Monster War."

Emerald wanted to say that she knew no more than they did, but perhaps they really did not know much. Wharshire was a long way from the center. News might be badly distorted by the time it arrived there.

"Do you all know what an elementary is?"

"A place for healing!"

"It can be. The place where sorcerers invoke the spirits is properly called an octogram, the eight-pointed star marked on the ground, but people do use the word 'elementary' to mean the building containing it. It can also mean the group or organization that owns the building, the *conjuring order.* They perform healings, yes, but they may do other things as well. Lately many conjuring orders have grown very rich, buying up land. They've begun putting on airs, too—the House of This and the Priory of That…. Last winter, the King decided the elementaries ought to pay taxes like other people do. Some wicked sorcerers banded together and tried to kill the King. They sent monsters—"

"Dogs big as horses—"

"Packs of them eating people in the palace—"

"Shush, shush!" Just when she had been getting them calmed down! "I'm sure the stories were exaggerated. Anyway, His Majesty set up a Court of Conjury, which is investigating all the conjuring orders and elementaries. Some of them do good, but many have turned out to be very wicked. They sell curses and bewitch people into giving them money. It's created a lot of worry about evil sorcery and that's why everyone suddenly wants a White Sister around. You will learn how to play your part. Now are you ready for bed, because…"

The stench was becoming nauseating, suggesting to Emerald huge quantities of rotting meat. Not being attuned to magic yet, her companions were noticing nothing amiss. But there must be qualified Sisters in some of the nearby trees, and they should be within range of anything this powerful. Anyone conjuring spirits right here in First Grove ought to have raised a hullabaloo audible in the next county.

She disentangled herself and stood up. "You get into bed. I'll be back in just a minute." She headed for the door.

Out on the platform, she could hear faint voices from neighboring trees, so she was not alone in the forest; she could see a few lights. Yet the stench of magic was even worse than before. She could detect air and death and a hint of time, but the combination felt gruesome and evil. She stood in the still night, almost gagging on it, barely able to concentrate well enough to try and locate it. It must be very close, perhaps right in this very tree. There was nothing below her, just the stair. Above her the steps went on, winding up to higher branches and the smaller huts.

Suddenly she saw the glint of eyes, too many eyes, up in the bracing that supported her sleeping cabin. A magical creation could be just as real and just as dangerous as any natural peril. When it saw that she had seen it, it came at her, scampering down out of the dark—a spider the size of a sheepdog with outspread legs like cables, mandibles big as daggers, eight eyes shining. It came on a wave of sorcery that was absolutely mind breaking.

Fire people might scream with rage, water people with fear, and air people just for the sake of the noise, but Emerald had always believed that earth people never screamed. She was wrong. She screamed at the top of her lungs. She hurled herself back into the dormitory, still screaming, and slammed the door against the horror outside. The six postulants, already very perturbed, quite understandably panicked. Three of them leaped out windows. A moment later came the sickening thump of a body hitting the ground.

6

Sentence

LATE THE FOLLOWING MORNING, SISTER EMERald was released from the meditation cell in which she had been confined overnight. She was led across the grove by way of many trees and bridges, coming at last to a large, mossy building set very high in one of the great forest giants. The tree was centuries old, and its buildings looked almost as ancient. She was taken to a gracious, dignified room, furnished with antiques, lined with ancient books. On this hot summer day it was cool and pleasant, bearing a homely smell of lavender and beeswax. Her guides—or perhaps they were jailers—showed her in without a word and then departed, leaving her alone with a white-robed woman, who sat writing at the big desk.

Emerald sank to her knees on the threadbare rug and waited as she had been taught, with hands clasped and eyes downcast. After a few moments of silence, she dared to glance up. She had expected the Prioress, but this was Mother Superior herself, the head of the Companionship. There could be no appeal from whatever verdict was to be announced here.

Eventually the older woman replaced her quill in the silver

inkstand and sat back to frown at her visitor. She wasted no time on pleasantries. "I have read your entire file, Sister—every report on you in the last four years. Your record is impressive. You were an exemplary student. I have also read the statement you gave last night, and that makes no sense whatsoever. Do you wish to recant?"

Mother Superior's control was the most perfect Emerald had ever met. Even here, high up in the ancient, enduring tree, with only insubstantial spirits of air and time around, any slight traces of the other elements should be as obvious as flying camels, and yet the lady was revealing no imbalances at all. She might be an earth person, or water, or fire, but Emerald could not venture a guess.

"I spoke only the truth, mistress."

Mother Superior drummed fingers on the desk. "Magic? Giant spiders conjured in the middle of Oakendown? This is rubbish! Nobody but you sensed anything at all, child. A dozen Sisters were so close to your location that they could not have missed detecting what you claim. So monstrous a sorcery must leave a taint that would linger for days, yet our most expert sniffers can find no trace of one. What you are claiming is rank impossibility!"

Someone was lying. Perhaps many people. Something terrible had happened in Oakendown and truth had been among the slain.

"May I speak with some of these reverend ladies?"

Mother Superior stiffened as if she could not believe her ears. "Are you accusing me of lying to you?"

"No, mistress." She was, of course. "But *I* am being accused—of falsehood or insanity or something. Do I not have the right to face my accusers?"

"There are no accusers," Mother Superior said menacingly. "Except me. Now, will you recant this absurd nonsense?"

Alas, Emerald had not been so named without reason. An emerald was a very hard jewel. The earth-time disposition was always marked by extreme stubbornness. "I regret I cannot tell a lie, my lady."

She met the angry stare and held it until Mother Superior

reddened and looked away. Fingers drummed again. The decision was made.

Before it could be announced, Emerald said, "May I ask how the children are?"

"The one who fell will survive. At worst she will have a slight limp. However she required such extensive healing that there can be no hope of her ever joining the Companionship. The others suffered a very considerable fright and are being counseled."

"I am truly sorry for what happened to them. I deeply regret my weakness in giving in to panic, but—"

Mother Superior pursed old lips. "If you had truly seen what you said you saw, then nobody would blame you for panicking." That was almost an offer of a second chance.

"I did see it, and I cannot say otherwise."

"Then I have no choice but to expel you from the Companionship. As is our custom, we shall provide transportation back to wherever you were recruited. You will be granted room and board until arrangements are made."

Emerald rose. Proper decorum required that she now curtsey, back up three steps, curtsey again. Angrily she just spun around and marched to the door.

7

Trials

THE NEXT FEW DAYS WERE THE MOST MISERABLE of her life. She was cut off from the only world and friends she had known for the last four years, abandoned in the heartless confusion of Tyton, outside even the familiar gatehouse. She had no money and nothing to do. Once or twice she saw Sisters she knew going about the Companionship's business in the town, but she could not bear to approach them in case they spurned her—or worse—offered sympathy.

Each dawn and sunset she had to report to the clerks at the gatehouse door. This involved joining a shoving, elbow-jabbing scrum with a hundred other people to reach the tables and a shouting match when she got there. Once a clerk had established that no transportation had yet been assigned to her, he would give her a token to exchange for food at a tavern. The food at Peter's was worse than the food at the Silver Hind, which was much worse than the Acorn's, and that was fit only for pigs. The fine fare of the refectory was not available to outsiders, which is what she now was. Gone, too, were the soft white robes. The drab gown and bonnet that she had been given in their stead were coarse and shapeless. The shoes pinched her feet.

Worst of all was the bitter taste of injustice. Something very wrong had happened in Oakendown that night. She *knew* she had detected a genuine magic; she was quite certain that Mother Superior knew she had. Others must know it also. A postulant had been injured, five others terrified half out of their minds, but the elaborate denial showed that much worse events must be involved. If Emerald were not so implacably stubborn she would have joined the chorus of liars and been spared this unfair banishment. On the second morning, when she saw the southbound stage leaving with half its seats empty, she realized that this was still what she was expected to do. She was being given a chance to write a note, begging for forgiveness and claiming a change of memory. Alas, earth and time were unbending rulers. Or was stubbornness only pride?

After Oakendown's serene solitude, the milling crowds seemed an unending nightmare, haunted by a pervasive reek of magic. She could rarely find a seat in the dining rooms without being close to an amulet of some kind. Most of those were merely phony good-luck charms—useless and relatively harmless—but several men tried to strike up friendships with her using glamours. Those sorceries were intended to make their wearers irresistible, but to her trained talent the results were as repulsive as hot dung heaps. Two of her encounters with magic were more noteworthy.

On the second evening, as she was bracing herself to fight her way into the mob at the gatehouse, a sudden odor of hot metal made her spin around. She would not have been surprised to see a huckster wheeling a brazier roasting chestnuts or even a farrier bearing a red-hot horseshoe in his tongs. What she observed instead were two dapper young men in green and silver livery. Curtly, but not roughly, they were clearing a path for an older man. She guessed at once that they were Blades and what she was detecting was the binding that kept them loyal to their ward, whoever he was. As they went by her, she glimpsed the gleaming cat's-eye gems on the pommels of their swords. They had no need to draw those weapons or display their renowned skill at using them. Their self-assurance alone was enough to make the bystanders yield, and in a few moments they and their ward had been passed through the door into the reception halls beyond. Emerald had never seen Blades before and probably never would again. They were a reminder of shattered dreams, for every novice in Oakendown hoped for an assignment to court one day, and she had been no exception.

The evening meal token also bought her a place to sleep, but the inns packed their guests in two or even three to a bed, four or five beds to a room. On her first night, Emerald was last to arrive and thus had to sleep nearest the door. Her five roommates seemed to spend the entire night climbing over her to get to the chamber pot. She vowed that henceforth she would retire right after eating.

Even that precaution was not proof against misfortune. On the third night of her exile, having been assigned a berth in the Acorn, she reached the room first and claimed a snug corner. Five women followed her and settled in with the usual jokes about bedbugs and snoring. One place seemed destined to remain empty, but just as they agreed to snuff out the candle, another woman bustled in, carrying a large carpetbag.

Hearing what seemed to be a continuous note blown on a very shrill whistle, Emerald sat up. "Pardon me, mistress, but are you wearing a sorcery of some sort?"

At a guess, the matron was the wife of a prosperous merchant—large, middle-aged, and surprisingly well dressed to be residing at the Acorn. Perhaps it was the best she had been able to find with the town so full. She simpered across the beds at Emerald. "Merely a charm of good fortune."

"Mistress, you have been gulled. That is no good-luck charm."

The woman glared. "It came from the Priory of Peace at Swampham. The brothers' prices are quite outrageous, but they have a countrywide reputation."

The lady would have done better hiring the brethren's magic to improve her teeth and remove her mustache, but to say so would require considerable tact.

"I never heard of that priory, mistress, or even of Swampham. But I do know something about magic. I know that there is no such thing as a true good-luck charm. All that any sorcery can do is drive away spirits of chance. They are so fickle that such charms rarely make much difference at all, and even if they do, they will keep away good luck just as much as bad."

"She's right!" one of the other women said. "If your charm worked, goodwife, then you wouldn't be in here with us."

The others laughed.

"Ask it for a room full of handsome men-at-arms!" said another.

"Insolence!" shrieked the woman with the amulet. "Nobody asked your opinions! Mind your own business, all of you."

The sorcerous racket was Emerald's business if she hoped to sleep tonight, but she did not try to explain that. "I can't imagine what business you have at Oakendown, mistress. If you try to speak with the Sisters while wearing that horror, they won't listen to a word you say."

But the problem was Emerald's not the woman's. She dressed and went down the creaking stairs to ask the innkeeper for another berth. She was directed to another room, but the beds were already filled, so she spent the night in a grubby blanket on a dirty floor. Her roommates all snored loudly.

On the following morning, the clerk found a note beside her name. "Ah, yes...Lucy Pillow. Greenwood Livery Stable. Ask for the Duke of Eastfare's man."

To leave Oakendown was tragedy, but she assumed that anything would be better than this shadowy nonexistence in Tyton.

8

The Open Road

THAT ASSUMPTION SOON BEGAN TO SEEM RASH. In the chilly dawn, the Greenwood yard was a clanking, clattering confusion of men and horses, reeking of ammonia, messy underfoot. Enormous animals were being led around, frequently at a run. Harnesses jingled, men shouted and cursed. In among the carts, drays, and wagons stood several grand carriages, but none of the footmen or postilions attending them would admit that his outfit belonged to the Duke of Eastfare.

By a process of elimination, she eventually arrived at a large gray horse harnessed to a shabby little wagon. The fresh-faced, cheeky-looking boy holding its harness strap was peering around, frowning. When he saw her horrified eye on him he said, "Pillow?"

"You may address me as Mistress Emerald."

"And I may not." To call him a youth would be premature. His shirt, breeches, and jerkin were all old and tattered, his floppy cap sat on hair of polished straw hanging down over his ears. He was only a finger-width taller than she was, although he drew himself up very straight to make the most of it. "You're the biddy going to Newhurst? Jump in."

This was too much! "You expect me to ride in *that*?" The

rig had no protection from the weather and its only seat was a plank across the front without even a back to lean on. It was loaded with two huge barrels, one behind the other, and a few anonymous cloth-wrapped bundles tucked in around them. It reeked. Even in that stinking yard, it reeked.

The boy shrugged. "It's good enough for me, missee. Run alongside if you prefer."

So that was it! Now Emerald could see the plan: *If the rack doesn't work use red-hot irons*! Having failed to subdue her victim with one humiliation, obviously Mother Superior was now trying something worse. Earth-time people rarely lost their tempers—they preferred to store grudges until they found a suitable chance to take revenge—but Emerald would certainly have resorted to violence now if the old hag were present. A handful of stable mire in the face would be a very promising opening. As she wasn't there, the only available victim for anger was this impudent brat. Emerald assumed he was in on the plot, although he did not *seem* to be laughing at her. Not yet, anyway. But there was quite a glint in his eye and he was likely to be better at roughhousing than she could ever be. Discretion prevailed—she restrained her temper.

"What is that appalling stink?"

"Garlic. You must know garlic!"

She did, but this was ridiculous. Those two great hogsheads could hold enough garlic to flavor every meal served in Chivial that year. Who would ever be transporting that amount of garlic around? The stench would be one more torment.

The boy laid one hand on the front wheel and vaulted over it. He grinned down at her triumphantly from the bench. "Coming or not?"

She tried to quell her anger enough to think rationally. He expected her to share that narrow bench with him, and most stable hands had very little idea what a bathtub was for. The garlic should provide some protection, depending on the wind. He was probably richly infested with fleas and lice, too, but after three nights in the cheapest inns of Tyton she must be well inhabited herself. He wasn't scratching too obviously.

If she refused he would drive away and she would be trapped. The Companionship would claim it had paid its debt. It had offered her transportation—who ever promised her padded seats or shelter from the weather? She would be stuck in Tyton with no money, no friends, nowhere to stay, nothing to eat. So she must choose between this whelp and Mother Superior; between his smelly wagon and complete surrender. She wasn't even certain that surrender was still an option. Perhaps she was just being punished out of spite. Furious, she stalked around to the other side, tossed her tiny bundle of possessions aboard, and climbed up beside him.

He smiled innocently at her. "Welcome aboard!"

"What's your name?"

"My friends call me Wart."

"Ug! Then what do your enemies call you?"

"*Sir!*"

He flashed an enormous grin to show that he had thought that up on the spur of the moment. She had to admit that it wasn't bad.

"Then until I know which I am, I'd better call you Sir Wart."

"*No!* I mean, please just call me Wart, mistress."

Why should her feeble joke alarm him so much?

Wart drove through Tyton standing up, so he could see over the horse. He did not speak, being intent on navigating the narrow, crowded streets. Admittedly the clearance was often closer than hairsbreadth, but his clenched teeth and the gleam of sweat on his face suggested that he lacked experience at urban driving. How could he have experience at anything? This was probably the first time his mother had let him go out alone. Once the horse had ambled out through the town gate, though, he sat down and began to whistle. When he wasn't whistling he chattered aimlessly about crops, herds, fine weather, and bad news of Baelish raiders attacking the coast.

Highways in Chivial were rarely more than rutted tracks and often less. The road out of Tyton was much less. The wagon had no springs, and Emerald was going to be thoroughly bruised when she reached Newhurst. That might not be until tomorrow at this pace, but she was in no great hurry to face her mother and admit defeat. Wart's whistling was tuneful and quite pleasant. Horsemen and sometimes coaches went jingling by. The fields were lush, starting to ripen into gold. There was not a cloud in the sky and if the sun had not been shining straight in her eyes—

"Where are you taking me?" she demanded angrily. "We should be going south!"

"You mean we're not?"

She should have noticed sooner. She bared her teeth at the gleam of mockery in his eye.

He laughed. "We'll get to Newhurst, I promise! Just sit back and admire the scenery. I call him Saxon. That isn't his name, but he reminds me of a friend of mine." He cracked his whip over the horse, whose large rear obscured the view directly ahead.

Just how foolish had she been? In her stubborn fury she had trusted herself to a boy she knew nothing about. Highways were so dangerous that stagecoaches carried men-at-arms. Wart himself seemed like no great threat, but he might have friends who were. Besides, how far would the White Sisters go to prevent ex-Sister Emerald from talking about the sorcery she had witnessed? Surely they wouldn't hire someone to cut her throat and leave her body in a ditch... would they?

They came to a toll bridge. Wart chatted for a while with the tollman—more about weather and harvests and rumors of another attempt of the King's life. As he paid up his copper penny, he said, "This is the road to Valglorious?"

"Aye, lad. Keep on to Three Roads and then go south."

"Not north?"

"No. North takes you to Farham. Valglorious is south, past Kysbury."

Wart thanked him and jingled the reins to start Saxon moving again.

"How long have you had this job?" Emerald inquired sweetly.

"Ever since I turned thirty," Wart said.

"If you get bored," he suggested an hour or so later, "I'll sing for you. Then you won't be bored. Or at least you won't *complain* of being bored."

"Try me. I'm sure you sing very well."

His juvenile blush burned up on his cheekbones again. "Um...truly?"

"I'd like to hear you sing."

Pleased, he cleared his throat and launched into "Marrying My Marion." His voice was a thin tenor, not strong but quite pleasant, although the jolting of the wagon naturally made it unsteady. Even Emerald could not fault his pitch or rhythm so he was probably another time person, like herself. When he reached the chorus she joined in. He shot her a delighted smile and switched to counterpoint and complex trills.

Truth be told, Wart was good company. His quick wit, cheeky humor, and bubbling energy showed that air was his dominant manifest element. His self-confidence puzzled her, although some of it must come from being an adolescent male—she had little experience at judging those. Although air people tended to brag when they were successful and whine excuses when they weren't, Wart seemed content with his world. He chattered, but not about himself. He had been wary when driving in the town, not unsure. The earth-time pairing made her stubborn and patient, but air-time people were usually flighty and impatient. He seemed too relaxed to fit that pattern, either. She would have several days to analyze him, though, as he deigned to explain when they had exhausted the possibilities of marrying off Marion.

"Vincent sent me to deliver a load of hides to Wail and pick up their salt fish. Phew! If you think garlic's bad, you should try sitting on top of that in the hot sun. I dropped the fish off at Undridge and picked up the garlic. He'd told me to stop in at Oakendown and see if they needed any loads delivered—know they're short-handed because of the Monster War, see? Got me and Saxon a free night's board, too. Now we're going to Valglorious...."

However much she might resent being called a load, his tale was believable. She gathered that the duchy of Eastfare owned dozens of estates scattered over half Chivial and ran its own cartage line, moving specialized produce from one manor to another or to a point of sale. Wart's planned itinerary would take him close to Newhurst in another four days.

"And who gets to keep my fare—you or the Duke?"

"Saxon and I ate it." He wasn't telling actual lies, but he wasn't revealing the whole truth, either. "I eat more than he does, as you'd expect. 'Sides, the Duke's dead, the old one. His son died before he did; his grandson's at court, being a squire. And if Good King Ambrose can teach that brat manners, then he's a better man than I am."

"I don't doubt he is."

He smirked. "Time will tell." Modesty was not one of Wart's burdens.

"So I have to endure four days of this bouncing? And who defends me from highwaymen and brigands?"

"How many highwaymen do you have in mind?"

"Three would be ample." One would be enough.

Wart grinned. "If it's more than three, I run for help. If it's only three, then I kill them myself." He reached behind him and hauled out a sword from under the bench. It was rusty and notched like a saw. Its point had been broken off, but it was a real sword, and she was surprised he had the strength to wave it around so.

"Please! *Don't* bother to brandish it. In fact I'd much rather you put it away before you killed me or the horse."

"You don't trust me!" he moaned, but he slid the weapon back out of sight.

She was starting to trust his motives a little, but she certainly would not trust herself to his arm yet. Give him ten years and he might make a competent defender. Air and time were good elements for a dancer, so they ought to make a nimble swordsman.

They came to a wide, stagnant-looking river and crossed on a ferry that was no more than a crude log raft. Emerald was glad to climb down and walk around, easing her aches. The ferryman on board was a grizzled, surly man whose job seemed to consist solely of tying up and casting off at the jetties and collecting the fare in between. The real work was done by the boy on the far bank, who led the donkey that turned the windlass that pulled the chains that moved the ferry.

"I'm heading to Valglorious," Wart said. "I turn left at Three Roads, yes?"

The ferryman spat overboard and watched what happened to his spittle before grunting, "No. That'll take you to Farham and Firnesse. Go south."

"South! Thanks."

"Do you think you've got it now?" Emerald inquired.

"See how flat the country is?" he said. "We're in Eastfare—flattest county in Chivial. And the most law-abiding. Vincent's peering over the sheriff's shoulder all the time, so no highwaymen!" He looked to see if she was reassured. "Besides, who'd want to steal two barrels of garlic?"

"It would not be an easy crime to conceal," she agreed. "You're telling me that there's no theft or violence here?" She had seen rows of peasants cutting hay, working their way across the meadows with their scythes and pitchforks, and their women following with sickles to collect what they had missed. She had seen herds of sheep, goats, cattle, and horses. But even in this poverty-stricken landscape, she had seen no houses, because the hamlets and villages all hid behind high stone walls. She said so.

"Ah, I meant *not much*. Remember that we're getting near the sea. Fens and salt marsh and cold gray fog. Where there's sea there's Baels—raiding and slaving, slipping up the creeks in their dragon ships. Even Vincent can't do much about them."

"Who is this Vincent you keep mentioning?"

"Sir Vincent. He was Blade to the Fifth Duke for umpteen years. You know how badly a Blade takes it when his ward dies, but he managed to weather the storm. The old man had named him his grandson's guardian, which probably helped save his reason, so now he runs everything." Wart was clearly enthusiastic about this Vincent. "He's a knight in the Order. Private Blades can only become knights after their wards die. The King summoned him to Grandon to dub him."

This talk of Blades was not out of place. She knew that there was an auxiliary corps of retired Blades who helped out the Companionship by performing odd jobs, although she was vague on the details. Squiring vulnerable ladies on long journeys might well be one such task. She also knew that some of these "Old Blades" had been conscripted into more strenuous duties during the present emergency. Possibly they also supplied boys with wagons as replacements. "Do you often transport Sisters?"

"No," Wart said indignantly, "but I can't afford to be fussy."

9

Minstrel Boy

THE MORNING AGED AND THE DAY GREW HOTter. Wart asked directions from two shepherds, one more toll keeper, and the drivers of three other wagons, always receiving the same answer. Emerald was astonished to discover that she was enjoying herself. Having never wandered this far from Oakendown since she'd first entered its gates, she had forgotten how interesting the world was.

"What about you?" Wart asked. "Why are you not going to Newhurst by coach?"

That was none of his business, but if she lied to him, he would be entitled to lie to her. She wasn't very good at lying anyway. "Someone used some nasty sorcery right in the heart of Oakendown. I detected it and wouldn't lie about it, so they threw me out."

"Oh, that's tough! What sort of sorcery?"

The inquisitors of the Dark Chamber claimed they could detect any spoken lie. Although they did not brag of it, most White Sisters could do the same, smelling the taint of death on the falsehood. Emerald had enough of the knack to know that Wart had faked his reaction. Sadly she concluded that he was not what he said he was. He was playing Mother Superior's evil games.

"Nasty. I was attacked by a spider bigger than you. I don't honestly know if it was meant to kill me or just frighten me. It certainly did that. No one else will admit it existed at all. I was outvoted."

"Not fair! What do you do now?"

"Find a rich husband."

"Truly?" He had not expected that. He looked at her doubtfully. "Mightn't that be even tougher? Not finding, I mean—I'm sure you won't have to look very long. I mean, finding a husband you want."

"Very likely."

"No parents, brothers?"

"My mother's still alive, but she hasn't got two copper mites to clink together." Either Emerald needed to hear her problem set out in words or else young Wart was just skilled at asking questions, but she found herself telling him all about her father's illness and the enchanters of Gentleholme Sanctuary. "They said they could cure him, but the pain grew worse and worse. Soon he was screaming all the time unless he got a fresh enchantment every day."

Wart's lip curled in horror. "They made his sickness worse?"

"Don't know. Some diseases act that way, so perhaps not. We certainly couldn't prove anything. But they did keep putting their price up."

"This is why the King is trying to suppress the elementaries!" he said indignantly. "His new Court of Conjury is turning up all sorts of horrible cases like that. They have some good sorcerers helping them, and some White Sisters, too. And the Old Blades, of course. You must've heard of Sir Snake, who used to be Deputy Commander of the Royal Guard? He's their leader…. Officially they're called the Commissioners of the Court of Conjury—but they're all knights in the Order, so everyone calls them the Old Blades—and they go in and investigate the elementaries. But often the sorcerers fight back with monsters and fireballs and terrible things. They're doing a wonderful job, and—" His baby face colored again. "I'm raving, aren't I?" he muttered. "But you have heard

about the White Sisters who help? They're not called the
Old Sisters, but…Well, you must know."

"I've heard of them." Emerald had volunteered to join
them, but so had a hundred others, so she had been turned
down. "Some of them have died, also."

"I didn't know that!"

"Why should you?" she asked quietly.

He gulped awkwardly. "Well, I'm interested." After a
moment he sneaked a look at her and evidently decided he
had failed to convince. "I met Sir Snake once. You should
tell him about this Gentleholme gang."

"I can't prove they made my father's sickness worse. They
did put their price up and up until they had taken all our
money. When he died there was nothing left." Not even
Peachyard, the estate her mother's family had owned for
generations.

"Or they let him die when there was nothing left to
take?" That was a surprisingly cynical remark. At times
Wart sounded much older than he looked. She sensed an
unexpected element in his makeup—a faint trumpet note
in the far distance, a whiff of familiar scent on the wind.
It might be the fading trace of some old magic, perhaps a
healing, but somehow she thought it went deeper than that.

"You may be right," she said.

Her brothers had gone off to war and died together in
their first campaign. The White Sisters offered almost the
only respectable profession open to a woman and would
pay even a novice a stipend if she had real promise and the
money was needed—as it was in her case. Her mother could
no longer see well enough to sew. She could do washing and
cleaning, but the rich folk who employed servants had no use
for elderly women with twisted hands. She had been living
on Emerald's wages. Now it was rich husband or nothing.
Trouble was, most rich suitors were old, ugly, crabby….

"If you can detect sorcery," Wart protested, "why can't
you get a job doing what White Sisters do? Protecting
warehouses from thieves and so on?"

"We don't—I mean *they* don't protect anything. All they

can do is warn. Who's going to take my word for what I can do? They'd assume I was in league with a gang of thieves." She smiled at him. "That's enough about me. Let's hear your story." He didn't look old enough to have one.

"Me? I'm a wandering minstrel. Hold this." Thrusting the reins into her hands, he squirmed around to rummage in the cargo. Saxon accepted the change of command without argument, although he twisted his ears nervously when Wart's legs waved in the air. In a few minutes he turned right side up again, clutching a contraption longer than himself.

"Is that a chitarrone?" she exclaimed.

"Almost—an archlute. Very similar. Its mother was a lute and its father an unscrupulous harp."

That described it well. It had the usual catgut strings and a lute's sound box in the normal half-pear shape, in this case beautifully inlaid with brass and mother-of-pearl rosettes. But instead of stopping at the keys, the neck continued for another three feet or more and ended in another set of keys that tuned a second course of strings—metal ones, running the whole length of the instrument.

Leaving Emerald to steer Saxon—who was quite capable of looking after himself—Wart went to work to tune the monster. That would have been a hard enough task on level ground. On a small and bouncing bench, it proved impossible, because the keys for the bass courses were out of his reach. But he tuned up the standard lute portion well enough and soon his fingers were dancing on it, plucking out torrents of melody. He played a few pieces, sometimes singing, sometimes not.

"Wonderful!" Emerald said when he paused to adjust the keys again. "You are as good as any minstrel!"

"Better than most."

"You could earn a living with that skill!"

He shook his head pityingly. "There are more worthy ways a man can earn a living. Any requests?"

She told him to play whatever he wanted.

He stopped at a ford to let the horse drink and eat from a

nose bag. From one of the bundles in the wagon he produced two meat pies and a flagon of small beer to share with his passenger. He played his archlute again, doing much better on steady ground, but she noticed he was making little use of the extra strings, and when he did the result was not always tuneful. It was a very beautifully crafted instrument, worth more than he would earn in years.

As their journey resumed, Emerald tried again. "What do you do the rest of the time, when you're not wrestling that lute or following Saxon around?"

He shrugged vaguely. "Odd jobs."

That was a very terse answer from an air person. Sterner measures were called for.

"Who cuts your hair?"

That alarmed him. "What?"

"All the stable boys I ever met looked like pitchforks in hay season. Your clothes are dirty enough and you remembered not to wash your face this morning, but those fingernails? You don't stink and scratch. A skilled barber cut your hair. You don't talk like a hayseed. You're interested in things a hayseed would not be—Sir Snake, for example."

He flushed yet again, this time obviously furious. His anger was directed at himself, though, not her. "I wait on table sometimes. Vincent's very particular about things like fingernails."

He was lying. She just shook her head.

"And I overhear the gentlefolk talking about things like the Old Blades."

"Go tell an owl, boy! You said earlier that you'd met Snake, one of the King's most trusted officers. And 'Vincent'?— you're on first-name terms with a man who runs a county?"

"That has nothing to do with...with you."

"Tell me anyway. All of it."

"You wouldn't believe me," Wart said, sounding as if he were trying to talk and keep his teeth clenched at the same time.

"Try me. We have several days to kill."

He sighed. "I ran away from home when I was ten. I

had to. My stepfather drank all the time and beat me. He was going to kill me or cripple me. My name was Wat in those days, Wat Hedgebury. I teamed up with a wandering minstrel. He showed me how to strum a lute. Owain was his name, kindest old man you'd ever hope to meet. I sang a bit and passed the hat for him; I learned to do a little juggling and tumbling and carried his bedroll on the road, so I wasn't just charity for him. One day we were performing in Firnesse Castle, which isn't very far from here, and he had a stroke. He died the next day. Baron Grimshank had no use for a minstrel's apprentice—I was ordered to try another county, and soon. On the other hand, he did fancy Owain's lute, which was a good one. Owain had told me I could have it, but no one listened when I said so." Wart grinned ruefully. "I became more than a little cheeky, I'm afraid."

"Not wise?"

"Very foolish. His lordship did not take kindly to being called a thief to his face. He had a henchman called Thrusk, a great hairy brute, big as a bull. They called him the Marshal, but he was just the thug who did the dirty work, grinding the faces of the poor and downtreading peasants. Grimshank told Thrusk to see me off. Thrusk's idea of a fond farewell involved a horsewhip. That left me really mad." Watching her out of the corner of his eye, he added, "So I decided to get my lute back, and that night I broke in."

"You broke into a *castle*?"

"Knew you wouldn't believe me!"

But she did. He had lied earlier and was telling the truth now. Perhaps he was testing her ability to tell the difference. "I didn't say I didn't. I'll decide whether I believe you when I've heard the rest."

That pleased him. He smirked as he said, "It gets stranger. Firnesse Castle sits on the lip of a cliff—not a very high cliff, but high enough and steep enough that they don't bother to post guards on that side. There's no beach, just rocks. Even Baelish raiders could never land a boat there, but at low tide it's no great feat to scramble around the base of the cliff. Climbing up by moonlight was a little trickier." He was bragging, not understanding that it was his dominant element, air, that made him good at climbing.

"Nobody could scale the walls. I didn't have to. Whoever built the castle had put all the latrines on that side—overhanging the drop, upside-down chimneys. It was chilly when the sea wind blew, but the sea did all the shoveling. I was small enough to wriggle up one of the shafts."

"Yucch!"

He scowled at her. "Ever been really hungry? Really, *really* hungry? So hungry you can hardly walk? I had. That lute was *mine* and I needed it to earn a living. I spent *hours* creeping around the Baron's castle hunting for it, terrified I would fall over something or rouse the dogs. When I eventually did locate it, I was too late. The tide had come in and the shore was white with breakers, real killer surf. I hid in a closet until the portcullis was raised at dawn, but they caught me trying to sneak out."

"With the lute, of course?"

"Of course."

And she had thought she was stubborn! "You were ten?"

"Oh, no. Twelve, almost thirteen."

"You were lucky you weren't hanged."

"I very nearly was," Wart said glumly. "Grimshank claimed to be a lord of the high justice and kept a gallows outside his gate to prove it. King Ambrose might argue about his right to use it, but Ambrose wasn't there. After breakfast the Baron held one of the briefest trials ever seen in Chivial and told Thrusk to take me out and string me up...."

For a few moments the wagon rattled on. Even Saxon twisted his ears around, waiting for the rest of the story.

"I wonder if that slime pit is still alive?" Wart muttered, and Emerald heard again that inexplicable wrong note, that faint trumpet.

"Baron Grimshank?"

"No, Thrusk. Grimshank was within his rights—or almost within them. The law says to hang criminals over the age of ten. But Thrusk had other ideas. He spoke up to say I was too young to be hanged. 'Your lordship should show mercy on a penniless orphan,' he said. 'Why not just send the poor lad back where he came from?' And Grimshank laughed and told him to go ahead. That—" Wart thought better of whatever word he'd been about to use. "That *cur*! He was jeering and chortling as he marched me off to the latrines. He was going to shove me down a shaft, he explained— *with* my hands tied and *with* the tide in and breakers all over the rocks. Headfirst, he said."

He looked at Emerald to see if she was going to accuse him of lying. She wasn't. Even without her Oakendown training, she would probably have believed him. The story was all too horribly credible. Noblemen in remote areas could do pretty much as they pleased, answering to no one, and a baron who'd been insulted and made to look foolish by a friendless juvenile vagabond could easily react with the sort of brutality Wart was describing.

"Maybe one day I'll find Thrusk and settle a score or two."

"How did you escape?"

"Just luck, no credit to me. When we got to the latrines, Sir Vincent intervened. He was a guest in the castle, so he shouldn't have meddled. He had no authority at all, except he was a Blade. His beard was gray and there were a dozen of them to one of him, but he didn't even draw his sword. Didn't need to. He told them he and his servant were leaving now and I was going with them—and so was the lute. And that's what happened. That's what it means to be a Blade."

Recalling the two cocksure young men she had briefly seen in Oakendown, Emerald did not doubt that part of the tale either. "They just let him walk out?"

"Yes. If they'd used violence on the Duke of Eastfare's guardian there would have been a hue and cry. He's a member of the White Star, so the King would probably have asked questions. The Lord Chancellor back then was Montpurse, another former Blade.... I wasn't worth that sort of trouble to them. Vincent put me on the back of his horse and took me to...a safe place."

She caught a whiff of evasion. "What safe place?"

"Valglorious." Wart flashed his most cocky, boyish smile.

"So virtue triumphed and I have never been back to see the Big Bad Baron! You believe my story?"

Not that mention of Valglorious. "Some of it," she said, "but not all."

He scowled and silently handed her the reins. He removed his hat, took out his knife. Everyone carried a knife to eat with, and his had seemed quite ordinary—a crude bone handle and a shabby leather sheath. When he drew it, though, she saw that it was a small dagger, with a point and two edges. He soon showed that it was as sharp as a razor, so the blade must be of much better quality than the hilt. Ignoring the bouncing of the wagon, he proceeded to cut his hair, lifting it a lock at a time and slicing it off close to the roots. Pretty soon he had trimmed his whole head to a hideous shaggy stubble.

"How's that?" he demanded, not looking at her.

"Horrible. You look as if you had head lice and your master told the shepherd to shear you."

"Good." He stuffed his hat back on his head. He had slightly protruding ears and now they showed.

"Who are you trying to deceive, if not me?" she demanded.

That question the normally chatty Wart would not answer.

Peculiarer and peculiarer!

10

Three Roads

T HE COUNTRYSIDE DETERIORATED FROM blacksoil farmland to a stony plain good only for sheep and goats, apparently uninhabited except for shepherds and their dogs. The only buildings were a few isolated hovels. However, its apparent flatness was deceptive, and it was tufted with patches of gorse and scrub not unlike the new condition of Wart's scalp. Emerald had already noticed that she could rarely see very far in any direction, but she was taken by surprise when a sizable stockade came into view almost as if it had sprung out of the ground.

"Three Roads," Wart announced. "Coaching inn. It's called Three Roads because one road leads from here west to Tyton, one goes north to Farham and Firnesse, and a third runs south to Kysbury and Valglorious."

"I am amazed by the depth of your knowledge."

"We'll spend the night here."

"We could cover a league or two more before dark."

"There isn't anywhere to go. Besides, Saxon wants his oats." *Do not argue with the driver!*

He drove the wagon through the gate to a dusty, stony yard surrounded by a variety of thatched buildings—housing, sheds, stables. A mob of ragged boys a little younger than he flocked around him, all yelling for his attention. In such a hubbub Emerald could not make out a word, but Wart obviously knew the proper procedure, for he aimed a finger at one of the largest and said, "You!" The chosen one scrambled aboard, grinning proudly. The rest fell back to wait for another customer.

"Stabling for the night," Wart demanded. "And which road do we take to Valglorious when we leave?"

"Best yer honor park over there under cover," said the guide, pointing with one hand and wiping his nose with the other. "South road goes to Valglorious, if it please you."

"I expect it will whether I'm pleased or not." Wart steered the wagon where he had been directed to park. The boy jumped down to begin unharnessing Saxon. Wart turned a complete somersault in the air before landing on his feet like a cat.

"Oo!" said the boy. "Do that again!" More of the hungry-looking urchins came running over to watch.

"Stand back, then." Wart vaulted up on the wagon again and repeated the feat. Laughing, he refused a third demonstration and turned serious to address the hostler who had appeared to take the guest's orders. "Oats and a good rub-down. Which way to Valglorious?"

"South road," the man said. "You could make Kysbury before dark. Cheaper board than here," he muttered quietly.

"The lady is weary," Wart explained, but he made no offer to play gentleman by helping the weary lady dismount. Instead he rummaged in the wagon for his archlute. Declining offers of help from the grubby boys, he slung it over his shoulder, took up a bundle of personal possessions, and swaggered off in the direction of the hostelry office, leaving his chosen helper guarding the wagon. Emerald followed, assuring the mob of skinny minions that she could carry her own skimpy baggage. She would have hired one of them as porter if she had possessed even a copper mite to pay him.

The door of the main building opened into a sizable timbered hall, dim after the brightness outside. Clattering noises and juicy smells drifted in from a kitchen area at the back, and Emerald guessed that the long tables and benches could probably seat at least two hundred people. Some men were already sitting there quaffing ale, and the big man standing chatting to them was almost certainly the inn-keeper. They broke off their argument to scowl at the newcomers.

"Don't need no flea-bitten minstrels here," growled the big one. "And no dancing girls neither."

Wart bristled. He stood the archlute on the floor and said, "Hold this."

"What are you going to do?" Emerald asked nervously. Oakendown did not prepare a girl very well for dealing with men. The world was full of men.

Without answering, Wart strutted forward like a bulldog stalking a bull. He put his fists on his hips and sneered up at the innkeeper, who stood a head taller and twice as wide.

"Are you insulting my companion?"

"You would know that better than me," said the big man. The ale drinkers chuckled.

"But you do offer hospitality to worthy travelers?"

"Them 'at has money to pay for it."

"Best board for two," Wart said. "Private room for the lady. I'll settle for no more than four in the room, but a bed to myself. A clean blanket. A candle for each of us. Cover and picket for the wagon; oats, water, and a rubdown for my horse."

"Two florins and I'll see the color of your silver now, son."

Not silver—the coin that appeared in Wart's fingers was gold. He flipped it at the innkeeper, who grabbed but missed it. It rolled under the table, and the big man dived for it as if frightened his customers might beat him to it. While he was down on hands and knees, Wart slapped him on the rump and said, "Good boy!" The ale drinkers guffawed. Emerald was quite certain that Wart had made it happen.

The innkeeper rose red faced and scowling at him with even more suspicion than before, but clearly gold excused anything. He slipped the coin in a pocket and fumbled for change.

"Beg yer pardon, young master. 'Scuse the misunderstanding. I can spare a private room for you also at no extra cost, if that'll make it up to you. Same one the Duke himself prefers when he honors us. Clean linen, of course, always. Best board tonight will be barley mash, roast swan, venison pie, and peaches poached in brandy, if that will be satisfactory, master? All the ale you can drink included. Bread and cheese and small beer to break your fast in the morning if you wish. And her ladyship has only to ask if there is anything at all that my women can do for her comfort." He bowed to her. "Honest Will Hobbs at your service, mistress!"

There was a faint odor of magic about Honest Will Hobbs, but nothing threatening. He probably wore a mild glamour charm to sweeten his customers' view of him.

Wart now looked quite blasé, as if this fawning was only his due. Doubting that she could achieve the same panache, Emerald said as haughtily as she could, "Have you such a thing as a bathtub?"

"Certainly, mistress! I'll have it brought to your room directly, and ample hot water too—no skimping on the hot water, I promise. Softest towels you've ever met, my lady."

"At no extra charge!" Wart said. "By the way, which is the road to Valglorious?"

Emerald's room was cramped and stuffy in the evening heat, but far better than anything she had been granted in Tyton. She enjoyed a long soak to wash off the road dust and ease her bruises. Fresh clothing would have been a joy, but she had nothing to wear except the same drab sack and toe-biting shoes. When she had done the best she could with her appearance, she went downstairs to explore the rest of the inn.

Three Roads was thriving. Four more wagons had arrived and been parked. Like Wart's, each was being guarded by one of the boys. As she watched, a grandiose coach in purple and gold came rattling and jingling into the yard, drawn by four matched chestnut mares. Two liveried grooms stood on the platform at the back and two men-at-arms sat on the roof. The boys swarmed around it like midges and were yelled at by the coachman. She wondered who could afford such an outfit.

On a loading dock outside one of the stable buildings sat Wart, astride a log, strumming his archlute. About a dozen boys were grouped cross-legged around him, singing as he directed. Some adults had drawn close to listen, keeping well back from Wart's hat, which lay invitingly on the edge of this impromptu stage. Emerald wandered over. On solid ground he played much better than he had on the wagon, understandably, although once in a while he still stumbled in the bass. As with an ordinary lute, his left hand had to steady the instrument and also stop the strings while the fingers of his right hand plucked them, but on the archlute he had to pluck the extra bass courses with his right thumb, and this knack he had not quite mastered. He was already better than he had been that morning, though. She wondered again how he had acquired a thing so precious. He had admitted stealing one lute in his brief life.

"Once more right through!" he said, and led his makeshift choir into the ballad again. When they reached the end, the audience clapped. "Take a bow!" Wart said, and the boys jumped up eagerly. "All donations go to the choir, gentlemen, not to me. This minstrel has earned his crust already today." Some men tossed coins into the hat. "Thank you, my lords! May the spirits cherish you all."

His fingers danced over the string. "Now, how many of you know 'Marrying My Marion'?" The show of hands disappointed him. "Suggest something, then." In a moment he had them singing again. He had not known the melody, but he quickly picked it up.

He was a real mystery, was young Wart, and not just because of that faint discordant spiritual element she kept detecting and failing to identify. He went out of his way to draw attention to himself with this public lute playing and by asking every man, bush, and tree the way to Valglorious. He tamed the innkeeper with gold. If he was really the sort of lowly stable hand he was pretending to be, he would never have touched gold in his life. A genuine wagoner would eat in the commons and sleep in his wagon, certainly not in a private bedchamber. Yet he had hacked off all his hair to make himself seem more in character!

Emerald could be sure of only two things. She was certain Wart was in league with Mother Superior, but she enjoyed his company in spite of that. Bother him! Villains were not supposed to be likable.

He wound up the song with a fancy arpeggio, and again a few men threw coppers. "May the spirits favor you, my lords!" He had not been exaggerating about his experience as a minstrel. He was working his audience like a seasoned performer. "This is only our first lesson, you understand, but what better solace than music to ease the cares of a long day? Madrigals and cantatas will have to wait for our second lesson, but if there is any country ballad or simple roundelay that your lordships especially favor, these honest men here will be happy to hazard it for you! Won't you, lads?"

A well-dressed man called for "The Baker's Kittens."

"'The Baker's Kittens'!" Wart exclaimed. "You all know 'The Baker's Kittens,' my hearties! So let's hear it—'The Baker's Kittens' for two silver florins!" He strummed a few chords, which were almost drowned out by the onlookers' laughter and a howl from the requester that he had never agreed to such a price. It was a good choice, a counting song that anyone could learn as it went along.

The boys had not reached the second kitten before Emerald was distracted by a thin, shrill whistling. Even as she wondered who would be so callous as to spoil a children's singsong like that, she realized that the sound was entirely in her own head. What she was hearing was magic, and the moment she looked around she saw the woman she had encountered at the Acorn in Tyton. She was still some distance away, but the recognition was mutual.

The woman's customary pout twisted into an expression of surprise. She said something to her companion, who

offered his arm to lead her over to Emerald. Her voluminous
scarlet gown was too heavy for such weather and much
too grand for traveling the dusty roads of Chivial. Under
a floppy bonnet, her face was shiny with sweat, and her
efforts to smile produced a bizarre leer. The steady scream
of her amulet was even shriller than Emerald remembered.

"Fancy meeting you here, child! The spirits of chance
keep throwing us together! Is this not good fortune?"

That would depend on one's point of view. Plank walls
would not keep out magic, so Emerald was in for a wretched
night if the innkeeper had assigned this woman a room near
hers.

"The pleasure is mine, mistress."

The woman simpered. "Just an hour ago I was telling
Doctor Skuldigger your theory that there could be no such
thing as a good luck charm. Wasn't I, Doctor? And now see
how my amulet has brought us both good fortune!"

"Perhaps it has." Emerald reminded herself that earth
people never lost their tempers. That sorcerous racket had
nothing to do with luck. She always heard spirits of chance
as a thin dry rattle like dead leaves in the wind—or like
dice being rolled. She could not guess the purpose of this
discordant whistle, only that it twisted every nerve in her
body.

"Your lack of faith surprises me." The man had the
saddest face she had ever seen, its flesh hanging in folds like
a bloodhound's under silver eyebrows. The sword he wore
was merely the badge of a gentleman; at his age he would
not be expected to use it. His hair was hidden by a wide-
brimmed hat, and his expensive, heavily padded doublet and
jerkin made his torso seem bulkier than it possibly could be.
His spindly shanks could not fill his silken hose, although
he stood straight enough. He uttered a sad moaning noise,
"Aw? Wherever did you get such a notion?"

None of his business! "From my dear, late grandmother.
A White Sister told her so, many years ago."

"Perhaps it was true in her day, but sorcery has made
great advances in the last twenty or thirty years." Doctor

Skuldigger's voice was as melancholy as his face, a deep groan. "Aw?" he moaned again. "Adepts now can separate the chance elementals, binding the favorable and dispersing the unfavorable." He waited courteously for her to comment. His eyes were bright enough, but the lower lids had sagged to reveal their red lining. Emerald found the effect so repulsive that she had difficulty looking at him.

"I thank you for correcting me, sir. Are you a practitioner of the arts magical?" If he was, then he must be one of the rogues the King had sworn to suppress, because he was talking nonsense. She could not tell whether he was merely ignorant or deliberately lying—the most skilled mother in the Companionship would have had difficulty detecting a death taint under the shrill screech of the woman's spell.

"Aw? Merely a doctor of natural philosophy."

"A scholar of international repute!" said the woman. "I am Mistress Murther."

Emerald curtseyed, as she was expected to. She had still not decided what name she would use in future. "Lucy" she detested. "Emerald Pillow" sounded absurd. And what title could she claim? In her father's day she had been Mistress Lucy of Peachyard. Now she was old enough to style herself Mistress Pillow. Alas, her present threadbare garments would allow her no such grandeur. "I am Emerald, may it please you, mistress."

She was bitterly aware that in the robes of a White Sister she would have outranked both Murther and Skuldigger handily. They would not have dared address her without first sending a servant to ask her permission.

"And what brings you to Three Roads, Emerald?" Mistress Murther inquired as sweetly as could anyone whose mouth was shaped like hers. All the screaming bad temper of their first meeting was now forgotten, apparently.

"I am on my way home."

"Way home to where, Emerald?"

"Newhurst, mistress."

Murther beamed. "Well! Did I not say that our encounter must be good fortune? I happen to be on my way to Grandon, and Doctor Skuldigger will accompany me only as far as Kysbury. Newbury is close by my road. I will let you ride in my coach, because any company is better than none. You will enjoy learning how the gentry travel."

"No!" The unexpectedness of this offer had sent presentiments of danger prickling all the way up Emerald's backbone. "I mean, I couldn't possibly impose on you like that, mistress...very kind...other arrangements with my friends." She had walked into a trap. She was not sure what sort of trap, but the sensation of a gate falling behind her was unmistakable. *Snap!*

Murther turned away quickly, as if to hide a smirk of satisfaction. "Come, Doctor. I should know better than to expect courtesy from the lower orders." She swept away with her red skirts brushing the dust and her bejeweled hand still resting on Skuldigger's arm. The ghastly sorcerous whistle faded as she moved out of range.

Emerald stared after her, struggling to understand her own unease. She had refused the offer too abruptly, but why had that been such a blunder? For all Murther knew, she was traveling with seven brothers and six grandparents— for all Murther *should* know, that is. If she had other information, then she must be another accomplice in the obscure Oakendown plot. She might have seen Emerald on the road, bouncing along in a farmer's wagon with only a boy for company; in that case her poxy chestnut mares ought to have reached Three Roads first, but the spectacular coach had not been parked in the yard when Wart and Emerald arrived.

Just *what* was going on?

11

Bad News

"THAT ENDS TODAY'S CONCERT, MY LORDS AND ladies." Wart sprang to his feet, archlute and all. The sun was setting, and Honest Will Hobbs would charge for every candle stub. "We thank you for honoring us with your attention, and I do believe that your generosity has provided almost enough to buy every one of these young nightingales a real meal in the commons this evening. From the look of them, it is a treat long overdue. I rashly promised it to them and I shall have to dig deep in my own pouch if the tariff exceeds the take. You, Ginger, take the hat around and see if some—Ah, thank you, mistress! And you, your honor..."

As the audience dispersed, Wart turned to Emerald, grinning happily. "Haven't sung for my supper in years! Even if I don't get to eat any of it."

"Why did you bother?" She fell into step beside him as he headed for the main lodging, closely convoyed by the choir. They were anxious to see if he would be true to his word. She was determined to get some truth out of him.

He shrugged. "I suspect Honest Will feeds them the plate scrapings, and not much of those. I've been hungry in my time. Who were your friends?"

She smiled to hide her anger. "I'll tell you when you stop lying to me."

Wart turned to the boy he'd named Ginger and held out a hand to get his hat back. "How much did we make?" He scooped out the coins. "That should do it. Off you go, all of you. Tell Honest Will you're eating at my expense tonight. He knows I'm good for it. You, Freckles, wait a moment." As the rest of the boys vanished in the direction of the kitchens, he said, "What do you know about the lady and gentleman who were talking to Mistress Emerald here a little while ago?"

Freckles looked worried. "Not much, y'r honor. She 'rived in that coach soon after you did. He and 'nother lady came in just after, but their coach left right away."

Wart shot Emerald a cryptic look. "Well, that's a start. Who's the other lady?"

"Just a lady." The boy scratched his tangled mop. "Haven't seen her since she got here."

"Not your fault. I'd guess that for a groat you could find out their names for me, couldn't you? And maybe other stuff too?"

Freckles nodded so eagerly that he almost shook a few off. "Yes, sir, y'r honor! I'll ask. I seen the gentleman around before with the Marshal."

Wart stumbled over a rut and recovered. "Which marshal is that?" His voice had risen half an octave.

"Marshal Thrusk, y'r honor—Baron Grimshank's man from Firnesse." He looked curiously at Wart and muttered, "'E's a rough sort, y'r honor."

"Yes. Yes, I know he is. So you be careful."

Wart stopped, only a few feet from the door now, and watched as his young spy ran off. He had lost color. Emerald found his pallor strangely worrying. She had assumed that Murther and Skuldigger—if those were their real names— were in league with Wart—if that was his—and thus with Mother Superior. If there were two factions involved, then she had some rethinking to do.

"Thrusk can't hurt you here," she said.

Wart looked at her disbelievingly and licked his lips. "He could, you know! Death and flames! He could ride in here with a dozen men at his back and do anything he liked. Grimshank may be only a baron, not a duke, but who's going to bring his henchmen to justice if one unknown youth dies in a drunken brawl? This is absolutely the worst thing that could have happened, the one thing we—he won't know my name if he hears it," he muttered, as if speaking only to himself. "He might not remember my face—spirits, it's been four years! But the poxy lute will remind him. Flames and death!"

"Four years ago? Getting our stories a little confused, aren't we? You told me you were thirteen then."

"Almost thirteen..." Wart's puzzled frown turned into a fierce scowl. "I'm a month older than you are!"

"Oh!" He wasn't lying. Boys matured later than girls, of course, but he certainly didn't look more than a tall twelve or thirteen. *"And just how do you know my age, Master Wart?"*

"I'm a good guesser. Let's go in and eat while there's still something there to gnaw on."

"No." At the end of a hard day, her resentment boiled over. "You are lying to me now. You have lied to me several times, and you have certainly not told me the whole truth of who you are and why or where you are taking me and who put you up to it. Now I'm going to ask some questions and you are going to answer them, or I shall go straight to Mistress Murther and tell her I shall be delighted to accept her offer of a ride in her coach."

Wart screwed up his eyes for a moment as if resisting a twinge of pain. Then he snarled at her. "No, I will not answer your questions. But you obviously know when I'm lying, so I'll tell you two things. One is that I'm the best protection you have got or can get, and the other is that you are in truly terrible danger. So you'd better just trust me. Now let's go in and eat."

"I'm in danger?" Emerald yelled, "and you won't tell me why or how or who? That is the most arrogant, insufferable—"

"It's too late," Wart said miserably. "Telling you would make the danger much worse, believe me. And if Thrusk and Grimshank turn out to be involved, that is sheer disaster. Everything will fall apart."

12

Good Offer

THE COMMONS HAD BEEN AN ECHOING BARN even when almost empty and would be unbearably noisy any evening, with wagoners and drovers all shouting for service from the overworked staff. Now it had been invaded by thirty skinny, hungry boys, shrilly clamoring for what they regarded as their due—the choir had doubled in size on the way in. Wart pushed his way into the riot to find out who was cheating whom.

Still seething, Emerald headed across to the gentles' dining room where best board was provided. This was a much smaller chamber with a single long table flanked on either side by benches and bearing two glimmering candles to brighten the evening shadows. The dozen or so guests already present were almost all men, and she paused in the doorway while trying to decide whether she should go in or wait for Wart. No doubt delicious odors were wafting from the loaded platters the hurrying servant wenches were delivering, but after a whole day in the wagon she could smell nothing except garlic. The cloying stench of glamours was not a real odor, of course, any more real than the rattling of good luck charms was a real sound. She could detect a faint screech from Mistress Murther's sorcery and see the lady in question sitting alone at the far end. King Ambrose would be having much less trouble suppressing the elementaries if fewer people were deceived by such quackery.

"Aw?" The melancholy noise right at her shoulder made her jump.

"Doctor Skuldigger!"

"Emerald?" Skuldigger attempted to smile at her, although with his spaniel eyes the result was gruesome. "Forgive my prying. My associate, Mistress Murther, is convinced that the reason you shun her is that you can detect sorcery and her good luck charm distresses you."

That was certainly part of it. "I am sorry if I gave offense. I have promised to drop in on an elderly aunt and stay some days with her."

"Aw?" He raised his silvery brows in surprise. "Then you cannot in fact detect sorcery as the White Sisters can?"

Wart's dire warnings rang in her head. "If I were a White Sister, Doctor, then I would not be traveling in my present style."

He sighed. He could not have looked sadder had he witnessed his entire family dying of some terrible disease. "Of course. Your sorrows are your own business and I should not meddle. However, pray grant me a moment to explain. You met Mistress Murther in Oakendown, yes?

"We are anxious to obtain the services of a Sister, and I am sure that you know how much in demand they are these days. We explained that our patron, a most distinguished member of the nobility, is grievously worried that he may be the victim of a curse planted upon him by unscrupulous enemies. Aw? We offered to pay a substantial sum—a very substantial sum, I should add—for a Sister to come and inspect his residence. It may be that there is nothing to this tale and then she would find no hex, aw? But success or failure would not affect the payment of the money." He blinked his droopy eyes at Emerald.

"Do continue, Doctor." She wished Wart would appear. This morbid old man frightened her.

"Alas, the Sisters are grossly overworked nowadays,"

Skuldigger mourned. "Our mission did not prosper. But if you do have this ability, Emerald, I can promise that a patron such as I have described would offer you the same generous terms as he would a qualified Sister. His house is large, but I assure you that you could visit every corner of it in less than a day. Do not fear that your journey would be unduly delayed."

He did not seem to be lying, but there was too much minor magic in the room for her to be certain of that. She suspected he was hedging his words most carefully.

"Who is this noble patron, Doctor?"

"It would not be advantageous for me to reveal that information at this stage in the proceedings." Skuldigger groaned. "I can, however, promise you that the honorarium he would be willing to pay—for less than two days' effort, I stress—would be at least a thousand crowns."

Emerald gulped. "That is princely!" She and her mother could live comfortably for two years on that.

"Indeed, and I will go further. Should you succeed in uncovering such a hex as I have mentioned concealed upon his premises, a wealthy aristocrat such as he would certainly consider a bonus of an additional thousand as fair reward."

Spirits! With that kind of incentive in the offing, it would take unusual honesty *not* to find a hex or two in the attic.

But...*Truly terrible danger* Wart had said, and she knew she must choose between them—the brash boy, who had certainly deceived and entrapped her, and this distinguished gentleman with his so-carefully chosen words. Fortunately Wart appeared at her side then, still wrestling the archlute. Youth and old man eyed each other with equal suspicion.

"I thank you, Doctor," she said, "for your most generous offer. I beg you to allow me time to consider it in the light of my other obligations." She bobbed a curtsey.

Wart offered her his arm—the first gentlemanly gesture she had seen from him. She laid her fingers on it and together they paraded into the dining room.

13

A Dangerous Thing

THE DECISION COULD NOT BE POSTPONED FORever. Next morning, when Emerald emerged from the inn in the mean, clammy light of dawn, she found the yard in predictable chaos, with scores of men and boys trying to harness or saddle at least a hundred horses. She had slept badly, tossing all night, and now was at the end of the line. She must choose. To remain here at Three Roads was not an option, unless she wanted to starve. Lacking a cloak, she shivered in the chill air.

At the far side of the yard at least a dozen youngsters were determinedly trying to help Wart put Saxon between the shafts. They were getting in one another's way and making the horse nervous. Closer to hand, Mistress Murther's grooms and coachman were attending to her team, with her two men-at-arms assisting. The smelly little wagon and the opulent coach could not have presented a greater contrast. Common sense insisted Emerald should grab at Doctor Skuldigger's fantastic offer. Why was she so suspicious? What seemed a great fortune to her might appear trivial to people who could travel in a coach like that one.

She had told Wart about that offer, but he had still refused to reveal any more about himself. She remained convinced that he was somehow in league with Mother Superior. Since she had no idea what Mother Superior was up to, that conclusion was hardly helpful. Most of what he had told her had been true. Murther and Skuldigger's truthfulness she had been unable to judge—which was suspicious in itself. But a thousand crowns was a fortune. It would be salvation to a girl without a penny to her name.

The coach was closer, so she went to it first. There was no sign of Mistress Murther yet, nor the woebegone Doctor, but perhaps she could gather information from the flunkies— exactly who Murther was, for example, and where she lived. It was the sort of vehicle she would expect only the King or maybe a duke to own. It had real glass windows and the body was slung on leather springs to give a smooth ride. A carriage like that one ought to have its owner's arms emblazoned on the doors, but even the men's livery bore no insignia. Very odd! She approached confidently, weaving between horses and men and vehicles, until she was within twenty paces or so of her destination. She stopped suddenly, causing a groom leading a big roan to curse at her and then mutter an apology as he went by.

Magic! Murther's magic or another like it?

Going more cautiously now, Emerald dodged around a couple of wagons and drew nearer. In a few moments she had it worked out. What she was hearing did not come from Mistress Murther lurking inside the coach. It came from the coachman and his helpers, as if all five of them were wearing the same sort of amulet as their mistress. Whatever it was, the magic gave Emerald goose bumps; it would still prevent her from detecting falsehood.

Watching the men, trying to analyze the elements of the spell, she noted that they were a curiously glum lot. Other crews in the yard were talking, joking, even cursing, but Murther's men slouched around in sullen silence. Recalling Mistress Murther's permanent pout, she wondered why this strange sorcery should make its wearers so morose.

She went on past the coach without stopping.

Wart was already sitting on the bench in his wagon.

His smile seemed genuine—and welcome. "Good chance, Emerald!" He had to shout over the racket as a four-horse dray loaded with lumber went clattering past, heading for the gate. "Have you made your decision?"

"Wart, I need the money!"

His face fell. "Don't believe in the money. Skuldigger is known to consort with Thrusk, Grimshank's man, and you know what I think of those two. I can't find out any more about Mistress Murther. Anyone rich enough to drive that carriage ought to be armigerous—and if you look very closely at the door, you can see that it used to bear a device, but it's been painted over. I could make out a swan and two badgers and those are not Grimshank's arms. It may mean only that Murther has just bought the vehicle. The boys haven't seen it around here before." He shrugged. "Or her. And the other woman seems to have disappeared altogether, but Skuldigger certainly arrived with another woman. Emerald, I'm sure your friends are up to mischief."

"I'm sure you are!"

His boyish face colored. "If you go with them, you may be heading into terrible danger."

"And if I stay with you I will not?"

"I told you that you were safer with me. I repeat that: *You are safer with me*! Am I telling the truth?"

Safer, not safe. She nodded, trying to keep her teeth from chattering. The sun was touching the roof ridges, so the world would warm soon. The sky was a glorious blue already. Saxon rattled his harness and stamped his great hooves, anxious to be gone.

"Wart, you're telling me what you think is the truth, but that doesn't mean it's necessarily right. Whoever's behind you may have lied to you." Mother Superior had lied to her.

Wart opened his mouth to protest and then shut it with a click. That was a bad sign—he was more or less admitting the truth of what she had just said. "What do you want?"

"The whole story."

He shook his head. "I swore I wouldn't tell you. And if

you're right, I may not even know the whole story. I'm sure I don't."

"Then I will take my chances with Doctor Skuldigger and Mistress Murther." She turned away. She was bluffing, because being shut up in the carriage with all that shrieking sorcery would be unbearable torture.

But Wart didn't know that. "Emerald! Come back!" He showed his teeth angrily. "I'll bend my promise this far. I will tell you *why* we're doing this and *why* it matters and *why* I can't tell you any more than that." He pulled a face. "I shouldn't! I don't like the situation any better than you do and I'm in much worse danger than you are. I almost hope you will run away from me, because then I'll be safe. Safer than I am now, anyway."

Burn him, he was still telling the truth! Emerald tossed her bundle into the wagon and lifted the edge of her skirt to climb over the wheel.

He turned Saxon out the gate onto the sunlit trail, but he had barely cleared the corner of the stockade before a shrill voice shouted, "Wart!" The boy he called Freckles came running.

Wart reined in Saxon, although with some difficulty, for the horse was frisky and eager. "What's the tumult, m'hearty?"

"The Doctor promised me a whole penny if I'd keep watch and see which road you took!"

Wart laughed and reached in his pouch. "Then this is your lucky day. Here's another for telling me you're going to tell him." A coin spun through the air.

"You want me to tell him wrong?"

"No. Tell him the truth. Be the good little boy your mother would be proud of."

Freckles curled his lip in disgust at this insult and examined his new treasure. "Me mom says telling truth is stupid and gets you in trouble."

"Go back and tell her she's wrong this time."

"Dunno know where she is."

"Then keep it a secret. I suspect the nasty Doctor will have more than one spy watching me, so you won't get your money from him if you tell him lies. And don't forget how I said you could earn a silver groat." He thumped the reins down on Saxon's back and the wagon rattled forward on the south road. "Beautiful morning!"

"Speak!" Emerald said menacingly.

"I hear and obey, Your Grace. Don't you know that a little knowledge is a *dangerous thing*?"

"I'll risk it."

He shrugged. "Don't say I didn't warn you. We are serving the King's Majesty. You did not volunteer for what you are doing, but you will be well rewarded at the end of it. If you die, then your family will be compensated. Will that satisfy you?"

It ought to surprise her. Curiously, it did not. One of the few conclusions that she had reached in the night was that young Wart talked a lot about the King's Blades and claimed to know at least two of them. If someone other than—or as well as—Mother Superior had put him up to this escapade, one of those men was probably the culprit. "No."

"You are safer not knowing."

"I don't care. You promised."

He sighed. "You've heard about the Night of Dogs. There have been other attempts on the King's life since then."

"Three, I heard."

"More than that." The wagon was leaping and bouncing as Saxon raced along the road, feeling his oats from the previous night. He would soon tire and slow down to his usual amble, but in the meantime his passengers might be beaten to pulp. "That's a state secret and I am telling you the truth. Do you still want me to go on?"

State secrets could be dangerous things to know. They were not normally passed on by juvenile stable hands. "Yes."

Wart sighed. "Are all girls so stubborn?"

"Are all boys so secretive?"

"Probably not. You must know this better than I do, but I'm told that not all White Sisters sniff magic quite the same

way—that the same spell may seem different to different
Sisters. Is that right?"

"Yes. It's very personal. What seems a scent to one may
be a sound to another, or a cold feeling, or almost anything."

He nodded. "Lately the attacks have been getting more
subtle. Two weeks ago someone slipped a poisoned shirt or
something into the royal laundry basket. The White Sisters
detected it and the whole batch was burned, but it's a safe
guess that the purpose was to kill the King." Wart shot
her a wry glance, as well as he could while the wagon was
bouncing so hard. "I trust you are a loyal subject of His
Majesty?"

"Of course!" If such an evil could be smuggled into the
palace, then the spider monster she had seen in Oakendown
was not so surprising after all.

A coach went rattling past them, but not Murther's
coach. It vanished southward in a cloud of dust. Then two
horsemen...Last night's residents at Three Roads were
scattering to the four winds. Three winds, actually, as little
but sea and salt marsh lay to the east.

"The problem is," Wart said grimly, "that the magic got
past two Sisters without being noticed and almost past a
third. A similar booby trap turned up in the royal stables
a few days later, and that one was even harder to detect—
had it not been for the laundry warning they would almost
certainly have overlooked it."

"This is nonsense you are talking."

"Oh? I'm lying?"

"No, but you have been misinformed. If the sorcery
was powerful enough to do real harm, that is. If all it
was designed to do was produce a faint itch, say, or a bad
smell, well, then it might slip by. But a White Sister should
recognize anything fatal at least twenty paces away. Easily!"

"Saxon, you idiot! Slow down!" Wart rose to peer over
the horse, then sat down again, as much as bouncing could
be classified as sitting. "Yes, that's what I was always told—
anything powerful enough to worry about will show up
to the sniffers like a dead pig in a bed. But that isn't true

anymore! Whoever the conspirators are, they're managing to mask one magic with another, a magic-invisibility spell, you could call it."

"Rubbish!" she protested. If what he said was true, then the entire Companionship of the White Sisters might find itself useless! "It can't be done."

"Why not?"

"Because the second magic—the magic wrapping, call it—would be detectable also, so you'd need to put another layer around that one and then another...." But was that necessarily so? The wrapping itself need not be a major sorcery, just a deception spell, and if the elements could be properly balanced, perhaps it would not show up very much at all. She had never heard such a thing mentioned in Oakendown, but even the possibility might be a forbidden topic, best never discussed. "Maybe it could be done," she admitted, "but it would be very difficult. It would need a team of very skilled sorcerers and..."

"And?" Wart waited for her to finish the thought.

"Oh no!" Horrors! "And a White Sister?" The novices and postulants at Oakendown were kept well away from magic until they became attuned to the natural flow of the elements. Sorcerers could never develop the same abilities because they were constantly in communion with spirits. The two crafts were direct opposites.

Wart sighed. "More than one. At least two, but the more the better. Suppose you want to kill the King and you devise a booby trap—a petition, for example, a roll of parchment, or a fishing rod, something he will handle in person. Suppose you then cloak its magic in a magic wrapping. You might find that the package would deceive two Sisters, yet still be detected by a third. Grand Wizard of the Royal College of Conjurers says that there must be at least two Sisters working with the conspirators, and he would guess four or five."

She could find no flaw in the logic. Sorcerers trying devise a magic wrapping would be like blind people trying to paint a picture. Only White Sisters could tell them how effective their work was, or how it should be improved.

"But we all take vows not to use our skills for evil purposes or for our own enrichment. *They* do, I mean."

Wart let the wagon rattle on—a little slower now—for several minutes before he spoke. He twisted around to stare back past the barrels. With the sun low in the east, the scrubby landscape was more obviously rolling than it had seemed the night before. A solitary flock of sheep grazed off to the west. Three Roads was no longer in sight.

"Renegade Sisters?" he said at last. "I didn't say they were cooperating willingly, although we think at least one of them must be."

"I refuse to believe *any* White—"

"We know of one who was kidnapped right out of her house. A former Sister, married, had a young baby. The baby went with her. I think she could be made to cooperate, don't you?"

Emerald shivered as if the day had suddenly turned cold again. "Would they really do that?"

"They're traitors!" Wart yelled. "They're trying to kill their king—and if they're caught, they will be hanged, drawn, and quartered!" He lowered his voice again. "They're evil enough and desperate enough to do anything you can imagine and a lot of things you can't. *That* is why I mustn't tell you any more. *That* is why I have already told you far too much."

"I don't see—" Suddenly she did see. It was like a shutter being thrown open to let daylight into a cellar. "*Bait*? Spirits! You set me up as *bait*!"

Wart muttered, "Oh, vomit!" under his breath.

"Arrogance!" she said. "Cold-blooded arrogance! You worked out that if the conspirators' masking spells are good enough to fool their own White Sisters but not all the Sisters at the palace, then what they need is more Sisters to help them. And the best place to find White Sisters is Oakendown, so you guessed that they would be snooping around there. *Snake*!" she shouted. "Sir Snake! You mentioned that you'd met him, but you made it sound like a long time ago. I bet the last time you saw *Sir* Snake wasn't any longer ago than the day you met me or the day before—was it?"

Wart stared straight ahead, not speaking. His face looked ready to burst into flames.

"And you got Mother Superior to—No, *Sir Snake* got Mother Superior to expel me! That was the only reason for the spider, wasn't it? You provided a sorcerer to create that spider and frighten me and six children out of their wits. I was trapped, wasn't I? Used! You had me thrown out with no money. Shamed, humiliated. You left me hanging around the gatehouse for days, hoping the traitors would be on the lookout for vulnerable White Sisters. I suppose you even spread rumors of my disgrace around town." She was so indignant she could hardly speak. "*Bait*! You used me as bait!"

Wart glanced at her miserably. "It wasn't my idea."

"But you helped. You're guilty too. You sold your soul to that precious Sir Snake and his Old Blades." Mother Superior was another and must have been helped in the deception by a fair number of senior Sisters. "How much did they pay you? Just the archlute? Is that your reward? And that gold you were flashing around so freely at the inn, I expect. I hope you enjoy your ill-gotten wealth, because it would choke me if I'd earned a penny than way. So Murther and Skuldigger are the first nibble? What happens now? If I'm the bait, then where's the hook?"

Wart stood up to peer over the horse and then look back over the barrels.

"Speak up!" Emerald shouted. "You've told me enough that you can't stop now. I don't have a baby to protect. I know not to try and lie to a White Sister—if they do have traitor Sisters on their team, which I don't believe. Tell me. I'll keep quiet."

Wart looked down at her. "Keep quiet? Will you keep quiet if they nail your hand to a bench and start cracking your fingers with a hammer?"

She shuddered. "I'll think of you when they do it. Come on! You wouldn't just trail bait without a net or a hook of some kind." Magic? No, if Wart had any magic up his sleeve she would have detected it right away. "Tell me! What happens now?"

"What happens now," Wart said harshly, "is that the armed men up ahead stop us and keep us there until the coach coming behind us arrives. Then you get carried off, I expect. You're valuable. You're what they want. If you behave yourself you should be all right, at least for a while. I'm no use to anyone, so the odds are that I get my throat cut. That's what happens now."

14

Ambush

IT WAS A BEAUTIFUL SITE FOR AN AMBUSH. THE trail ran along a very gentle ridge, a stony swell on the landscape; and the dips on either hand were marshy, with reeds and bulrushes. Saxon could not haul the wagon across a swamp, no matter how narrow. Furthermore, the next ridge to the east was slightly higher and the one to the west bore a mane of thorny scrub along its crest, so the site was hidden from any distant onlookers. Perfect.

Wart hauled on the reins; the wagon rattled to a halt.

About a hundred paces ahead, a line of men-at-arms blocked the road. Five of them were busily moving their arms as if working a pump or a bellows, but Emerald realized that they were actually winding up crossbows, the bows standing upright in front of them, each steadied by a stirrup. Another man in the background held the horses. The seventh was obviously the leader, standing on the verge with folded arms.

About the same distance to the north—back the way they had come—a large coach was approaching. The trap was closed.

The bowmen finished spanning their bows and lifted them to the horizontal. On the leader's command, each one pulled a steel-tipped quarrel from his quiver and laid it in the firing groove. The sight of loaded weapons pointed at her made Emerald's skin try to crawl right off her.

"What's the range of those things?"

"Farther than us, but they're only accurate close up." Wart's voice sounded very thin. His blush had totally gone now. He was pale to the lips.

Another command and the men raised their bows, laying the stocks against their cheeks, ready to shoot. They wore swords, steel breastplates, helmets shaped like hats with wide brims. They began to advance in line abreast, and Emerald could not help but imagine one of them stumbling in a rut and accidentally pulling the trigger of his bow. Their leader swaggered close behind, staying out of their line of fire. His red cloak was bright and grand; his helmet was more elaborate than theirs, with cheek pieces and a flange covering the back of his neck. He was a very large man, bushily bearded, armed with only a sword and dagger.

"Thrusk," Wart said hoarsely. He turned and reached under the bench.

"Oh, no!" Emerald muttered. Then she saw that Wart had found the sword and repeated, much louder, "No!"

He was staring at the advancing enemy with hate in his eyes and teeth bared like a dog. At least he had enough sense to hold the sword out of sight behind him—so far.

"Wart, you're crazy! Throw it away right now! *Now,* before they get here. You show that thing and they'll put five bolts through you in an instant." Her protest produced no result at all, as if he had become completely deaf. *Men! Why did men always think violence could solve anything?* "Wart, please! They're in armor—you're not! Even if they didn't have bows, they're trained men-at-arms! You wouldn't have a hope against one of them, let alone six!" She could hear the coach in the distance behind her, coming slowly. Thrusk and his bowmen were going to arrive first.

"Run, Wart! Leave me and the wagon. Just run! See those bushes up—"

"*Run?* Run from bowmen? Run from horsemen?" He did not add, *Run through a swamp?* as he might have done.

"At least throw that wretched old sword away. Be polite, don't annoy them, then maybe Thrusk won't remember you, maybe they'll just leave you here and take me. And I'll be all right—you said so yourself. Then you can go and...and..."

It wasn't working. Wart still snarled, never taking his eyes off his old enemy approaching. "*Now* do you see why I didn't want to tell you? *Now* do you understand why I was strictly ordered *not* to tell you anything *at all?* If you breathe one word, one hint that you were staked out for them to find, then we're both cold meat."

"Yes, Wart. I'm sorry I didn't trust you."

"At least you have a chance."

"So do you, if you'll just throw away that sword. Now, please let go of it and get down from the wagon. *Don't* make them see you as a threat, Wart! Be humble, Wart, please." She had a sudden clear image of him sitting there nailed to the garlic barrel by a bolt through his head. And the shot might hit her by mistake.

"As far as Thrusk is concerned, I'm already under sentence of death." His voice had dropped to a growl.

She had never seen real hate on a man's face before—she could no longer think of Wart as a boy when he looked like that. Yet his only hope of survival lay in seeming harmless to the brigands.

The shrill wailing of that awful sorcery was back, but it was coming from the Marshal and his men—all of them, as far as she could tell.

"Halt!" Thrusk barked.

His little troop halted. They were only a few feet in front of Saxon's nose now—two on the left and three on the right, placed to shoot past the horse at the passengers. The squeaks and hoofbeats in the rear died away as the coach stopped. Horses whinnied greetings. Emerald risked a glance behind her and was not at all surprised to see Murther's purple monster and its four beautiful chestnuts. One of the grooms was opening the door and pulling down the steps, and the armed guards were clambering down from the rooftop seat. Wart with his rusty sword was seriously outnumbered.

Thrusk walked along the verge, staying clear of his men's line of fire, on Wart's side of the wagon. "Get down, both of you."

As Emerald began to move, Wart said, "Stay where you are! By what right do you contest our passage on the King's highway, fat man?"

Thrusk showed yellow teeth in his black jungle of beard. "By right of might, shrimp. Now get down or I'll have my men—Huh?" He took one step closer, peering harder at Wart. So tall was he and so low the wagon that he was looking down, rather than up. "By the eight! It's the minstrel brat, the sneak thief! Well, well, well!" His roar of laughter sent avalanches of ice down Emerald's backbone.

Wart glanced back. So did Emerald.

And so did Thrusk.

Doctor Skuldigger was just emerging from the coach.

Taking advantage of that momentary distraction, Wart made a flying leap from the wagon, swinging the rusty sword in a murderous slash. What he might have achieved with it against a man wearing breastplate and helmet was never established, because he caught a toe on the wheel. His war cry became a howl of despair and he pitched headlong, sprawling in the dirt like a wagonload of firewood. He rolled and his sword rattled away across the gravel.

Emerald ducked, but no crossbow bolts flashed through the air.

"*Flames!*" Thrusk roared. "Try to kill me, would you?" He grabbed the front of Wart's jerkin and hoisted him up bodily with one hand, as if he weighed no more than a blanket.

Wart sagged in his grasp like a rag doll, half stunned by his fall, eyes wobbling, but evidently undaunted. "Killing's too good for you, stinkard!"

Thrusk roared in fury and slammed a fist the size of a loaf of bread against Wart's jaw.

Emerald screamed at such brutality. Wart hit the ground

again, flat on his back. But Thrusk then drew his sword as if
to chop off his opponent's head and the time for screaming
was past. "*Leave him alone!*" She was down on the road
between the two of them with no clear recollection of
hitching up her skirts and completing the sort of mad leap
that Wart had attempted, even in her ill-fitting shoes. "You
get back!" she yelled, spreading her arms.

Thrusk snarled and drew back his free hand to swat her
aside. An instant before he would have spread her as flat as
he had spread Wart, a sepulchral voice spoke at her back.

"Stop!"

At that soft moan, the giant froze.

"Incompetent oaf!" Doctor Skuldigger came mincing
forward, followed a few paces behind by Mistress Murther
and another woman. "Aw? What are you doing, Marshal?
Tell your men to unload those bows at once."

Thrusk barked an order at his troop. "This trash tried
to kill me." He gestured with his sword at the unconscious
Wart, the move being close enough to Emerald's knee that
she jumped aside. His attitude to the Doctor was one of
sulky deference.

Skuldigger was in charge. He sighed. "Aw? I instructed
you that there was to be no bloodshed."

Blood was still being shed. Emerald knelt to examine
Wart. He was out cold and bleeding badly from the mouth.
Whether he had lost teeth or simply split his lips she could
not tell, but his jaw was swelling up like a red cabbage.
Perhaps this experience would cure some of his tricky habits.
Having seen him do midair somersaults off the wagon, she
could not believe he could fall flat on his face like that. He
must have been faking, although she could not guess why.

"Doctor!" she shouted. "This man has been injured and
needs attention."

"I know that brat of old," Thrusk growled. "He's a felon!
He was sentenced to hang years ago. Now he tried to kill
me. Let me have him, master, and—"

The Doctor moaned. "Must I always be served by idiots?
He is half your size, ninny."

The giant growled defiantly. "He attacked me with a sword. You told us we could defend ourselves."

"Bah! He could not hurt you if you had both hands tied behind your back." Skuldigger seemed moved close to tears. He turned to the two women. "Well?"

Murther stayed silent, regarding the world with her inevitable pout. The other woman was younger and might have been judged beautiful if she had made an effort to dress better, comb her hair, stand up straight. Her gown and cloak had originally been of good quality but looked old and abused, as if handed down from a mistress to a servant. She herself was strangely hunched, arms tightly folded across her breast like someone freezing, although the day was warming rapidly. She might be seriously ill. She shook her head and mumbled something Emerald did not catch.

"Stand back!" Skuldigger commanded. "Go, Murther!"

"Back to the horses!" Thrusk roared. He marched off with his bowmen. Mistress Murther stalked back to the coach with her nose in the air. The sorcerous whistling faded almost to nothing.

"Well?" the Doctor demanded again.

The woman looked Emerald over without ever meeting her eyes. She gazed down at Wart, then shuffled over to lay a hand on the wagon. "Nothing," she muttered.

Skuldigger moaned. "You are quite sure of that, Sister? You do remember that any carelessness on your part will have terrible consequences?"

For a moment fire glinted in her eyes, and she bared her teeth at him in fury or hatred. Then the former hopelessness fell over her face like a veil. "Yes, Doctor, I remember."

For a moment the horrible old man seemed almost about to smile. "Then you do not need to worry about being rescued, do you? Sir Snake has outsmarted himself again. Go back to the carriage."

She obeyed, shuffling away as if she carried all the sorrows of the world on her shoulders. Thrusk returned.

Skuldigger sighed heavily, scowling down at the

unconscious Wart. "Your mindless brutality has put a serious hitch in my plans. This boy cannot ride, and I will not have him bleeding all over my coach."

"Tie him across a saddle," Thrusk suggested.

"And if we are seen, idiot?"

"He was condemned to hang years ago, little vermin. Let me hang him, or chop his head off, master. Please?"

Skuldigger sighed mournfully. "No, he will be of use in our experiments. Here is what we shall do. Bring him in the wagon. Lay him face-down so he does not choke on his own blood, aw? You will escort us to the turnoff and wait there for the wagon, as previously planned. If you are quite sure that there is no pursuit, you will bring the boy to the boat."

"And if there is?" the Marshal demanded, his eyes narrowing to shadowed slits inside his helmet.

"I already ordered you to slay as many of them as you can, did I not? But in that case you may kill the boy first. Will that satisfy your blood lust, brute?"

"If I have time to do it properly."

"And see there is not one spot of blood left on the road here—you understand?"

"Yes, master. Not a drop."

"Now we must hurry or we shall miss the tide." The old man turned his agonized, droopy eyes on Emerald. "Give me your bonnet."

"I certainly will not! And I'll thank you to explain by what right you behave like a common brigand on the King's—"

"Hit her."

Thrusk raised a huge fist.

"No!" Emerald cried, stumbling back.

"If you are hurt," the Doctor moaned, "you will have only yourself to blame. Now, the bonnet."

Emerald hauled off her bonnet without ever taking her gaze away from the leering Thrusk; she handed it to the Doctor.

"Now get in the carriage."

"I will not! Are these highwaymen yours, Doctor, because—"

She did not see Thrusk move. One minute he was two paces away from her and the next he was standing over her, chuckling, and she was flat in the dirt. Her head rang. The shock of it left her gasping like a landed fish.

"Aw? I said, 'Get in the carriage.' Now you will force me to have the Marshal kick you in the ribs until you obey. One..."

Emerald scrambled giddily to her feet and lurched along the road to the coach. She might not know for certain who headed the conspiracy against the King, but she could name a convincing suspect. The other woman was obviously the kidnapped Sister whom Wart had mentioned, the one whose child had been taken hostage. Now Emerald was in the same boat. The bait had been taken, but where was the hook?

15

Knights to Remember

STALWART WAS NEVER AWARE OF RECOVERING consciousness. He just gradually understood that he was in a lot of pain and helpless to do anything about it. For one thing he was face-down in a very smelly box, being bounced up and down on bare boards; he could see nothing except chinks of daylight between them. For another, he was bound hand and foot with a noose around his neck, so he dared not try to sit up in case it would choke him and he would not be able to loosen it again. The rope around his wrists was so tight that he could feel nothing at all in his hands. If the blood supply was cut off too long they would die and rot. What use was a swordsman with no hands?

His mouth and jaw felt as if Saxon had kicked him there with all four shoes at once; some of his teeth were loose on that side and the taste of old blood was nauseating. To make it worse, his mouth was held open by a gag, a rag tied around his head. Guess who had done that—no prize offered? He could hear hooves and sometimes two voices, although he could not make out what was being said. The strings of the archlute murmured somewhere close to his ear. Under a heap of smelly sacks he was sweltering, but even in this poorly inhabited part of Chivial, no one could drive around with a corpse in plain view and not get asked questions.

So he was alive, when he had not really expected to be. That situation did not seem much of an advantage at the moment, and Thrusk would make sure it did not last long.

Someone cleverer than Thrusk was in charge, though.

"We mustn't let the enemy suspect that the wagon is being followed," Snake had said. "So we'll stay well back. One of us may ride forward and pass you from time to time, but don't react. Don't show you recognize us. Talk to people whenever you get the chance, because we'll ask the ferrymen and other locals if they remember seeing you going past."

It was a good plan, but someone had been smart enough to see through it. Now the wagon was still trundling along the highway and it still had a man and a woman on the bench. It might be a long time before the Old Blades realized that a switch had been made and Emerald was gone.

Stalwart had known right from the moment Bandit swore him into the Guard that he was destined for danger, and Snake had spelled it out for him an hour or so after that. He had known it but never really believed it—not like he believed now. That morning the prospect of adventure had blinded him to everything else.

He left Ironhall in public shame, head down to avoid the disbelieving stares of the few juniors who happened to be around. There were no seniors in sight—thanks to Bandit and Grand Master, probably—but Bandit himself was at the gate, talking with the Blades guarding it. He did not even look around as Stalwart slunk past, but some of the others scowled and made biting remarks about quitters and cowards. It was not a happy moment.

As soon as he was off by himself amid the lonely wilds of Starkmoor, his usual cheerful spirits returned. Hope and adventure put a spring in his stride and the wind danced with his cloak. He raced along the dusty track, jogging and walking by turns, bothered little by the weight of the lute on his back and not much more by the hunger in his belly.

He never did reach Broom Tarn. About half an hour up the road he turned off on the shortcut over the Rockheap; on the far side of that, safely out of sight of Ironhall, two saddled horses grazed the wiry moorland grass. The man lying on his back nearby seemed intent on the hawks circling in the blue heavens, but he must have been keeping a eye on the horses, too. When Wart came in sight they raised their heads and he sprang up.

He came striding over, hand out in welcome. His clothes were nondescript, almost shabby, but the sword at his side bore a cat's-eye on the pommel. He was not only a Blade, he was the one Stalwart had been desperately hoping he would be, Sir Snake himself—Deputy Commander of the Guard during Stalwart's first years at Ironhall, later dubbed knight and released, then called back to lead the volunteer group they called "the Old Blades." The name he had chosen long ago still fitted him, for he was exceedingly lean; he had a knife-blade nose and a thin mustache. He was devious, they said, clever as a forestful of foxes. He had not named his sword anything obvious like *Fang* or *Venom*. No, she was called *Stealth*, and that said a lot about him.

His eyes twinkled as he pumped Wart's hand and thumped his shoulder.

"Was counting on you," he said. "Never thought you'd fail us. Welcome to the Blades, brother!" He laughed, joyous as the summer morning. "And welcome, O Youngest of All Blades, to the *Old* Blades, the unbound Blades! I have a job for you that will make your hair stand on end!" He made that sound like a great virtue. He led the way over to the horses—and what horses they were! The King himself rode nothing better.

"I brought a sword for you to wear. Not a cat's-eye, I'm afraid, but we'll get your real sword to you shortly. Can't have a Blade walking around unarmed, like a peasant."

"That's very kind of you, Sir Snake."

"Oh, you go pile *that* manure elsewhere, my lad! You're one of us now. You call me 'Snake' or 'brother,' understand? There's food in the saddlebags and you can eat as we ride…. The King is 'sire' to his face and 'Fat Man' when he's not around. Bandit is 'Leader.' You can be polite to Dreadnought and Grand Master when you feel like it, but don't ever give me titles. Now let's—" He paused for an instant. "And Durendal. Him we honor because he's still the greatest of us all. No one else. Now get your tender young behind on that saddle. We have the width of Chivial to ride before we'll see a bed tonight. Yes, I'll tell you all about it as we go." He went to put his foot back in his stirrup and then paused again. "I'm told they call you Wart. Which do you want to be from now on—Wart or Stalwart?"

"Wart's more fitting…Snake. Call me Stalwart when I grow into it."

The glittery eyes studied him for a moment. "You may have earned it by next week."

"Then call me Stalwart next week," the boy said crossly, and swung himself up into the saddle. He wished they would all stop talking about danger and tell him what it was they wanted him to do.

If they did not ride the whole width of Chivial that day, they certainly crossed most of it, thundering along on the finest horses Stalwart had ever ridden. Until that journey he had rather fancied his skills in the saddle, but Snake was superb. Every hour or so they had changed mounts at a posting inn, taking horses reserved for the Royal Couriers, the best steeds in the land. As they rode, Snake spelled out the plan.

"It's risky, of course," he admitted, "but I think we've thought of most things that can go wrong." He had not foreseen Thrusk.

Stalwart had blundered, yes. He had thrown his expense money around at Three Roads. That had been a stupid childish impulse, exactly the sort of mistake that might warn an enemy he was not what he was pretending to be. Nor should he have told Emerald that she was being used as bait. Yet he might still have pulled it off if Thrusk had not come on the scene. Thrusk's involvement had been the worst of all possible luck, misfortune that could never have been predicted.

He remembered how Thrusk had sworn to get even with him, that day at Firnesse Castle. On the way to the latrines, Thrusk had collected a dozen men to come and watch the fun. Public executions were always a big draw, and no one had ever seen a thief executed quite this way before. The jokes were flying thick and fast.

When they reached their destination, one man blocked their path. He had gray in his beard and weather lines etched in his face, but a cat's-eye shone yellow on the pommel of his sword, and a diamond Star on his jerkin warned that he was in royal favor.

"This joke is not funny, Marshal," Sir Vincent said quietly. "Untie the boy. I'm taking him off your hands."

Thrusk responded with a drum roll of oaths. Vincent took hold of his sword hilt and there was silence.

"If you call me one more bad name I shall draw. If you force me to draw, for any reason whatsoever, then you die first. This I swear."

That was all it took. That was what it meant to be a Blade, even a Blade with a grizzled beard facing a dozen young men-at-arms. Thrusk sent a page to tell the Baron what was happening. He came at once and followed them all the way to the gate, screaming outrage. "Arrest that man! I am a lord of the high justice! This is rebellion against the King's Peace! I shall complain to the Privy Council!" On and on. He was a plump little man with absurdly bowed legs and a very shrill voice. Sir Vincent mostly ignored him, and nobody dared interfere with Sir Vincent.

Unable to believe this change in his fortunes, little Wat Hedgebury the minstrel's apprentice walked out under the portcullis clutching the lute he had almost died for—in hands that would not stop trembling. Vincent's servant was waiting there with two horses. The knight gave the man the lute to bring and pulled the boy up behind him on his own mount, although he still stank mightily of his climb up the sewer in the night.

Before Vincent could urge his mount forward, Thrusk's voice bellowed down from the battlements: "Don't think you're going to get away with this, thief! You can't hide behind that old brigand forever. One day I'll catch you and give you what you deserve."

Vincent turned his horse to get a better view. "You want to come down here and repeat that?"

"Go while you can, old man. We're about to loose the dogs on you. And if you do take that trash with you, don't be surprised when your silverware starts disappearing. One day we'll stretch his neck for him."

"Don't be so sure of that!" Vincent roared, the first time he had raised his voice. "Boys grow up. Next time you meet it may be his turn to jeer." He kicked in his heels and the two horses cantered off along the road. For the next hour a gang of Thrusk's flunkies rode at a safe distance behind them, shouting threats and insults.

They were leagues from Firnesse before Wat Hedgebury could speak at all. Then he just said, "Thank you, sir," in a small whisper. His hands were *still* shaking.

The old man did not look around. "You are most welcome, lad. I enjoyed that little episode more than I have enjoyed anything for a long time. And you earned it."

He did not explain that remark then. They stopped at the first Eastfare estate they came to, and he had his new friend throughly scrubbed and clad in fresh clothes. He ordered the old ones burned, and perhaps his own also. And it was there, when the two of them were eating a meal in a humble farmhouse kitchen, that he first spoke the magic name of Ironhall.

"You have wonderful agility," he said. "You most certainly have courage. And you have a sense of justice. I think you would make an excellent Blade to serve your King."

The future Stalwart had laughed heartily, convinced that the knight was joking.

The old man smiled, knowing that he was being misunderstood. "Was Owain a relative?"

"No, sir."

"Have you any family at all?"

Wat shook his head, munching bread and cold roast goose.

"How old are you?"

"Almost thirteen, master."

"'Almost' may be good enough. We must put you somewhere out of those men's reach. The Baron is just a windbag, but that Thrusk is pure poison. He carries grudges. Somewhere far away. Do you really want to be a minstrel all your life, singing for the gentry, cap in hand for a copper penny? Sleeping in stables, trudging winter roads in leaky boots? Wouldn't you rather be one of the gentles yourself?"

And Wat—he was always to remember that stunning moment when he realized that this talk was not just a gentleman's joke—stopped chewing and stared in disbelief.

Sir Vincent shuddered. "Close your mouth, boy!"

After a swallow that almost choked him, the boy whispered, "Me?"

"You."

"*A gentleman?* Is that possible?"

"I'd say the King's right hand itself is possible. If you want, I'll take you to Ironhall. Grand Master will accept you, I promise. You're much too good to waste." He chuckled at the boy's stare of disbelief. "Weather looks good. They don't expect me back at Valglorious for a few days yet. We can start right now if you're ready."

16

Unpleasant Journey

SKULDIGGER'S COACH-AND-FOUR MADE NO great speed along the dusty, rutted trail, but for comfort it could not be surpassed. It could seat four people at ease and six at a pinch on softly padded benches upholstered in mauve silk. Yet Emerald wished fervently that she were back in Wart's smelly wagon. Thrusk's blow had left the side of her head swollen and throbbing; she was going to have a black eye from it.

The bait had been taken. If the mysterious Sir Snake was hoping to catch her kidnappers red-handed, he had better pounce soon. While she hated to concede a point to anyone as odious as Doctor Skuldigger, it did seem that he had won the bout, that Snake had been outwitted and must still be watching the wagon. She had last seen it being driven by one of Skuldigger's coach guards clad in Wart's cap and jerkin, with Murther beside him sporting Emerald's bonnet.

To increase her misery, she was a prisoner in a vehicle screaming with magic. It came from the coachman on his box, the grooms on the back, the remaining man-at-arms on the roof. At times she could even hear it from Thrusk's escort when they rode close.

Skuldigger sat on the rear bench of the carriage, facing

his two captives, and for a long time he seemed to be lost in thought, staring at nothing with the woebegone look of a basset hound. After an hour or so, the carriage left the rutted trail which was flattered with the name of highway and began following a barely visible path over the rolling moorland. Now it moved slowly, often splashing through shallow ponds and streams. The wind brought a scent of the sea. He roused himself.

"Well, Sister Emerald, I am ready to hear your—"

"I told you last night, Doctor! If I were a White Sister I should never have been riding in that wagon."

He groaned. "Aw? Emerald, you must never, never interrupt me when I am speaking, or I shall be forced to punish you. If you do not answer all my questions courteously and truthfully, without attempt to mislead or omit pertinent information, then you will have only yourself to blame for what you will have to endure in consequence. Is this not correct, Sister Swan?"

Swan had been staring fixedly out the window. She turned toward Emerald but did not meet her eye. "He will have you flogged or branded. He is utterly without compassion, utterly ruthless. He is also completely crazy, but no one can defy him. Resist him and he will break you."

Skuldigger showed no resentment at being called a madman. "A very exact description of the situation—if you disobey you must be punished. You cannot hope to escape from Quagmarsh, where we are headed, so you may as well accept reality now and save yourself unnecessary suffering. I cannot use sorcery on you without destroying the abilities I need in you, so I am forced to resort to brutality." His tone and manner implied this was an unavoidable tragedy. "Marshal Thrusk supplies this quite willingly and in much greater quantities than you can possibly withstand. Clear?"

"Yes, Doctor." Her mouth was very dry.

"Sister Swan cooperates with me, you see? Her daughter, Belle, is a beautiful child, but she has the sort of fair skin that scars easily. Her mother knows that I left strict orders to feed the girl to the chimeras tomorrow, so it is essential that

I return safely to Quagmarsh in good time to countermand those orders."

Swan was staring out the window again. She seemed to be weeping.

"Now, Emerald," Skuldigger moaned, "I want the true story. I am aware that Sister Swan cannot judge your truthfulness under the present circumstances, but when we reach Quagmarsh, I shall ask you if you lied to me. Swan can tell me then how truthfully you respond; if her reports are not favorable, terrible things will happen to you."

Emerald had made a grave mistake in worming even a small part of the story out of Wart. If she were still as ignorant as she had been when she left Oakendown, she could talk freely. Now she knew things that she must not mention: Sir Snake, attempts on the King's life that were not generally known, poisoned shirts, ensorcelled saddles, and even previous knowledge that Swan and her daughter had been kidnapped. If she lied she would be detected. If she refused to talk, she would be tortured.

"I am not a Sister. I was—for one whole day. Then I was expelled. The Companionship was shipping me home in that farm cart."

The improbability of this tale made Doctor Skuldigger even sadder than before. "But you must have known you were being set out as lure for me?"

"No. I never heard of you—I knew nothing about you. And still don't."

He pouted. "Expelled for what cause?"

"I witnessed a sorcery and was ordered to lie about it. And wouldn't."

"Expelled? Expelled when half the country is screaming for White Sisters to protect them from myself and some of my colleagues? You wouldn't be expelled if you committed multiple murders. Then you just happen to be billeted in the same room as Mistress Murther, who is my agent looking out for potential recruits. Are you so stupid that you believe this to be mere coincidence?"

"Not now I don't. Now I think as you do, that I was

deliberately set out as bait. But I am an innocent victim. I never saw the boy before and know nothing about him except what he told me." She had spoken the truth so far.

"The boy will be questioned, do not worry." The Doctor uttered another of his moans. "Aw? I am sure you are right. It is tragic that you must suffer so, but the fault lies entirely with the King and that bullyboy of his called Snake. He is a fool, though, and easily outwitted. Swan could find no trace of magic on you or the wagon or even the boy. I hope you do not disagree with her evaluation?" The bleary, red-rimmed eyes peered inquiringly at Emerald.

"I detected no sorcery." Except an indefinable something about Wart...but lots of people bore such imbalances. It was certainly too faint to be of any importance.

Skuldigger showed his lower teeth in what was apparently a smile. "So Snake was relying on purely secular means to track you, my dear, and I have now outsmarted him. It is not the first time, and I am sure it will not be the last."

"I am sure you are right, master." Still she was telling no lies!

"When Murther sent word that she had located a suitable recruit, I suspected right away that you were a decoy. I detected the unsubtle hand of Snake, but I came anyway, because the man is nothing but a trained sword swinger, without finesse or ability. I suppose that eventually even the King will see that. But perhaps not, because Ambrose himself is a bigger fool than any. For years this fair land of Chivial has been molested by the evil Baels, and when someone attempts to do something about them, he is harried and persecuted. The King is not just a fool but also a profligate, power-crazy tyrant!"

Swan glanced very briefly at Emerald and then returned to staring out the window.

Emerald said, "I don't think I understand, Doctor." She would rather have the madman gloating over his own cleverness than interrogating her.

"The Baels, child! For years these pirates and slavers have molested our coasts at will. Foolish Ambrose can do nothing about them. Only superior sorcery will defeat them; yet I and others like me, who strive to develop this magic, are hounded by his government. Such research takes years and vast amounts of gold, yet we are persecuted by rapacious tax gatherers. And when some of my colleagues attempted to remonstrate, they were denounced as traitors!"

He was probably referring to the Night of Dogs, but Emerald did not need to comment. He was ranting, paying no attention to her or Swan.

"Now this despot is attempting to put us out of business altogether and ban our research! Well, we have ways of dealing with such incompetents, and you will have the honor of assisting us. Soon, I promise you, the crown will sit on the head of a three-year-old boy, and a regency council will certainly display more sense than his father ever did. The bungling Snakes and Durendals will be swept aside, and the government of this country will be in the hands of more rational men. Aw? I believe we have arrived."

17

Reluctant Ally

HOW MANY HOURS HAD HE BEEN LYING IN THE wagon? His feet were as numb as his hands now, but the waves of pain around the gag in his mouth were worse than ever.

The wagon had left the road, and that was bad—very, very bad. That was disaster. He had laid the best trail he could, as he had been instructed, but it had turned out to be the *wrong* trail. At Three Roads he had bribed four separate boys to look out for men wearing cat's-eye swords and tell them about the mysterious Mistress Murther and Doctor Skuldigger, a man with a Grimshank connection. *Do not forget to mention Thrusk!* he had warned them all.

And that had been a terrible mistake. The wagon was rocking over hillocks, it was splashing through streams and ponds. It was not on the public road at all. It was not going to Firnesse, so when Snake and his men learned that they had been hoodwinked, they would go looking in the wrong direction entirely.

That was exactly the sort of foul-up Sir Vincent had predicted.

About halfway on that other journey, the one from

Ironhall to Valglorious, and about the time Stalwart realized that Snake was serious when he said they were going to ride right across the country that day, they picked up another of the Old Blades, Sir Chefney. He had been a fencer of renown and Deputy Commander back when Montpurse was leader. There was something utterly unreal in riding stirrup to stirrup with such men and casually saying, "Tell me about the times you won the King's Cup, brother."

Brother!

Chefney laughed. "Just twice—353 and 357. What was different those years was that Durendal wasn't competing. I came second to him a couple of times, but I could never beat him. Never did, not once, even in practice. Then Jarvis came on the scene and turned me into a has-been. I hear you're pretty fast yourself, brother."

Brother!

After twelve hours in the saddle, Wart staggered into the great hall at Valglorious and the arms of Sir Vincent. The old man's beard was pure white now, but his back was still straight and his eyes were bright as a child's. Indeed they glistened and Wart could hardly see them for his own tears. Brushing aside the congratulations, he fell on his knees and took Vincent's hand to kiss.

"It is your doing, sir! If I have achieved anything, it was because I had to be worthy of your trust."

"Get up, you young rascal!" the knight said gruffly. "And no more of this 'sir' talk. You're my brother in the Order now."

"Never!" Wart said. "If you will not allow 'sir,' then I shall call you 'father' and nothing less."

"Listen to that!" Snake said. "I can't wait to hear how he talks when he starts chasing girls. Are you going to feed us, brother, or lay our bones in the ossuary?"

"Food's coming," Vincent said. "I don't know any man who can eat like you and stay so thin. If you were my horse I would worm you. But first I want to see what Ironhall has made of this minstrel trash I picked up. Come along, all of you."

"Good idea," Snake said blithely. "Work out some of the knots."

It was unbelievable. It was inhuman! Twelve hours in the saddle and they expected a man to fence? Of course they did. He was a Blade now.

The great hall, to which Vincent now led his guests, could have been used for horse racing or indoor archery. Lit that evening only by flickering candles, its walls soared up into mysterious darkness. There would be ample space, but light was going to be a problem. Even with blunt épées, fencing practice was never totally without danger. By the time they reached the senior class at Ironhall, future Blades scorned the use of padded garments or even face masks. Swordsmanship was not a game to them, and a few bangs with a steel bar taught the importance of a good defense like nothing else could. But Ironhall had an octogram and skilled enchanters ready to treat injuries right away. Valglorious almost certainly did not, so what Stalwart's new brothers were proposing seemed utterly crazy. He wondered if it was his fencing they wanted to test or his courage. Poking out a friend's eye would be a poor start to his career in the Guard.

Jerkins and doublets were shed. Wart faced off against Sir Vincent. His instinct was to let the old man win, of course, but he knew that such courtesy would be no kindness in this case. Furthermore, to deceive any man about his fencing ranked as mortal sin in the Blades' code, and these men would not be taken in. He began cautiously, parrying every stroke and making little effort to riposte until he could judge the light. The swords clattered and clanged. Then he flashed in with Rainbow, one of his favorite routines. It was easy.

"A hit!"

Vincent laughed. "It was indeed. Try that again."

Clink, clatter—Cockroach! "Another!" *There! This is what you made of me!*

"I'm dead!" the old man agreed. "I think my judgment

has been vindicated." He looked to Chefney. "Show us how your wind is standing up to the years, brother?"

"Not worth a glob of pond slime," Chefney retorted. "Snake, you found this whippersnapper. You cut him down to size for us."

"Obviously I must teach him respect for his betters," said Snake, removing his doublet. He accepted the épée, raised it briefly in salute, and then went for Wart like a wildcat.

Back and forth the two of them danced on the flagstones, and their blades rang to the rafters. Now Boy Wonder had a real battle on his hands, because Snake was only two years past his release from the Guard, still very much in his prime. He had never won the King's Cup, but he had always been a respected fencer and he could call on many times Stalwart's experience. Every routine had its counter, and Snake knew them all—Violet...Willow...Steeple...Butterfly.... Lunge and parry, engagement and envelopment and *froissement*...

How about *Woodpecker*, then?

Snake yelped in surprise as Stalwart's blade tapped the side of his throat. "Do that again!"

Clatter...*Vulture*?

"*Ouch*!"

"Sorry," Stalwart said. "A little harder than I intended."

"Again!" Snake roared, sounding seriously annoyed now.

He was outclassed, though. Four times his new protégé scored, and at last he conceded defeat, puffing mightily.

Wart had beaten Snake himself! Wow! What would they say back in Ironhall if they knew that?

"Give me!" Chefney said, reaching for the blade. "Show *me* how you do it, brother."

To go up against the great Chefney would have seemed like insanity a mere ten minutes ago, but now Stalwart's dander was up. He fizzed with excitement. "At you, then!"

Clitter, clatter...Oops..."A hit!" Stalwart admitted. "Again!"

Another hit...

And another...He tried Vulture again, and even Castanet, but nothing worked. After the fifth point he lowered his foil, resisting the temptation to hurl it to the floor. He had forgotten what humiliation felt like. Five to nothing and in about two minutes! The old man was not even breathing hard, and he must be three times Stalwart's age. *Has-been* indeed! Boy Wonder could feel his face burning with shame.

"What's he doing wrong, Chef?" Snake asked. "What did I miss?"

Chefney did not answer him. He spoke instead to Stalwart as the two of them were resuming their doublets. "Where did you get all that complicated rubbish?"

"From Sir Quinn," Stalwart admitted. The recently appointed Master of Rapiers had a collection of highly unusual routines he called Fancy Stuff, which he claimed had won duels against skilled opponents in the past. He warned that they must only be used as a last resort, and he taught them only to the best, those who had already mastered the standard Ironhall style. They had worked against Snake well enough.

Snake was not Chefney.

"Forget the flimflammery!" Chefney said sourly. "Stick with what works. If you can't beat an outsider with Ironhall basics, then nothing is going to save you."

"Yes, brother," Stalwart said as humbly as he could, donning his cloak. "I'll remember." *No more Fancy Stuff!*

"Good. Do that and you'll be a serious contender for the Cup inside three years."

"I *will?*" Stalwart asked, suspecting mockery.

"Certainly. Your speed's incredible—lightning in a bottle— and your footwork's the best I've seen since Durendal. You'd have wiped me clean just now if you hadn't tried to be so fandangle clever." The expert turned away, leaving Stalwart gaping. "Where's that meal you promised, Vincent?"

Snake grinned. "I'm going to start putting money on him now."

"You won't get any takers here," Sir Vincent said proudly, thumping Stalwart's shoulder. "Never met a wolf looked so like a rabbit."

So losing didn't matter after all. It was a gloriously

unbelievable ending to an unbelievable day. Unfortunately the deadly Sir Stalwart spoiled it all by falling asleep at the table with his head among the dishes. He did not wake even when Snake and Chefney carried him upstairs and put him to bed.

Sir Vincent was a knight in the Order, castellan of Valglorious, regent of the Duchy of Eastfare, member of the White Star, a baronet in his own right, one of the most honored men in the realm. He was too old to join the Old Blades and fight in the Monster War, even had he not had a dukedom to run. Although he had politely refrained from asking questions when three brother Blades dropped in on him, he knew that theirs was not just a sentimental visit. They wanted something.

The next morning he called them to account. And since this meeting was business and not social, he held it with all four of them standing in the great hall, in front of the gigantic fireplace. There was no one else present. He was dressed more formally than he had been the previous evening; a four-pointed diamond star glinted on his jerkin. Snake, to Wart's great amusement, was flaunting an identical bauble. It had not been in evidence a few minutes earlier, during breakfast.

The thin man outlined the problem of the unknown assassins. Chefney explained how a White Sister was to be offered as bait and how she would be watched during the two or three days she would be made to wait in Tyton. "If no approach is made to her there, then the Companionship will provide transportation to her home, which is near Newhurst. Rather than sending her by stage, though, we thought we would make her seem more vulnerable."

"Let Wart outline this part," Snake said.

So Wart took over the tale, showing that he understood the role he was to play and the various contingency plans Snake and Chefney had devised. He threw in a couple of suggestions of his own, which won thoughtful nods from his superiors.

"And if the evildoers still ignore her," Snake concluded, "we shall have her watched for two or three weeks after she arrives in Newhurst. But that may be too late. The King may well be dead by then."

Vincent's face had been growing darker and darker. Now he said, "And what do you want from me?"

Snake nodded to Wart to answer that one, too.

"Well, sir, mostly we need a reasonable excuse for me to be driving a wagon south from Oakendown by a fairly roundabout route, so the conspirators have time to organize the grab, if that's what they decide to do. We hope you will loan us the horse and wagon and let me pose as one of your hands. Your knowledge of the area, of course...a really rusty, hacked-up sword if you can find one, and..." He wilted under the old man's glare. "And your blessing on our venture, father."

"You *cut* that *out!*" the old castellan snapped. "I am not your father, and if I were I would forbid this nonsense absolutely." He turned his anger on Snake. "No blessing from me! I think the entire scheme is disgraceful and unworkable. The trick you propose playing on the girl is utterly base, unworthy of our Order. The danger to both her and the boy is unconscionable. He'll end in a ditch with his throat cut. I cannot imagine how you can be so unscrupulous as even to consider such a monstrous fraud."

His visitors exchanged glum glances.

"Because we're desperate," Snake said. "Four attempts in the last month? Leader is going out of his mind. We honestly believe they, whoever *they* are, will succeed next time or the one after."

Vincent bent his head and began to pace back and forth before the great stone mantel. After a moment he stopped and scowled at Snake. "You're telling me the Companionship has agreed to this?"

"With distaste, obviously, but they would rather stage a kidnapping under controlled conditions than lose any more Sisters completely. Mother Superior selected the—hmm—

the victim herself and has been cooperating with Brother Chefney in the planning."

What Snake had told Wart the previous day was that Mother Superior's audience with the King had been extremely noisy, with much royal shouting. The Blades on duty outside the door had reported that she came out in tears. But she was cooperating now.

Vincent grunted and went back to his pacing. Then he reached a decision. "No. I will not be associated with such deceit. I bid you good chance, brothers, and safe journey."

He was not the sort to be talked into changing his mind once he had made it up. Snake shrugged hopelessly and looked at Chefney to see if he had any suggestions, but it was Wart who spoke up.

"It shocked me, too, sir, until I thought about it. I haven't met a White Sister yet, but I'm told they're honorable, dedicated women. I agree that it's unkind to involve one without her consent, but her sisters in the Companionship are probably being tortured into cooperating and one of them has a child with her. If this Sister Emerald is at all typical, she should support our efforts wholeheartedly. She won't be in as much danger as I will, because she will be the prize. And if it is me you are worried about, remember that I am the only man in the Guard who has a hope of pulling this off. It has to be me. Binding leaves a scar and it also marks a man so the Sisters can detect him. Anyone but me will be slaughtered on the spot. Me, I'm just a kid. Who could suspect me of being dangerous? Only yesterday, father, I swore to set my life as nothing to—"

Vincent's face had turned very red. "*I am not your father!*"

Wart shouted right back at him. "Then stop behaving as if you are! Think, *brother!* When you were my age and a senior at Ironhall, if you had been offered this chance to serve your king, wouldn't you have grabbed it with both hands, danger or no danger? This is what Blades are for! You made me what I am. Don't destroy me now!"

"Destroy you? *They* will destroy you!—these two

scoundrels. Boy, I'm as old as both of them put together and I say they've dazzled you with all their clever planning—contingency this and supposition that. It's too complicated. They've forgotten that chance is elemental, and sooner or later chance always outsmarts us, all of us. Something totally unforeseen will trip you up and ruin it all."

That should have been the end of it. Wart thought it was the end, and it was with no great hope that he added, "Well, we'll do the best we can without you, sir. If I die, I'll be in good company. Twenty-four brothers in the last half year! That's one a week."

Vincent glared at him, then at Snake. "You're really determined to go through with this whether I help or not?"

"I have no choice, brother."

"Of course we'll do it," Wart said, "*brother.*"

"Flames and death!" The old man shook his head. "Then we'd better talk about it a little more.... Let me get my steward." He stalked over to a bell rope.

Under his breath, Snake hissed, "You sing a sweet song, minstrel."

"Don't I!" Wart whispered happily.

He had won Sir Vincent over, but the song he sang had turned out to be his own funeral dirge.

18

Chimeras

THE COACH HALTED ON VERY MARSHY GROUND near the edge of a wood. Descending the steps behind Doctor Skuldigger, Emerald found herself enveloped in dense clouds of insects. Horses lashed tails and angrily splashed their hooves in the mud. Certainly the sea was not far off, for its tangy scent was detectable even under the fetid stench of swamp. The view inland was blocked by a gentle rise in the land, but no buildings or landmarks explained why this place was significant. As soon as Swan came down, one of the grooms folded up the steps and closed the door.

Swan's eyes were red with weeping. She stood hunched and downcast, making no effort to sidle out of the group, even ignoring the tormenting bugs. Emerald hoped the two of them might move off by themselves so she could ask a few private questions. She also wanted to escape the nerve-racking shriek of sorcery emanating from the men.

"Herrick and Thatcher, you will return with me," Skuldigger decreed. Without a word the remaining guard clambered up beside the coachman on the box. Why were all these men so surly? It must have something to do with the magic they bore.

The four horses leaned into their collars and the big vehicle began to squelch forward. In moments it gathered speed and dwindled into the distance.

One of the grooms headed toward the woods on a very faint trail that had been trampled through the reeds and sedge. Swan followed him without being told. Emerald hesitated, wondering if she should make a break for freedom now, whether she could outrun the men and hide in the trees.

Then something roared in the wood—from the sound of it, something very large and very fierce. The groom leading the way screamed and came racing back, with Swan close behind, both of them looking over their shoulders. Whatever it was roared again and the undergrowth swayed. Emerald caught a whiff of sorcery like a foul animal stink.

"There's one in the trees!" the other man yelled. "It's coming!"

"No need for panic!" said Skuldigger testily.

From a pouch at his belt he produced a small golden object, which he put to his lips like a whistle. The result was not sound but a blast of magic, a bolt of pain straight through Emerald's head, making her cry out. *Something* went crashing away through the wood. There was a splash in the distance, silence.

"*What* was that?" she demanded.

All the men ignored her. Swan said, "A chimera," and turned her back, unwilling to explain what a chimera was.

"It's gone now!" Skuldigger sighed. "Bring the prisoners." He stalked off with his sword swinging at his side.

Swan followed him. The grooms, Herrick and Thatcher, closed in on Emerald as if intending to resort to violence without further ado. Slipping and splashing and cursing her ill-fitting shoes, she let herself be shepherded after the Doctor.

The wood itself turned out to be a mere fringe of shrubbery and sickly saplings along the bank of a river or tidal channel—dark, still, and unwholesome. The far bank was similarly wooded. On the black mud beach lay a flat-bottomed boat, which doomed any remaining hope that Snake and his men might be able to track the kidnappers back to their lair. Skuldigger climbed over the side and paused to look with distaste at the seating. It was wet.

Granted that the punt lay in shadow, the day was too hot for the thwarts to stay damp very long. Recalling the splash she had heard a few moments earlier, Emerald went to inspect the narrow mud flat beside the boat. She did not have to look hard to find the footprint. There was only one, for the crushed weeds nearby would not hold an impression. Here the chimera had come, fleeing from Skuldigger's magical whistle, and here it had planted one foot as it dived into the river. The indentation was very deep, made by a heavy animal moving fast, but it was still clearly visible, for the water seeping in had not yet filled it. It was about the length of a human print, although much wider, and it had the same five toes grouped together at the front. She was no woodsman, but her father had often shown her animal tracks in snow and identified them for her, and this was like nothing she had ever seen. Each of those five clearly defined toes must bear a talon as big as her thumb. A bear? She was not familiar with bear spoor.

She took a few steps back along the way the thing had come, trying to imagine what sort of monster might have inspired such fright in Swan and the two grooms. Hearing a drone of flies like a pipe organ in the trees to one side of the trail, she turned that way.

"Emerald, where are you going?" Skuldigger called.

"To look at...*this!*"

This was a carcass, bloody and shredded, with bones and meat scattered around. Scraps of white fat and gray fur lay in a separate pile. The chimera had been interrupted while feeding on whatever that litter of flesh had been.

"Harbor seal," Skuldigger announced, joining her. He sounded almost pleased, less mournful than usual. "I wonder if it wandered into the river or if my pets are venturing out to sea now?"

"Chimeras?"

"I call them that, yes." He was wearing the golden whistle on a gold chain around his neck.

"I do not see," Emerald said as calmly as she could manage, "any signs that the carcass was dragged there." It had been carried in, then. There had been only one splash, one chimera. "How much would a harbor seal weigh, Doctor?"

"This appears to have been an adult male. Substantially more than Marshal Thrusk."

"Chimeras are large animals?"

He uttered a peculiar choking noise that was probably a laugh. "Large, yes. Animals...not entirely."

The Doctor sat on one of the punt's two thwarts. The women took the other, at his back, while Herrick and Thatcher stripped off their road-stained and uncomfortable livery. Wearing only knee breeches, they waded into the mud and then pushed, heaved, and grunted in efforts to launch the ungainly craft.

"We are a little early for the tide," Skuldigger announced without turning around. "It may be necessary for you two to disembark and—Ah, here we go!"

The boat moved, and once it had started the two men easily slid it the rest of the way into the water. They scrambled aboard, mud caked from the knees down, and grabbed up poles in time to stop the awkward craft from running aground on the far bank. Then they turned her and began poling her along the channel. Although there was no visible current, Emerald decided that they were heading downstream. She was judging by the height of the sun at her back, a feeling that the day was aging into late afternoon, and knowledge that the sea lay to the east. After a few moments the channel curved around so that she had the sun in her face. Another channel came in on the right. At that point she gave up trying to memorize the way through the maze. Thatcher and Herrick heaved on their poles, working their hearts out. She at least could fan the flies away from her face. Their sweating torsos were peppered with bugs like black freckles.

Skuldigger glanced around briefly. "I advise you to sit nearer the center," he moaned.

Emerald realized that he and the two boatmen were keeping careful watch on the black, oily water and the sinister woods. She hastily moved away from the side. Swan had needed no warning. The punt suddenly seemed very narrow. "Can a chimera snatch people out of boats?"

Swan just nodded.

Emerald tried again. "Doctor, what exactly is a chimera?"

Without turning his head, he replied in a loud lament, as if he were addressing a large funeral. "Quagmarsh used to be a fishing village. I cannot call it a 'humble' fishing village, because in fact it was extremely arrogant, denying allegiance to any lord and claiming an ancient history. There was a token stockade around it, but the foolish inhabitants relied for their safety on the assumption that only they had the specialized geographic knowledge and boats of sufficiently shallow draft to navigate these marshes. Possibly they also assumed that they owned nothing worth stealing. Aw! They learned the magnitude of their folly about ten years ago, when a party of Baelish raiders came in on a spring tide. Baels are slavers and their longships draw very little water. They stripped Quagmarsh of everyone except old people. You can still see where they tried to burn it down, but there must have been rain that day. The survivors fled inland and Quagmarsh stood empty until my colleagues and I moved in a few months ago."

He paused to stare suspiciously at an unexplained ripple until the punt was safely past it. "If the Baels would just try to repeat their success now, the results would be very interesting, a foretaste of what will happen when I launch my attack on Baelmark itself. The most important thing you must learn in Quagmarsh, Emerald—other than total loyalty to myself and instant obedience to my wishes—is to stay inside the stockade at all times. This is true even in daylight, but at night it is essential. Several people have ignored that rule and paid dearly for their imprudence, including two of your predecessors. We rarely find more than fragments of bloodstained fabric or some well-gnawed bones."

After a moment he added, "The same fate befalls any outsider who wanders close to the village. This may seem unkind, but it is the fault of King Ambrose. While he persecutes us, we are forced to defend ourselves as best we can with our limited resources. Chimeras are always hungry. This must have something to do with their extraordinary growth, which I cannot as yet explain."

This time the silence remained unbroken. The punt moved on. Apparently the lecture was over, but he had not said exactly what a chimera was or looked like. Swan would know, but she was clearly too cowed to speak at all.

19

Quagmarsh

THE FIRST SIGN OF THE VILLAGE WAS A LOW DOCK of rotting wooden pilings lining the left-hand shore. Behind that stood a wooden palisade, so mossy and ramshackle that it seemed like part of the forest. When Herrick and Thatcher brought the punt in against the wharf and held it there with their poles, Skuldigger removed the golden whistle from his neck and dropped the chain over the head of the taller of the two, whichever one he was. "Go back and wait for the Marshal. Obey his orders. If he does not come, do not wait long enough to miss the tide."

"Master." The man's reply was little more than a grunt.

With the tide in, it was possible to step from the side of the punt straight onto the dock, and thus Emerald followed Swan and the Doctor ashore. The bank was treacherous, a mixture of mud and decayed timber, and in some places the pilings had collapsed to let the soil slide away, leaving gaps like giant bite marks. Nevertheless Swan took off at a run for the gate, going in search of her daughter. Skuldigger strode along behind her, making no effort to call her back.

Emerald followed more cautiously. She was unimpressed by the palisade leaning over her, which had obviously been built many years ago out of the spindly trunks of local trees.

It was a mossy, half-rotten fence, not much more than head height, sagging like the flesh on a dowager's neck. She could not imagine how such a wreck could keep out monsters capable of killing and eating full-grown seals. Anyone could knock a hole through that if she had to.

Just before the Doctor reached the gate, two middle-aged men and a young woman came hurrying out. They greeted him warmly—very warmly in the woman's case. Flames! It had never occurred to Emerald that there could be a Mistress Skuldigger. Would she be as crazy as her husband? This question should soon be answered, because the men vanished inside, chatting busily, while the lady waited for Emerald.

First impressions were not favorable. Her rose-and-gold gown was crafted of the finest silk and decorated with innumerable sequins and seed pearls—far better suited for court than a backwater in the swamps. As a concession to reality, the toes of black leather boots showed under the hem of its widely spread skirt, but nothing of the lady herself was visible, being hidden by long sleeves, white gloves, and a red straw hat inside a veil of muslin that completely enveloped her head like a bag. Granted that the overall effect was bizarre, the outfit was practical enough to protect her from both insects and the mire underfoot. She did catch the eye in a little place like this.

"I am Sister Carmine!" she announced in the imperious tones of a herald proclaiming the entry of the Gevilian ambassador. Her face remained a blur behind the muslin.

"Sister Emerald, Sister." Emerald had realized at some point in this interminable day that if her expulsion from Oakendown had been a fraud, as Wart admitted, then she was entitled to ignore it and claim the rank she had earned.

"Welcome to Quagmarsh, Sister."

"My visit here is not by choice."

"Come, I will show you around." Sister Carmine turned and led the way to the gate, being careful not to let her skirt brush against any of the debris. "Choice or not, here you will be privileged to assist in a magnificent extension of the frontiers of human knowledge, combined with a struggle for personal freedom against tyrannical oppression." That answered the question. She was at least as crazy as her husband—birds of a feather flip together.

Inside the gateway, hidden from outside view, lay another punt and two small boats. There was no street as such, merely narrow passages between squalid huts of wattle and thatch. The air stank of sewage.

Waving away the swarming insects, Emerald said, "Pray explain to me the magic in the amulets Marshal Thrusk and his men wear. I am much relieved to be free of it at last."

"Amulets?" Mistress Skuldigger laughed gaily. "They wear no amulets, child! They have themselves been bespelled with loyalty to Doctor Skuldigger. It is one of his greatest magics, based on the enthrallment sorcery that the Baels use to tame their slaves. The Baels are satisfied to turn their victims into human sheep, incapable of doing anything except obey orders. Doctor Skuldigger has succeeded in imposing absolute obedience without damaging the subjects' intelligence—not to any great extent that is. Yet the tyrant Ambrose seeks to crush all such progress! His oppression is intolerable. It has taken Doctor Skuldigger many years and hundreds of attempts to perfect this sorcery, and the value of it to society could be inestimable."

Well now, there was a debatable statement! The value of such a spell to the sorcerers who owned it would certainly be beyond measure, but Emerald shuddered at the thought of the evil being made available to anyone who could afford it. Landowners would enslave their workers, householders their servants; generals would make troops fearless.... This was exactly the sort of magical barbarity the King was trying to stamp out.

"I cannot imagine why a man like Marshal Thrusk would submit to such treatment."

Inside her veils, Mistress Skuldigger laughed. "He did not know he was submitting. A year or so ago he came to the Priory to have a wound healed, a nasty puncture made by a pitchfork tine. Of course Doctor Skuldigger recognized his value right away and enlisted him."

"Thrusk did not mind being tricked like that?"

"He cannot complain. He recruited all his men as well—the Baron's men, really. And the Baron, too, is now a supporter."

Her name, her choice of colors, her burning enthusiasm—they all proved beyond doubt that fire was Carmine's dominant manifest element. Wart had said that there must be at least one Sister cooperating willingly with the traitors. A little thought showed the logic of that, because the captors would need to know when the captives were lying to them. Carmine was that traitor, the Sister who had married the corrupt sorcerer. Emerald wondered if her dominant virtual element was love, which could make its children do anything. No, in that case she should not be so indifferent to the suffering her husband's work created. Chance, more likely. Fire-chance people were so unpredictable and uncontrollable that the Companionship rarely admitted them.

Carmine followed a complex winding path through the shacks. Some of them were collapsed ruins; others had recently been repaired, and sounds of hammering and sawing not far off suggested that the work continued. The few people in sight were obviously servants and laborers, the telltale discordant whistle of enchantment indicating that they had all been bespelled. But there had to be other inhabitants in this den of horrors. The men who had greeted Skuldigger at the gate must have been colleagues, for eight people were needed to conjure the eight elements. The slaves' loyalty spells would disrupt the balance of elements too much for them ever to work magic. Masters and slaves alike seemed to be prisoners of the monsters roaming the swamps.

"What does a chimera look like?"

"Depends on the ingredients Doctor Skuldigger used to make it. He has warned you about them, I hope?"

"In a general sense. They attack on sight?"

"Oh yes. Most of them are flesh eaters and they all seem to be permanently ravenous. To venture far from the stockade by day is very dangerous. By night it is suicide. You will be eaten alive, and not just by mosquitoes!" Sister Carmine found her own humor irresistibly funny. Love was certainly not a major element in her makeup.

"Why do creatures so powerful not break into the village?"

"Because they were ordered not to do so when they were assembled, of course. Doctor Skuldigger has also made a device that drives them away. Without that we should all be trapped in here forever."

"Only one 'device'? Isn't that rather risky?" If a prisoner could steal that magical whistle....

"We have several copies. You will note," Sister Carmine said, changing the subject abruptly, "that I am not taking you by the shortest route. If you are as sensitive as I am, you will have detected the conjuration presently underway in the elementary. I wish to avoid it."

Emerald had certainly noted it—magic like a stench of rotting fish—and now she could hear chanting. A few moments later her guide led her into a small open area, an irregular patch of weeds and mud that seemed to serve as a village square. A woman was turning a windlass on a well, making horrible squeaking noises, and a gang of four men was repairing thatch on one of the huts.

"Do come and see this!" Carmine said excitedly. "One of our trappers brought in an *otter* this morning! Very rare! Usually they just catch water rats or squirrels. In fact, the trap lines are often quite empty now. The chimeras have scared everything away."

Or eaten everything, Emerald thought. What would happen when there was nothing left for them to eat in the woods?

Carmine stopped at a small open-fronted shed containing a collection of metal cages. She peered into them until she found the one she wanted and then banged on it. The lump of fur in one corner did not move. "There it is. Poor thing! They say its paw is injured and of course they never eat in captivity. I expect Doctor Skuldigger will want to use it tonight, before it starves itself to death."

Emerald did not ask *Use how?* She did not want to know.
She was more interested in two solid posts outside and the
rusty chains dangling from them.

"And this?"

Although Sister Carmine's face was concealed by her veil,
her smile could be heard in her voice. "Well, those serve
several purposes. New recruits usually have to be restrained
until Doctor Skuldigger and his assistants have time to
attend to them. On occasion they also serve as a whipping
post. You have met Marshal Thrusk?"

Emerald did not answer.

"This way." Sister Carmine set off through the weeds in
her fine gown. "You will find that the cost of defiance rises
swiftly. Doctor Skuldigger will question you later, and I
expect he will introduce you to your duties. They are very
simple and quite harmless if performed correctly."

Past two or three more huts, they came to a woman sitting
on a bench outside a doorway, cuddling a child of about
two. It was Sister Swan, and both she and her daughter were
so intent on each other that they did not notice the arrivals
until Carmine spoke.

"There you are!" she said cheerfully.

Swan jumped. The child screamed. And screamed. She
tried to burrow into her mother's neck, screaming all the
time. Swan picked her up and ran into the hut, just as another
woman came out to see what was happening. It was quite
understandable that a two-year-old girl might be frightened
by a woman with a bag over her head, but somehow Emerald
thought that Belle knew exactly who was under the veil, and
that was why she had screamed. And was still screaming
inside the hut, despite all her mother could do to calm her.

But the other woman—large, plump, grandmotherly...

"Cloud!"

"Emerald!"

They fell into each other's arms.

"Oh, how nice!" Carmine declaimed. "I am so glad you
know each other. This will help you to settle down in your
new home, Emerald."

20

Stalwart Unbound

THE WAGON BROKE ITS REAR AXLE ON A ROCK
and tipped. The barrels slid, broke open the tailgate, and
fell out, one after the other, exploding in a fog of powdered
garlic. Fortunately Stalwart was on the uphill side, or he
would certainly have been flattened. As he began to move,
he expected the noose around his neck to choke him, but
the rope had been tied around one of the barrels, so it went
with him. Trussed so he could do nothing to save himself, he
slid within a torrent of bags and clothes and one archlute to
land in the heap of staves and garlic.

"Now you've done it!" Murther screamed. "Thrusk'll
have the skin off your back for this. And look at the poor
boy! Dead he is!" She came closer, fussing and coughing.

Stalwart was coughing also, and his eyes were full of
burning garlic.

"You come here and help, Cordwainer, right now!" she
yelled.

The man's voice, farther away, bellowed that he was busy
with the horse. Saxon agreed loudly. The woman, to her
credit, waded into the debris and dragged Stalwart out. He
lay on his side, which was a wonderful experience after so
long facedown, and he coughed around the gag. At least his

torment in the wagon was over. Almost anything would be better than that. But oh, his eyes!

"Poor boy!" she muttered. She struggled, trying to unfasten the gag, having trouble with Thrusk's knots. "Not our fault. Have to do what we're told, see. 'Don't stop,' he said. 'Take him all the way to the landing if you can.' Well, that's Thrusk for you—mean as they come."

The wagon creaked and settled as Saxon was freed from the shafts.

"Never said we could untie him," the man growled, coming to see.

"Well, and how are we to get him to the landing if we don't? You going to carry him, Cordwainer?"

"Could put him over the horse."

"I'll ride the horse, thank you. Don't you just stand there like a dumb mule. Bring the canteen, if there's anything left in it. Look at his face! And then cut his hands free so— *Look* at his hands, won't you! And his feet'll be no better, I'm sure. Oh, his poor face!"

The woman, querulous sourpuss though she was, treated Stalwart with consideration, wiping his tongue and cracked lips with a wet rag. Had she just put the bottle to his mouth, he would probably have choked himself. He wanted her to wash out his eyes, but he couldn't speak, so he waited.

"Thrusk never say we're to cut him loose, Murther." The man continued his growl, but he was sawing at Stalwart's bonds as he did so.

Stalwart managed a swallow. He must be alive. No one dead could hurt so much.

His troubles were far from over. When his mouth had been cared for and he had drunk his fill, when his eyes had been washed out and he could see again—although still not very well—then it was time for the blood to start returning to his hands and feet. His fingers looked like pig guts, except they were blue. Hurt? His jaw hurt, but the pain of the blood returning to his hands was going to be worse than that.

Murther and Cordwainer fretted and muttered and wanted to continue their journey.

"Any more water?" he croaked. The woman handed him the canteen and he emptied it. "Is my lute all right?" What good was a lute to him with his hands like this?

"Looks fine," the man said. He twanged the strings. "That's a wondrous strange-looking lute." Then he stiffened and looked around.

Hooves! Horsemen were coming from the west, from the way the wagon had come—could it be *Snake*? Stalwart struggled upright and managed to stand up with some help from Murther. No, it was not rescue coming. It was Thrusk and his band, who had stayed behind to look out for pursuit. How they must have laughed if they had watched Snake and the Old Blades galloping past along the highway, chasing nothing! Stalwart squared his shoulders and tried to look more defiant than he felt. Should be easy—a dead jellyfish would look more defiant than he felt. His hands were useless balls of sheer agony and his feet not much better. He still wore a rope around his neck, which did not help his dignity much.

Thrusk reined in, enormous on horseback, a mountain against the sky. "Have a nice nap, did you?" he inquired.

"You are a bucket of dog vomit and your mother ate rats."

The big man studied him for a moment and then smiled. He swung a leg over and slid down from his horse. He walked closer, very close. Even on level ground he could fill the sky.

"What did you say, runt?"

"You are a stinking barrel of dog vomit and your mother ate rats raw."

Someone sniggered. Thrusk looked around quickly and the laughter stopped at once.

He turned back to Stalwart. "I'm not allowed to pull that rope over a branch, which is what I'd like to do, slipgibbet. But I got no orders not to teach you manners."

"You couldn't teach manners to a pig."

"That's quite a lute you got this time. Who'd you steal that one from?"

"It belongs to a friend of mine and you keep your paws off it, you oversized latrine worm!"

The men-at-arms sitting around on their horses were watching to see if their leader would control his temper or hit a man half his size. Stalwart was too mad to care which happened. But he jumped when Thrusk's huge hands grabbed at his neck and in one swift motion ripped his shirt and doublet open to the waist.

"What's that for?"

The giant shrugged. "Just a precaution." He had guessed about Ironhall. Thanks to Snake's cleverness, he had found the only Blade who did not have a binding scar over his heart, but he was still suspicious. "I could flog you, for starters."

"Sure you could, but the reckoning is coming and it's a lot closer than you think. You're in over your head, animal."

Thrusk guffawed and appealed to his audience. "Listen to who's calling me an animal!" Some of them laughed, too, although the humor escaped Stalwart. "Well, you won't be around to sing any songs about it, sonny. The good Doctor has a very special treat in store for you." Chuckling, Thrusk took the rope and walked back to his horse. Stalwart had no choice but to stagger along behind him on feet that felt like two red-hot bricks.

"Because," Thrusk said as he tied the other end to his saddle, "in future you are going to help guard our little nest for us. You'll be one of our watchdogs. Right now I'm going to take the dog for a run."

21

Sic Cloud

SISTER CLOUD HAD BEEN EMERALD'S FIRST
GUIDE in Oakendown. She was caring and affectionate
and did not have a mean bone in her body—and not
many other bones either. She was exactly what one would
expect an air-love person to be, but she was also exactly
what Emerald needed under the present circumstances. She
provided sympathy, wash water, fresh clothes, and even her
own spare pair of shoes, which were a better fit than those
Emerald had been enduring for days. After that she busied
herself preparing a meal; she answered questions.

She had been the first Sister kidnapped, back in the spring.
Two others taken after her had tried to escape and been eaten
by the chimeras. Swan and her daughter had arrived only a
few weeks ago. Emerald told them of her own experiences
without mentioning Snake's conspiracy.

Cloud, in turn, told her all about Quagmarsh. There
were a dozen sorcerers living there. The Doctor was their
leader, or possibly his wife was, because it was her fire
element that drove their partnership. He was a water-time
person, infinitely patient. The rest of the inhabitants, men
and women both, were bespelled to complete obedience.

Emerald asked about chimeras.

"Abominations! Monsters! He makes them by blending people and animals. Wants to mix human intelligence with animal speed and toughness; thinks he can produce an army of unbeatable warriors and send it to conquer Baelmark and win the war."

"What sort of animals?"

"Anything. He keeps experimenting—rats, dogs, birds. Even cattle and pigs."

"So some of them are big?" Emerald, asked, thinking of the seal.

Cloud rolled her eyes. "They're all big and keep getting bigger! They roam the fens, eating everything they can get their claws on. And we're reduced to eating gruel," she added, handing Emerald a bowl. "All we got. Used to get nice fish."

The shadows were growing long, but the bugs were not as bad as before, for the sailors' wind had risen—the breeze sent by the sea at evening to hasten the boats home. It was taken for granted that Emerald would move in with her fellow hostages, although she had the option of cleaning out one of the empty hovels for herself. The hut would suffice for all of them at a pinch, and company was comfort.

As the three women and one child sat around on the floor eating their meager supper, Swan began to join in the talk and show a little vivacity, recovering from the agony of being separated from Belle. She might be a very charming woman in normal times, but her disposition was water-love, which was about the worst possible combination to withstand such an ordeal. Her daughter was unwilling even to look at Emerald or sit anywhere but on her mother's lap. Whatever abuse had provoked their terrors could not be discussed while the child was present.

Obviously neither Cloud nor Swan would offer much resistance to the traitors' demands. Emerald vowed that she, as an earth type, would be made of sterner stuff. She did not think this den of horrors could remain secret very much longer. If Sir Snake and his Old Blades did not find it by themselves, the starving chimeras would lead them to it, preying farther and farther afield until they began eating farmers' livestock. All she had to do was endure until rescue arrived.

"What exactly will I be required to do?" she demanded.

Swan's arms closed protectively around Belle.

Cloud sighed. "Two or three times a day you get called up to what they call the hall—it's just a big hut, really. They will have four or five sacks laid out. Without opening them, you have to say which contain something bespelled and which don't. That's all."

"But you mustn't lie!" Swan cried. "Carmine will ask you if you have lied, and Cloud and I will be given the same test. You can't cheat them."

"Sometimes they give you the same ones again," Cloud agreed. "There's no way to cheat. They get brutal if they think you're trying to deceive them or if you refuse to cooperate." She glanced at Belle, who was sucking a finger. "And you may not be the one they make suffer."

Emerald pointed in horror at the child, and Cloud nodded. *Fair skin that scars easily*, Skuldigger had said.

"I have never heard anything so despicable," Emerald said. "But I have never witnessed a public execution either. I do hope I can start soon."

"Not just watch," Swan snarled. "I'd like to *do* it."

"Slowly," said Cloud, and that was the first time Emerald had ever heard her utter a harsh word against anyone.

22

Reunion

EMERALD WAS SUMMONED JUST AFTER SUNSET. The messenger was a vacant-faced youth who bore the discordant whistle of the obedience spell. He seemed little better than half-witted, but when they reached their destination he pointed it out to her and ran off into the twilight. Perhaps he was not as stupid as he seemed.

"Hall" was an absurd name for what was merely a large shed. It had no door on its hinges or shutters on its windows; its floor was packed dirt, and birds nested in the rafters of a badly sagging roof. There was no furniture, nowhere to sit. It did boast a stone chimney with a fire crackling on the hearth—ominously, on this still-warm summer night. The long metal rod that lay with one end in the coals looked suspiciously like a branding iron. Emerald stopped just inside the door and surveyed the people standing there.

To her left were Doctor Skuldigger, his over-dressed wife, and two elderly men she did not know. Since they bore no enthrallment spell, she assumed they were sorcerers. Opposite stood Marshal Thrusk and a man-at-arms she recognized from the morning. Between them was Wart, looking much the worse for wear. His eyes were scarlet and swollen, his jaw was puffed out and already turning purple, and his doublet and shirt hung in rags, tattered and grass-stained as if he had been dragged. In an insanity of insanities, he was still clutching his precious archlute, hugging it to him with both arms, not using his hands. But he was still alive, which was a relief; and he smiled lopsidedly at her. She tried to return the smile, being reminded that her face, also, had been bruised by Thrusk's fist, although not nearly so badly as his.

She knew why the conspirators wanted her. She was horribly afraid she also knew why they wanted Wart, because the cage with the otter stood just outside the door. She braced herself for whatever was coming, wishing her lower lip did not keep trying to tremble.

"Aw?" sighed the Doctor. "Here she is. Emerald, I must ask you some questions. Mistress Skuldigger will know if you try to lie to us, and in that case I shall have no choice but to order Marshal Thrusk and man-at-arms Foster to punish you severely. I hope you understand that it is kinder to settle the matter once and for all, and teach you obedience right at the beginning. Now, why were you expelled from Oakendown?"

She told the truth as she knew it—if she had been the victim of a plot, it had not been knowingly.

"What do you know of Sir Snake?"

"That he is very stupid and incompetent."

"Ah, that is a lie!" Carmine said.

"Your husband told me so himself."

The only person who found that exchange funny was Wart, who laughed. "Don't believe that one if he tells you day follows—"

Thrusk hit him. It was not a killer blow, just a backhand slap across the mouth, but it must have hurt like fury on top of the existing bruise. Wart staggered and almost dropped his archlute. When he straightened, he was blinking away tears of pain; blood trickled from his torn lips.

"Can't you control that animal, Doctor?" Emerald shouted.

Thrusk laughed. "I'm not as much animal as he's going to be very shortly."

Skuldigger ignored him. "Aw? What do you know about Snake that I did not tell you?"

"Nothing but hearsay," Emerald said. "I never met him."

And so on. For a long time she managed to answer without lying. But finally Skuldigger brought her to a fence she could not jump. "Do you think the boy knew that you were bait?"

"What value have my guesses to you?"

"Aw? You are evading the question. Marshal, you may start using the iron now."

"Yes, sir," The big man stalked over to the hearth. He showed no signs of reluctance or distaste at what he was about to do. "Hold her, Foster."

Before Emerald could turn on her heel and run, the man-at-arms stepped between her and the door, although he did not lay hands on her—not yet. There was nowhere to run to, anyway. She would soon be caught and dragged back, and then either she would be made to suffer more or—much worse!—little Belle would.

"Of course I knew," Wart said hoarsely. "I helped Snake plan it all."

All eyes went to him. He seemed astonishingly unworried by his peril, brave beyond his years, even if he was as old as he claimed. Again Emerald sensed that odd disturbing something about him that had bothered her before, only this time stronger than ever. There was death in it, and a trace of love, time…it reminded her of some sorcery she had met somewhere recently.

"Do tell us," Skuldigger moaned, "everything."

Wart shrugged. "What is there to tell? The original idea was Snake's. The King approved it. Sir Chefney did most of the organizing. I added a couple of details." He showed no signs of lying, but he was certainly bragging. How could he be so bold? Did he have no idea what the otter was for? "We arranged for Emerald to be expelled from the school with no money and no way out except whatever the Sisters offered. Meanwhile, the Sisters were noting who in Tyton was wearing magic, and Mistress Murther's was a very unusual magic. So Emerald was put in her path. Bedroom, I mean. When nothing significant happened, I came forward with the wagon and we trailed the bait.... Sorry, Emerald. But it's true, isn't it? We trailed the bait until you swallowed it, Skuldigger. Snake and his men made no effort to stop you, of course, because they wanted you to lead them to your lair—which you did. Thank you. They'll be here shortly." He stopped, grinning as well as his bruise would let him.

He was *not* lying! And now Emerald remembered where she had met that sorcery—on the two Blades she had seen so briefly in the gatehouse. Not that Wart was bound as they had been, but whatever she was detecting on him was strangely similar.

"Mostly true," Sister Carmine said uncertainly. "That last...he's not sure...but he's not really lying...."

"Explain," wailed the Doctor. "Marshal Thrusk and his men waited behind to see if anyone followed the wagon when it left the main road. No one did. There was no magic on it or on you. If you are not lying to us, then Snake lied to you. You were misled!"

"Well, if you won't believe me," Wart said haughtily, "then I won't play your silly games. So there!"

"Aw? You force us to use force. The iron, Marshal—on the girl."

Thrusk chuckled and bent to test the cool end of the iron with a cautious finger, preparatory to picking it up. Wart turned his archlute so the soundbox was on top. Gripping it by its neck, he raised it like a giant club.

Foster cried out a warning. Thrusk straightened and spun around. They both reached for their swords as Wart swung the long instrument in a great arc overhead. The soundbox crashed into a rafter, exploding in a shower of splinters and inlay—mingled with a deluge of dust and bird droppings. The strings twanged a sonorous dying dirge.

Thrusk guffawed and let go his hilt. "Didn't judge that too well, did you, shrimp?"

Wart reached into the remains of the lute and pulled out a sword. "In the King's name," he shouted—voice quavering with excitement—"I, Stalwart, companion in the Loyal and

Ancient Order of the King's Blades, by virtue of the authority vested in me as a commissioner of His Majesty's Court of Conjury, command that all present do now lay down arms and submit to the Royal Justice."

Thrusk drew.

"Kill him!" one of the older men shouted.

Wart said, "If you insist," and bounded across the room.

23

Fight

IT TOOK STALWART THREE STEPS TO REACH HIS foe—and those three steps seemed to last the rest of eternity, as if all time elementals had fled away in terror and the world would never change again.

On the first step he realized that he was heading into his first-ever real fight with real edges and real points, so he might get killed or maimed very soon. Speed counted for far more than strength, and even Sir Chefney had agreed he was fast, so he would not normally be worried by Thrusk's size. But this was not *normally* at all. His hands were not back to their full strength, and he could not even trust his feet, which were just as important. His neck had not recovered from Thrusk's little dragging games on the horse. He would be slower and weaker than usual; Foster was drawing at his back; both men were wearing armor. *This was going to be very tricky indeed*! As he completed the step he remembered the latrines at Firnesse and promised himself that he would kill Thrusk if he had to run up the brute's sword to do it.

On the second step he was assessing the grip and weight of the weapon he bore. He had never seen it or touched it before and yet it was comfortingly familiar, thanks to Snake's fore-sight.

On that wonderful first morning, just after they had changed mounts at the first posting inn and Snake finished outlining the plan, he had said, "You didn't look at that sword I gave you."

In Ironhall, drawing a real sword—as opposed to a practice weapon—while on horseback was cause for some of the most ghastly punishments that could be inflicted on a senior, such as teaching courtly dancing to the soprano class. But Stalwart wasn't a candidate anymore and an order was an order, so he drew. The blade was long and slender, a thrusting sword almost like a rapier with a single edge added. He didn't like it much; it was heavier and less wieldy than a pure rapier and not sturdy enough for really serious slashing.

Beside, the edge was dull and the point rounded!

He howled in outrage.

Snake laughed. "No insult intended! That's as close a match as we could find to the sword you'll be using on this outing. Want you to get used to it and shaped up on it, too. You have very little time. We'll give you all the fencing we can—me and Chefney and another couple of hotshots to give you some real workouts. If you're going to need a sword, brother, you're going to need it *fast*. No time for tryouts or practice."

That made sense. Mollified, he waved the weapon a few times and managed to slide it back in the scabbard at full canter. "I prefer a rapier."

"I know. Just thought something a little more versatile might be useful on this outing. This isn't going to be any courtly duel, brother. This'll be mixing it up, roughhousing." Snake reined in to a trot to give the horses a break. "And you can't have the real one. It's inside a lute."

"It's *where*?"

"Inside a lute—an archlute, actually, because we needed the length and the extra weight won't show as much. Lovely thing, cost more than you'll earn in a ten-year stint with the Guard. We had our man disassemble it and hollow out the neck to take the blade. The hilt's inside the soundbox. Then he put it all back together and the varnish is still drying. When in need, smash and draw. Just hope it doesn't bind..."

It hadn't, and on his third step Stalwart was assessing his opponent. Thrusk was encased in a helmet and a simple cuirass of breastplate and backplate. There might be gaps where those met, but only a desperate man would gamble on finding them. Below the waist he wore no steel, only breeches well padded with linen, which might not stop a sword stroke completely but would probably save him from serious hurt. Heavy leather riding boots covered his legs to above the knee. There were very few places where Thrusk could be effectively damaged.

He knew how to handle a sword, too, advancing right foot and right shoulder to meet the attack, holding a hand-and-a-half broadsword one-handed, and raising it to a guard position that in Ironhall's own distinctive terminology would be approximately Butterfly. He had it a little too high for his opponent's height, though.

Hoping to make him raise it even farther, Stalwart lunged at Steeple and was parried to Stickleback. Hmm! Man Mountain was quick in spite of his bulk, and his power was hair-raising. There was no resisting his pressure when the blades engaged. Stalwart parried Thrusk's riposte with the neck of the archlute and tried Osprey, which was a tricky compound riposte involving a double feint and a lunge under the opponent's guard. Surprisingly, it did not end with his sword in Thrusk's armpit as it should have done, but he felt his point catch Thrusk's upper arm. Whether it just cut the cloth or nicked the skin he could not tell—and it barely mattered, because Thrusk's recovery put his left foot in the fire. No matter how much a man might trust his boots, that situation would make him lose his focus.

Stalwart left him and spun around with a wild slash that wasn't in the Ironhall repertoire at all—except that instinct was always permitted and in this case the windmill stroke parried a lunge from Foster, who hadn't expected it and obviously didn't know one end of a sword from another. Before he could even go to guard, Stalwart feinted at his eyes with the remains of the archlute and slipped the sword in underneath it to cut his throat.

He turned again with a backward spring away from Thrusk's downward cut, staggering as his feet refused his orders. No one else in the room had even moved a step yet, but this affair had better be settled quickly. He threw the archlute ruin like a javelin. Thrusk let it bounce harmlessly off his armor and lunged, sending Stalwart back yet again. There was very little room here, and if he let himself be cornered he would be a fond memory. He feinted, was parried, and lunged again, very nearly losing an ear. He was fencing like a cripple! Thrusk showed his teeth in a grin. Parry, riposte, parry...Lily, Violet...*clang—clang—clang—* The man's strength and reach were incredible. Eggbeater. One misjudgment and this flimsy thrusting sword would be cut in half. *Clang—clang—*

He would have to gamble the farm on one roll of the dice.

In desperation he discarded Chefney's advice and reached for Sir Quinn's Fancy Stuff. There was one compound attack called Beartrap that would work best—if it worked at all— for a short man against a very tall opponent. Stalwart lunged, parried, feinted, and ducked under Thrusk's riposte to cut at his right leg, slicing through his boot just above the knee as if he were carving meat. (*Thank you, Snake, for giving me a sword with an edge!*) The hamstring parted; Thrusk cried out and toppled. Even better—as he sprawled forward and Stalwart straightened, for an instant Thrusk had his head back to expose a glimpse of naked throat under his beard. Stalwart rammed his sword in past the collarbone, down among lungs and gullet and major blood vessels. The weapon was almost wrenched out of his hand as Thrust completed his fall, face-first into the floor, but that just meant that the blade was able to do more damage in there.

It was done! It was over! He was bubbling so hard with excitement that he could barely keep from dancing. That was what a real fight was like? And the battle was a long way from over yet. Sir Hawkney had told him that after the Night of Dogs he hadn't been able to sit down for two days.

He kicked Thrusk's helmet. "Die, you dreg!" he shouted. "You hear me, brute? You're dying. I killed you. I wish I could do it again."

24

Flight

SORRY ONLY THAT HE COULD NOT GLOAT longer over the death throes, he turned to survey the glazed eyes and open mouths of the five spectators. Obviously they had never seen a Blade in action before. One boy and two dead or dying men, and it had taken less than a minute. Skuldigger still wore his sword.

"I told you to throw down your weapons!" Unfortunately Stalwart's voice came out as a shrill squeak.

That didn't matter. Screaming in terror, the four traitors turned and rushed for the doorway with the woman in the lead. Emerald, bless her, stuck out a foot and tripped her. Skuldigger fell on her and the other two men jammed in the doorway. No time to laugh. No way to take hostages, either, because it might be days before Snake rode in.

"Let them go!" he shouted and headed for the fireplace.

Foster was unconscious, bleeding to death very messily—an incredible river of blood. Stalwart could feel sorry for him, because he had probably been tricked into being enslaved, and after that he would have had no choice.

He was not sorry for Thrusk, who had been just as bad before Skuldigger bespelled him. Incredibly, the giant had managed to sit up. He was hardly bleeding at all, just blowing red froth out from under his beard, gurgling and coughing blood. Stalwart went around him and took up the branding iron, resisting a powerful temptation to let Thrusk have a taste of it. He poked it into the roof instead.

Thrusk reached feebly for his fallen sword.

Stalwart kicked it out of reach. "I told you," he said. "You're dying! Outsmarted by a kid. I'm glad." The antique thatch flared up. "Can't stay to watch, but take all the time you want."

Emerald was staring at Stalwart as if he'd sprouted antlers. "You really are a Blade! That was what I was detecting—all those years of training!"

"If you say so. Come on." He pointed at Foster's sword. "Bring that."

He ran to the door and hurled the iron onto the roof of the next shack. The sea breeze was still blowing, and all the village thatch was old and dry. A good blaze or two would distract the pursuit. People were shouting in the distance, but no one had come in sight yet. The moon was ...*there*...and just short of the full, so that was east. When they brought him in through the gate the sun had just set on his left so the river must be over...*there*. "This way!"

He stretched out his left hand behind him. "Hang on and don't trip me with that sword, but keep it. You may need it." It was dark in the alleyways and the footing was made treacherous by garbage, firewood, wheelbarrows, chicken coops—all sorts of clutter. He went as fast as he dared, feeling out the clearance with his sword and judging direction by the moon-light on the clouds.

"Wart, there are monsters out there!"

"There are worse monsters in here."

He ducked under windows and turned away from candlelight spilling from doorways. He collided with a hurdle across his path and wakened a litter of piglets on the other side of it to terrified squealing. He kept heading west.

"There are two Sisters and a child, Wart! We can't leave them."

Oh, death and flames! "We must leave them! They'll be

safer here for a few more days than they will be out in the
woods with us." His job was to rescue Emerald and lead
Snake to the traitors' lair, in that order.

The shouting in the background was increasing, and
sometimes when he looked back he could see two red pillars of
sparks. Glowing fragments were floating away in the breeze,
threatening half the village. With any luck Skuldigger and
his cronies would concentrate their own efforts on putting
out the fire and rely on the chimeras to catch the fugitives
for them. With a lot more luck they would be wrong.

The unbroken wall on his right must be the palisade. "The
gate's that way," he whispered, "but they'll be watching it.
We need a place to climb over."

"Why not just push it down? It's rotten."

He tried a shoulder against it. "I'm not stalwart enough."
The individual posts might be no thicker than a man's arm,
but they were still sturdy hunks of timber.

"Keep trying. There are places where it's mush."

Emerald had seen it in daylight and probably seen more
of it than he had. Together they crept along the perimeter
of the village, hunting for a weak point, often having to
detour around heaps of garbage. Unfortunately none of the
obstacles was high enough to let them climb over the wall.
As he began to worry that they were drawing too close to
the gate and its inevitable guards, he almost collided with a
pole angled across his path. Fumbling and peering, he made
out that there were four of them, and they were bracing up
a section of the palisade that was anxious to fall inward.

He handed his sword to Emerald and set to work. The
props came loose easily enough. Then the wall sagged farther,
but its cross-rails still held it together. He was certain his
time was running out fast. He took up one of the props and
tried to find a place he could insert it to use as a pry bar.

"Wart!"

"What?"

"There's something out there!" Emerald's voice was shrill.

"Good." *Got it!*—he forced the lever between two posts.
"Need all the help we can get."

"Wart! I am telling you! There is a chimera outside that fence. And at least one more not far away."

"Help me!" He heaved with all his strength.

Emerald, having her hands full of swords, put her shoulder to the pole. Timber groaned, and then a single post cracked off and toppled, bringing two lengths of cross-rail with it. Not enough. He was about to put his lever back and try again when a wailing animal howl froze him solid. It went on and on until his scalp prickled. The lungs on that thing! Whatever was creating that racket was not close, but it must be big—*very* big.

Something grunted just outside the narrow gap he had made. He dropped the pole and grabbed his sword back. Another post creaked, snapped, and fell. No need to break out now. The thing outside was breaking in.

25

Fright

IT WAS UNFORTUNATE THAT THE MOON CHOSE that moment to wander into a cloud, so that Stalwart and Emerald, watching from behind a chicken coop some distance away, were unable to make out many details of what happened. Or perhaps that was fortunate. Whatever the new-comer looked like, it roared and growled, it made the entire stockade shake, it broke off posts and threw them away like straws. And finally it lurched in through the gap it had created and paused to sniff and snuffle. It was about the size of a bull and seemed uncertain whether it should stand on two legs or four. Its bushy tail was as large as a feather bed. Eventually it decided to go straight ahead and lumbered off between two huts.

Stalwart wiped his forehead. He managed to swallow at his third attempt. The weapon of choice against a thing like that would be a lance with warhorse and full plate mail included. "I am inclined to get out of here."

"Wait for the next one," Emerald whispered. They were kneeling very close together and he could feel her shaking. He had an arm around her, was why. She had one around him and they could shake in unison. "It's coming."

"You're sure? The fire must have drawn them." He could hear it. The sky was red over the center of the village.

"Possibly, but also they've eaten the fens bare. They either have to go after farmers' livestock or come back here. They're spelled to stay away, but hunger—"

"Sh!" Something was snuffling outside the stockade. The moonlight was brightening rapidly.

A couple of houses away someone screamed terribly—the newcomer had made its presence known. Then the second chimera entered. It leaped through the gap and ran after the first one so quickly that Stalwart wasn't *quite* sure what he'd seen. It was bigger than the first. A rat with arms walking on its hind legs would about sum it up. Tusks? Well, he wasn't sure about the tusks. Its tread had made the ground tremble.

"Let's go," he said, finding his throat drier than ever. "Outside is the lesser of two evils."

"I wish I knew that," Emerald said, but she was with him as he scrambled through the gap in the stockade. "You're not going to go right out in the woods, are you?"

"I'm going back to report to Snake. I'm going to hand you over to him and tell him I've brought you back safe and sound, so I've carried out my mission and please can I go off and do something much safer for the next ten years, like guarding the King from attacks by lion-size dogs...." He followed the stockade around, through a young growth of saplings and spindly weeds, hoping he might find an unguarded boat on the river. "And he can take his Old Blades and turn them into sausages for all I care."

"Wart! You'll—I'm sorry! I should be calling you 'Sir Stalwart.'"

"My friends still call me Wart." *And my enemies die!* "And you're going to be Sister Emerald again—if you still want to be."

"Ha! I shall tell Mother Superior she can stuff her precious Sisters and use them for garden furniture."

He chuckled and said, "Sh!" There were voices ahead.

He crept forward as quietly as he could. All dry twigs near the settlement had long since been gathered up for kindling, but total silence was still impossible.

"There's more chimeras around," Emerald whispered.

"Which way?"

"Hmm...All around."

He reached the corner of the stockade and knelt to peer along the waterfront. With the tide out a silvery trickle in the center of the channel was all that remained of the river. The rest was black mud. There could be no thought of boating home.

The voices he had heard came from a gang of men gathering water to fight the fire. They were too few to form a proper chain. The one on the end filled a bucket and trudged over to meet the next, who gave him an empty one in exchange, then walked the full one to the next man, and so on. They were all quite visible in the moon-light and the glow of the fire. Their cause seemed hopeless. Probably they were trying to wet down the other roofs and the village wells couldn't keep up with demand.

"I'm going to take my shoes off," Stalwart whispered. "That mud'll suck 'em off if I don't. It'll be horrible going but still easier than trying to force a way through the brush." They would have moonlight; the woods were dark.

"Wart, Wart! That is crazy! We'll wander for days and days and go around in circles."

"You do that if you want," he said, pulling off his left shoe. "I'm going back the way we came." Right shoe. "Didn't you take note?"

"I got dizzy in the first few minutes." Emerald was removing her shoes too. Perhaps girls just enjoyed arguing. There were no girls at Ironhall, but there would be lots of them at court.

"When we embarked we went to the left and the village was on the left bank. We passed six channels on the right and only two on the left. So we go right, stay on this bank, cross channels twice, and then look for our tracks. If we can't find those, we'll cut inland at dawn. Ready?"

She stood up, holding her shoes. "You think you're pretty smart, don't you?"

"Oh yes. Also brave, handsome, witty, charming, trustworthy, and modest. Now let's—"

Two chimeras burst out of the trees on the far bank and flashed across the empty channel. The bucket gang fled, screaming, but one of them was run down. A chimera knocked him flat, and—as far as Stalwart could make out at that distance—bit through his spinal cord with its beak. Then it picked him up in its arms and walked back the way it had come. The second chimera seemed to have two heads. It loped on all fours into Quagmarsh and the gate remained open and unguarded behind it.

"Cloud!" Emerald said. "And Swan and her baby!"

"They'll be all right. They can tell where the chimeras are, can't they, just like you can? Besides, Skuldigger values them, so he'll see they're protected. Now let's go."

The mud made for horrible walking, every step sinking ankle deep into frigid muck full of rotten branches and old shells. But it was better than fighting through bushes, and there was room to see danger approaching—anything Emerald's sensitivity missed. There was room to swing a sword.

The night was alive. Owls still hunted; the bat population was intact, with its creepy whistling cries. Chimeras were howling all over the fens, but Stalwart had no way of knowing whether they were calling to one another or just expressing rage and hunger. The fire's glow remained visible behind them for a long time.

Emerald held her sword in her left hand and clung to him with her right, which he found quite flattering. He could even admit it was comforting under the circumstance, although poor tactics. It certainly was not a romantic moment. Their feet went *squoosh—squoosh—squoosh*...and monsters howled, *arrrgh—arrrgh—*

She began turning her head a lot, searching....

"Trouble?" he murmured.

"Close." After a few more steps she muttered, "Very close."

Then she stopped. "Wart, we're heading for a chimera. It's just up ahead a little, waiting for us."

He had that swallowing problem again. "Then it knows we're here. Let's keep going. We should just show it that we're not afraid of it."

"You show it. I'm scared to death."

"So am I, but the chimera doesn't know that."

Her nails dug into his arm. "Wart! There!" She transferred her sword to her right hand.

It took him a moment to see what she had made out in the tricky silver moonlight. Something huge and dark stood within the trees, watching them. If Thrusk had been a five-year-old, that is what he would have looked like when he grew up. Except its eyes were too far apart. It had a muzzle...and horns. It was furry. He couldn't hope to win against that thing—chimeras were just too fast, too strong, and probably much too loathe to die. Obviously the thing Dreadnought had killed had been a chimera, but he had been one of three Blades at the start of the fight. The other two hadn't won any jeweled stars to wear on their jerkins.

This was what real fear felt like. Hard to breathe.

Seeing that it had been noticed, the monster displayed a mouthful of fangs like an ivory chess set, and growled a low, rumbling, deathly sound.

"Speak to it!" Emerald said.

"*Speak* to it?"

"Poor wretch! He must have some human intelligence still lurking inside there. He should be at least as smart as a dog."

Well, it was worth a try. Stalwart strained his throat to sound deep and commanding. "Go home!" He pointed back to the village. "Food there! Go home. Go to the Doctor. Doctor Skuldigger. He has food for you. Go home!" He added under his breath, "Eat him, for all I care...Bad Boy."

The chimera turned its head to look where he had pointed.

"Go home!" Stalwart repeated. He went through the message again.

The monster threw back its head and uttered a great,

long, pitiable howl that raised the hair on his neck. Then it
vanished, without sound or any sense of motion. It just was
not there any more.

It could probably return the same way.

"Come along, Sister." Stalwart resumed the trek. "You
will," he said—and for some reason he was whispering—
"tell me if it changes its mind and comes after us?" She
probably wouldn't have time to get two words out.

"I'll try to remember."

"Let me get him at first and *poke* with that sword. Don't
swing it or you're liable to get me instead."

But nothing more happened. They walked on unmolested.
He had not died of fright—Stalwart, *Sir* Stalwart. He was
going to be a hero if his luck would just hold a little longer.
But then...

They were approaching a fork in the mud highway. Hmm!
If the punt had brought him along the branch presently to
his left, then the branch to his right must be one of the two
he had seen joining from his (then) left, so he and Emerald
should now cross and go down the other. But if the punt
had come along the one now to his right, then the one to
his (now) left must be one of the several he had seen joining
from his (then) right and should be ignored. All the channels
looked the same by moonlight. His wonderful clever plan
had just collapsed and all his bragging to Emerald had been
vanity and wind. The safest thing to do was to stay on the
right bank and keep walking. If Quagmarsh was on an island
they would eventually come back to it, although they might
reach the sea first. And the best that could happen would be
the two channels he had seen on his left earlier turning out
to be the same channel, a loop around an island, and in that
case this new plan would get them where they wanted to
be anyway, although they probably wouldn't recognize the
spot in the dark.

Trusting him, Emerald did not comment as they went past
the fork, bearing right. Instead she said, "Was the archlute
your idea?"

"No, that was Snake's. I wondered if I'd ever be able to

bring myself to smash a beautiful thing like that. You know, it wasn't difficult at all?"

"You said you added some ideas."

"Just one, I think. The rusty old sword. They wanted me to be unarmed, saying I would be less likely to get my throat cut if I seemed harmless. I argued that carters always carry some sort of a weapon, so I would seem unusual if I didn't. I settled for a really absurd old relic that Vincent found in a stable."

"And you very nearly got both of us filled full of crossbow bolts!"

He laughed, although he knew he had not been laughing at the time. "No I didn't! They weren't going to shoot with Skuldigger's coach right behind us; not to mention the Doctor himself and all those splendid horses."

"That fall you took off the wagon…?"

"Cute, wasn't it? I told you I learned some tumbling and juggling and stuff when I was with Owain, and I kept it up at Ironhall. Even taught some of the others. It helps keep you supple."

"You were faking?"

"Of course. Owain taught me some sleight of hand— pulling coins out of kids' ears and so on. The secret to that sort of trick is that you set it up beforehand and you distract the viewers at the critical moment. That was what I was doing. I played the fool with the sword so I would be written off as a fool." His jaw still throbbed. "I didn't expect Thrusk to take it quite so seriously."

They squelched on for a while, and then Emerald said, "You're very brave."

He thought about it. "I'd like to believe that, but I wouldn't do it again. Crazy, more than brave. I've learned a lot these last two days…. Besides, you should talk—you've been marvelous!"

"I," Emerald said grimly, "was given no choice."

"I didn't have much," he admitted. Bandit and then Snake had flattered him into it. He would never fall for that trick again!

They came to another fork and again he kept to the right. The night was lasting forever. His feet hurt, every muscle in his legs ached, and he wasn't going to suggest stopping before she did.

"At least we seem to be past all the chimeras," he said. "I don't hear any howling ahead of us, do you?"

"I hear something."

Oh! So did he.

After a moment she said, "What *is* that?" And after another, "Oh, Wart! There must be hundreds of them! They're coming this way, Wart!"

He stopped. Suddenly reaction set in and he felt so limp he wondered how he was managing to stay upright. Maybe it was the mud holding him up. "The garlic was Vincent's idea."

"*Wart*!?" she cried. "What do you mean?"

"You don't have such a thing as a dog biscuit on you, do you?"

"Dogs? Those are dogs coming?"

"Garlic doesn't smell all that strong if you keep it in cloves, or bulbs," he said wearily. "It's when you cut it up it stinks. Nobody wanting to transport garlic would ever dream of grinding it up and mixing it with salt first."

"Oh!" she said. "The barrels leaked? Gaps between the planks in the wagon and the road was very bumpy? You left a trail of garlic!"

"Dogs love garlic. Absolutely crazy about it. And we didn't plan this part, but I fell in the stuff when the wagon broke down. Then Thrusk made me run the rest of the way to the river. It wasn't much fun while it lasted, but if he'd put me on a horse, the dogs might have lost the trail."

The dogs were clearly audible now, Snake and his men coming at last. If old Sir Vincent was with them, as he probably was, he would have remembered the abandoned hamlet of Quagmarsh and guessed that was where the conspirators were holed up. Not having boats, the Old Blades would have had to wait for the tide to go out. It occurred to Sir Stalwart that he had left very little for them to do.

26

Valglorious

FROM THE OUTSIDE VALGLORIOUS LOOKED LIKE a castle, and it had withstood sieges in the past. Inside, it was a ducal palace. After two days of luxury, Emerald began to feel spoiled for any lesser existence. She had been assigned a bedchamber the size of a ballroom, she had maids to attend her, she chose her clothes from a finer wardrobe than she had ever imagined, and the entire resources of the palace were available to amuse her. She seriously considered writing herself a note, *Memo: Marry a duke.*

From Wart's stories she had expected her host to be big, but Sir Vincent was sturdy and short, wearing his years well. He was also brusque, charming, considerate, and took no nonsense from anyone. His wife, whom Wart had not mentioned at all, was everybody's idea of what a grandmother ought to be. She could not have been kinder.

On the third morning Emerald went riding with Wart, who looked much better since he'd been healed at the elementary in Kysbury but was still steamingly furious at having been kept out of the fighting at Quagmarsh. When they returned, they were informed that Sir Vincent wished to see them. They found him standing in his favorite place, before the fireplace in the great hall. He was chatting to another man, who was exceedingly lean, with a supercilious manner and a thin mustache to match. Emerald had met him only once and then briefly, by moonlight in a swamp. He was clean and neatly dressed, but his eyes looked as if they had been propped open for a week. He bowed very low to her.

"You are in good health, I trust, Sister?"

She gave him a bob in return. "Recovering, Sir Snake." No thanks to him! "And I am not a Sister." Thanks to him!

"Yes, you are. The annals of the Companionship record nothing to the contrary."

She would see about that. "Cloud? Swan?"

"Both safe!" Snake beamed triumphantly. "Sister Cloud is upstairs being bathed and scented and pampered and whatever else ladies' maids do to ladies. Sister Swan and her daughter have been joyously reunited with their family." He pouted briefly in Wart's direction. "Skuldigger and a few others eluded us, I am afraid. But we caught enough of the ringleaders to stage an impressive public execution." And to Emerald, "With all the usual barbarities imposed on traitors. Let me know if you want tickets."

"I'll think about it."

"You may be called to give evidence at the trial. Ten minutes ought to do it."

"Casualties?" asked Sir Vincent.

"A few. Not too bad," Snake said evasively. He turned his bleary, red-rimmed eyes back to Wart. "Fetch your lute and anything else you need, brother. We ride for Grandon at once."

"Yes, *brother*!" Wart turned and ran. He hurtled up the staircase in a tattoo of boots on timber.

The Blades exchanged amused glances that Emerald found excessively irritating. Wart was a *hero* and they were still thinking of him a child. It was his courage that had made this victory possible.

"You have a visitor, Sister," said Sir Vincent. "Mother Superior is waiting upstairs in the solarium."

Oh! She had been expecting a summons to Oakendown.

Having the queen bee come to her was probably an epochal honor and breach of tradition. "Let her wait."

Snake pursed his lips disapprovingly. "Is that a sensible attitude under the circumstances?"

"I may drop in later and spit in her eye."

He sank down gracefully, kneeling to her. "If there is eye spitting to be done, mistress, then I am the guilty party. Which eye do you want—right or left?"

She did not look at Sir Vincent, but she knew he was amused. "You were merely doing your duty. Mother Superior betrayed my trust!"

Snake shrugged and rose, still moving with a fencer's grace. "As she will freely admit, although the King did threaten to clap her in irons. I am quite sure she will kneel to you and beg your forgiveness. What else do you want? Now is the time to ask."

"Gentleholme Sanctuary!" she said. "My father—"

"Already done!" Snake smiled his infuriatingly condescending smile again. "We received more complaints about Gentleholme than almost any other elementary in all Chivial. It was one of the first we raided, back in Thirdmoon. A couple of the rogues turned king's evidence and the rest were hanged."

"So they did murder my father?"

"We cannot be certain in specific cases." He shrugged. He was waiting for her to say something....

"And what of the money they stole from him, then?" she asked. "What of the land?" What of her mother, aging in poverty these past four years?

He sighed. "There have been thousands of such cases over the years, Sister. To locate and compensate the victims would be an impossible task. Under the law, all assets are forfeit to the Crown."

"How nice for His Majesty! Perhaps Doctor Skuldigger does have a valid point or two!"

Sir Vincent cleared his throat warningly. "May I suggest, Sister? Sir Snake, Mother Superior, and of course the King— they are all persons of power and authority. Such people frequently have to stray outside the normal bounds of conscience in performing their duties. What I mean is that you will not get very far by trying to shame any of them into admitting guilt. You certainly will gain nothing by spitting in eyes."

"But…?" she said cautiously, wondering if the old man was trying to be helpful or was in league with his fellow Blade.

"But if this story should come out, then Mother Superior would certainly have to resign her high office. The King would be forced to dismiss Sir Snake, possibly commit him to trial. Ambrose himself would look like a coward who had sent a girl into terrible danger just to save his own skin."

Snake shuddered dramatically but said nothing.

"Do continue, Sir Vincent. Your discourse is most interesting," she said.

Vincent shrugged. "Now, while you have Mother Superior on her knees, you could ask for immediate restitution as Sister, a solemn promise of promotion to Mother within a year, a posting to court, if that is your wish—just about anything that takes your fancy. As for our sovereign lord the King, if he has fallen heir to lands stolen from your family, you might offer to take them off his hands as compensation for your suffering." He smiled then. "You would have to promise to keep your mouth shut, of course—not about Stalwart's valor but about how you were deliberately exposed to danger. That must never be revealed."

She looked at Snake, whose face would have seemed as innocent as a baby's had babies sported supercilious mustaches. "Would the King give up Peachyard?"

"Give up Peachyard?" he echoed incredulously. "And I suppose you would also expect all appurtenances pertaining thereto, including but not limited to all livestock, standing crops, indentured laborers, vehicles, implements, existing buildings, and improvements? You might even demand a five-year relief from taxes and a cash grant of, say, ten thousand crowns for necessary repairs?"

It would not bring back her father, nor yet her brothers,

but it would be fun breaking this news to her mother.... She blinked away some tears. She nodded. "Not a penny less."

"No spreading naughty stories?"

"My lips are sealed."

"No spitting on Mother Superior?"

"I may drool a bit, but no more than that."

Snake took her fingers and kissed them. "Consider it done, mistress. You were most helpful."

Wart came down the grand staircase like a landslide and seemed to bounce across the floor until he came to a panting stop beside Sir Snake. "Ready!" He had his lute on his back.

"Then we must be on our way," Snake said. He offered a hand to Vincent. "Thank you for all your help, brother. Where is your dear lady? Anything we can do for you in return?"

"You can tell Fat Man to keep that spotty duke out of my hair for another year or ten."

"I'll see if I can get him kidnapped."

"Preferably by Baels."

Emerald held out both hands to Wart. "Thanks for saving me from the monsters, even if you did throw me to them in the first place. I'm truly grateful. Good chance, Sir Stalwart! See you at court."

He blinked and then grinned. "So you will!"

27

Star

WHATEVER ONE MIGHT THINK OF SNAKE AS taskmaster, the man never spared himself either. It was almost midnight when he and Stalwart thundered into the King's favorite palace of No-care, west of Grandon. He had not had a proper night's sleep in a week, but he saw Stalwart temporarily quartered in the guest wing, ordered a tailor dragged out of bed to measure him, and then went off in his road-stained clothes to report to the Lord Chancellor.

Soon after dawn the tailor got his revenge by dragging Stalwart out of bed to try on his Guard livery, all blue and silver. It was much too loose on him, so the man fussed angrily with chalk and a mouthful of pins, marking it for alteration. Probably it was the smallest uniform ever cut and he had not been able to believe his own measurements. During this ordeal, surveying himself in the mirror, Stalwart was more depressed than impressed. He *felt* a great deal older than he had done when he left Ironhall two weeks ago, but he didn't *look* it. His moorland haircut helped not at all. Those ears of his were definitely better kept out of sight. He had Sleight hanging at his thigh, a magnificent rapier with a cat's eye pommel, and he looked...*ridiculous*!

This way to the children's pageant.

Snake walked in without knocking. He beamed, fresh as dew on a mushroom. "Good chance, brother! Oh, very smart! How is it?"

"A few minor adjustments," the tailor mumbled around the pins.

"Don't take too long. He's going to be presented at noon."

The tailor practically screamed. He ripped the livery off Stalwart and vanished out the door with it, leaving scissors and tape and other tools strewn everywhere. Stalwart looked around for other clothes. There weren't any, because his riding outfit had gone to be washed. He perched on the edge of the bed in his briefs and regarded Snake's contented smile with considerable suspicion.

Snake leaned against the wall and looked as guiltless as paint. He was wearing full court dress, with pearls and gold trim and his White Star order. "While I remember," he said, "you will sup with His Majesty this evening. Bring your lute. Private party, with music. I advise you to stay sober and not to eat too much at the state banquet this afternoon."

"I always sick up at state banquets," Stalwart said sourly.

"I look forward to that, then. At noon the Fat Man will be *holding court.* A very big event—heralds and trumpets and the best gravy. It will begin with the new ambassador from Isilond presenting his credentials. Then the Lord Chancellor—that's Durendal now, of course—will present me."

"*You?* Does the K—does Fat Man have such a short memory?"

"Two more points," Snake said smugly, flicking the four-pointed star on his breast. He meant he had been promoted from member to officer.

"Wonderful!" Stalwart said. It was a rare honor for any Blade, very rare. He jumped up and pumped Snake's hand and tried to look and sound excited. "Well earned, too!" No need to say *who* had done the earning.

"Thank you, brother. It's an acknowledgment of all the Old Blades' efforts, of course." Snake did not believe that, obviously, but he must enjoy saying it that way so you

knew he didn't believe it. "You'll go next. This is a breach
of precedent and tradition, so we had to make it up. We
gave you extra trumpets. Leader will present you. When
he announces you—Bandit, I mean, not the herald—then
you advance doing the three bows thing. You kneel on the
cushion—"

"*I do what?*" Stalwart yelled, leaping up from the bed
again.

"Kneel on the cushion," Snake repeated, as if surprised by
his surprise. "His Majesty will place the ribbon over your
head and—"

"What *ribbon?*"

"Member of the White Star, of course." A grin broke
through, and now it was Snake's turn to pump hands.
"Congratulations! The King's own idea, not mine. He is
really impressed by what you did, brother. You are only the
seventh Blade ever admitted to the Star. The heralds think
you must be the youngest member ever, by about ten years."

Stalwart muttered, "Flames!" a few times and flopped
down on the bed again. If he'd been earning *that* then he
must have been in much worse danger than he'd realized.
How low had they rated his chances? He shivered all over.

"You deserve it, brother."

"That's what I'm afraid of." But had he earned it? Or
was he being given a diamond-studded bauble so that he
wouldn't provoke too many smirks when he strutted around
the palace dressed up as a Blade?

"The bad news," Snake added, "is that Fat Man says he
may just create a junior order of chivalry especially for you
and Sister Emerald—the Order of the King's Daggers."

"Oh, funny! Very, *very* funny!"

"It's funny when he says it, brother! Kings' jokes are
always hilarious. If he says it again tonight, you laugh your
head off!"

"I don't, he'll chop it off?"

"Could be," Snake agreed with a smirk. "Now this
afternoon...at these highfalutin formal affairs, it is
customary to have four Blades in attendance on the dais.

Leader has assigned today's duty to Sir Orvil, Sir Panther, Sir Dragon, and Sir Rufus."

"*Flames*!" Stalwart was saying that a lot this morning. Those four, who thought he had been chucked out or had run off with his tail between his legs, were going to watch him being inducted into the Star? Bandit would be there, and the great Durendal. Flames, flames, flames! Life was *never* going to get sweeter than this.

Snake wandered over to the window and peered out. "That's if you want it that way," he said offhandedly.

Warning gongs clanged. "What other way might I want it?" Stalwart asked warily.

Snake shrugged. Even in formal court finery he was skinny. "We haven't nabbed Skuldigger yet or his wife. We think Baron Grimshank is worth a hard look. And there are many, many others out there almost as bad."

"Oh, no! *No!* You are not going to talk me into any more of your crazy suicide missions!"

"Of course not," Snake said blandly to the window pane. "You'll enjoy hanging around here with a hundred other men, all guarding the King. Standing on the sidelines at balls, masques, banquets...You'll love it, I'm sure. Ten years of crushing boredom to look forward to. I admit it isn't as boring as it used to be, but it's we Old Blades who are really doing the work—the cutting edge you might say. Out there in the real world battling evil, defeating the King's enemies—"

"I am not an Old Blade! I am the youngest Blade of them all, perhaps the youngest ever bound.... When am I going to be bound?"

"When Ambrose gets around to it. Next time he goes to Ironhall. Of course you can't wear a sword in his presence until you are bound. Neither can I these days, but I don't care, because I'm not in the Royal Guard. That *will* be embarrassing, an unarmed Blade! Goodness! Still, I'm sure you can find lots of other boys in the palace to play with."

"Burn you!" Stalwart muttered.

"Meanwhile I need a man who can handle a really tricky

mission. He has to be the sort who won't attract suspicion, who can think on his feet, a superlative—"

"No! No, no, no! You are trying to sucker me into volunteering again! You and the King! You are going to cheat me out of my reward!"

Snake turned, looking indignant. "Not at all! Just a brief postponement. We'd keep you under wraps for a week or two longer, that's all. The Star is yours, only you would receive it at that private supper tonight instead of in public. We'd put the livery away in a drawer for now. That's all." He picked up the tailor's shears and tested their edge with his thumb.

There was a long silence.

"Of course, you did swear an oath...but if you're not interested you're not interested." He turned back to the window.

Still silence.

Snake sighed. "It is so hard to find really firstrate men! Superlative fencers, I mean—great swordsmen who are also men of courage. Above all, courage. Tremendous courage. You're the only man I know who could possibly have achieved what I had in mind."

Oh, flames!

"What do you want me to do this time?" Stalwart asked glumly.

BOOK TWO

THE CROOKED HOUSE

There was a crooked man,
  Who walked a crooked mile.
He found a crooked sixpence
  Against a crooked stile.

He bought a crooked cat
  Which caught a crooked mouse;
And they all lived together
  In a little crooked house.

—TRADITIONAL

1

Murder in the Court

IT began with a murder. Stalwart saw it happen. He was watching a formal court reception, a grand state function held only three or four times a year. That was the last place anyone would expect to see such a gruesome crime.

The day's pomp had been staged in honor of the new ambassador from Isilond. King Ambrose had set out to impress him with spectacle and splendor, sparing no expense—drum rolls and trumpeters and heralds wearing gaudy tabards. Every ambassador in the diplomatic corps was there, as were scores of great lords and ladies, bejeweled and decked out in finery. They had all been escorted in from the gates of Nocare Palace by glittering honor guards of the Household Yeomen in silver-bright breastplates and plumed helmets. At the doors of the reception hall they had observed White Sisters in their snowy robes and high pointed hats— no one would sneak any evil magic into the King's presence while the Sisters were on duty. The inside of the hall was patrolled by Blades of the Royal Guard, the world's finest swordsmen.

And yet a murder!

After welcoming the new ambassador, the King began handing out honors and appointments. The first man the heralds called forward was Sir Snake. In recognition of his triumph over the traitors at Quagmarsh, he was being promoted from member to officer in the Order of the White Star, the greatest order of chivalry in the realm. It was an honor very few Blades had ever achieved. As he knelt to receive the diamond-studded brooch from the King, the assembled courtiers clapped and cheered.

Hidden away by himself on a screened balcony, Stalwart kept his hands in his armpits. *He* should have been down there as well, and he had let Snake talk him out of it. It was *he* who had made Snake's triumph at Quagmarsh possible! The King had been so impressed by that exploit that he had appointed Stalwart to the White Star, although he was *at least* ten years younger than anyone else who had ever been so honored. And stupid Stalwart had let Snake talk him out of public recognition for the time being. His undercover work for the Old Blades was too important to give up so soon, Snake had insisted, so why not just accept the star this evening during a private supper with the King? He could watch from this private box, seeing without being seen, hidden away like a shameful secret.

He had seen the King often enough at Ironhall, although never wearing his crown and swathed in a robe so massive that it needed four pages to carry its train. Ambrose was a huge man, towering over everyone else as he stood in front of his throne. At his back, with swords drawn, stood the newest Blades, who only two weeks ago had been Stalwart's classmates at Ironhall: Sir Rufus, Sir Orvil, Sir Panther, and Sir Dragon. They looked very smart in their blue and silver livery. He kept imagining the expressions on their faces if they heard his name proclaimed and saw him strutting forward before the entire court, honored as no man of his age had ever been honored.

Sigh!

And tomorrow he would ride off to a paltry little town called Horselea to investigate rumors of black magic there. In spite of all Snake's efforts to make it seem dangerous and exciting, this sounded like a very dull mission, not the sort of thing to challenge an eager young swordsman. He could not help wondering if Snake just did not know what to do with his young helper now and was sending him off to horrible Horselea to age a few years.

Sigh again!

The reception that should have been the greatest moment of his life proceeded without him, dribbling down in boredom through awards, titles, and appointments to mere acknowledgments. Peers presented stripling sons and new wives to the King. Very subtly, people were fidgeting. Even Ambrose seemed to be hurrying things along, as if hungry for the roast boar, stuffed peacock, and other delights of the state banquet that was to follow.

The herald was close to the end of the list now. In a voice like a trumpet he proclaimed, "Lord Digby of Chase, Warden of the King's Forests, knight in the Loyal and Ancient Order of the King's Blades, most humbly craves Your Majesty's gracious leave to return to court."

Digby had visited Ironhall a year or two back, and thus was one of the very few people in the hall, other than Blades, whom Stalwart recognized. He began his advance to the steps of the throne. His petition was a mere formality, because he was one of the King's personal friends. Having just returned from a brief absence, he was required by protocol to pay his respects to His Majesty at a public function. In fact he had supped with the King the previous evening and reported on his travels at that time. So it should have all been over in a few seconds. He made the first of the three low bows required. He took two more steps.

He dropped dead.

All the White Sisters standing around the hall screamed in unison. Heralds rushed forward to help the stricken man. One of them leaped up in horror with blood on his hands. Lord Digby had been stabbed through the heart. There had been no one near him; there was no weapon in sight.

It was only a wild guess, but Stalwart was instantly certain that he would not be riding to Horselea after all. He was going to be needed.

2

His Majesty's Displeasure

KING Ambrose of Chivial was not merely very large, he was often very loud as well. Royally enraged by the murder of his friend, he canceled the banquet, sent the distinguished guests away, and summoned the Privy Council. Its members needed time to assemble, and he was not accustomed to waiting for anyone. He strode up and down his council chamber, roaring like a thunderstorm, while those councillors who had been foolish enough to be prompt stood back against the walls, staying out of his way.

Kings have few real friends, so Ambrose's grief was genuine. He raved that he had been grossly insulted in his own throne room and Chivial would be the laughingstock of all Eurania. Although he would never admit it, he had received a severe shock, because obviously the evil sorcery had really been directed at him. Digby had died by mistake.

"Disgraced! Shamed! Sorcery most foul!" Like a gigantic bluebottle circling a kitchen, the King came to a sudden and unheralded halt. He was in front of Commander Bandit, who stood at his post in front of the door. "Why did the Guard not prevent this outrage?"

Swordsmen must be nimble, so no Blade was ever very large; Sir Bandit had to bend his head back to meet the royal glare. He said calmly, "If Your Majesty believes that the Guard is at fault, then I humbly beg leave to surrender my commission to Your Majesty."

The King seemed to swell even more. His already inflamed face turned a deeper shade of purple. "You are responsible for our safety!"

Bandit was popular with his guardsmen because he never lost his temper. Nor would he allow them to be unfairly blamed. "With all respect, sire, your Blades cannot defend you against sorcery unless it is identified for them. That responsibility rests with the Sisters."

Ambrose flashed a look around the room to confirm what he already knew. "And where is Mother Superior?"

"Her Excellency was absent from court, Your Grace, and had only just returned to the palace when she was informed of the incident and Your Majesty's summons. I believe she wished to ascertain—"

A tap on the door made even the imperturbable Bandit look relieved. "With Your Grace's permission..."

The King moved just enough to let him peer out and then admit the lady in question. Mother Superior was a national monument, who had been around court longer than anyone could remember—tall, imperious, unsmiling, and relentlessly efficient. Her white robes were invariably spotless and uncreased, and the high hennin that all White Sisters wore seemed to brush the lintel of the tall doorway. Finding herself trapped between the paneled wall and the King's angry glare, she dropped without hesitation into a curtsey that almost poked that white conical hat right in his piggy little eyes. Ambrose perforce backed up.

"Well, Mother?" he bellowed. "Who brought such sorcery into the hall? Why did your women not give warning? They were guarding the doors. What do I pay you for, if not protection, eh? Explain your failure!"

Rising, she inspected his rage with matronly disapproval, as if it were a child's tantrum. "The Sisters failed to give warning because the sorcery was *not* brought into the hall, sire."

"A courtier is struck down on the steps of the throne by an invisible assassin and you claim there was no sorcery present?"

She raised her chin. "With respect, sire, there was no *invisible assassin.* I have spoken with the Prioress and most of the Sisters who were present. They are adamant that there was no sorcery present until the instant Lord Digby died."

"How can that be? What sort of magic works like that?"

She met the royal glare with one of her own. "I do not know what sort of magic, sire! None of the Sisters has ever met anything quite like it. They detected no death elementals. Air and fire, they think. And love! A large measure of love."

"Love?" roared the King. "A spell drops a man dead and you say it is made of *love?*"

Even the formidable Mother Superior flinched before that enormous bellow. "So they claim."

"And it kills when it is not there? Instantaneously? From a distance? *What sort of magic does that?*"

"The Sisters can only determine the presence of elemental spirits, Your Majesty, not analyze the compulsions laid on them. That is the job of the College."

With a snarl of fury, King Ambrose swung around to survey the assembled councillors. The Lord High Admiral was there, the Lord Chamberlain, several dukes, the Earl Marshal...but not the head of the Royal College of Conjury. Inevitably, the royal eye sought out the crimson robes and gold chain of Lord Chancellor Roland. "Where is Grand Wizard, Chancellor? He was at the investiture."

As Sir Durendal, Lord Roland had been the most famous Blade of them all, commander of the Guard before Bandit. He bowed calmly. "Sire, the learned adept is deeply concerned about Your Grace's safety in the face of this unprecedented threat. He wished to consult urgently with the entire faculty, so I gave him leave—" He was cut off by a royal bellow. Everyone knew that Grand Wizard was a mild-tempered scholar who became flustered when the King shouted at him, whereas Lord Roland accepted that

his duties sometimes included acting as royal punching bag.
Like now, for instance.

"Bah! He dared not face us, you mean! Does he have the
faintest idea how that evil was worked?"

"I suspect not, Your Grace. But the sooner he can set the
College to work the better."

"*Snake!*" The royal anger turned on Lord Roland's
companion. As thin as his namesake, Snake was dandily
dressed in a green velvet jerkin, cloth-of-gold britches, silk
hose, furtrimmed robe, and osprey-plumed hat. He made a
leg with a fencer's fluid grace. "Sire?"

"That!" The King poked a meaty finger at him.

Snake looked down. "Oh, that."

"Yes! *That!*" Ambrose had dropped his voice to a low
growl. He was much more dangerous when he was quiet
than when he was shouting. The *that* in question was the
glittering six-pointed star he had hung around Snake's neck
not two hours ago. "I gave you that because you told me you
had wiped out the traitor sorcerers who keep trying to kill
me. It would seem that you lied."

Snake would never have made such a claim, but he did
not deny the accusation. He just quirked his eyebrows as if
puzzled. His features were narrow and bony, like the rest
of him; he had an extraordinarily arrogant nose and a thin,
disdainful mustache. "It would seem we missed a few, sire."

"And what are you doing about them now?"

"I consulted with Grand Wizard as he was leaving, and he
agreed that action at a distance like that is a highly original,
if not unique, application of magic. He is also of the opinion,
Your Grace, that the range of such an enchantment must
be limited, and therefore the spell must have been cast
from somewhere very close to the palace—probably within
Grandon itself or its suburbs."

Everyone knew that Ambrose detested being lectured,
but Snake blithely continued and was not struck down by
any royal thunderclaps. The King listened, scowling intently.

"Of course Your Majesty is aware that powerful spells
tend to leave traces on the octogram where they were cast,

at least for a short while. I therefore suggested to Mother Superior that the Sisters who were present in the hall at the time of the crime, and who should therefore be able to recognize the, er, *smell* of the murderous enchantment, be sent to inspect every known octogram within an hour's coach ride of the palace. Fortunately, we had already compiled such a list, so this program is now under way. I sent Old Blades along to defend the good ladies. A dozen carriages are even now making the rounds, and they will visit every elementary in or near the capital."

That was incredibly fast work, and could not be faulted.

"Bah! Anyone can make an octogram with a piece of chalk and a reasonably clean floor."

Snake bowed again. "Your Majesty's expertise is legendary."

The King's glare turned even darker. "So why would the traitors not have created a new octogram, one you don't know about?"

"Of course they may have done so, sire. However, Grand Wizard did point out that great time and effort are required to season a new octogram before it will work predictably. He suggested we begin by inspecting the known sites."

"*Harumph*! But you have no idea who was behind this foul attempt on our life?"

Snake pursed his lips, as if he had somehow tugged the ends of that arrogant mustache. "Has Your Majesty considered the possibility that the attack was directed at the man it slew?"

The King's mouth opened and shut a few times. His eyes seemed to shrink even smaller, retreating into their nests of blubber.

"I may be quite wrong, of course." Snake obviously did not believe that. "But this is a new and very horrible sort of conjuration. Would the evil genius who could devise such a weapon be so clumsy as to mistake Digby for Your Grace?"

"Why," Ambrose growled, even quieter, "would he be so perverse as to want to kill our Warden of Forests?" Only loyalty to his late friend would keep him from pointing out that Digby had been an amiable blockhead—a fine sportsman, but of no real importance.

Snake glanced around as if to see who was listening. Predictably, the entire Privy Council was hanging on every word. "Possibly because he knew something, sire? Something dangerous to the traitors?"

"*Harumph*! He spent the last month counting stags and partridges all over the realm. What could possibly be dangerous about that information?"

"Er, nothing, sire…. He mentioned nothing untoward last night?"

Monarchs were not accustomed to being questioned, and Snake's presumption did not soothe the royal temper. The only answer was a head shake and a dangerous glare.

"It is unfortunate, sire, that I just returned to court myself last night and had no chance to speak with the late lord."

"Indeed?" the King said with menace. "And what exactly would *you* have had to discuss with Lord Digby?"

Again Snake glanced around the room, then peered up hopefully at the King. "May I answer that question in private audience, sire?"

"You believe there are *spies* in our Privy Council?"

"Of course not, sire." But the traitors must have eyes and ears at court. Rumors spread faster than bad smells. The palace swarmed with servants, all of whom knew enough to keep their ears open for any good scrap of news or gossip, and where to take it to turn it into gold. Ambrose knew as well as anyone that the more people who knew a secret, the greater the chance that everyone soon would.

With a sigh, Snake said, "Lord Digby was always eager to further Your Majesty's interests. Before he left on his inspection of forests, he asked me if there was anything he might do to assist the Old Blades. I did mention one place he might look at if he was in the vicinity—"

"Oh, you did?" the King raged. "We recall giving strict orders that the Old Blades were to be old Blades and nothing but old Blades, that you were to recruit no one who was not a knight in the Order."

That remark was met by an awkward pause, because of course Digby had indeed been a knight in the Loyal and Ancient Order of the King's Blades, although he had been the same age as the King himself, so his youthful days of swaggering around in livery were twenty years in the past. Then Ambrose realized his mistake. The royal roar returned, fit to rattle the windows. "*We expressly forbade Lord Digby to join the Old Blades!*"

Snake did not say that he had never been told of that edict, although his eyebrows hinted it. "There was no question of joining, Your Grace, just a small and very harmless favor that he—"

"And what was the place he was to scout for you?"

"The name escapes me for the moment," Snake said crossly, and did not flinch under his liege lord's disbelieving scowl. "I shall put my best man to work on it right away."

"Meaning who?" The King rarely bothered with details. Anger was making him meddlesome.

This time Snake balked openly. "I prefer not to mention the name here, sire. But Your Majesty will know who I mean when I refer to 'the King's Daggers.'"

"Stalwart?" roared the King, making Snake wince. "He's only a child!"

"With respect, Your Grace, for this job he is the best man you have."

3

Posthaste

THE storm had been building over Starkmoor for hours. It broke just before sunset, sweeping down in fury on the Blackwater valley, flaunting flames of lightning and drum rolls of thunder. It hurled apples from trees and flattened corn, as if to warn that summer was over at last. Long before it hit, though, Osbert had rounded up the horses from the meadow. By the time the rain and hail began thundering on the slates, he had them all combed and curried and comfortably bedded down in their stalls.

Obviously no travelers would be coming by on a night like this, but he could not just run for the house and take the rest of the evening off. Not yet. Thunder made horses restless. So he found a comfortable seat on a bale of straw in the covered saddling area outside the tack shed. From there he could see into most of the stalls that lined either side of the yard, and hear the remarks being whinnied back and forth. If there was any panic, he could move to stop it before it grew serious. He was contentedly munching an apple and marveling at the white haze of hail rebounding from every hard surface, when he heard an answering whinny from the lane.

In through the gate came three horses. Two of them bore

bedraggled riders; the third was a well-laden sumpter. He scrambled to his feet and watched angrily as they splashed along the yard toward him.

Osbert Longberry ran the Blackwater post house as his father and grandfather had run it before him. He loved horses so dearly that he could imagine no better life. He made sure his charges ate well, even when he and his family did not. When a sickly or weary horse was brought in—one that any sensible hostler would trade out again as fast as possible—he would often keep it for weeks, until he had wormed it, pampered it, and nursed it back to health. A post-horse might be traded from house to house across the length and breadth of Chivial, but if one that had spent time at Blackwater ever came back, Osbert always remembered it.

The village lay only an hour's ride from the King's great school of Ironhall. Every few days some Blade or royal courier would go by on Crown business. They liked to have a fresh mount for the climb up Starkmoor, which was a steep trek. Coming back down was equally hard on a horse, so they would change mounts again on the way home. Osbert approved of the Blades; Ironhall taught them almost as much about horses as about swords, and they treated their mounts with almost as much respect. They spurned the common posting animals. The King boarded a string of royal horses with Osbert Longberry and came by every few months with his Royal Guard escort. His Majesty never failed to hail Osbert by name and wish him good chance.

These new arrivals were quality stock—he could tell that just by watching their approach, although the storm was naturally making them skittish. In Osbert's opinion, any responsible rider would have taken shelter under trees or in the lee of a building until the worst of the weather had blown over—certainly until the hail ended. He would perhaps forgive a royal courier for treating a horse so, because his business might be urgent, with every hour counting. He could see that these two were mere boys, but old enough to know better.

As soon as they were safely in under cover, the visitors dismounted. One of them jumped down nimbly and removed his hat to shake off the water, revealing a very clumsily cropped head of blond stubble. The other moved more circumspectly, but he was no older or taller. He had a chubbier face and dark hair down to his shoulders. Neither of them could be a day more than fourteen. Osbert looked them over suspiciously—it was not unknown for horse thieves to visit a post house and try to exchange their loot for honest animals. These two were too well dressed for that, he decided. The blond one's fur-trimmed cloak stuck out at the back, proof that he was wearing a sword. The other appeared to be unarmed, although his clothes were equally fine. They must be just rich young gentlemen, who had never been taught proper respect for horseflesh.

"Terrible weather you keep around here," the blond kid said cheekily, wiping his face and thrusting reins at Osbert. "I need your three best right away. There'll be a silver groat for you if you're quick!"

Osbert scowled. "Can't send honest animals out in this weather, lad."

The blond boy had already set off toward the stalls to see what mounts were available. He stopped and spun around, frowning.

"I'm in a hurry."

"It won't kill you to be an hour late for dinner. Might kill a horse to catch a chill."

The rich brat smirked. "*Please? Pretty* please?"

Mockery infuriated Osbert. "No! Go and choose a horse if you like, but I won't let it out of here until the storm passes."

The two boys exchanged cryptic glances, but the dark-haired boy said nothing. The blond boy shrugged and turned.

"Not that way. Those are the King's horses." Osbert pointed to the other side of the yard. "Choose from there."

The kid drew himself up to his full height, which wasn't very much. He tried to look stern and succeeded only in seeming sulky. "We are on the King's business. We ride to Ironhall."

Spoiled brat! Osbert knew his type. All his life his father's money had let him have anything he wanted, so now he just fancied some fencing lessons, did he? Well, if he thought money would get him into Ironhall, he was sadly mistaken. They didn't take rich trash there, because rich trash wouldn't last a week under the discipline.

"Another hour won't hurt much, sonny. It takes five years to make a Blade."

The kid's face flamed scarlet. He reached under his cloak for his sword. Osbert yelped in fright and leaped backward, colliding with the sumpter.

"Wart!" shouted the other boy. "Don't!"

"Don't what?" The would-be swordsman scowled.

"He's not armed."

The blond boy's scowl turned to exasperation, as if all the world was crazy except him. "I can see that! You think I'd draw on...on him?" He turned to Osbert. "Know what this is?"

He was showing the hilt of his sword, and it bore a yellow jewel. Osbert had seen hundreds like it. Only Blades sported cat's-eye swords. The kid wasn't hoping to *enroll* in Ironhall.... Osbert gaped at him in disbelief.

"You can't be!"

The boy's eyes narrowed in fury. "Yes, I am! And whether I am of the Royal Guard or a private Blade, by law I can take any horse in your stable. Right?"

"Yes, Sir Blade."

"Any horse!"

"Yes, Your Honor!"

"I could take *all* of them!"

"Yes, yes! Beg pardon. I didn't...Sorry."

The boy turned his back angrily and strode off to inspect the King's horses.

The other boy was smiling apologetically. "He's sensitive about his looks. He's older than he seems, obviously." Since he was unarmed, he must be the Blade's ward, but he was far too young to be a minister of the Crown or an ambassador. Most likely he was some obscure member of the royal family, to have been honored with such a bodyguard.

"Yes, my lord. Sorry about the misunderstanding. I did hear that the King was taking them younger than usual, because of the Monster War." But, even so...

"He's a very good swordsman," said the boy, "and he truly is on urgent business for the King."

"Yes, my lord." Osbert hurried off after the baby-faced Blade to help him select his horses.

By the time they were saddled and the baggage had been transferred to the new sumpter, the storm had faded to a heavy rain, so the argument had been unnecessary. Surprisingly, the Blade did give Osbert the silver groat he had promised, and he did sign for the horses: *Stalwart, companion.* Some of his brethren would not have been so forgiving.

As he rode out of the gate, he turned to the companion riding beside him. "Just so you know, I do *not* use my sword on unarmed yokels. I'd only do that if they attacked me first."

"I'm sorry. You startled me. And you scared him half to death!"

Stalwart chuckled. "He thought you were a boy!"

"Am I supposed to feel flattered?" she asked.

The hostler had not been the first to mistake Emerald for a boy that day, although Stalwart had refrained from mentioning the fact sooner. It was a natural mistake when she was dressed like a man, for she was as tall as he was (or he was as short as she was, depending on how one looked at the problem). She had fooled even him for a moment when they had met before dawn in the palace stables. Only then had he realized that she obviously could not ride a horse in a White Sister's flowing draperies, not to mention the absurd steeple hat. When he asked where she had found such garments in the middle of the night, she had become strangely vague. Who could guess what deceptions the

White Sisters might get up to that no man ever heard about? Perhaps they made a habit of masquerading as men. He would ask Snake when he got back.

It had been Snake who had suggested Emerald come along. He must have learned at Valglorious that she could ride like a trooper, but Snake always knew everything. Stalwart had not cared much for the idea. After all, his new mission was merely to find out whatever it was Lord Digby had discovered earlier, the secret that had caused him to be murdered. Digby had not needed a White Sister to help him. If an old man like Digby could do it, Stalwart could. But the King had thought it was a good idea, and that had settled it.

She was doing remarkably well, although Stalwart knew better than to say so—she would bite his face off. She had not uttered one word of complaint, and she looked no more tired than he felt. Of course he was leading the packhorse, so he had to have an eye in the back of his head all the time; that made his job a little harder, but not much.

It had been a very long day. The King's little supper party had not finished until well after midnight. They had set out at first light and ridden all the way from Grandon without a break, pausing only to change horses. That was how Snake traveled. *Never give your enemies time to find out you're coming,* he said. Besides, this mission was urgent. If the traitor sorcerers had learned how to kill people at a distance, then the King might drop dead at any minute. It was up to Sir Stalwart to track down the evil in time, a *huge* responsibility!

As they left Blackwater and walked the horses up the winding hill trail, Emerald said, "You never said we were bound for Ironhall. I thought we were going to Prail, to catch the ferry."

"We are. Ironhall is only a little way off the Prail road."

"Why?" she asked suspiciously. "You just want to go back and gloat?"

"Of course not!" He mustn't, but he had been thinking wistfully about the idea all afternoon. He kept imagining himself strolling into the hall when everyone was at dinner, wandering up to the high table to sit with the knights and masters, since he was a real Blade now. He would have *Sleight*, his cat's-eye rapier, slung at his thigh and the White Star jewel glittering on his jerkin. Very few Blades had ever earned that honor, and he had done it in less than two weeks. He kept thinking of Grand Master's face when he saw it.... He would have to tell them about Quagmarsh. He might mention in passing how he had taken on two swordsmen at once and killed both of them. That was not a Blade record, but not something that happened every day, either. And if the conversation should happen to touch on that party last night with him and the King playing duets on their lutes... then he might let slip the complimentary remarks the great Durendal had made, Lord Roland, the greatest Blade of—

"Then why are we going there?" Emerald snapped.

"What? Where?"

"Ironhall!"

"Oh, for Badger."

"A horse?"

"A man. Good friend, next behind me in seniority, so he must be Prime now."

The sun had set. A streak of red sky showed through the rain, squeezed between the lowering clouds above and the bleak moor below. The school would be eating dinner, so he was too late to make the dramatic entrance, even had it been permissible. It wasn't. He must remain a coward a little longer, the secret swordsman, the *boy* who looked too young to be dangerous. However humiliating that was, his mission was too important to risk. But he *was* growing now. At last! In another few months he'd have a mustache....

"Why?" Emerald persisted.

"Why what?"

"Badger."

"Oh, Badger." Badger had a beard like a farrier's rasp. "He knows where we're going. He's been there. I remember him mentioning it. We'll take him along as a guide."

"Will Grand Master let him go?"

"Of course," Stalwart said confidently. If Grand Master

refused, Stalwart could overrule him. He would enjoy doing that. He did not like Grand Master. Nobody did. Even the old knights, the retired Blades who hung around Ironhall, disapproved of him. He was surly and unpredictable, known behind his back as Small Master. For Stalwart to pull out his commission with the King's seal and start giving Grand Master orders would help make up for some of the miseries old sour face had inflicted on him over the last four years.

"Why didn't you mention him sooner?"

"Didn't I?" In fact the Badger brainwave had hit him about noon. He hadn't mentioned it then because it was such a good idea that he should have thought of it much sooner.

"Suppose this Badger doesn't want to come?"

"I shall appeal to his loyalty." That was something else Snake had taught him—you never *ordered* a man into mortal danger. You asked him. In Snake's case you shamed him, outwitted him, or flattered him until he found himself volunteering, but you never ordered. Badger might refuse, because he was a moody, self-contained loner who had made few friends at Ironhall. He was older than Stalwart and would not enjoy taking his orders. On the other hand, he was going to be offered a chance to do a real service for his king, plus a chance to see the world again after being shut up on Starkmoor for four years. He would be a fool to refuse.

They had reached the top of the first slope, and the trail ran level ahead into the gloom. The rain was easing off.

"Giddyap!" Stalwart said, digging in his heels. They would reach Ironhall about curfew, and Prail around midnight. Perfect timing! Snake would approve of his progress so far.

4

Prime

UNAWARE of the dread destiny bearing down on him, Badger lay stretched out on his cot in the seniors' dormitory, staring at the boards of the ceiling. He was flaming mad. Had he flamed any hotter, he would have set his blanket on fire. He had very nearly punched Grand Master in the nose. He was seriously wondering if he should go back down and finish the job.

No day was good for him now, and the nights were worse, but this day had been especially irksome. Until two weeks ago, he had been comfortably anonymous, sixth man in a senior class of nine. Now he was Prime, meaning he was saddled with a million ill-defined duties, of which the worst was being den mother to the whole school.

That morning, as he'd come out of a dreary-dull lecture on court protocol, he had been accosted by a deputation of sopranos, the most junior class. They had complained shrilly that Travers was still wetting the bed every night and making their dorm stink. So Badger had taken young Travers aside for yet another heart-to-heart talk. Travers was barely thirteen and ought to be home with his mother, if he had one. He wasn't even showing much promise as a fencer. Grand Master should never have admitted him.

"Bad dreams?" Badger asked.

Travers wailed, "Monsters!" and started to weep.

Every candidate in Ironhall was having bad dreams about monsters—except, ironically, Badger himself, who had worse things to dream about.

"Are you still quite certain that you want to be a Blade?" he asked patiently. "If you made a mistake, then it's better to admit it to yourself now than five years from now. Look at Stalwart. He ran away, but only after he'd wasted four years of his life."

There was something very suspicious about that story, though. At times Wart had been a smart aleck, rambunctious, immature pest, but he had never impressed Badger as a quitter. Most people believed Grand Master had thrown him out in one of his petty temper tantrums.

"But what can I do?" Travers wailed, his eyes wide and red as his mouth. "If I leave, I'll be sent out onto the moors by myself and I'll starve to death!" Only orphans or rejects or rebels came to Ironhall. Very few had family to go back to.

"That's hog swill. Carters bring food to Ironhall every single day, yes? If they see a boy on the road they give him a ride into Prail or Blackwater, depending which way they're going."

The kid gasped like a convicted felon receiving a royal pardon on the steps of the gallows. "*Honest?*"

"Honest. And when they get him there, they see he gets a job in the fields or the mines or on a boat. Ironhall pays them to do this, because the Blades don't want to be accused of littering the countryside with beggars." Or skeletons; Badger didn't say that. "It will be lowly labor, not glamorous like strutting around beside the King, but there won't be any monsters."

Travers gaped at him, struck dumb by the immensity of the decision required.

Badger sighed. "Why don't you think it over for a couple of days? If you do decide to go, I'll see you get a packet of food to take, and perhaps we can steal a warm cloak for you. Don't tell anyone I told you all this."

The storm struck soon after, cascading white hail off the gloomy black walls and towers, sending peals of thunder echoing through the hills. A riding class of fuzzies and beansprouts was caught out on the moors and soaked to the skin. No one was injured, but the thunder made three horses bolt. Losing control of a horse was a serious offense. Master of Horse sentenced the riders to triple stable duties for a week, which meant that all of their free time and part of their sleeping time would be spent shoveling *horse stuffing*. News of this ghastly punishment was whispered around.

The main result of the bad weather was to move fencing classes indoors, and that brought problems for everyone, including Prime. The gym was crowded, noisy, and poorly lit. Men became testy. The juniors began clowning or goofing off. People could get hurt.

Swords clattered from dawn until dusk in Ironhall. The candidates were drilled with swords every day from their admission as spindly-limbed urchins until the night they strode out into the world behind their wards, deadly Blades bound to absolute loyalty. Master of Rapiers and Master of Sabers and their assistant knights taught fundamentals to the beginners, coached the seniors in the finer points, and tried to keep track of every one of the hundred candidates' progress. They simply did not have time to conduct all the daily practice sessions, so older boys were required to drill younger. There was no escaping that chore, although every candidate in three centuries had cursed it in his time.

In this year 368 of the House of Ranulf the problem was acute. Twenty-four men of the Order had died in the Monster War so far—eight guardsmen and sixteen knights—and Commander Bandit was screaming for more Blades to defend the King and his children. Ironhall had supplied forty in less than a year, but now it had reached its limit. The normal five-year course had been cut to four. There were only six seniors, instead of about twenty, and not one of the six was completely up to standard. They knew that. Everyone knew it. Yet they also knew that their binding could not be long delayed. The Guard would soon lick their fencing into shape for them, even if they had to work at it twenty-four hours a day, but they might find themselves facing mortal peril even sooner, ready or not. The seniors were worried young men. They grudged the hours they were forced to spend coaching juniors. Tempers were growing steadily shorter.

There was no rule that said Prime was responsible for keeping order in the fencing gym, but Grand Master was nowhere to be seen, typically. The fencing masters were demonstrating basic moves to teams of juniors. Everyone else was dueling, one on one, far too many men in far too small a space, and all the coaches were yelling directions at all the students. The result was earsplitting confusion: "Violet!" "Eggbeater!" "Higher!" "No, you *never* use Cockroach against Willow!" "Lower!" "Watch that wrist!" "That was Steeple, I said Rainbow...." Feet stamped up choking clouds of dust. Thunder roared outside.

Chaos. Someone was sure to get hurt.

No sooner thought than done. Marlon, who was Second, appeared with a split lip and a broken tooth. He was the best fencer in the school at the moment, but even his agility had failed to parry a wild and unpredictable stroke. Of course he should have been wearing a mask, but it was easier to instruct without one. Badger sent him off to find Master of Rituals, who would have to assemble a team of eight to chant a healing conjuration over him in the Forge, where the school octogram was located. That would take most of the afternoon and tie up masters or knights who could have helped here.

To relieve the pressure on space, Badger conscripted about thirty of the middle classes—beardless and fuzzies— and started drilling them in calisthenics, which needed a lot less room than fencing. He had no authority to do so, but no master objected. The boys welcomed the change of routine when he assured them this was how to build muscles. They

all seemed like children to him. None was as old as he had
been when he was first admitted, brazenly lying about his
age.

Having exhausted his first thirty victims, he began
collecting another thirty. He was preempted by Master of
Rapiers, Sir Quinn. Quinn often had strange ideas. His
current notion was that Badger needed a lesson in Isilondian
rapier technique. Badger despised rapiers. He was a saber
man, a slasher. He wanted to smite a foe, not poke at him.
Nor could he see any reason for learning all the various
styles that Ironhall liked to teach when Ironhall's own style
was the best. A man who had mastered that could beat any
opponent.

Furthermore, he already knew a fair bit about Isilondian-
style rapier fencing. To conceal that fact from Quinn he had
to play clumsy, which required superhuman reflexes when
fencing at that level. By the time the fading light brought the
session to an end, he had developed a throbbing headache.

"Excellent, excellent!" Quinn blathered. "We'll make a
rapier man out of you yet."

Over Badger's dead body.

Of course his dead body was going to be available quite
soon now....

"Prime?" The voice at elbow came from a fuzzy named
Audley. His face was wet and he looked worried. "There's
something nasty going on in the bath house."

"What sort of nasty?"

"The Brat. It sounds like Servian."

Badger hesitated only a moment. Discipline was Second's
responsibility, not his; but Marlon had not reported back
yet, and the healing would probably leave him dazed for
a while. The Brat was always the newest recruit, who had
no name because he had left his old one behind when he
was admitted and had not yet chosen another. Hazing the
Brat was the juniors' favorite occupation. It was supposed
to weed out the weaklings, so the masters usually turned a
blind eye; everyone had been the Brat once.

But Audley was a good man, almost ready to hang a

sword on and be a senior. If he said "nasty" then it must *be* nasty. Servian had been warned before.

"Thanks." Badger ran.

From the gym to the bath house was no distance, but he was soaked by the time he pounded up the steps. He could hear the kid's screams from there.

It was very nasty, far beyond normal hazing. Servian's meanness was the sort of disease that could infect others and turn them into henchmen. He had three of them with him now. They had the Brat's clothes off; they were holding him down and "cleaning" him with wet sand.

Badger lost his temper.

He waded into all four of them, fists flying. The three disciples were only kids, who could be sent flying with a slap; but Servian himself was a burly, sulky brute, as big as Badger himself. It took a couple of real punches to lay him on the floor, where he belonged.

"Put your clothes on, lad," he told the victim, who was starting to grin through his tears at this rough justice so unexpectedly imposed on his tormentors. Servian tried to rise; Badger pinned one of his hands to the flagstones with a boot, not gently. "You stay there for now. The rest of you, on your feet!" He made a mental note of their names. "Go to your dorms and stay there until I say otherwise. Don't expect to eat tonight. Do expect more bad things to happen. Run!"

When the weeping accomplices had gone, it was safe to deal with the pervert himself. "Get up! What you should have realized by now, scum, is that the Brat isn't the only one being tested."

Servian scrambled to his feet. For a moment he seemed ready for a second round, but when he saw that his supporters had gone and Badger was willing, he lowered his fists and just scowled.

"What 'ju mean?"

"I mean you're gone, lost, blown. The King has no use for sadists. You can't be trusted with a Blade's skills." It was unfortunate, because horrible Servian had the makings of an excellent swordsman.

Having confirmed that the Brat was more frightened than hurt, Badger sent him off to the infirmary to have his scrapes bandaged, and then marched Servian out to the quad. And over to the stocks. In his four years in Ironhall, he had never seen the stocks used, except sometimes to torment the Brat. He couldn't think of anything else bad enough for Servian at the moment. He rather hoped the thug would resist, but he submitted without a word. Badger locked him in, wrists and neck pinned between the boards, and left him there, standing in the storm. Then he went in search of Grand Master.

Grand Master, it seemed, was looking for Prime.

Badger tried First House, then West House, then back to Main House. They must have missed each other several times, because they were both well soaked when they eventually met. Their encounter took place back in the gym, before an audience of knights who had lingered to chat, plus a few juniors still tidying away equipment. Grand Master was obviously in one of his ogre moods.

Badger was alone, very much alone. Grand Master had a retinue. On one side of him stood Travers and some of his soprano friends; on the other Servian and his three stooges. Servian's face was swelling nicely, but he smirked at Badger as if to remind him of that ancient principle: *The enemy of my enemy is my friend.*

"Prime! You have been using violence on other candidates!"

"I admit I lost my temper, Grand Master. I was rescuing a boy these four were torturing."

"Even if that were true, it would be no excuse."

"There were four of them. Should I have drawn my sword?"

"Insolence! You should have used your authority. You have betrayed the trust placed in you—attacking boys, abusing Candidate Servian by locking him in the stocks." The old man's manner implied that the worst was yet to come. "*And* you deceived Candidate Travers with some nonsensical tale that has started a flood of absurd rumors."

Travers failed to meet Prime's eye. He had not kept the secret.

"I told him the truth." Badger could never understand why the Order had chosen Sir Saxon its Grand Master. He had been a compromise candidate, apparently, but even that did not excuse such a blunder. He always seemed so *small*, although he was quite tall for a Blade. Some days he greeted Badger by name, thumped his shoulder, made jokes, asked his advice. Other days, as now, he spluttered and squeaked like a mad tyrannical bat.

"You did not! You deceived him. You proved unworthy of the honor conferred on you."

Badger cared nothing for the honor of being Prime. He cared nothing for the Order, nor Ironhall and its inhabitants. He never had. "I told him that candidates who elect to leave are picked up by teamsters on the road. I also told him that the Order pays for this mercy, and also finds them work in Prail or Blackwater. Do you deny this?"

The old goat gibbered for a moment. Then, "Who ever told you such nonsense?"

"I have known that for years. I made it my business to find out before I turned up on your doorstep, Grand Master. Even then I knew better than to put myself in a trap that had no way out."

Grand Master grew redder and shriller, while the audience watched in amazement. "This is rubbish! You have betrayed the trust I placed in you when I appointed you Prime."

"You appointed me Prime? By puking Stalwart, you mean?"

"Insolence! Go to your room and stay there until I give you leave!"

Oh, flames! "You are a bucket head," Badger said sadly. "If you must be so petty, why do it in public?" He turned to go.

"And leave your sword!" Grand Master squealed.

Badger went, leaving his sword. He resisted the temptation to leave it in Grand Master. He even resisted the temptation to do to him what he had done to Servian.

Later, sprawled on his cot, he was seriously tempted to go back down to the hall and correct that mistake. By doing so, he would throw away four years' grinding hard work. He would ruin all his plans. But he would not die after all.

5

Return of the Lost Lamb

"WE'RE almost there!" Wart said cheerfully.
Emerald thought, *And about time*!
Ironhall was a vague something to her left. The rain had
almost stopped, but the wind still blew, and the night was
far too dark for any sane person to be riding over rocky
country like Starkmoor. Of course sanity was an illusive
concept when applied to a not-quite-seventeen-year-old-
male; and when that man had just become *Sir* Stalwart,
member of the White Star, companion in the Loyal and
Ancient Order of the King's Blades, official hero, an expert
swordsman who had recently won his first mortal duel and
been sent on a vital state mission with almost unrestricted
authority, sanity was about the last thing to expect. She was
cold and battered and one big blister from ankles to hips.
But if Master Smarty Warty had thought he could outride
her, he now knew better. She had not screamed for mercy
once and was not about to start now.

"I smell magic!"

"Right!" he said, sounding either surprised or admiring.
"We're passing the Forge."

That was where the boys were bound, she knew, and it
spoke to her as the Blades themselves did. No White Sister

could ever describe her reaction to a specific sorcery exactly, and *"hot metal"* was as close as she could come to classifying this one. It was something between an odor and a feeling. She could not see the building itself in the darkness, but an octogram that had been in use for several centuries would have a very wide aura.

A few moments later Wart said, "See that light? Grand Master's study. That's where we're going."

Several windows were showing faint glimmers of candlelight, but if he was pointing, she could not see his hand. The packhorse whinnied wearily, smelling stables ahead.

Her life had been *so* peaceful until Sir Snake had interfered in it! Just two weeks ago, she had been a deaconess in the White Sisters' tree city of Oakendown, nearing the end of her training. The nightmare had begun when she was unexpectedly summoned before Mother Superior and sworn in as a full Sister on the spot. Four years' quiet study had been followed by days of mad confusion and mortal peril. She had been rescued in the end by Wart, this peach-faced stripling who had turned out to have so many unexpected skills. She would have been more grateful if he had not helped put her into the danger in the first place.

Yesterday had seemed like the start of a fine new life at court. She had ridden in from Valglorious with Mother Superior in that lady's magnificent coach. Mother Superior had turned out to be a much nicer person than her reputation suggested. She had insisted on going around by Newhurst so that Emerald could visit her mother and break the marvelous news that the family home at Peachyard was to be returned to them. Poverty had turned overnight back to wealth—and that good fortune they owed in large part to Wart.

Was that why she was setting off on another mad adventure with him? She was certainly not doing so just to please the King. In the evening she had supped with the King. Wart had been there, as had Commander Bandit; Mother Superior; Lord Chancellor Roland and his delightful wife, Lady Kate; also the devious Sir Snake. Between the conversation and music, they had planned Wart's mission to investigate the suspected sorcerers' lair in Nythia. Emerald had agreed to accompany him, and she was not certain how that had happened.

Snake—he gave snakes a bad name—had pointed out that Wart would need help from the White Sisters to detect magic. Mother Superior had promised to write to the prioress in Lomouth. She could not send a Sister with him, she had said, because he would be traveling on horseback and almost no White Sister knew how to ride. But the old lady knew very well that Emerald could, because they had discussed such things that morning on the coach ride. And the look she had given Emerald had been a clear invitation to volunteer; whereas that morning she had sounded very much against any more such shenanigans. Wart had said nothing, ignoring Emerald completely, although they had gone riding together at Valglorious. So she had spoken up, admitting that she had grown up with horses at Peachyard. At once the King had asked her to accompany Wart.

And she had agreed. *Not* just because Wart had pulled a face at the idea of having to share his mission with her—she hoped she was not so childish. (Although that might have been a *small* part of it...) And *not* just to please the King. She had found Ambrose IV much too big and too loud. He had kept repeating the same joke about Wart and her being the King's Daggers, which everyone had to laugh at. He fancied himself a musician, and the funniest part of the evening had been watching the other guests trying to keep straight faces while he and Wart played duets on their lutes. As a former minstrel, Wart had been tying his fingers in knots in his efforts to follow the King's scrambled keys and timing.

All in all, it had been an exhausting evening. When the party finally broke up, Emerald headed back to the Sisters' quarters with Mother Superior.

"You wanted me to go with Stalwart, my lady," Emerald said. "May I ask why?"

Mother Superior sighed. "Because I am worried about

that boy. He did so amazingly well at Quagmarsh! I am afraid it has made him dangerously overconfident. He will get himself killed. He needs someone sensible to look after him." She regarded Emerald with a pair of old but extremely shrewd gray eyes. "And why did you agree to go?"

"For that exact same reason!"

They had both laughed.

After fourteen hours in the saddle, the joke was no longer funny.

Wart dismounted and for once remembered his manners enough to hold Emerald's horse while she did. Faint rays glimmered through a small barred window. Below it was a hitching rail. A latch clattered, hinges creaked, and she followed Wart's silhouette inside.

"This's called the Royal Door," he said. "There's always a light in here...." He took the lantern down off its hook and turned up the wick. The golden glow brightened to reveal a large circular chamber, completely empty except for a narrow stone staircase spiraling up the wall.

"For the King?"

"And other visitors. Ah!" He had found a bell rope. He hauled on it, but the masonry absorbed any sound he may have produced. "Can you come back out and hold the light for me? If he assigns a Blade to someone—an ambassador or a duke, f'r instance—then this is the way they come."

He fussed over the packhorse's load while Emerald held the light for him. She was shivering. Judging by his angry growls, his fingers were too cold to work properly, but eventually he managed to detach one long bundle.

"What about the horses?"

"Small Master will send someone, of course. Come on."

He led the way back inside. Although he must be as tired and sore as she was, he ran up the steps two at a time, eager for the coming interview. She knew he detested Grand Master, who had held despotic authority over him for four years. Was he hoping to get some of his own back? The bell had been heard somewhere, because a door halfway up the stair stood ajar, waiting for them. Pushing it wide, Wart strode forward into the brightness of candles and a crackling fire.

"Stalwart!" Grand Master was not as old as Emerald had expected. His face was bleak and bony, and what flesh there was on it had settled into grooves and lines, but there was no gray in the narrow fringe of beard. He gaped in amazement at his visitor.

"Good chance to you, Grand Master! Glad we didn't drag you out of bed. My companion, Luke of Peachyard...."

Luke? Emerald bristled. Before the Sisterhood renamed her Emerald, she had been Lucy Pillow, but that hated name was supposed to be dead and forgotten. The great Sir Stalwart would scream in fury if she referred to him as Wat Hedgebury! He had not warned her that he expected her to masquerade as a boy. Mother Superior had advised male clothing for comfort on horseback, although she had admitted it would also deflect unwanted questions. Real ladies were expected to travel by coach; other women never had reason to go anywhere. The Sisters had their own priorities.

Grand Master barely spared a glance for "Luke," who must be a child or servant, because he was not wearing a sword. "Good chance to you, Stalwart. This is a pleasant surprise." That was not a lie, just sarcasm. His initial amazement had given way to anger and disapproval. Emerald suspected his face often expressed disapproval; he had that sort of a mouth.

Wart tossed his sodden cloak over a stool. "A surprise to me also. If you would have the horses cared for, please? Do not mention my name."

Grand Master went to the other door and paused with his hand on the latch. "And yourselves? Food? Beds? Are you and the boy staying?"

The *boy* removed her cloak also and headed for the fire to thaw out her hands.

"Can't," Wart said cheerfully. "I must be on my way

directly. If you would kindly have replacements saddled up? And one extra mount."

The older man glared at him, but when no explanation followed, he opened the door and stuck his head out to give instructions. Wart joined Emerald at the fire, shivering and rubbing his hands. He did not even look at her, but his eyes were gleaming; he was enjoying himself enormously. She saw him check the hang of his jerkin, making sure the edge concealed the diamond star pinned on his doublet. He went to the table and began untying the long package he had brought.

The room dearly needed a woman's touch. Stone walls and plank floors made it grim; there were cobwebs in the window niches. Its aging furniture was ugly and mismatched, none of it comfortable—a settle by the fireplace, a very ancient leather chair facing it, three stools around a table. Grand Master himself had the same shabby, neglected appearance.

He finished giving orders, closed the door, and went to join Wart at the table. "You bring sad tidings. I should send for Master of Archives."

"No! My presence here tonight must be known only to yourself and one other." The covering of oiled cloth fell open, revealing three swords. Swords coming back to Ironhall meant dead Blades, but Wart now ignored them, donning his most innocent expression, which made him look about twelve and invariably signaled trouble ahead. "To save time, would you be so kind as to summon Candidate Badger?"

Grand Master dropped any pretense of enjoying the evening. "No."

Wart smiled at this show of resistance. "I must insist, Grand Master."

"Not until I know why you want him."

"I need to borrow him for a few days."

"What! Why?"

The smile grew wider. "I am sorry I cannot answer that."

"The charter decrees that all candidates reside within the school until completion of their training."

Confrontation.

Emerald waited to see what Wart would do next. His White Star would probably be enough authority by itself, but she knew that he also carried his commission from the Court of Conjury. That bore the royal seal and identified the bearer as "our trusty and well-beloved Stalwart, companion in our Loyal and Ancient Order of the King's Blades...." It commanded "our servants, officers, vassals, and loyal subjects without exception" to aid him in "all his dread purposes and ventures." With that backing, Wart could practically order Grand Master to jump down a well.

But Grand Master had just noticed the sword dangling at Wart's thigh with its hilt toward him. It bore a cat's-eye stone on the pommel—quite a large one, because it was a rapier, whose point of balance had to be well back toward the user's hand. He had explained all that to Emerald at least twice. He was very proud of his sword, was Wart. He called it *Sleight*.

"Where did you get that?"

Amazingly, Wart's smile could grow even wider, and did. "From Leader." That was the Blades' own name for Commander Bandit. "And he got it from Master Armorer. Didn't they tell you about this, Grand Master?"

The older man's face was red enough to set his beard on fire. He seemed to keep his teeth clenched while he said, "I do not recall your being bound."

"No? Well, that was because Fat Man postponed my binding. Master of Archives has the edict somewhere in the records."

More confrontation.

Obviously Wart was just dying to pull out his commission and smash Grand Master to bits with it. Grand Master, in turn, was wondering how much authority Wart really had. He chose not to take the risk of asking.

"I must know what business you think you have with Prime."

Wart tried to stick out his jaw, but it was not a very convincing jaw yet. "I will explain when he gets here."

Grand Master sighed. "I do not wish to trouble him, you see. Some boys...candidates...have trouble as they approach their binding. Badger is one of them, I fear, poor lad. He has not been a success as Prime. He has become very jumpy and short-tempered."

"Badger? Never! The man's a rock."

Grand Master shook his head sadly. "You would be quite shocked by the change in him."

Wart said softly, "I will judge him for myself."

Confrontation again. Again it was the older man who yielded.

"I will be present while you speak with him."

Wart shrugged. "I am on the King's business, and I bind you to secrecy by your oath of allegiance."

That was a slight retreat, probably designed to trap the other man into demanding to see his credentials, but Grand Master refused to take the bait.

"And I do not agree that he may accompany you when you leave."

Wart just smiled. Grand Master swung around and went back to the door. Wart closed his eyes for a moment and sighed as if his joy was almost too much to bear. He did not look at Emerald; he might have forgotten she was there.

Having given the orders, Grand Master returned to the table with a thin smile nailed on his face. "Well, well, brother! You must have been having some interesting experiences since you left us so unexpectedly."

If he had been a girl being admitted to Oakendown and in need of a new name, Emerald would have suggested "Minnow"— small, slithery, and skittish. His abrupt reversals told her that he was a water person. Although all the manifest elements—air, fire, earth, and water—were present in everyone, one was always dominant. White Sisters were trained to identify elementals, and only a water person could run through so many moods so quickly. The virtual elements were harder to assess, but she was detecting a strong component of chance, which always seemed to her like a faint rattling of dice being rolled. Water-chance people should never be put in positions of responsibility, but their combination of luck and malleability often won them appointments for which they were totally unsuited.

"Life has been interesting," Wart agreed. "These swords... fallen Blades. They all gave their lives for their King." He drew a sword and raised it. "I bring *Woe*," he proclaimed, "the sword of Sir Beaumont, knight in our Order, who died three days ago at a place called Quagmarsh while serving as a commissioner of His Majesty's Court of Conjury. Cherish this sword in his memory." He sheathed *Woe* and passed it with both hands to Grand Master, who took it the same way.

"It shall hang in its proper place forever."

The confrontation had been set aside for now. These were fellow Blades mourning their brethren.

"You see the hilt is partly melted? He was struck by hellfire." Wart drew another. "I bring *Quester*, the sword of Sir Guy, knight in our Order, who died three days ago at a place called Quagmarsh while serving as a commissioner of His Majesty's Court of Conjury. Cherish this sword in his memory."

Grand Master shuddered and repeated his formula: "It shall hang in its proper place forever. What happened to him?"

"He was trying to save a woman from a chimera."

"Chimera?"

"Magical monster. They vary, depending on the ingredients. They can be quite scary, especially at night; can't they, Luke? This one tore Guy's throat out before Snake got it. By the way...news of a brother. Yesterday Snake was promoted from member to officer in the White Star."

"Wonderful!" Grand Master said. "I shall announce that in the hall with great pride."

The falsehood made death elementals flutter on the edge of Emerald's awareness. Inquisitors were not the only ones who could detect lies; most White Sisters could do it too. Grand Master was jealous of Snake's success.

Wart raised the third sword. "I bring *Durance*, the sword

of Digby, knight in our Order and First Lord Digby of Chase, Warden of the King's Forests, who died yesterday, struck down by sorcery in the presence of His Majesty."

"*What?*" Grand Master screeched, ceremony forgotten. "How?"

"That we don't know...yet."

"You're serious? Where was the Guard? Who did it?"

"Nobody. I saw it. The whole court saw it. He was stabbed through the heart and there was no one within four paces of him."

Grand Master scowled in disbelief. "That is outrageous!"

"We're working on it."

"This Quagmarsh place—were you there too?"

"Not during the fighting," Wart said with disgust. "Just—"

Knuckles rapped on the door.

6

Pilot on Board

A MAN stepped in and slammed the door behind him, while fixing a dangerous glower on Grand Master. He was of average height, but heavyset, huskier than any of the Blades Emerald had seen during her brief stay at court. She knew that seniority in Ironhall depended entirely on order of admittance, not on age or ability, and the newcomer sported a murky beard shadow that made him look ten years older than Stalwart. He saw Wart and stiffened. His dark gaze flickered quickly over the cat's-eye sword, the courtly clothes so much more splendid than his own Ironhall rags, the unarmed youth by the fire, the three swords on the table.

"Good chance!" He had a harsh, unmusical voice. "*Sir* Stalwart, I presume?"

Wart made a leg. "The same."

Badger doffed his hat and offered a full court bow. His black and very curly hair was blazoned by a startling white patch right above his forehead. If he had not chosen the name of Badger for himself, the other boys had hung it on him. "Congratulations." He awarded Emerald a second, slower, inspection, then looked back at Wart. "Private?"

"Guard. Until my enlistment becomes official, I am assisting Sir Snake in some confidential matters."

"Indeed!" Badger looked impressed, but Emerald detected a glimmer of something false, a wrongness. "I never believed the lies some dishonest people were spreading around here about you."

"Thank you." Wart was enjoying himself again. "You are not wearing a sword, Prime."

"No, I'm not."

"Grand Master, why is Prime Candidate Badger running around naked?"

The mercurial Grand Master was red with fury again. "A disciplinary matter."

Wart said, "*Tsk*! Then perhaps my timing is appropriate. I came to offer you a break from routine, brother. By the way, over there is my assistant, Luke of Peachyard. Sh—*he* has certain skills that may be useful to me. Candidate Badger, Luke."

Emerald and Badger exchanged nods. This time his appraisal was even longer, as if something about Luke puzzled him.

Wart and Badger were presently united in baiting Grand Master, but they were very dissimilar people. Either Wart had invented their former friendship, because it suited him to believe in it at the moment, or they were a striking case of opposites attracting. He was an air-time person, which was why he was so incredibly agile with a sword and such a fine musician. Badger was bone and muscle, probably tenacious or at least stubborn, not much humor.... Yes, even his name...Badger was an earth person, like Emerald herself. And his virtual element? Wart had called him a loner, so not love. Not *chance* by any stretch of the imagination; he was the sort of plodder who calculated every step.

"I'm on my way," Wart said airily, "to investigate a suspected nest of traitor sorcerers, and I know you used to be familiar with the area. There shouldn't be any fighting, just a little snooping and riding around. I'll have you back here in four or five days."

"And did Grand Master say I could go out to play?"

"Grand Master?" Wart asked vaguely. "Oh, yes, Grand

Master. Well, I'm sure he will not deny you this opportunity of serving His Maj—Fat Man, I mean. We of the Guard always call him Fat Man. There's nothing Grand Master *can* do about it, really, since the King has forbidden him to expel any more kids without royal permission in writing."

"Indeed?" Badger said thoughtfully. "I don't believe I knew that."

"Leader told me; perhaps I shouldn't have mentioned it. Grand Master, what do you—"

"What is *that*?"

Wart looked down to see where the older man was pointing. "Oh, that!" If he had exposed his star deliberately, it had been very skillfully done and he ruined the effect by blushing. Emerald was certain he had just forgotten to keep it hidden. "A token of His—of Fat Man's appreciation. For services to the Crown."

Badger and Grand Master exchanged looks of amazement.

"Flames and death!" Badger growled. "You must have had a busy couple of weeks, brother Stalwart!"

"It was strenuous at times," Wart said with unusual modesty.

"Well, I am sure Grand Master will not deny you any reasonable request now. He and I could use a break from each other, certainly." Even if Badger was not much of a humorist, he could help Wart hammer on Grand Master's coffin. "I'll need a sword. I won't come without a sword."

"Of course not. You need a *good* sword. I suppose you still hanker after those woodchopping sabers? Try this." Wart offered the one he had been holding all this time.

"That sword belongs here!" Grand Master bleated angrily.

Badger hefted it and tried a couple of swings. "A little lighter than I prefer, but very fine!" He peered at the blade. "*Durance*? Whose was she?"

"Digby's."

"Digby? I remember him! Warden of Forests? He gave the Durendal Night speech last year. No, two years ago."

Grand Master tried again. "His sword has been Returned and belongs here!"

"I didn't finish Returning it." Wart gave Badger the scabbard also. "You had not accepted it. Besides, it's Digby's killers we're hunting, so I'm sure he would have been happy to lend us *Durance* for a few days."

"Candidate Badger is not bound!" Grand Master protested. "He is not entitled to wear a cat's-eye sword. Did the King give you permission to hand out cat's-eye swords?"

"Fat Man pretty much gave me a free hand. *Durance* is a good name for a badger's sword."

Badger looped the baldric over his shoulder and adjusted it to fit his thick chest. "I hope I can help her to avenge her master."

There was something about him that set Emerald's teeth on edge. An earth person, certainly. And his dominant virtual? Not love, not chance. And it could not be time, because she was an earth-time person herself, and another would not give her this scratchy, unsettled feeling. That left only death. She had never met any earth-death people; there had been none at Oakendown. They made the finest warriors, of course. Human landslides. Ruthless, probably possessed of unlimited courage. Deadly.

"I'll go and get my cloak and razor," Badger said in his harsh growl. "Meet you downstairs?"

"Be so kind as to send for our horses now," Wart told Grand Master.

The older man seemed to be building up to an apoplectic fit. "By what right do you presume to give me orders?" he roared.

Wart beamed and reached inside his jerkin to produce the scroll with the royal seal. The sight of it was enough. Grand Master muttered an oath. Spinning on his heel, he headed to the door.

Badger smiled for the first time, reflecting Wart's triumphant grin. "What is this place we're going to scout?"

Wart checked to make sure Grand Master was outside. "It's in Nythia. A house called Smealey Hole."

All the color drained out of Badger's face.

7

Nythia

BY the time they rode into Prail next morning, Wart was wondering whether Snake's way of traveling was quite as admirable as he had at first believed. Of course Snake would not have lost the trail after leaving Ironhall and thus would not have been forced to wander the moors in a downpour all night. Snake would not have had to put up with Badger's sarcastic comments. Emerald's had been even worse, but by dawn she had stopped speaking to him altogether, which was an improvement. Chilled and exhausted and bad tempered, they came down to the cold gray waters of the Westuary. Not far out from the shore stood a wall of white sea fog, hiding the hills of Nythia beyond.

Possibly some traitorous Nythians still believed that Nythia should be a separate country, but it had been a province of Chivial for centuries, despite many attempted revolutions. The last uprising, when Stalwart was a child, had been suppressed by King Ambrose in person. He had ridden through the breach at the storming of Kirkwain with his Blades around him, and Ironhall's *Litany of Heroes* included several stirring tales of that campaign.

Nythia was a peninsula. It could be reached by a short ferry trip across the Westuary inlet or by a daylong ride

around it. Until very recently any seafarer risked capture
and enslavement by Baelish pirates, but now there were
strong rumors that a treaty had been negotiated to end the
war. The raiding seemed to have stopped, and Digby had
reported that ferrymen were willing to risk the crossing
again.

The fare had to be bargained over, the baggage loaded,
and the horses turned in to a posting house. Badger took
care of all that, because he was the least weary of the three
of them. He could also look fiercer. Nevertheless, Stalwart
was already wishing he had never involved Badger in his
mission. He was being much less helpful than expected.

That problem could wait. The boat was small, smelly,
and bouncy, but the moment the master and his boy cast
off the lines, Stalwart rolled himself up on the deck in his
blanket and let the world disappear.

By afternoon, life had become a little brighter. The sleep on
the boat had helped. So had a truly enormous meal at an
inn in Buran, where they disembarked. Now the sun was
shining and the road was dry, winding through prosperous
farmland flanked by rolling green hills speckled with sheep.
The horses they had hired were fine beasts and well fitted
out. It was time to form a plan of campaign.

Stalwart rode in the middle, keeping the other two
apart. When they had been properly introduced, Badger
had remarked that honorable warriors did not take women
along on dangerous missions and ladies did not dress like
that. Emerald had been snarling and snapping at him ever
since. He had always been a bit of a churl; becoming Prime
seemed to have made him a lot worse, so perhaps there had
been something in what Grand Master said.

"Why don't you begin at the beginning again?" he growled.
"You weren't making much sense last night."

"I'll use nice short words this time," Stalwart said
cheerfully. "The elementaries that sell black magic are
mostly located near Grandon or other big cities, because
that's where the rich customers are. The sorcerers themselves

come from all over. It takes eight of them to chant a spell, and they have to learn their nasty trade somewhere. Snake has discovered that a lot of them were trained by an order that calls itself the Fellowship of Wisdom. It inhabits a house called Smealey Hole."

"On the south edge of Brakwood," Badger agreed, "near Waterby."

"Snake's even found letters hinting that its members organized the Night of Dogs attack. He also suspects that some of the villains who slipped through his nets may have gone back there. The Fellowship is hiding them. So when Lord Digby set off on his tour of the King's western forests, Snake asked him to take a look at Smealey Hole."

Badger snorted disbelievingly. "A peer-over-the-wall look at it or a climb-through-the-pantry-window-at-midnight look at it?"

"Probably a can-you-sell-me-something-to-get-rid-of-my-mother-in-law look at it."

"And that's why he was murdered a week later? Do they kill the minstrel who comes to sing or the tinker who mends pots? Wart, are you quite sure Snake doesn't just want to keep you out of harm's way until you've grown up enough to wear Guard livery without making everyone die laughing?"

"Quite sure. If you don't want to help, go home to Ironhall and wipe the juniors' noses."

"Grand Wizard thinks this new sorcery is a short-range weapon, so all the Old Blades are frantically rounding up suspects around Grandon, but you get blown away to the other side of the kingdom?"

"Grand Wizard is just guessing," Stalwart said with as much confidence as he could summon. "So's Snake, I suppose, but his guesses *work!*"

Badger would not give up. "But you don't know what Digby found at Smealey or if he went there at all."

"We do know he went there. His retinue says so—he had clerks, huntsmen, grooms, and squires with him. But he left them all behind in Waterby and went to Smealey with just one local guide, so we don't know what he saw or who he talked to. He died before he could report to Snake. He didn't mention anything to the King, but he wouldn't, because Fat Man had forbidden him to join the Old Blades."

"Doing-a-favor-for isn't joining."

"Brother, you do *not* argue that sort of point with kings!"

No need to tell Badger that Snake was now in royally hot water. If Digby's death was not explained and avenged very soon, he might find himself in the Bastion, rattling every time he scratched his fleabites.

Badger thought for a while as they cantered along the trail. "If Digby found evidence of treason, why didn't he send a courier to Snake? Why didn't he rush home himself? He can't have found much if he just carried on with his tour, counting antlers hither and yon across Chivial."

"We're puzzled by that. He didn't do either! He went to Smealey on the twelfth. He was expected back in Grandon about the thirtieth, but instead he arrived on the seventeenth. Next day he died. So he did cut his tour short, but not as short as he could have done. Nor did he tell his men why he was in such a hurry to get back."

"If these sorcerers were so frightened that Digby was going to tattle bad stories about them, why would they not just have someone put an arrow through him in the forest? Why do anything as risky as putting a curse on him?"

"He was not cursed!" Emerald shouted. "The Sisters would have detected a curse as soon as he entered the palace. This is a new sort of magic."

"And if Wart drops dead when he gets back to Nocare, that will prove it."

Stalwart still held on to his temper. "When Snake told me about Smealey Hole, I recalled the name. How could I ever forget it? You mentioned it one night when we were juniors. We were discussing secret passages. Orvil told a story about being shown one, then you said that you'd *found* one. You'd been exploring caves, you said, and discovered a man-made tunnel, with steps carved into the rock, and you followed it up to a door. You learned later that this was a smuggler's route, leading into the local lord's house, Smealey Hole."

Badger shrugged. "I don't remember. If I said that, then I was lying. I suppose I thought Orvil was bragging and I could top his story with a better one—we were only kids, remember."

Most of them had been kids, but not him. He'd claimed to be fifteen when he was admitted, but no one had believed him. He'd been shaving, even then.

"You sounded very convincing."

"I'm a good liar. It's quite likely that there is such a passage, so perhaps I'd heard about it and claimed to have seen it. The house is really Smealey *Hall* but it's always known as Smealey Hole, which is the name of the pothole where the Smealey River disappears. There's lots of caves south of Brakwood, and a secret back door is never a bad idea in wild and whiskery country like that. But my home was at Kirkwain, north of the forest. I've never been near Smealey Hole or Waterby. What I do know about the Hole is that there's a curse on it."

"What sort of curse?" Emerald asked, looking skeptical.

"Terrible things happen to people who live there. It's very old, but no family has ever owned it for long. They all die nastily."

"For instance?"

"For instance...if you knew the name of Smealey, Wart, you must have recognized Waterby, too. I mean, you'd heard about it before this Digby murder?"

"Just that Durendal was named Baron Roland of Waterby because it was there he saved the King's life."

"You remember what it says in the *Litany*?"

"Of course." Stalwart had heard it read out often enough, like all the other great tales of Blades who had saved their wards' lives or lost their own in trying. Durendal's was special. "'*Number 444: Sir Durendal, who on the sixth day of Sixthmoon, 355, in a meadow outside Waterby single-handedly opposed four swordsmen seeking to kill his ward and slew them all without his ward or himself taking hurt.*' That's the only time a Blade has ever managed four at once," he explained for Emerald's benefit, "and to do it on open ground was just incredible. In a narrow passage—"

"Two of the men he killed," said Badger, "were sons of Baron Smealey of Smealey Hole. Another brother was executed later in Grandon Bastion, but only after he'd murdered his father, the Baron. *That's* the sort of curse I mean."

Stalwart waited for Emerald to comment on the magic of curses, but what she said was, "So it has a long history of treason?"

"Possibly. Look, there's a corner of Brakwood now!" Badger pointed at hills ahead.

Although Brakwood was a royal forest, it was not an unbroken expanse of trees from Waterby to Kirkwain. It was rough country, partly wooded, partly open; most of it hilly, none of it cultivated. It included lakes and rivers. It all belonged to the King, who would come and hunt there every three or four years. He allowed no one else to do so, or even to cut wood without his permission. Enforcing the unpopular forest laws was the responsibility—and principal headache—of Lord Florian, the Sheriff of Waterby, and it was to him that Stalwart must look for assistance in his mission.

Snake's instructions had been simple enough. "You proved your courage at Quagmarsh. I do *not* want heroics this time, understand? *Don't* go blundering into Smealey Hole yourself, or we'll have two deaths to investigate. Just track down that local guide who escorted Digby there. Find out from him whom Digby saw and what was said. Then talk around. Find out all you can about the Fellowship. If you can lay your hands on evidence of black magic—at least two independent witnesses—send a courier posthaste back here, and I'll bring the Old Blades at a gallop. At *that* point you can start to scout out the country, so you can help us plan our attack."

Then Snake had skewered Stalwart with a glittery stare. "Can I trust you to take your commission along? Theoretically,

that gives you almost unlimited power, you know. It would
let you put the Sheriff and all his men under your command
and go in with swords flashing. Try anything like that, my
lad, for any reason short of absolute proof of treason and an
imminent attack upon His Majesty, and I'll feed you alive
to the palace rats!"

Snake had described Waterby as a pleasant little town on
the Brakwater. It had long since recovered from the siege of
355, he said, but its walls had never been rebuilt; instead the
stones had been put to use in a considerable enlargement of
the castle. As the Stalwart expedition rode along the river
meadow—probably passing the very spot where Durendal
had worked his miracle thirteen years ago—that grim
edifice seemed to grow ever more menacing, looming higher
over the houses clustered below its towers.

"Master Luke," Stalwart said, "the castellan may board
us with the men-at-arms. You'd better dress up as a girl
pretty soon."

"The sooner the better. How can you wear these awful
clothes all the time?"

"I'd be a wondrous weird swordsman in yours. You,
brother, ought to be *Sir* Badger with that sword."

Badger thought for a moment. "'Suppose. Can't see how
not."

"Isn't it illegal," Emerald asked, "for any man except a
Blade to wear a cat's-eye sword?"

"Very," Stalwart admitted. "No one except snarly old
Grand Master will object to Digby's sword helping avenge
his murder, but a candidate should not be passing himself
off as a companion." Giving Badger the sword might have
been a mistake, although a reasonable one, because all
other swords in Ironhall were kept blunter than shovels. By
wearing it he was committing a major imposture, a crime
that could in theory bring the death penalty. The entire
Order would scream like rabid dragons. Wart's own status
as the first unbound Blade in history was scandalous enough,
although it was backed by royal edict and Leader's approval.

"Then introduce him just as plain Badger of Kirkwain, and let everyone jump to the wrong conclusion. And exchange swords."

"Huh?"

She sighed as if he were being unspeakably stupid. "Surely there would be very little objection if *you* carried Lord Digby's sword?"

"Just about none."

"And surely you can lend yours to Badger?"

The men exchanged thoughtful glances. Badger pulled one of his sour smiles. "How can you stand it, brother?"

"Nice bit of hairsplitting," Stalwart agreed, grinning at Emerald to show he was actually grateful. "Let's try that."

Durance and *Sleight* were drawn, exchanged, hefted, swung.

Frowns were frowned, pouts pouted.

"All right if you want to chop meat," Stalwart said. He detested sabers. He was built for speed, not strength.

"Useful if you need to darn socks," Badger countered.

Sleight went back to her owner and *Durance* to the imposter.

"Nice idea," Stalwart told Emerald, "but really good swordsmen like me are all rapier men; Badger's just a blacksmith—beef and no brain. You're right about names, though. Brother, you'll be Master Badger of Kirkwain. If anyone gives you titles, pretend not to notice. Keep the hilt under your cloak whenever possible. And let me do the talking."

"I shall be silent and invisible, Great Leader." Badger pulled his hat down over his eyes.

They rode through the town to the castle. The road ended abruptly at a very smelly moat, a canal from the river. It was spanned by a draw-bridge guarded by men-at-arms bearing pikes, but they made no move to challenge the strangers riding through. Hooves drummed on the planks of the bridge, then echoed in the low tunnel through the barbican. Passing under the grisly portcullis and through a final massive door, the visitors emerged into the sunlit bailey. This was a busy little town square in its own right, with washing being dried, horses groomed, men-at-arms drilled, and various wares sold from stalls. Amid all that, women gossiped, men argued, children screamed, dogs barked, and pigeons cooed.

The newcomers barely had time to dismount in front of the door of the keep before a crowd congealed around them to gape. Boys came running to take the horses. A chubby man in servants' garb hurried out, wiping his hands on his apron. He bowed—to Badger, naturally. He probably thought Stalwart was his squire.

"My lords...Cuthbert the steward is not available. I am the bottler, Caplin. May I be of assistance?"

Stalwart said, "Pray inform the Sheriff that Sir Stalwart is here and would hold converse with him."

The bottler bowed again, but to the space between the two, as if uncertain which was which. "I will see if his lordship is available, Sir Stalwart."

Badger roared. "*He had better be*! We come on urgent business for His Majesty."

Flustered, Caplin backed away a few steps, then turned and scurried indoors.

"I told you to keep your mouth shut!" Stalwart said bleakly, being careful not to shout. Wrong, wrong, all wrong! Badger's blustering was how a royal official would normally behave, but Snake had sent Stalwart on this mission because he knew how to be inconspicuous. Badger's bellow had been overheard by so many onlookers that the news that the King's men had arrived would be all over the town in an hour. The Fellowship would be sure to have spies near the Sheriff.

8

The Sheriff of Waterby

A S a page led the visitors across a gloomy dining hall filled with plank tables and benches, Emerald found her chance to poke Wart in the ribs. He nodded without speaking. The boy disappeared up a very narrow spiral staircase built into the wall of the keep. Wart gestured Badger to go first, then for her to follow. She held back until Badger had disappeared.

"He's betraying you!" she whispered. "When he shouted at the bottler, that was deliberate mischief. Not quite a lie, but I'm sure he's playing you false."

Wart, surprisingly, did not look surprised. He pushed her forward and came up the steps after her, as close as it was possible for two people to go together in that cramped space. "What has he said that's not true?" he asked her shoulder.

"I can't be certain," she told his hat. Badger's dominant element confused her ability to detect falsehood. He had confessed to being a good liar; he might have been joking, but any death person must be a good liar. "But I don't think he's from Kirkwain. Why is he doing this?" She passed a loophole that let in a little light; she wondered if anyone had ever shot arrows out of it, and marveled at the thickness of the wall.

"He's always been sort of surly," Wart said sadly. "He may be jealous of my success. It can't have anything to do with Digby, Sister. It just can't! Any crimes Badger committed before he came to Ironhall are forgotten and will be automatically pardoned when he's bound. For four years, he's had no contact with the world, and why would he spend all that time there if he did not want to be a Blade?"

"Digby went there two years ago."

"Just to give the Durendal Night speech. As I recall, his was even duller than most. Badger and I were only beansprouts then. They keep the riffraff away from important visitors."

The logic seemed inescapable: Whatever was troubling Badger could have nothing to do with Wart's mission. The sound of boots up ahead suddenly stopped. She hurried.

"There you are!" Badger said as she reached him. Did he suspect that she suspected him? The White Sisters did not advertise their ability to detect falsehood, but it must be known in Ironhall.

"The stair's making me giddy."

He turned to continue and she followed. It wasn't the stair making her head spin, she realized—it was magic, growing stronger with every step she climbed. She opened her mouth to shout a warning. But then there was light, and an open door, with the page holding it for her.

Emerald followed Badger in and Wart came at her heels. The boy departed, closing the door. The solar was located high in the keep, with large windows facing safely inward, overlooking the bailey. Sunshine alone would have warmed it comfortably by that time in the afternoon, for it was a small chamber, but the huge fire blazing on the hearth had heated it almost beyond endurance. Incredibly, the sole inhabitant was hunched in a chair directly in front of this inferno. It seemed a wonder that he did not burst into flames himself. He was swaddled in thick robes, wrapped in blankets. His sparse hair was white; his face was hollowed by a loss of teeth, and wrinkled like cedar bark. Obviously Lord Florian was a very sick man; he was also the source of the magic.

Emerald detected healing spells as a sickly-sweet odor.

They were all much the same—air and water, a little fire, and much love to nullify the opposing death element—but this mixture represented a very unbalanced octogram, and she always found it unsettling.

Wart was bowing and introducing himself. He did not name his companions.

The Sheriff turned his face from the fire to peer at him with dull, rheumy eyes. "So the King sends children now?" He spoke in a hoarse, painful whisper, barely audible over the logs' crackling.

Wart, who was already turning pink from the heat, turned even pinker. "I repeat: I am a Blade in the Royal Guard, and on His Majesty's business as a commissioner of the Court of Conjury. Here is my warrant."

Florian waved the scroll away with a frail, age-spotted hand. Once he must have been a towering and imposing man, probably a very handsome one, for the bones of his face were craggy. Now he was a ruin, a heap in a chair.

"I care not for your fancy seals and parchment," he whispered. "What does the King want of me now? I have kept his peace here these thirteen years, gathered his taxes, hanged men who took his deer. Must he harass me now, in my last days?"

Badger and Emerald had gone to stand beside the windows, but even there the heat was stifling. To see the Sheriff's face, poor Wart must stay close. He shifted uneasily from foot to foot.

"My lord, the Warden of the King's Forests visited here nine or ten days ago."

"Digby. Known him for years. Comes around every year or two and makes a thorough nuisance of himself. He was underfoot during the rebellion, too. Don't recall he ever did any good then either. He stayed two days and left by the Buran road. Get to the point." Florian's memory was in better shape than the rest of him.

"Day before yesterday he was murdered."

Pause. The old man stared hard at Wart. "So?" he croaked.

"We have reason to believe that his death was connected with his visit here, specifically with the so-called Fellowship of Wisdom. "Wart's face was streaming sweat.

"Why? Why do you think that, boy, eh?"

"I am not at liberty to reveal that information, my lord. Lord Digby visited Smealey Hole, or Hall, while he was here?"

"Yes."

"And who went with him?"

"Rhys, one of my foresters. Sent him to make sure Digby didn't get lost or cause trouble." His voice sounded as if it were bubbling through gruel. Why didn't he cough and clear it?

Emerald wished she could warn Wart about the healing magic. If it came from the sorcerers of Smealey Hole, then Lord Florian was probably in their power, just as her father had been bespelled in his final illness by the enchanters of Gentleholme.

"And what happened?" Wart persisted.

"He talked with the Prior and came back here." *Bubble.*

"That's all? Do you know what they discussed?"

"No. And I don't care."

"I want to speak with this Rhys Forester."

"Well you can't." *Bubble.* "He went off somewhere—" *gurgle* "—couple' a' days ago. Want him myself. Can't find him. Run off after some—" *glug, glug* "—girl, most like. Have him whipped when he shows up." *Gurgle.*

Emerald watched Wart's eyes light up.

"So two men went to the Hole. One has been murdered and the other has disappeared. Is Rhys in the habit of disappearing for days at a time?"

For a long moment the dying Sheriff just sat and made his horrible bubbling noises. Finally he said, "No."

"Has he parents or friends who might know—"

"Pestilence, boy, you're talking rubbish! Young mud-head! Just like Digby. He came back here frothing about raiding the Hole and arresting the brethren, lock, stock, and barrel!" Anger seemed to give Florian strength to ignore his drowning lungs. "Wanted me to call up my Yeomanry and send them in! Had to tell him that Smealey Hole wasn't in the forest, so he'd no authority over it. No one's lodged any complaints of black magic, so can't invoke the Suppression of Magic Act either. There's laws in Chivial, I tell you! And they don't allow arbitrary house...searches—" He crumpled into a long paroxysm of painful coughing and spitting. Eventually he gasped, "Stupid idiot!"

Emerald stole a look at Badger, beside her, but Badger was an earth person. "Inscrutable" didn't begin to describe Badger. Wart was beaming, because Snake's guess had been proved right. Digby *had* discovered something suspicious at the Hole. Perhaps he had just asked to buy black magic and the sorcerers had sold him something. Whether that something worked or not would not matter; purveying anything purported to be black magic was a crime. Emerald kept frowning warnings, still wanting to tell him about the healing spell on the Sheriff.

Then Wart showed that he had thought of it for himself. "Tell me about this Fellowship, my lord. You say it isn't known for black magic. Does it do good works, then, like healing?"

"No," Florian mumbled. "Mind their own business, don't poach the King's beasts, pay their taxes and their bills. I got no cause to bother them." He still might have cause to protect them.

"I thank you for your time, my lord," Wart said with a bow. "If I wish to go and speak with the Prior, who will provide me with a horse and a guide?"

Florian stared at the fire for a while as if he had not heard, but at last he whispered. "See Mervyn."

The visitors left him as they had found him, huddled in his chair, slowly dying in front of the fire.

9

Stalwart Sends a Message

WART halted at the bottom of the stairs, and for a moment just stood there, staring across the dining hall as if wondering where the stench of boiled cabbage came from. Maids were laying out wooden platters and mugs, but no one paid heed to the strangers. Emerald could tell he was excited; he was taut as a lute string.

"I have everything Snake needs for a raid on the Hole," he said. "Digby wanted to do it, so he must have found something seriously wrong. The forester witness has disappeared. Lord Florian is incompetent and perhaps in the traitors' power. That's enough evidence."

Badger groaned. "You only have Florian's word for it that Digby wanted to stage a raid, and you admit that he's too sick to be trusted. He may be hallucinating. Anyway, Digby had the brains of a pony; he probably wanted to play Old Blade all by himself. You have absolutely no reason to believe that Forester Rhys has been murdered."

Wart pouted. Emerald tried not to grin. This was a classic case of an air person wanting to fly and an earth person holding him down. Yet Badger's death dominant still troubled her. Death people were dangerous to both others and themselves. She could imagine him as a great rock that might stand a whole lifetime, poised but unmoving, or might come crashing down at any minute to destroy everything it encountered.

He was certainly persistent. "If Digby really did find evidence of treason or black magic at the Hole and the Sheriff blocked him, then why didn't he rush home posthaste? Or write to Snake?"

"Maybe he did," Emerald said. "Write to Snake, I mean. If you wanted to do that now, Wart, how would you send the letter?"

Wart's scowl turned to a wicked leer of triumph. "I'd give it to someone here in the castle—the castellan or that bottler man or the steward. And he'd probably hand it to the marshal, who'd pass it on to the sergeant-at-arms or the stable manager...and eventually a boy on a horse would carry it down to the ferry at Buran. There he'd give it to the boatman, or perhaps take it across to Prail. It would go to the Royal Mail office in Lomouth, so it could travel on the mail coach or by special courier.... That's if it ever left Waterby Castle! Or the courier died on the road, maybe. *Digby's letter never arrived!*"

"And Digby?" she asked. "He wouldn't think of that, but he would want to hurry home and deliver a report in person as well. But he daren't neglect his duties, in case the King took offense at his meddling. On the other hand, he wouldn't dally to socialize. So he'd make a very quick trip, but not posthaste. And that's exactly what he did."

Now it was Badger who was frowning, but he did not dispute her logic. "So what do you do now, *Leader*? Write to Snake?"

"That doesn't work!" Wart said, grinning dangerously. "There are traitors right here in Waterby Castle. I send you, Brother Badger."

Even an earth person could show astonishment sometimes. "Me? Grand Master will lay duck eggs!"

"Leave Grand Master to me. Go to Grandon, Candidate Badger, and find Snake, wherever he is. Failing him, report to Durendal—if a sheriff's incompetent, that's the Lord

Chancellor's business, isn't it? And take care! You may need your Ironhall skills on the road. That sword will get you the best mounts in the—"

Badger's always squarish face seemed to develop more stubborn planes and angles. "No. It won't work, Sir Wart. I'll never make it. The law says any man wearing a cat's-eye sword must be able to show a scar over his heart. You've got that fancy commission with the King's seal, but I don't. I'm not wearing Guard livery. I'm not attending a ward. Why not go yourself?"

Emerald knew that that would never do. Wart wanted to snoop around Smealey Hole and get into trouble: fight monsters, kill traitors, be a hero again. He reached in his jerkin and brought out his precious star. "Then take this. That's enough authority to get you into the King's bedroom if you want."

Badger stared at the glittering bauble with wide eyes. He took it as if it were a dangerous scorpion. "These jewels are worth a fortune, Wart! How do you know I won't just steal it?"

"Don't be ridiculous." Wart strode off across the hall with fast strides, making the others run to catch him. "Let's go find this Mervyn the Sheriff mentioned. Hope you don't mind a few more days in those same clothes, because I'm going to sneak you out of here. We'll say we're all heading over to the Hole; when I give you the signal, you turn around and tear down the Buran road before anyone can move to stop you!"

Badger caught Emerald's eye and now the two earth people were in complete agreement: Wart was flying.

10

Mervyn

EMERALD knew that Wart could be almost as devious as his hero, Snake. It was no coincidence that the name he had given his sword, *Sleight*, was similar to Snake's *Stealth*. She just hoped that he had some hidden purpose in giving Badger the star, because the more she saw of the man the less she was inclined to trust him.

After several inquiries, Wart was directed to an obscure corner of the bailey, to a tiny shed sporting a dozen or more sets of weathered antlers. Emerald and Badger peeked over his shoulders as he peered in the doorway. The gloomy inside was packed to the ceiling with bows, rods, spears, arrows, nets, mounted heads, horse tack, horns, stuffed birds, sample branches of a dozen different trees, a boar's skull with tusks attached, stuffed birds, and mysterious sacks. Three white-muzzled dogs sprawled asleep underfoot, and the cubicle reeked of animal. In the center of this midden stood a small, bent, white-haired man wearing the green garments of a forester. He had the customary horn hung on his belt, too. What he could actually be doing in there was a mystery, because there was barely room for him to stand, let alone move anything.

"I was told to speak with someone called Mervyn."

The ancient blinked at him. "Eh?"

Wart raised his voice. "The sheriff told me to see someone called Mervyn."

"Ah, he ain't the man he was 'fore his wife died." The forester shook his head sadly.

"Who isn't?"

"Ah, who is?"

"Are you he?"

"Who? What? Speak up, boy, you sound like a wood dove."

The back of Wart's neck was turning pink as he decided that the Sheriff had palmed him off on a doddering antique. He shouted, "Where can I get horses to go to Smealey Hall?"

"Horses live in stables, boy."

"And who'll give them to me?"

"No one. You buy your own horses."

"Do you know a forester named Rhys?"

"That's a cheeky question, boy. Very cheeky. You think I'm so old you can come 'round here making fun of an old man who's been at his trade these three score years and more, almost four score?"

Emerald was having trouble suppressing a snigger.

"I'm not making fun of you!" Wart howled. "Do you know where Rhys is?"

"Didn't sell it! He was proud of it, you hear?"

"Proud of what?"

"Speak up, boy. Stop mumbling."

"Tell him," Emerald whispered in Wart's ear, "that you think Rhys was murdered."

"Eh?" said the old man sharply. "What's that about murder?"

Deafness could only be carried so far, evidently.

"Rhys guided Lord Digby to Smealey Hall," Wart said in quieter tones, "and Lord Digby has been murdered. The King sent me to find out why, and I want to speak with Rhys."

"He's disappeared," the forester said sulkily. "But he's a good boy and it ain't right what Sheriff says about him selling the horn and going off drinking or chasing women. Wouldn't do that, Rhys wouldn't. He's a fine lad and I says so even if he is my grandson."

"I'm afraid he may have been murdered, too."

Mervyn nodded sadly. "So'm I." Suddenly he advanced on his visitors so that they backed away, into the light. He stood in the doorway and looked them over. "You're the King's men. They said the baby one was in charge. Name of Stalwart. A Blade."

Wart showed his sword. "This is Badger—this is Luke. The King sent us, Forester. If your grandson's been hurt, we'll see that the criminals hang. What were you saying about a horn?"

"He guided earl there. Lordship gave him a horn. It's seemly for lords to reward good service, isn't it? Fine bull horn with gold 'round the top, tooled leather strap. Blows a lovely call, it do. Rhys got lungs! Could hear the boy all the way to Kirkwain on that horn. He wouldn't sell it for all the gold in Chivial."

Wart glanced up at the sun, which was dipping behind the castle wall. "I'm sure he wouldn't. How far is it to Smealey Hole?"

"'Bout a league."

"North?"

"An' a bit west."

"You know if there's more than one way in?"

"And why wouldn't I know?" the old man said indignantly, drawing himself up as straight as he could. "Me being bred and buttered in Brakwood, lived here more'n four score years? You want to go and root out those sorcerers, boy?"

"I'd like to go and take a look at the place."

"Why didn't you say so sooner?" From somewhere the old man produced a green cap with a pheasant feather in it. He stuck this on his head and set off across the bailey, head down, at a lightning-fast shuffle. The dogs snored on unheeding.

After a day and a half in the saddle, the last thing Emerald wanted to see again was the backs of a horse's ears. The second last thing was Wart blundering into trouble because she wasn't there to warn him. If she complained, he would just leave her behind, so horse's ears it would have to be. She was going to remain Master Luke for a while yet.

At the stables old Mervyn shot off orders like an archer firing arrows. "Patches for him, Snowbird for Sir Stalwart. You've not been skimping on his oats, have you? And Daydream for this one. Fine gentle ride she has. I'll try Daisy, see what you've done to her." The hands jumped to obey.

In the confusion of choosing saddles and watching the fresh horses being readied, Emerald managed to sidle close to Wart at a moment when Badger was out of earshot. "You are a flaming air-head! Why did you give him that star? If he's a traitor, you'll never see it again. It's worth a fortune!"

"It's not worth as much as my life," he said glumly. "Or the King's. Do you think I'd ever let Badger have it if I didn't trust him?"

"You mean you *do* trust him?"

"Y...es," Wart said warily. "I think Grand Master's gotten to him. He wouldn't be the first Prime who got driven up a tree by that nump. But I've known Badger for years, Em. If he says he'll do something, he'll do it. He's solid as a rock."

"Perceptive of you to see that. Your brooch is worth a fortune. He'll be set for life."

"He'll be hanged for larceny, you mean." Wart was watching the horses, avoiding her eye. "I'm giving him a chance to show his stuff. If he staggers into the palace, dead on his feet and shouting treason and foul play, he's going to come to Snake's attention, and Leader's. Durendal's, perhaps. Even the King's. It's a *big* chance for him!"

"Do you trust him or don't you?"

Wart shrugged. "Well, yes! Of course. Sort of. Here comes your horse, Luke."

11

The House of Smealey

OLD Mervyn set a cracking pace; the horses thundered through the barbican, over the draw-bridge, and up into the town. Dogs, pigs, and chickens fled in noisy alarm; pedestrians leaped to safety. In moments the riders had left the houses and were out in open country, lit by a low sun ahead. Wart gave Badger a sign; Badger nodded without a smile, and turned his mount away to head back to Buran and the ferry. The old man did not seem to notice that one of his charges had departed; he rode as he walked, with his head well down. It was almost in the horse's mane.

Although the plain was wide and fertile, the river forced the trail steadily northward, toward wooded bluffs on their right. The old man cut the pace before he winded the horses, and then Wart was able to pull Snowbird alongside and shout a conversation.

"Tell me about this Fellowship of Wisdom, grandfather."

"Don't know nothing 'bout them, lad. Standoffish lot. Teachers, so they say."

"Do they sell conjurations—good-luck charms, healing?"

"Not so's I've heard."

Was he telling the truth or defending a bespelled Sheriff?

"You don't go there much?"

"Nobody does, lad. Haven't been there in ten years. Foresters don't go, even. It's near the forest, not in it." After a brief pause, Mervyn added, "Saw lot of swordsmen around, Rhys said. Sheriff keeps the King's peace! Why'd a gabble of enchanters need swordsmen around?"

As if he timed the interruption for maximum annoyance, he then turned Daisy off the main trail onto a rough path that disappeared into the steep bluffs on the right. Daisy was a very fat mare, almost as old as he was from the look of her, and she made little speed on the slope. Only when the track emerged in open parkland up on the bench, could Stalwart urge Snowbird alongside again.

"How many swordsmen?"

"A score or more, he said."

Bad odds. "What else did Rhys tell you? This was when he went there with Lord Digby?"

"Aye. Nothing much, lad. He was left outside while his haughtiness went in to talk with them. Boy said the swordsmen stood guard on him as if they didn't want him snooping. Not that he would have, of course. Honest lad—"

"Did Digby say anything when he came out? Did he seem angry, or frightened...?"

"Boy said he was white, like he'd had a real shock. He wasn't talking, though. Didn't say hardly a word all the way back to Waterby; lad couldn't tell if he was mad or scared, his wife says."

"Rhys is married?" Stalwart had thought they were discussing someone of his own age.

"Got three sprats," the forester said proudly. "Eight great-grandchildren I got now. His three, and—"

"But as far as you know, the brothers are good and loyal subjects of the King?"

Mervyn rode in silence until Stalwart repeated the question. His deafness seemed to come and go according to his mood. He shot Stalwart a scornful look.

"How can they be, living in that house?"

The house was more important than its inhabitants now.

Stalwart must become familiar with the surroundings so he could lead the Old Blades in.

"Tell me about the house."

"Ah!" the old man said, launching his tale with every sign of intending to enjoy the telling of it. "There's a curse on it, there is! Bad place. Been lots of families own it, but never for long. Baron Modred, now...well he got it from his father, Gwyn. Gwyn came from out west aways, somewhere around Ghyll. Rough type—said to have been a highwayman or worse. There's tales 'bout him...." He told some. Obviously Gwyn of Ghyll had been born with poison fangs and gone to the bad thereafter. "There was a real Earl of Smealey back then. I wooed one of his serving maids for a while. Married a soldier, she did, and much good—"

"The Earl of Smealey?" Stalwart prompted when he could get a word in.

"No saying what happened to him, exactly. River runs right under the windows, see? Smealey River. It runs down the Hole and never comes up. Water probably joins the Brakwater underground—least, that's what Sheriff thinks—but *things* don't even come back up. Like bodies. No saying how many bodies gone down there in the last few hun'red year."

"The Earl's was one of them?"

"Who can say, see? Gwyn claimed he won the house at dice. Leastways he moved in and nobody felt like moving him out. Started callin' himself the earl. Nobody else did, 'cept to his face. Then came the uprising of 308. First time I handled a sword, that was." Mervyn sighed nostalgically, without saying which side he had fought for. "Gwyn pretended to join and then sold it out. Or else he saw which way the tide ran. An'ways, he betrayed the leaders. The old king created him Baron Smealey for that."

"He sounds utterly charming," Emerald remarked on his other side.

"Aye, that he was, lass," Mervyn agreed, and carried on without showing any awareness that he had supposedly been addressing a boy named Luke. "He had two sons and a bushel of daughters. Eldest was another Gwyn. He and his father died in…around 320, must of been. In same night, so they say."

"Did they also die of too much proximity to the river?" Stalwart asked.

"Who knows, when there were no bodies to examine? The second son was Modred, who became the second baron. Had several wives."

"One at a time?"

"Mostly. River's good for divorce, too. Bred seven sons. Ceri was eldest."

Stalwart knew he ought to recognize that name, but he was distracted by the landscape, realizing that it was a very good site for an ambush. The valley had become a canyon—enclosed by rocky walls and shadowed now, as the sun set. The floor was tufted with scattered trees and enough scrub to hide several dozen swordsmen. Was the old man leading him into a trap? He considered the timing, and decided it would have been impossible for Lord Florian to order any such betrayal at such short notice. If there was going to be treachery, it would happen when he went back to Waterby. He would have to sleep with his eyes open. He hoped Badger had made a safe getaway.

"Is this the main road into Smealey Hole?"

Mervyn pouted at having his reminiscences interrupted. "No. This is back door I'm showing you. Not many know of it. Main road comes in from the east, fords the Smealey. Mustn't do that too near the Hole, see?"

"Of course not. Tell me about Ceri."

"Was ringleader in uprising of 354. Folks hereabout figured they worked it out between them—the boy would raise rebellion while his father crawled around King Ambrose, kissing his horseshoes. That way, whichever way things went, one of them would come out on top and rescue the other."

This tied in with Badger's story. "Then it was Ceri and one of his brothers that Durendal slaughtered when they tried to kill Ambrose outside Waterby?"

"Naw, that was Kendrick and Lloyd, other brothers. Another of the seven, Edryd, died in the siege of Kirkwain."

"Then what did happen to Ceri?"

"Well, after the rebels lost, he was an outlaw for a while, roaming the hills. Till he made the mistake of dropping home for a bite of food and a chat, that is."

"He went down the Hole, too?"

"He'd have been better off," Mervyn said sourly. "His father sold him to King Ambrose. They say the price he got was his own head left on his shoulders. That an' his lands."

"So Ceri was executed?"

"Beheaded in the Bastion, side by side with Aneirin."

"Another brother?" Badger had mentioned only one brother dying in the Bastion.

Mervyn nodded with the satisfaction of a storyteller whose tale has reached a fitting conclusion. "Aneirin was second son. He murdered Modred for betraying Ceri, you see. Strangled his own father with his bare hands! That pretty much finished the line of Gwyn."

Stalwart counted on his fingers. "Two Gwyns, one Modred, then Ceri, Aneirin, Edryd, Kendrick, and Lloyd." That put the score at: Curse eight, Smealeys two. "You left two unaccounted for."

The old man shrugged. "There were a couple'a kids left over. Don't know what happened to them. The Crown seized the lands. They say King thought of using the house as a hunting lodge, decided was too risky—the curse'd get him. Eventually he put it up for sale and yon bunch of sorcerers bought it."

It was as gruesome a tale as Stalwart had ever heard. "How well do you know the grounds right close to the house?"

The old man nailed him with his usual shrewd stare. "Told you I hadn' been here for ten years or more. As a kid I hung around some, courting that girl I told you about." He shrugged.

Wart laughed. "And a bit of poaching."

"Maybe."

"I won't tell the Sheriff. How much do you know about the secret passage?"

"What secret passage?"

"I was told that it was common knowledge that a secret passage—" That did not make much sense. "There's a back door from Smealey Hole into a cave."

"First I heard of it. Doesn't mean there isn't one, though. Whoa, boy! Here's the Hole."

12

The Hole

STALWART realized that he had been shouting louder than ever, because a dull roaring had added itself to the problem of Mervyn's deafness. Mist laid a chill dampness on his face. The sides of the valley had been rising steadily, and now the ground fell away precipitously right in front of him. The deeper canyon continued on, curving so that its extent could not be seen; it was no wider but it held a river. Coming into sight around the bend, the stream was darkly smooth; soon it frothed over white rapids, vanished in a clear fall into the great pit almost directly under his toes. No wonder nothing ever reappeared! Anything that went down there would be smashed to fragments in the cavern below.

"Not far to the house," Mervyn bellowed. "You can take a look without being seen. Come on, I'll show you."

Without waiting for an answer, he urged old Daisy down the slope and disappeared. Stalwart's mount declined to commit suicide, balking, tossing its head, backing away. To his intense fury, Emerald easily persuaded her horse to follow the old forester, so she disappeared also.

"You," Stalwart said through clenched teeth, "are going to go down there if I have to carry you! In pieces!" He drew

Sleight. A rapier made a very good riding crop, because it was flexible and had no cutting edge. In this case he did not even need to use it; he demonstrated the swishing noise it could make, and Snowbird whinnied surrender and agreed to proceed.

There was a path of sorts, but slippery with moss and tangled with ferns. It angled northward at first, down the steep slope to the canyon wall, and then became even steeper, a ledge with a sheer face above and the ghastly maw of the Hole below. The worst part came after that, when it reached water level and the rapids. Cold spray blew in his eyes and the horse's, while a terrible roar echoed back and forth until he thought the noise would burst his skull. At that point there was little pretense of a road, just rocks scoured clean and smooth by the river, part of its bed when it was in spate. The passage was obstructed by tangles of driftwood. On his left rose a carved and polished wall of stone, sculpted into fantastic niches and pillars; on the other side white water fell away into nothing.

Why had he ever gone to Ironhall? Why hadn't he stayed a minstrel?

Worse, Emerald had stopped, blocking the way. Old Mervyn was past the horrors and waiting for them up ahead, perceptibly higher than they were. From him the river fell, swirling and leaping, raising white cockscombs against the rocks, spinning in dark whirlpools. Just behind Stalwart, it disappeared altogether.... His horse was trembling even harder than he was.

It was not a good place for a chat.

Emerald looked around, her eyes wide. She shouted something. He saw her mouth move, but could hear nothing. He yelled back to demonstrate. She understood, and pulled her right foot out of her stirrup as if she was going to dismount.

"Don't!" Stalwart screamed. "You're crazy!"

There was no room for such nonsense. The horses were growing more terrified by the second. If one hoof slipped on the slick-wet rocks, the Hole was going to have two more victims, or even four. Fortunately Emerald worked that out and let her horse proceed up the slope, out of that madness.

The path continued upriver, still too narrow for two horses abreast, while the noise gradually dwindled behind them. The trail rose higher above the water as it rounded the bend of the canyon and entered a wide valley, bereft of real trees but shaggy with brush and saplings. Mervyn reined in and pointed a bony hand at a knoll some distance ahead. Its river side was a cliff, but the rest of its slopes seemed gentle enough. It bore buildings on its crest.

"Smealey Hole," he explained needlessly, then scowled at Emerald. "What was wrong with you, lass, back there? All that tomfoolery?"

"There's something down there," she said, speaking to Stalwart. "I can't see what it is, but I know there's something. I'm going back to see."

Whereupon, she slid down from the saddle, knotted her reins around a sapling, and ran back the way she had come. The old man just sat his horse, looking puzzled, but Stalwart was right on her heels.

"What sort of something?"

"Magic, of course. I don't know what. Not a sort I've ever met before."

Night was falling. Seen from this side, the path they had followed down the great step was barely visible in the shrubbery. It showed as a narrow ledge around the side of the Hole, and then disappeared into that jumble of rocks between the base of the cliff and the plunging rapids. It was hard to know exactly where Emerald had stopped. But there *was* something there, pinned under a shadowed overhang, half in and half out of the torrent.

Hoping for a better view, Stalwart stepped onto a flattish boulder in the stream. He jumped to another beyond it... and another...then a larger one, a tiny island in midstream with water rushing by on both sides. Emerald followed him, tried to join him, and missed her footing. He grabbed; she grabbed. They teetered in mortal peril for a long and horrible moment before regaining their balance. He swallowed his heart back down where it belonged.

She put her mouth to his ear and yelled, "Thanks!"

He wanted to make a joking response and couldn't think of one, so he pointed instead. Now they had a clear view, except that spray kept blowing in their eyes.

"It's a body!" she shouted.

He nodded. It might well be a body. If it was a body, he was most utterly, completely, positively sure that it was a *dead* body. He was going to be very surprised if it was not the missing Rhys. To let the old man see his grandson in that position would be horribly unkind. Common sense said to say nothing more, go back to Waterby, and return with a team in the morning. On the other hand, if the water rose in the night, the river would take that corpse away, never to be seen again. Had Emerald not sensed the magic, they would have missed it altogether. Why should there be magic associated with a corpse?

He recalled that Mervyn had a coil of rope hung on his saddle.

On horseback, the old forester had seemed younger than his years. Back on ground level, he was again tiny, frail, and stooped. There was not a thing wrong with his wits, though. His bleak expression showed that he had guessed what they had seen.

"I think it may be a body, grandfather," Stalwart said. "We can't get it out, but if we had some rope we could tether it so it won't wash away."

The old man turned to his horse. "No forester ever goes anywhere without a bit o' rope, lad."

That was a pity. Someone was going to have to do some death-defying acrobatics, and Stalwart knew who that someone was. He was a skilled juggler and tumbler, but he had never performed on the lip of a giant sewer before.

He told Emerald, "It'll be dark by the time I'm finished. So you may as well go back up that cliff before the light goes. I don't intend to disappear into that pit, but if I do, one of us must get back to report. And I'll be beyond help. So no dramatic rescues! You go back to Waterby and wait for Snake. Understood?"

She gave him a hard stare. "Yes, Sir Stalwart."

He distrusted her when she called him that. "Promise?"

"Didn't you just give me an order, *sir*?"

"Yes."

"Then why do you need to ask me for a promise?"

He was never going to understand girls.

He gave her his sword and commission for safekeeping. He stowed his cloak, hat, and jerkin on Snowbird and handed the reins to Mervyn. When the horses set off back down the trail, he followed on foot with the rope slung over his shoulder. He watched them pass safely around the edge of the Hole and start the climb up the big step. As he drew close to the falls, the roar of the waters grew ever more menacing. He was aware of being frightened, and that made him angry. To delay would be cowardice. *Get on with it*!

He clambered along the water-slick rocks to what he thought must be about the right place. Back in his soprano year in Ironhall, he had learned some good knots from Sailor, who had been Prime then—a lesson in knots in exchange for a lesson in juggling. Sailor had died on the Night of Dogs, last Firstmoon, battling monsters in the King's bedchamber.

For this job, Stalwart needed nothing fancy. A clove hitch was enough to fasten one end around a well-wedged tree trunk. He used a simple bowline to fashion a noose and fitted it loosely around himself under his arms. That might stop him being swept over the falls if he slipped. A running bowline would pull tight and hold more firmly, but might also cut him in half if he was trapped in the full force of the torrent. More likely the river would smash him to a jelly first. Already spray had soaked through his hose and doublet and his hands were aching with the cold; there was so much noise he couldn't hear his teeth chattering.

He started down the rock pile. It was not a long climb, no more than the height of a cottage, and the river offered him a convenient ladder—a tree lodged almost vertically inside a smooth circular chimney that the falls had carved out of bedrock. It had not been in the river long enough to lose all its branches, and the stubs stuck out like rungs. All in all, it seemed so handy that he wondered if it could be some fiendish trap. It worked, though. He made his way almost to water level without trouble, but there his view was blocked by the sides of the chimney.

With silent thanks to the memory of Sailor and that knot lesson, he bent the line around the tree and secured it. Then he let the noose take his weight while he braced his feet against the trunk and leaned outward. He ended almost horizontal, with his head practically at water level. Downstream there was nothing except a ghastly, shiny-smooth black slide down...down...down....

Shuddering, he turned to look upstream. There was the body, just out of reach, and higher than he was. It had been swept in under the overhang and run aground on a sloping rock, but most of it was still underwater. It looked very precarious, ready to cast off at any minute. Its feet were toward him, and the legs were moving in the current, as if Rhys were marching, marching, marching to the country of the dead. That it was Rhys there could be no doubt. What was left of the clothing was visibly a forester's green, even in that gloom.

Meanwhile, Stalwart was soaked and exhausted and a long way from home. Also a long way from that corpse he had come to save. He hauled himself upright with rapidly numbing hands. He untied the rope from the tree and started climbing. The rope kept snagging, of course, and delaying him.

He really ought to leave Rhys where he was. The man's spirit had already returned to the elements, and the underground river might dispose of his corpse even faster than a proper funeral pyre would. It was wrong to risk a live man for a dead one. But the body was important evidence against the Fellowship of traitors. Also there was old Mervyn, who had been helpful. There were Rhys's wife and three children...

Reaching the top of his rope, Stalwart crouched for a moment on his hands and knees, catching his breath. Then he secured the rope to a boulder, a few steps farther upstream. He paused to plan what he would do. Even if he could get close to the body—and he had no great confidence that he could—he was certainly not going to crawl in under the overhang. It was lying with its head upstream.... He would have to try to lasso it with a hangman's noose. A gruesome way to treat a corpse, yes, but he had no other means to secure it by himself in near darkness. He tied a slip knot, put the loop around his upper arm so he would not lose it, and started down the cliff again, this time working his way spiderlike, with his face to the rocks.

A savage tug at his right boot warned him that he had put it in the river. He returned that foot to its previous position and then clung there, sprawled on a rock face, not quite vertical and very insecurely attached. An adjacent boulder was flattish and stuck out over the water—he was almost certain that it was the one pinning poor Rhys. Of the body itself, however, there was no sign.

Inch by inch, Stalwart transferred himself to the ledge, which was just barely wide enough for him to stand on. Once he was on it, he then had to lie down. Having achieved that, gripping tight to the rope with one hand and the rock with the other, he wriggled forward and hung over the edge to peer in under the overhang. He found himself staring into two lifeless eyes just above water level.

It wasn't Rhys after all. It was Lord Digby. Stalwart was so startled that he almost let go of the cliff.

13

Homecoming

THE horse they had given Badger was a mean, ugly piebald whose high, hard trot made him ride like a sack of rocks. Badger barely noticed. His mind was roiled by the staggering realization that *now he did not have to die!* Eventually, yes. Of course. Everyone must die, but for most people it was a distant prospect, something that need not happen for fifty years. Facing certain death in a month or two changed life considerably.

Beset by his thoughts, he reached the ford over the Swallowbeck long before he expected it. He reined in Sack-of-rocks and sat for a moment, debating. Fortunately the Buran road here was a mere track through trees and presently deserted, so no one observed the young traveler's strange indecision. This was his moment of choice, the turning point of his life. Why had that young pest given him the jeweled star? The decision would have been easy without Wart's unwelcome display of trust.

If Badger carried on to Buran he would catch the evening ferry, then do as the uppity kid had ordered—ride to Grandon and the court, tell Snake what had happened. And the next time Ambrose came to Ironhall, Badger would die.

The alternative was to head up the Swallowbeck, the road

to Smealey Hole. Then he would not have to die, because
there, too, he would deliver news: news that the Fellowship
was suspected of murdering Lord Digby and conspiring to
assassinate the King; news that there was a White Sister
in the area, sniffing out magic, and also a swordsman of
the Royal Guard—even if he did stand shoulder high and
still had his milk teeth. *Not fair!* whispered his conscience.
*Stalwart is not as young as that. In a fair fight, rapier against
saber, he would beat you every time.*

If he went home to Smealey, Badger might not die.

Home?

Yes, home. To see his home again, even if it must be for
the last time...With a groan, Badger turned his horse's head
to the north and set off up the Swallowbeck.

Few people would have noticed that road. The streambed
itself was the path, a winding course of shingle holding a
few small ponds. In the spring the stream was more evident,
but rarely fierce enough to bother a horse. Pebbles crunched
under his mount's hooves.

The cards were dealt, the decision made. He was *not*
going to die in the Forge at Ironhall! As wild relief surged
through him, he rose in his stirrups, waved his hat in the air,
and let out a long howl of triumph. *He would live!* Sack-of-
rocks whinnied in terror at this madness and broke into a
gallop. Badger gave him his head and went racing along the
Swallowbeck, screaming with joy.

All too soon he had to regain control and soothe the stupid
animal, for he came to the second turning. The Smealey
road branched off, becoming an obvious man-made track
through the trees. It seemed smaller and meaner than he
remembered, though, more overgrown. It climbed steeply
to cross Chestnut Ridge, then plunged down into the valley
of the Smealey.

Only now did he consider the possibility that Owen might
not be there. Owen might very well be somewhere in or near
Grandon, preparing to strike down King Ambrose as he had
struck down Lord Digby. Never for a moment since Wart

had told him of the murder and the connection to Smealey Hall had Badger doubted that the Fellowship was guilty, or that Ambrose was its true quarry. Digby, he assumed, had seen or heard something that had tipped the Fellowship's hand. They had perhaps been forced to strike before they were completely ready. The Blades kept nattering about the Monster War, but the Monster War was less than a year old. Owen's campaign went back a lot further than that. Owen's implacable purpose had always been to kill the Chivian tyrant.

But if Owen wasn't *here*, right *now*, then things might become complicated.

No matter, he had made his decision....

Halfway down the slope, the trail went by the ruins of a massive beech tree, perhaps a hundred years dead. Long ago it had rotted, or been struck by a lightning bolt and burned. All that was left was a huge columnar stump about three man-heights high. It was also hollow, although the opening was not visible from the trail.

Badger reined in with his sight blurred by tears and a lump in his throat big enough to choke him. He remembered the day Lloyd and Kendrick had decided to turn the hollow tree into a castle and had lit a fire in it to clean out the ants and make it bigger. They had come so close to setting the whole forest ablaze that the Baron had whipped them till they howled, sending little Bevan into a fit of screaming terror. Then there was the day little Bevan, grown old enough to apply the family talent for devilry, had hidden in that tree until the entire population of Smealey had been turned out to beat the woods in search of him. Memories— much later memories—of leaving food there to feed an outlaw Ceri...

He dismounted and led Sack-of-rocks over to the verge. The hollow tree would still be an excellent hiding place. Its wormy, dirty interior looked as if no one had been there since the last time he had peered in and found a pathetic cache of Ceri's personal treasures: his pouch, his sword, his hunting horn, his dagger. Ceri had left them there on the day he rode off to Waterby to die, knowing that Bevan would find them. Ceri, twelve years dead. *Vengeance is coming soon now, Ceri. One way or the other, you will be avenged. You and the others...*

To ride into Smealey Hole today wearing a cat's-eye sword might be fast suicide. Badger laid *Durance* in the tree; it could endure there until he returned for it. If Owen sent him back, he would retrieve it on the way out. If not—if he was to live—then an Ironhall sword was worth a fortune anywhere outside the country; only in Chivial were cat's-eyes reserved to the King's Blades.

He swung himself up into the saddle and urged Sack-of-rocks into a canter. The sun was very close to setting as he forded the river. Memories came thick as midges at twilight now...the meadow where Kendrick taught him to ride, where Aneirin taught him to shoot a longbow...the hayloft where young Bevan hid to watch Lloyd kissing the plowman's daughter...the still pools of the Smealey, where the Baron went fishing.

The valley was a bowl enclosed by a rampart of rock, lowest on the west. Its bottomland had long since been stripped of trees, but it had never been fertile enough to farm. The Smealeys had grazed cattle there. Evidently the Fellowship of Wisdom did not, probably because herds needed herders, who would be unnecessary witnesses to things better left unseen. Bracken, saplings, and man-high thistles had taken over the pasture. The river snaked across the plain in a steep-sided channel, plunged along a canyon cutting through that low western side, then vanished into a bottomless pit.

Smealey Hall stood on a flat-topped knoll. On two sides the ground dropped almost sheer to the treacherous river; to north and east it sloped gently. Some of the mismatched cluster of buildings had been built by Baron Modred or his father, others were centuries old. It was not a castle, because fortification required royal permission to crenulate and King Ambrose would not grant that to Smealey Hole in the next ten thousand years. A site so defensible must have been a fortress many times in the past, though. Traces of ancient walls could still be found in the turf.

No dogs barked as the stranger rode up the trail, which was another change from the old days. No guards challenged, but Badger was certain his arrival would have been noted. Thoughts of archers waiting with strung bows made the back of his neck prickle as he rode across the flat summit to the residence door. He could hear chanting coming from somewhere, voices taking turns at evoking spirits, in the way of conjuration everywhere.

There was not as much as a cat in sight when he halted Sack-of-rocks beside the steps. He swung his leg over the saddle, dropped down, turned, and found himself facing three grim swordsmen. He could almost believe they had used magic to make that dramatic arrival, except that magic was too valuable to waste on party tricks.

They were not wearing armor. Even this backwood scholastic retreat must receive visitors sometimes, and the Privy Council would jump cloud high if it heard rumors of a private army in Nythia. So they bore no visible steel except their swords and daggers, but their jerkins and britches were of stout leather, padded to deflect all but the heaviest or most skillful strokes. There might be metal under their floppy plumed hats. If he had kept *Durance* with him, he could have demonstrated what an Ironhall man thought of three scowling yokels. But then four more came strolling around the corner of the house to take up position in the outfield. Even an Ironhall man must shun those odds.

"Identify yourself," growled the one wearing a sergeant's red sash. He was big, powerful. His face was a hideous ruin, an untidy wad of hair and twisted leather, decorated with old scar tissue. One eye was a gaping hole and half his nose had gone. He looked as if he had been used for broadsword practice by all the Ironhall fuzzies at once.

"I am a friend of Brother Owen."

"No brother here by that name."

"Have I misjudged his title? Have you another Owen?"

"None."

Owen might be using another name or the man might be lying.

"Identify yourself," the sergeant repeated, laying a hand on his sword hilt.

Badger cursed his folly in coming unarmed. He could not hope to fight so many, but they would not bully him like this if he bore a sword. The distant chanting had ended, he noticed.

"My name is my business," he said stubbornly. "Go to Owen and describe me." He removed his hat.

He had worried that Owen might have started losing his hair now, but it was clear at once that the gamble had paid off. All three jaws dropped.

The Sergeant recovered first, a sneer pulling up his scarred lip to display wide gaps in his teeth. "If you're not who I think you are, sonny, I'll rearrange you until you look worse than I do."

"I am."

The man grunted. "Gavin, run and tell the Prior his brother's here to see him."

14

Reunion

THE youngster called Gavin ran—not into the residence, but across the yard to the elementary. The sergeant gestured for Badger to follow and then walked just behind him, within striking distance. He was being extraordinarily cautious, but that was a strong hint that Owen was in charge. Owen never left anything to chance.

The elementary was the oldest building on the site, dating from dark ages long ago. Originally it must have been a warriors' feasting hall, but Badger could recall it being used for that purpose only once. In some more recent time, an octogram had been inset in the floor to turn it into an elementary. Serious sickness or injury had been treated there by healers summoned from Waterby. Most of the time it had just stood empty, a marvelous haunt for bats, rats, and small boys.

The man who emerged just as Badger reached the steps was clad in the floor-length gown of a sorcerer, black in his case. The cord around his waist was gold, which was usually the mark of a prior. He halted and stared down at the visitor, then reached up and threw back his hood to reveal a face very similar—rugged rather than handsome, stubborn, distrustful, wearing at the moment a wry, slightly lopsided smile. His dark hair was blazoned with a silver streak.

"Owen!"

"Bevan!"

They met in a rib-cracking embrace halfway up the steps and pummeled each other in the delight of reunion. It had been four years since they'd parted at the doors of Ironhall.

They went inside with their arms around each other, babbling the nonsense that is evoked on such occasions: "By the spirits, you're not the boy I remember." "You haven't changed a bit." "It's been a lifetime!"...The joy became unbearable, Badger-Bevan's eyes flooded and his voice cracked.

Owen released him abruptly, mood changing like a whip crack. "What's wrong? *Why are you here?*" He had never approved of unmanly displays of emotion, even from a small boy. Tears had always provoked him to harsher punishment.

Badger drew one shuddering, deep breath and had himself under control again. "Sorry. My...seeing you...home..."

The elementary had been built entirely of vertical oak timbers, from an uneven stone floor to a too-high roof, whose rafters were home to bats and birds. It could never have been a comfortable place. Smoke would have filled it whenever the open hearth was lit, and the windows admitted little light, being mere slots through the massive walls. The small room at the back had perhaps been the master's sleeping quarters, but it had been a later addition, of inferior timber. The minstrel gallery along one side was probably even more recent, but it listed badly.

The Fellowship had made some effort to clean it up. The eight-pointed star of the octogram was more obvious. Walls, which had no doubt once borne displays of weapons, battle honors, and hunting trophies, were now hung with cabalistic inscriptions on long scrolls. Since a lesson had just ended, the novices in their white gowns stood clustered around adepts, hearing of their failings and successes. They all had their hoods up, so only varying heights suggested which were men and which women—black and white, like pieces in some gigantic board game.

Yes, Owen had wrought changes, but bring back a roasting ox and a hundred drunken warriors swilling mead and the elementary would again be barbarically impressive. Badger had seen it like that once, the night Ceri raised the banner of rebellion, proclaiming Nythian independence to the cheers of his patriot zealots. Ceri was twelve years dead and the child who had hidden up in that minstrel gallery that momentous night was a grown man now. Yet he felt himself quail under Owen's terrible stare, and was amazed to discover that Owen could still terrify him. Owen was quite capable of sending him back to Ironhall to die.

"I came to warn you that you're under investigation. The Privy Council is after you."

"The Council? Not just the Old Blades?"

"The Council."

The Prior's eye gleamed. "Why?"

"For the murder of Lord Dig—"

"It worked?" Owen shouted. "He did die? How? How do you know?" He grabbed his brother's shoulders as if to crush them. Four years of scholarship had not weakened the demonic grip he had earned in a lifetime of weapons training.

Badger winced and squirmed loose. "You don't know this? He dropped dead in the middle of a state reception, in full view of the entire court, practically at the King's toes."

Owen closed his eyes in ecstasy. "I did not know. We were still waiting to hear. And a court reception...We did not plan *that*! How wonderful are these tidings!"

"You did it from *here*? Across the whole width of Chivial?"

The Prior smiled like a well-fed wolf. "Oh, we have some greatly devious sorcerers in the Fellowship, believe me." Abruptly his mood changed again, and he impaled his brother with a dark and deadly stare. "But how do *you* know, mm? Ironhall hears the news and you leave your post?" They who plot treason must be ever on guard against treachery, and a naked sword would have been no greater

threat than his suspicion. "Come and let us talk, brother!"
he said softly.

"Of course, brother." *He is going to send me back*, Badger
thought, and the terror rose again like fire in his throat.

The Prior's office in the residence had once been the Baron's
office. Here, too, ancient clutter had been replaced by new.
The brothers sat on opposite sides of a table heaped high
with papers, while Badger told the story of how he came to
be there, back home at Smealey Hole. Owen did not offer
food and drink, as one should to a guest who has traveled
far. He just sat, still as a corpse, staring at his brother as if
watching the words emerge from his lips.

He will send me back! Badger had sworn an oath. He
wondered if he would hold Owen to his word, were their
positions reversed. They were very much alike, so alike that
he had always assumed they shared the same mother. He
did not know that and never could. Although the Baron had
collected several luscious beauties during his life and flaunted
each in turn as his wife, there had in fact been only one
true Baroness. Anwen had been an extraordinary woman,
tough as iron and ugly as a plowman's boot. Rumor, those
terrible stories that sprouted like weeds around the House
of Smealey, insisted that she had disposed of her rivals, one
after another, by way of the river. She had certainly reared
all of Modred's sons, but how many had been hers she
had somehow kept a secret, even from them. Perhaps none,
because none had looked in the least like her. They had all
been handsome: Ceri, Aneirin, Edryd, Kendrick, Lloyd, and
Owen. Then Bevan, nine years later. Owen and Bevan, the
last two born, the last two still living, two too much alike.

Outside the tiny window, the light was fading fast. Only
when Badger ended his story did Owen speak.

"So you have delivered your warning. What do you do
now?"

With dry mouth, Badger said, "Whatever you wish. I
can catch the morning ferry and ride to Grandon. If asked
to explain the delay, I can claim my horse went lame. But

the Old Blades will be here within two days, I promise you. Did you buy off the Sheriff of Waterby, or just frighten him away?"

Owen sneered contempt. "None of my doing. The cold shadow of death has shriveled his manhood." He clasped his thick hands, as he did when he was thinking. "Where do you stand in Ironhall?"

"I am Prime." There was the agony.

"Already?"

Four years ago he had sworn his oath. He would claim to be only fifteen, he had said. Get him enrolled, he had promised Owen, and he would work his heart out every day for the next five years. He would be one of the best. The best went into the Guard, bound by the King himself. Bevan Smealey had been no stranger to a sword, even then, although what Owen had been teaching him was Isilondian technique, quite different from Ironhall style; in some ways it had been a hindrance. But he had done well and won praise. Ironically, his success had hardly mattered. Every live body went into the Guard now, to make up the losses of the Monster War. He had been granted only four years, not five.

"Already. Leader told me they would have bound more of us last time except the Guard cannot strip Ironhall of all its seniors. They need us to coach the kids." Two months, no more, Bandit had said, and that had been two weeks ago. "But you, brother? What of *your* oath?"

Owen's eyes shone wolflike in the gloom. "Close, very close! I did what I promised, I collected the finest team of enchanters ever brought together. Digby was our final test. We have learned how to slay at a distance—any distance. If the tyrant flees to the ends of the earth, he cannot escape me!"

He is going to send me back. They had sworn to slay King Ambrose. They had shaken hands on it, that the oath would bind both until one succeeded. They had agreed that Owen would set up the school of magic he planned and Bevan would enroll in Ironhall. When King Ambrose tried to bind

Candidate Badger, Badger would kill him, but then he must die as well, cut down by the Guard. No more than six weeks left—was it so surprising that he slept poorly now?

"How soon can you do this?" He was ashamed to hear a tremor in his voice. He did not want to die.

Owen sighed. "As soon as I can find the link I need, and that is a matter of chance. As when Digby came here last week. He recognized me—not me personally, but this." The Prior's fingers touched the silver streak in his hair. "Ceri and Kendrick had it also, remember? Anwen told me once that the Baron had it in his youth, but he lost his hair early. Digby was Ambrose's Master of Horse in the Nythia campaign. The day Lloyd and Kendrick and the others ambushed the King outside Waterby, he saw the bodies after Durendal had finished with them. He probably saw Ceri the following year when they cut his head off, if not before." Owen bared his teeth. "And then he saw this badge of ours again, right here in Smealey Hole. He knew the Privy Council would not rejoice to hear that a Smealey was running a school of magic in the traitors' nest."

"He wanted the Sheriff to bring his Yeomanry against you."

Owen shrugged. "I gambled that the decrepit Florian would not heed his bluster."

"It's amazing he did not send a letter to Snake."

"He did send a letter. The boy taking it to the ferry was very happy to exchange it for a handful of gold. We used Lord Digby as a test of our new sorcery, and it worked. It worked!" He licked his lips. "Wonderful news!"

Struggling to seem calmer than he felt, Badger asked, "What is this link you need to slay Ambrose?" *And to free me from my oath.*

"A gift," his brother said. "The subject must be linked to another person by the giving or receiving of a gift. The link does not last long, as you may guess, just a few days. Like gratitude. We need the gift itself and the other person. Digby's guide here was a forester named Rhys. He gave him a gratuity, of course, as expected."

"A hunting horn. I heard of it. I don't understand how that—"

"It is just the way the sorcery works," Owen said dismissively. "It strengthens the spiritual link between them, making it so strong that when we kill one, the other dies also. We needed a few days to lure Rhys within our reach, but we got him, and the sorcery worked. I ran Rhys through with a sword myself, and you tell me that Digby fell dead in front of the King! Wonderful! But it may take a long time to locate someone linked that way to the tyrant, and then snare him while the link is still effective."

A wild surge of excitement made Badger stutter. "G-g-gift? Someone the King's given a gift to recently?"

Owen's eyes narrowed suspiciously. "A physical object, not just a title or a word of praise. And it must be freely given."

Badger chuckled. The chuckle became a snigger, then laughter. Tears came to his eyes as all his pent-up terror was released in helpless bellows of mirth.

"Stop it!" his brother roared, rising. "What's the matter with you! Pull yourself together!"

Badger pulled himself together. He gasped, choked, and then wiped his eyes. "I have exactly what you need, Prior Owen, and the man you want is undoubtedly snooping around the valley at this very moment. He was coming in by the canyon road. The King hung this on him just the night before last." He tossed out on the table a diamond-studded brooch in the form of a star.

15

Unwelcome Discovery

IT was a small miracle that Sir Stalwart, companion in the Loyal and Ancient Order of the King's Blades, did not topple off the rock and perform a graceful seal dive into the black water racing right under his head. He hauled himself up with the aid of the rope and wriggled backward until more of him was supported. He felt giddy—from being upside down, or the shock, or both.

He had first seen Digby more than two years ago, droning on about honor and service on Durendal Night. He had seen him again in the palace. Although they had not been close on either occasion, he was absolutely certain that the man in the water was Digby—and Digby clad in the remains of a forester's green. This was madness! No one could have spirited that corpse from Grandon all the way here. And for what purpose? Just to flush it down Smealey Hole?

The body in the water must be the real Lord Digby, and the man who had died in Nocare had been an imposter. Just because no one had ever heard of an enchantment that would make one man look exactly like another did not mean that one could not be invented. The switch had been made when he'd visited Smealey Hall, and the phony had been sent back with Rhys....

There were maggots in that theory. Why had none of Digby's retainers detected the change? Or the King, his friend? Why had the White Sisters not sensed the magic on him when he entered the hall...? And the wrong man had died anyway! Why? How? Had the fake Lord Digby intended to kill the King and somehow turned the sorcery on himself? And why had the White Sisters not detected *that* piece of magic when he brought it in? Why had the imposter not made his move the previous evening, when he'd supped with the King?

Shivering on the rough slab with his head and shoulders still overhanging the river, Stalwart realized that no one would believe his story without evidence. He edged forward and downward again and took another look at the corpse. The only part of it that he could possibly hope to catch with a noose was the head, but that was resting on the rock below, with only the face out of water. It wouldn't work.

He had to try at least once. He stretched the noose wide, then lowered it into the water. The current swept it away, twirling the rope like a spinner's yarn. He hauled it in and tried again, this time casting it upstream in the hope it would have time to sink before it was washed down to the body. That worked no better. What he needed was a pole with a hook. Not having one, he must just come back in the morning with helpers and hope the body was still there.

Wearily he began to clamber up the rocks. Shock and disappointment lay on him like a wagonload of tiles. Two nights without—no, really *three* nights without enough sleep. Plus two long rides—Valglorious to Grandon, then Grandon to Waterby. He needed a soft, warm bed more than anything.

He reached the top, where he had tied the rope. He pulled his shoulders over the edge and was about to grab a handy branch of driftwood to pull himself farther when he realized that the branch was, in fact, one of a pair of boots. Emerald! He had given her strict orders not to come back to help.

Yelling over the roar of the falls: "I thought I told you—"

Those boots were far too large to be hers. And there were

more of them. Eight in all. Balanced on one foot and the toes of another, gripping rocks with bloody, frozen hands, he felt himself freeze in a rush of despair. He had failed.

He had left *Sleight* with Emerald.

But that hardly mattered, because a sword now advanced until its point was right between his eyes.

"You must be Wart," said an unfamiliar voice. "Do you want to die now or later?"

16

Meanwhile, His Sword

EMERALD had ridden to the top of the cliff with Mervyn, but there she reined in. "I'm going to wait here for Wart—I mean Sir Stalwart. Do you want to go on?"

The old man chuckled. "No, er...Master Luke. My eyes aren't what they were, but I can find the path in the dark and doubt you could. Nor yon stripling Blade neither."

"You were right earlier, Master Mervyn, when you called me 'lass.' I'm no Luke." She had decided that she could trust him, unlike his enchanted master, the Sheriff.

He cackled. "Your legs are wrong shape for a boy's, miss, but very fine indeed for girl's."

"Um...thank you." That was the first time a man had ever told her that. Of course until yesterday she had never displayed them in hose. So what if he was two hundred years old? It was a start.

"'Course a forester's trained to see what he's looking at, unlike most folk."

"Er, yes. My real name is Sister Emerald."

He coughed an *oof*! of surprise. "My lady! I did not dream—"

"That's all right. You could not know. That was how I

found that body. It has magic on it. I am sorry, Forester, but I greatly fear it will prove to be your grandson."

He sighed. "Aye." And there was silence.

She dismounted and sat on a rock to wait. The old forester hobbled the horses and removed their bridles so they could graze. He perched on another boulder and time seemed to freeze.

Night fell. Wart did not come. She could see nothing down in the canyon shadows where the angry waters roared. She kept telling herself that he was an air person, nimble as a squirrel when it came to climbing.

Mother Superior had called him, "dangerously overconfident."

At last she said, "He should be here by now."

"Reckon so, my lady."

"I greatly fear that treason and black magic both are plotted in Smealey Hole these days."

"Aye, milady. Evil is a common crop there."

"Outsiders must visit it sometimes, though? Tinkers who mend pots?" That had been Badger's suggestion and she still had a painful distrust of that dismal man.

"Not many. Milady, Sheriff told us to stay away from the Hole. Got no cause to vex the conjurers, he says. But if they're behind Rhys going missing, and if they harm yon boy, then I know the lads will rally to my horn. Dozen of us, an' I can find half as many again, given a day."

Another day would be far too late. If the intruder had been spotted and those mysterious swordsmen had gone to investigate, Wart might be dead already. She was horribly conscious of the awkward weight of his sword at her side and his commission with the royal seal tucked away in her jerkin. His only hope was to be taken in for questioning, and that would provide only a brief and highly unpleasant delay before the same watery ending. He carried nothing to prove that he was anything more than a common poacher. What happened to petty poachers in Smealey country, anyway?

No court could summon evidence from the bottom of the Hole.

When the stars came out, she knew that she could not go back to Waterby without finding out what had happened to Wart.

"Forester, Sir Stalwart has been delayed."

"Aye, milady."

"Detained, likely."

"Aye, milady."

"That's a breach of the King's peace, because he's an officer of the Crown. Will you please go back to Waterby and bring a posse? I leave it up to you whether you tell the Sheriff or just round up a bunch of your friends. Meet me here at sunup. If I'm not here, then I have been detained also. Come and rescue us."

She expected fifteen minutes of argument, but the old man cackled approvingly.

"Aye, milady! That I will. You can count on Mervyn."

This instant agreement was a little disconcerting. Suddenly she had no more reason to delay. "Then please leave the other two horses here. Thank you."

"Spirits keep you—Master Luke!"

"And good chance to you, Mervyn Forester," she said, striding off down the hill with the cat's-eye sword swaying at her side.

17

Baron Smealey

"I ASKED you, Wart," said the mocking voice, "if you want to die now or later?"

"Later would be better." He was probably not audible over the din of the falls. That his captors knew his name was the worst news of all. Lord Florian or almost anyone in Waterby Castle might have betrayed him, but only Badger and Emerald knew him as Wart. Enlisting Badger had been entirely his own idea, not one approved by Snake. This disaster was all his own fault.

"Come up," the man yelled, removing his sword from the end of Stalwart's nose. "I was told not to maltreat you as long as you behave yourself. If you give any trouble, I am to thrash you within an inch of your life. Clear enough?"

"Very transparent." Stalwart hauled himself wearily up, boots scrabbling on the rocks. He made such hard work of it that powerful hands grabbed his arms and lifted him bodily, then steadied him as he staggered. He was looking at the laces of a leather jerkin.

"This un's not big enough, Sarge!" roared a new voice. "Ought to throw it back."

All four of them stood head and shoulders above Stalwart,

and twice as wide. All were stoutly clad in padded leather, armed with swords and daggers.

"Hands behind you," the leader shouted in his ear. "I'm told you're a lot more dangerous than you look."

"Wouldn't be hard," yelled one of the others, and they all hooted.

Who was Stalwart to disagree, stumbling, bumbling idiot that he was? He submitted in silence as his wrists were bound, and then a few turns taken around his elbows as well. Were they seriously worried that he might snatch a man's sword from his scabbard? That they felt the need to take such precautions was a compliment to the Blades' reputation—no credit to him.

"Move!" the Sergeant shouted, and off they all went along the rocky ledge, skirting driftwood and ankle-breaking gaps in the footing. Stalwart had trouble balancing, but his captors stayed close and steadied him.

It was only a week since the last time he'd been led around like a performing bear with a noose around his neck. He really should try and break the habit. His captor then had been the odious Marshal Thrusk, whom he had joyfully obliterated soon after. Thrusk had gone so far as to tow Stalwart behind his horse and had never tied a knot that did not hurt; but these men were being surprisingly considerate, as if they really had been ordered not to damage him.

When they had climbed up out of the canyon into the wider valley, they came to more men waiting with horses. Stalwart was lifted into a saddle like a child. He ought to feel flattered that whoever was in charge of this had felt the need to send so many men for him. He should have been more modest when he described his Quagmarsh exploits to Badger.

He would not be bragging much about this mission.

The Hall seemed to be a cluster of buildings arrayed around a central yard. From the way the rooflines blotted out the stars, some were two stories high; a few poorly shuttered windows showed chinks of candlelight. Bats squeaked and flittered overhead, which was common enough around country dwellings, but no dogs barked or came to greet the visitors. That was curious.

More leather-clad swordsmen appeared with lanterns. The prisoner was lifted from his horse's back, then led by his tether down some steps, with a lantern behind making shadows dance ahead. He noted a door of timbers as thick as his fist, a flagstone floor, glimpses of solid masonry walls, but it was the chill and the cloying scent of recently harvested apples that told him he was in a root cellar. Onions and carrots hung in nets overhead. Stacked casks and barrels took up at least half the space, but in the area left empty stood a single wooden chair. On an upturned bucket beside it were a pitcher, a loaf, and some cheese. His mouth started to water, traitor that it was.

The Sergeant hung a lantern on a chain dangling from the ceiling. "You'll be needing a blanket. Or two. We wouldn't," he added wryly, "want you to die of cold."

Stalwart was wet to the skin and shuddering, lacking cloak and jerkin. "Be nice," he admitted humbly. He would not be too proud to eat that food, either. When the bonds fell from his hands, he shot a quick glance behind him. Two other men were blocking the doorway, fore-stalling any attempt to dodge past the Sergeant and make a break.

The man was even larger than he had seemed in the dark. His features had been so horribly mangled that they seemed barely human. His remaining eye looked the prisoner up and down curiously. Mostly down, naturally.

"You really a *Blade*, sonny?"

"Naw! Give me a sword and I'll show you how bad I am with it."

"What's your second wish?"

"Yes, I am a Blade. And I'm on His Majesty's business. What you're doing here is treason."

"Yes, lad. I know." He chuckled. "I enjoy it. I also need the money, because I'll have to be very, very rich to find me a wife at my age. Don't bother trying to escape. This place was built to keep mice out. It can keep one dagger-sized

Blade in. I'll send a man with the blankets. No, I'll send three men with the blankets, just so you won't be tempted."

He left, his subordinates backing away before him. The door shut with a squeal and a boom, followed by muffled sounds of bolts and bars rattling and thumping. By that time Stalwart was eating.

He had barely taken the edge of his hunger when the same racket recurred in reverse order, ending when the door squeaked open. A man entered and the whole performance was repeated. Someone was fanatically determined that the prisoner not escape.

That someone was almost certainly the man who was now locked in with him, for his sorcerer's cowled gown of midnight black was bound by the golden cord of a prior. He stood under the lantern so that his face was shadowed. Stalwart could make out only a square, clean-shaven chin and two dark, deep-set eyes.

"The King sends children against me!"

Stalwart leaned back, crossed his ankles, and continued to chew. "Traitors deserve nothing better."

"I am no traitor, for he was never my king! Look! I will demonstrate a little magic for you." From his sleeve the conjurer produced a horseshoe, seemingly a perfectly ordinary iron horseshoe, large enough to fit a cart horse or a knight's destrier. "Watch!"

He had very large hands, and his gown was stretched over an enormous chest and shoulders. Grunting with effort, he slowly wrenched the arms of the shoe apart. He did not quite straighten it, but he opened it to a crescent. This was a legendary test of strength that Master Armorer at Ironhall always declined to try, although he could sometimes be persuaded to lift anvils. To complete his act, the Prior threw the shoe on the flagstones, making it ring convincingly.

"*Ta-rah!*" Stalwart clapped his hands slowly. As a former gleeman, he could appreciate a good routine. But why bother performing for him?

A fine set of teeth flashed angrily in the shadow of the

hood. "I wished to show you the wisdom of obeying my commands. Give me trouble, and I will break your arms with my bare hands. I can make you suffer unbelievable torments. Indeed, I intend to, but I prefer not to start just yet. It might lower your resistance."

Stalwart was locked in with a raving maniac, and the stench of madness made his scalp prickle. He shrugged. "You enjoy making others suffer?"

"No. It is because I have seen so much suffering that I intend to punish the criminal responsible. I understand that you claim to be a Blade, and yet you have never been bound."

"Yes."

"Show me."

Stalwart rose uneasily and unlaced his doublet, then opened his shirt to show that he bore no binding scar over his heart. "Satisfied?"

"Yes. A major conjuration like that would interfere with the enchantment I have planned for you."

As he dressed again, Stalwart recalled the late and unlamented Marshal Thrusk. He, too, had checked his prisoner for a binding scar, and would have slain him instantly had he found one. Now the situation was apparently reversed: it was the absence of one that had landed him in trouble this time.

"So when does the show begin?" The cellar was icy. He was trying as hard as he could not to shiver, lest this demented sorcerer think he was afraid. In fact, of course, he was absolutely terrified. Fortunately threats always raised his dander and made him smart-alecky.

"As soon as the novices have been sent off to bed. Where are the woman and the old forester?"

"When I found the body, I sent them for help." Oh, flames! He should not have mentioned the body. There went the evidence! To hide his dismay, he sat down and tore another hunk off the loaf with his teeth.

The Prior chuckled. "I guessed that was what you were doing in the rapids with a rope. I shall see that the corpse is properly disposed of as soon as there is light. Your remains may even make it down the Hole before his do, but I hope you will last longer than that."

What sort of man gloated over a helpless captive like this? It was a serious defect of character and there ought to be some way to exploit it. His identity was an easy guess.

"I assume your spite against me is because I am a Blade? You will take revenge on me because Sir Durendal slew two of your brothers?"

"I had not thought of that. Now you mention it, it will add to my pleasure."

"You are Badger's last remaining brother, of course?"

"His name is Bevan!" The sorcerer threw back his hood. The family resemblance would have been noticeable even without the white lock above the forehead. In his case it showed more as a streak than a tuft, because his hair was not curly. "I am Owen, fourth Baron Smealey."

"No you're not." Stalwart spoke with his mouth full, waving a chunk of cheese in one hand and an onion in the other. "When—which one was it? I lost count. When another of your awful brothers strangled your old man, Ceri was still alive. He would have inherited the title. Then he was convicted of treason, so all his lands and goods were forfeit and the title revoked. There is no Baron Smealey."

The Prior lunged forward, grabbed him by the front of his doublet and lifted him one-handed. Stalwart forced himself to keep still and just hang there, feet dangling, although he was choking as the mighty fist pressed up under his chin.

"But I am still rightful Prince of Nythia, aren't I? Say it: Yes, Your Highness!"

With all the breath he had left, Stalwart let him have the whole mouthful—cheese, onion, and a great spray of spit.

The Prior roared in revulsion and threw him away. Stalwart struck the chair, rolled off sideways, and bounced to his feet, grabbing the water pitcher to use as a weapon. He had acted without weighing the cost, and he realized now that it might be very high indeed.

But the madman did not leap at him. He wiped his face on his sleeve and laughed. "You will pay for that, runt—

pay and pay! You swore to die for your tyrant king. Well, tonight you will die for him, I promise. Over and over, hour after hour!"

Wheeling around, the madman beat on the door with his fist, and the guards outside began clattering locks and bolts again to open it.

Had the rest of the awful brood been as bad as this one? Or had some been more like Badger, who was decent enough under his surly manner? Owen was obviously madder than a bated bear. Why had Badger come home to aid his hopeless cause?

18

Sir Emerald

BEFORE she was halfway down the precipice, Emerald realized that her madcap rescue effort was unwise, but carrying on already seemed easier than turning back. The sword had taken on a fiendish, spiteful life of its own. It stuck out in front and behind, tangled in the undergrowth, and not infrequently managed to find its way between her knees. Now she understood why Wart had discarded it before going after the body in the river, and why the seniors at Ironhall were allowed a year's practice in wearing the accursed things.

By the time she was three-quarters of the way down, the light had failed completely and she was calling herself every kind of raving lunatic. She slithered and slipped and stumbled, no longer sure she was even on the trail and very much aware of the roaring waterfall below her. What could she really hope to accomplish by setting herself up as a knight errant? The chances that she might manage to return Wart's sword to him in a situation where he could use it were closer to invisible than the feathers on an egg. And reading out his commission to impress a gang of murderers did not seem a very promising program either.

* * * *

She could not believe that Wart had been so clumsy as to fall in the river, but there was no sign of him on the path. Bruised, exhausted, and filthy, she came at last to the wide valley beyond the canyon, and the river of stars overhead spread out as a sea. There she could at least walk upright instead of scrambling along on all fours. Soaked by spray and too cold to stop, she had no other purpose than to continue her trek in search of Smealey Hall. She soon lost the trail, but if she stayed close to the riverbank—and not close enough to fall in—she must inevitably come to the little hill she had seen earlier. She set off through the rocks and weeds, waving the rapier in front of her like a blind person's cane.

An isolated dwelling on the edge of Brakwood would certainly have dogs, but the wind was toward her, so her scent ought to escape their notice for a while yet. She struggled through thistles and brambles, with every new step a chance to sprain an ankle. Eventually a toothy black shape rose ahead of her, cutting off the stars to become the roofline of the buildings she sought. Soon she could even see pale gleams of candlelight in windows and a puzzling flicker of firelight at ground level.

Bats squeaked and wheeled overhead. She heard a horse whinny. She stopped. Horses reminded her of dogs. One bark and she would be lost—or found, rather—with nowhere to run, men coming to see what the trouble was…. She could not imagine herself fighting off a pack of mastiffs with a rapier, although she would probably try if the need arose.

The fire was certainly a bonfire. Why would anyone waste valuable fuel outdoors at night? The smoke was drifting toward her, so the dogs should not scent her yet. Unable to think of anything better to do, she decided to risk going halfway up the slope in the hope that she might find out something—*anything*—useful.

Five or six steps later, she scented magic. Very faint. Very subtle, too. A peppery smell, was it? Or a gentle humming?

Hard to say. She had been shown something like it in Oakendown, as an example of...of...of what?

She stepped a little closer. To her right? Closer yet? Ah! It was a warding. Not identical to the classroom example but very similar. There was a hint of death in it, too weak for it to be a physical threat. Most of it was air and fire, the elements of motion. If she went too close, it would set off an alarm somewhere. Any moving body would trigger it, including a dog's, so there would be no dogs here. It would be a very local spell, probably imprinted on a rock or a post, but there would be others, forming an enchanted fence all around the complex. Only a White Sister would even know the barrier was there.

Only a White Sister could hope to find a way past it!

To her right was the river. She set off to her left around the hill, staying at the very limit of her ability to sense the conjuration. As she expected, her path curved in toward the buildings until she sensed another source ahead of her. She proceeded in a series of arcs, skirting each ward in turn. That there would be a gap somewhere she did not doubt. The conjurations would weaken with time and have to be replaced often. In a sorcery school like this, that would certainly be a task for the novices. They would enchant the posts, or stones, or whatever it was they used, inside their octogram, then bring them out to repair the barrier. But the only way they could test their work would be to set off the alarms deliberately. Almost certainly they would have missed a spot or two.

They had. A stone wall could not stop magic altogether, but it would weaken an air spell, and she found a stub of an old stone wall. It had perhaps been an ancient fortification, because there was a ditch alongside it. In that, down at ground level, the warding was negligible. Slithering on her belly, Sister Emerald made a secret but extremely undignified entry into the compound of Smealey Hole.

A dozen or more buildings were grouped about a central yard. She had come a long way from the bonfire she had been tracking, so she skulked back around the dark perimeter toward it. The high building with lighted windows must be the main house, probably where the adepts lived. Her ears soon tracked voices to a couple of long sheds with many illuminated windows—she decided those were bunkhouses for servants or novices. Her nose identified the stable, brewhouse, chicken coop, bakery. But she also detected a nasty stench of magic as she went by a large, high building, which must therefore be the elementary.

She paused at the corner of a hay shed to inspect the bonfire that had guided her in. The three men sitting around it were serving no purpose she could think of unless they were guards, and the thing they were guarding was a low slate roof. The building itself must be mostly underground, either an ice house or a root cellar. The realization that Wart was still alive gave her a great rush of relief that made all the pain and fear and effort of the last few hours seem worthwhile.

Now, how could she get him out?

Behind the shed was a high tangle of weeds. Dropping to hands and knees again, she began to crawl. Unfortunately, the brush included a fair share of thorns, thistles, and sharp stones. Fortunately, the stinging nettles were past their stinging stage. Every few minutes she raised her head to look around, but the men were engrossed in a dice game, unaware of the curious local wind disturbing the vegetation. She had almost reached the building when she heard new voices, two men approaching from the main house. They were heading for the fire, though, and did not seem to have noticed her at all. If the prisoner was about to be moved elsewhere, she had arrived too late, but perhaps she could manage to throw him his sword while he was out in the open. She had seen Wart in action and knew how deadly he was.

Voices, mocking and resentful...a snarly order...then a clattering of bolts and bars. Emerald slithered faster, confident that the newcomers were making too much noise themselves to hear the rustles and crackles of her progress.

Puffing, she reached the back of the roof just as the door was slammed shut again.

Through a small grille set in the stonework, she heard Wart's voice, and then Badger's.

19

The Seventh Brother

SINCE Owen's departure, Stalwart had been curled up on a sack of goose feathers—which was unfortunately the only one of its kind in the root cellar. He had built himself a cave out of apple barrels and boxes of sun-dried plums. In this lair he huddled around the lantern, hungry for any trace of warmth. The blankets he had been promised had not appeared. When he tried shouting through the door, the guards outside either did not hear or would not heed. If he put an ear to the jamb he could hear them out there, cursing over their dice, so he knew they had not gone away.

His stocktaking of his cell had not taken long. Although the building was old, it was solidly built of fieldstone and massive timbers, and he found no weaknesses he could use. The absence of mouse droppings proved that the roof was sound and the door was snug in its frame. There was no window, the only ventilation came through a shaft in the masonry of the rear wall, and that was barely wide enough to admit his arm. He reached in past his elbow before his fingers found a mesh of metal wire covering it on the outside. If he lit a fire to keep warm, he would suffocate.

He brooded on failure, which had an unfamiliar taste. Quagmarsh had been such a triumph! Now he had hatched a total calamity, and all because he had put too much trust in an old friend and not enough in a new one. Badger's horrified reaction to the first mention of Smealey Hole should have been a giveaway. So should his denial of his previous story that he had found a secret passage there. So should his announcement in Waterby Castle, shouted for the Fellowship's spies to hear. He had claimed to be unfamiliar with the area and then identified landmarks. Unwilling to believe an Ironhall brother would betray him, Stalwart had ignored Emerald's warnings.

Idiot! Sucker! As punishment for his stupidity, the youngest-ever Blade was going to have the shortest-ever career with the Guard. Alas, *Sleight* would never hang in the sky of swords at Ironhall, and the name of her owner would not be inscribed in the *Litany of Heroes*. He would vanish unheralded down the Hole, after whatever horrors the sorcerers had in store for him. Perhaps, as a last request, he would ask the traitors to explain how Lord Digby had managed to die twice.

The usual clattering of bolts and locks warned him of visitors. By the time they entered, the lantern was back on its chain and the prisoner was seated on the chair with his arms folded and ankles crossed, desperately trying not to shiver, although he was sure his lips must be blue. The first man in was Badger, wearing a sorcerer's black gown. On his heels came the big, hideous-faced sergeant, carrying a bundle. "Brought you some dry clothes," he said.

The door was being closed and barred again as usual. Neither man was armed; the soldier's scabbard dangled empty at his side. Prior Owen took precautions to lunatic extremes.

Stalwart had never wanted anything as he wanted those dry clothes. Perversely, therefore, he made no move when the Sergeant dropped the heap at his feet.

"What's the price?"

"No price," the ugly man growled. "You got splat-all to pay with."

Taking his time, Stalwart began unlacing his doublet. "It took you long enough."

"Been busy."

"Sergeant Eilir has been working on your behalf," Badger said.

Stalwart stopped for a moment to stare at him. "I used to have a friend who looked just like you."

"You still do. I can't save your life, but I've arranged so you'll die quickly."

Wart peeled off his doublet. His fingers were almost too numb to manage shirt buttons. "You have curious ideas of friendship."

"I've been arguing for the last hour with a dozen sorcerers and a score of men-at-arms. It was only when Eilir backed me that Owen and his cronies yielded. They wanted to kill you by inches. Now he's agreed that he'll just cut your head off."

"Why?" Stalwart took up the clothes provided and discovered a hooded gown of black wool and a brown fur cloak, nothing else. He pulled on the gown. "It's murder. And treason. You can't expect to get away with this. What have I done?"

Badger sighed. He did look miserable, give him that. "You won that star from the King, that's what. The Fellowship has a spell that needs a link between the victim and someone else, and that link must be a gift. The star in your case—"

"And Digby gave Rhys a hunting horn?"

"Exactly. Did you get a good look at the body in the river?"

"It was—It *seemed* to be Digby."

Badger glanced at Eilir, who shrugged as if to say that revealing secrets to a man in Stalwart's position really could not matter.

"It wasn't him," the Sergeant growled. "It was the forester. The sorcery turns one man into a *simulacrum* of the other. By itself, the change is harmless and doesn't last long. The adepts practiced on one another and some of the novices, and they all changed back in a few days. But while the spell holds, whatever happens to the simulacrum happens to the original, or the other way round. Stick a pin in one and both will yell. Nobody knew if the effect went as far as causing death, so when they'd made the Digby simulacrum, Owen put a sword through his heart. He sent a man off to Grandon to find out what had happened, to see if the sorcery reached that far."

Stalwart stared in disbelief as he tried to comprehend this insanity. Trouble was, he *did* believe it. It was the implications....

"Are you saying they're going to make me into a copy of King Ambrose? Me and what ox? He's three times my size."

This time it was Badger who shrugged. "They say that size doesn't matter. I brought you the biggest robe I could find. And they're certain it doesn't hurt."

"Except when that mad brother of yours cuts off my head! I bet that stings." He dropped his britches and hose and wrapped himself up in the cloak, shivering more than ever.

"Yes!" Badger snapped. "We're going to cut Ambrose's head off just the way he cut off Ceri's and Aneirin's. You'll die by a sword, the way they did, and Kendrick and Edryd and Lloyd did! Owen and I are the only ones left, and we will have our revenge."

"The King's head will fall off while he's at breakfast?"

"Perhaps. He'll certainly die."

So would Stalwart. There were worse ways to die than having your head cut off. There were a lot more good ways to keep on living instead. "As I recall, Aneirin was executed for strangling your dad. I'm not saying your father didn't deserve it. I'm sure he did. But why wasn't Aneirin hanged like any other common killer?"

Eilir answered. "He asked to die beside his brother, and the King graciously granted his request."

Badger was scowling. "Listen, Wart. I'm sorry this has to happen, truly. I swore an oath..." He shot an uneasy glance at the Sergeant. "I was the baby, much younger than even Owen. I was only a child when Nythia rose against the tyrant. I worshiped my brothers—Ceri was the oldest, and the leader by right of perfection. There was nothing

Ceri could not do, nothing he did not excel in. Everyone worshiped Ceri, so you can imagine how he seemed to me. And the rest were little behind him. Kendrick was a swordsman; Lloyd already a sorcerer of note, although only an amateur; Edryd an artist...But that doesn't do them justice. They were strong and skilled in a thousand ways and beautiful as the stars. They taught me everything.... Ceri rallied all Nythia and kindled the torch of freedom. Monster Ambrose brought in his army to stamp it out.

"By winter, half of my wonderful brothers were dead. Owen was at home, being passed off as just a boy, although he was fifteen and had seen some fighting near the end. Ceri and Aneirin were outlawed, hiding out in Brakwood. I was seven, old enough to help smuggle food to them. The wolves closed in. Sheriff Florian was sure that the fugitives were in the area; and he came here, to Smealey Hole, violating guarantees the King had given the Baron. He took Owen and me away, and Anwen, our mother. He swore to the Baron that none of us would eat or drink until Ceri was turned over to him. Ceri surrendered, of course. He would have died for any one of us, let alone three." Badger fell silent.

No boy in Ironhall discussed his own past openly. Some of them had very lurid pasts and the others wanted everyone to think they did, too. So hints were allowed, but open bragging was cause for disbelief and retaliation. That way, everyone could pass as a murderer until proved guilty of innocence. Stalwart had never heard this terrible story; he did not want to hear it now. It was full of deceit and distortion, possibly direct lies, but it was also grievous and he did not want to feel sympathy for traitors.

"You're saying Aneirin was a little hasty when he strangled Daddy?"

"Aneirin was fine until the siege of Kirkwain. What he saw there unhinged him. He seemed to be recovered, but he had a brainstorm when he heard about Ceri. Owen wasn't there. Mother and I weren't strong enough to stop him."

"You *saw* it?" Stalwart squealed. "You were there?"

Badger chuckled, sounding not quite sane himself. "Oh, we had exciting times in our family! When Aneirin realized what he'd done, he went to Waterby and asked to die in Ceri's stead. The King allowed them to die together. Kind of him, wasn't it? Understanding, you must agree?"

There was no answer to that.

"Tell him what happened next," Eilir said.

"After Father's death?" Badger was pale and his voice almost shrill, as the telling dug up memories he had buried long ago. "Ceri was the new baron. He had never sworn loyalty to the House of Ranulf, but he was found guilty of treason—the trial took all of half an hour. His life, title, and estates were forfeit. The very afternoon the news reached Waterby, the Sheriff came with his men and drove us out of the house in the clothes we had on our backs. Literally! Not even a cloak or hat. Yes, it was snowing." He stared defiantly at Stalwart, who said nothing.

"Owen, and Anwen, and me. Anwen's health was poor. She and I would certainly have died without Owen. He had just turned sixteen, but he kept us alive that winter. The next year he got us across the sea to Isilond. He hired on as a mercenary, and we all starved together on a man-at-arms's pay. For eight years he lived by the sword. Do you wonder that I love my brother, *Sir Wart?*"

Stalwart wasn't going to admit that. "He isn't worth spitting on, let alone loving! He doesn't trust you, Badger! How can you trust him? He sends this hired pikeman along with you and even disarms him. Did he think I'd grab the man's sword out of its scabbard? Or you would? Or we both would? He's crazy, raving, deranged!"

"He's careful," Eilir said, "the finest warrior I ever knew. No man ever outsmarts or outfights Owen Smealey. I hired him as a raw recruit and discovered he was already a match for half the men in the troop. Within a year he was my captain. I could tell tales..." He shrugged.

Stalwart ignored him and concentrated on the man he'd thought was his friend. "How did you end up in Ironhall?

And why? You couldn't seriously have wanted to join the Guard."

Badger chuckled again, a sound to raise the hair on the back of a man's neck. "Owen made his fortune in loot eventually, but too late for Anwen. On her deathbed she made us both swear that we would be avenged on Ambrose of Chivial."

Stalwart shuddered. "Plague and corruption, man! Owen maybe. He was a mature, veteran soldier. But you? How old?"

"Sixteen."

"You were too young to—"

"Bah! How old are you now, Sir Wart?"

That was another question with no good answer. Not now. In a few more weeks the answer would be different. *There weren't going to be any more weeks*! There wasn't even going to be a tomorrow.

Badger sneered at the lack of response. "We came back to Chivial, Owen and I. He'd had enough of soldiering, and he'd conceived the idea of the Fellowship. The only real school of sorcery in Chivial was the College, and there were many sorts of enchantments it wouldn't teach that people wanted and would pay for. Owen, although no great enchanter himself, had the dream and the money and the leadership. The Crown had put Smealey Hole on the market; it would be an ideal location. And when he had built his team of sorcerers, he could move against the tyrant, as he had sworn. That left me. How does an eager young man go about assassinating a monarch guarded at all times by the finest swordsmen in the world?

He quirked an eyebrow. "No guesses? Need a hint? No man can bear arms in the King's presence, right?"

Stalwart said, "Oh, no!" but obviously the answer was *Oh, yes*! In the ritual of binding, the Brat gave the candidate his sword; the candidate stood on the anvil to swear loyalty to the King, and then the King struck the sword through his heart to bind him. The same sword. The candidate had to pass that sword to the King. If he leaped down from the anvil and passed it point first, even the Blades present could never move fast enough to block him. "You're Prime!"

Badger's smile was right out of nightmare. "I hope that tonight you will relieve me of the need to go back, friend Wart." His eyes were too bright, his teeth too big. "But if I must go, I will go, because when Owen and I parted at the door of Ironhall, we swore to each other that we would not step off our chosen paths until Ambrose was dead. If I do go back, then the next binding he attempts will be his last. The sword will go through the *other* heart."

Stalwart was aghast. It was unthinkable. "All these years? All the time I have known you, you've been plotting this? But it's suicide! The Blades will kill you right away, and even if they don't, then you'll die a traitor's death." He shivered. They were all crazy, the whole Smealey brood. The curse on the Hole was plain insanity, nothing more. "No wonder Grand Master said you were jumpy! Fates, man! You put yourself under sentence of death?" He stared in horror at Badger's mocking smile. "All these years?"

"All these years. But now my good friend Wart has come along to save me at the last minute. It's you or me, Wart. More exactly, it's you for certain and possibly me as well, if tonight's attempt doesn't work. Tomorrow at dawn I carry on to Grandon with your message to Snake. If Owen has failed and the King lives, then I must return to Ironhall and the binding. They'll be starting very soon." He turned away.

"Wait!" Stalwart yelled, jumping up. "Badger, this is madness! It wasn't Ambrose who caused all the deaths and suffering, it was your precious Ceri! Nythia didn't rally to his banner, you know that. You heard the history lectures in Ironhall. Very few people supported him. Even your own father didn't!"

Badger kicked the door with his boot. Bolts and bars began clanking.

"He had no claim to the throne of Nythia!" Stalwart shouted. "The royal line died out ages ago. If anyone is heir to the old princes, it is Ambrose himself, through his great-umpteenth-great-grandmother. The people didn't want Ceri and his mad ambitions, nor his sinister friends, either."

Badger had his face to the planks, his back to Stalwart, refusing to listen. Eilir was watching the argument with what might have been meant to be a smile.

"And you?" Stalwart yelled, turning on him. "Where does your loyalty come from? Just money? Friendship? Or are you as mad as the rest of them?"

"See this?" The Sergeant pointed to the nightmare ruin of his face. "I was about your age once, sonny. I looked human, those days. Quite good-looking, in fact." He took a step closer. "Not now, though! I lived in Waterby, see? I wasn't a soldier, not then. I was a glassblower's apprentice. Then the war came, and the siege." Another step made Stalwart recoil from the abhorrence leering closer. "Your precious Ambrose set his Destroyer General on us, hurling great rocks at the town. It was one of them hit a wall and exploded right in front of me." Another step, and Stalwart was back against the chair. "All the rest of my family died, so I was lucky, wasn't I?"

The door creaked. Stalwart ducked nimbly past the Sergeant and grabbed Badger as he tried to leave.

"Listen! Your darling Owen's unstable as a two-legged horse. Maybe he was a father to you, but he cared so little for you later that he made you swear to kill yourself. He wants to torture me to death! He's curdled in his wits. He's a raving, demented—"

Eilir's iron hand took him by the shoulder and hurled him back. His leg caught the chair and he pitched headlong. It was fortunate that he knew how to fall; perhaps even more fortunate that he was well padded by the thick gown and fur cloak. He didn't break anything. The door boomed shut behind the two men. Then came all the noisy rigmarole of shutting it.

Groaning, the prisoner sat up and rubbed his knee, his shoulder. His elbow hurt, too. He was starting to shiver again. Dead men didn't shiver.

A very soft whisper said, "Wart?"

20

A Sleight Problem

STALWART hurtled to his feet, knocked over the chair, banged his head on a dangling net full of onions, and hit the back wall at a gallop. He would have hit it with both shoulders had it been possible for his head to fit in the air shaft. "Em? That you?"

"Sh! Can you hear me—I mean, are you free to move around?"

"Yes!" His heart pounded. Funny—he felt almost more scared now than he had before. Now he had a friend out there. Now, just maybe, there was a chance of *not* dying?

She whispered, "I heard what they were saying, Wart, most of it. I sent old Mervyn for help, but they won't get here until after dawn. Can you hang on until then somehow?"

Oh, *good* idea! As soon as help appeared in the valley, he would be tossed in the river. Dangerous evidence would never be left lying around Smealey Hole. He forced himself to speak slowly and calmly.

"Personally, I'm in no hurry, but they'll move as soon as the novices have gone to sleep." Owen had said that, implying that not all the residents of Smealey Hole were traitors. Stalwart would not repeat that to Emerald in case she developed some crazy idea of organizing a revolution. It would never work, because Eilir was certainly loyal to the Prior and his swordsmen controlled the valley. "Em, you've got to leave! One of us must survive to be a witness. Please go!" He found that horribly hard to say: *Please go away and leave me alone again.*

He was more frightened now than he had been in Quagmarsh. There he had been so buoyed up by his hatred of Thrusk that he'd had no time to despair. Besides, Thrusk had been a clod; Owen was freakishly clever. No one out-smarted Owen Smealey.

The whisper came again. "There's a grille over this vent."

"I know."

"If I can get it off, I could give you your sword. Do you want it?"

Want it? "Yes please." *Yesyesyesyesyes...*If he had *Sleight* in his hand, he'd take on Badger and Eilir both. He could hold the door against the whole troop of men-at-arms for hours. It would change everything. They'd have to burn him out. Mervyn's men coming at dawn...He tried not to cackle.

"Just a minute," she whispered. "I'll try a rock."

"Wait! I'll go and make a noise."

Emerald said, "Right."

Stalwart hurried across to the door. He could still hear faint voices out there, probably three of them. Men-at-arms soldiered for money and did not necessarily believe in their leader's cause. He thumped the chair against the planks. "Traitors!" he yelled. "You're going to lose your heads for this, all of you. I'm an officer of the Crown. Let me out and I'll see you get royal pardons!" And so on—bang, yell, bang, yell...His efforts were ignored. Owen would have selected the guards with his usual care.

Eventually the prisoner decided that he had given Emerald enough time. If she had not opened the air shaft by now, she couldn't. He went back to it. "Em?"

"Ready," she said. "Stand clear."

A faint scraping sound...then *Sleight's* needle point came into view. He reached out and clasped the steel lovingly, pulled...*Clink!*...It stopped. His heart hit the floor. He felt

Emerald ease the blade back, turn it, try again.... But he could visualize *Sleight's* wide quillons and the narrow shaft and he knew that nothing was going to work. He would have known sooner if he had allowed himself to think about it. In a moment the blade was withdrawn.

"Wart?" Emerald whispered. "It won't fit."

"No." He must try to think clearly. Ironhall taught that courage wasn't just not being afraid, it was being afraid and doing your duty anyway. The more fear you felt, the braver you were. No shame in not wanting to die. Great honor in dying if you had to. "Nice try. Thanks. How much did you hear of what Badger said?"

"All of it, I think."

"Good. Then I needn't explain. I'm very grateful you came, but you really *must* go now! Please? Promise? No more heroics. It's very important that you get back safely to explain what happened. That sorcery is terrible! So please go now."

He probably wouldn't rank a mention in the *Litany of Heroes*, but it would be nice if *Sleight* got to hang in the sky of swords.

21

Faces from the Past

AFTER leaving the prisoner, Badger and Eilir walked back to the residence in silence, not sharing their thoughts. Badger felt awkward without the weight of a sword at his side. He hated the stupid sorcerer's gown that Owen insisted he wear so he would not stand out and provoke questions. That was either an admission that not everyone in the Hole was completely trusted or just a reminder that Owen never completely trusted anyone.

As they walked into the candlelight entrance, the first person they saw was Owen himself—waiting for them, of course. Suspicious, of course. Standing so his hood shadowed his face, of course.

"Well?" he demanded.

"Nothing," Badger said.

The only reason Owen had let him go to speak with Wart was to find out if Wart had anything up his sleeve. Frighten a man enough and he might blurt out secrets. It was unheard of for Ironhall candidates to be taken from the school before their binding, so of course Owen suspected that Wart had not been totally honest. Owen could not imagine anyone being totally honest. He was convinced that the kid was just bait on a hook and the Old Blades were skulking around, waiting to pounce.

"I still want to know why Snake sent a boy!"

Badger groaned. "Just what I said before—the Old Blades are run off their feet and this Smealey lead was a long shot. They sent the boy because he wouldn't attract attention. Wart isn't capable of lying on that scale. Snake is, certainly, but the kid is scared spitless. If he knew anything about a rescue coming he'd have told us."

Owen's restless gaze flickered to Eilir.

"I agree," the one-eyed man said. "He didn't try to bribe me, which I expected, but I'm sure he just didn't think of it. He certainly wasn't gloating as if we'd fallen into a trap."

"He may not know about the trap."

"Prior," Eilir said patiently, "I really don't think there is a trap."

The sorcerer pouted. "Very well. Another half hour or so. Stay in here until then," he told Badger. He stalked away.

Without looking at Eilir, Badger headed for the stairs. Treads creaked as he climbed—the same treads that had creaked when he was a child: the third, eighth, twelfth.... Half an hour gave him just enough time to do what he wanted to do. His bones ached from lack of sleep, but that was not the main reason he felt so miserable.

He would not describe Wart as a close friend, or even a friend at all. He didn't have friends. But the kid was amusing company and not halfwitted like some Ironhall inmates. He was a fine lutenist, juggler, acrobat. He'd earned his living as a minstrel's helper before he was even in his teens, whereas most of the others arrived there as useless trash. At times he had been a pest, but he didn't deserve this death. At least it would be quick, now that Owen had been talked out of his more savage intentions.

Carrying his lantern high ahead of him, Badger started up a second staircase, a very narrow one.

Kill Ambrose by all means. But to do it by killing another man—or boy—seemed so unfair! Not that Badger was about to insist on sparing Wart so he could carry out his own suicidal assassination plot. One way or another, Wart must die. He knew too much now. It was not a happy thought. All right for Owen; as a soldier, he'd killed before.

The stair brought him to a narrow, cramped space under the ridge of the roof. Low doors led to attics where servants had slept in the old days, but there were no servants in the Hole anymore, and the novices occupied the old fieldworkers' bunkhouses. Beyond these squalid sleeping quarters, angular nooks under the eaves provided hideaways for a billion spiders, storage for generations of junk, and play areas for small boys on wet days.

Badger went to the one he wanted and broke a fingernail prying open the access panel. It had not been moved since the day the last of the Smealeys were driven from their home. With less than an hour's warning that the Sheriff was on his way, they had hidden their most precious keepsakes in these attic cubbyholes—nothing of real value, though. Golden plates and silver candlesticks had stayed on display because the King's men would certainly have resorted to torture if they had not found the loot they expected. Here were only sentimental treasures, like the pictures Badger had come for. They were stacked exactly as he remembered leaving them. No one was less sentimental than Owen.

But the other things he had left on top of them were still there too, because he had never told Owen or even Anwen about those. Sword, horn, and dagger—personal treasures Ceri had left in the hollow tree. The horn and sword were ordinary, but the dagger was special.

Ceri's claim to be rightful Prince of Nythia had relied on a very flimsy tale, the drunken ravings of a half-mad grandfather, and not the terrible Grandfather Gwyn, either. It was through Anwen that the royal pretension had come, descent from an illegitimate royal daughter, who had been ignored by historians and perhaps invented long after her death. No one had put much stock in this dubious ancestor, but she had been necessary, and had been accepted by the patriots. One of those supporters had presented Ceri with an ancient dagger bearing the green dragon emblem of the royal house of Nythia worked into the hilt in gold and jade. Ceri had worn it ever after, until that final night when he had shed his last hopes and finery and ridden off to ransom his mother and brothers. It was a beautiful thing still, and much too valuable to be abandoned. Owen should have it, for he was the pretender now, Prince of Nythia. Badger put it aside to take with him.

He took up the topmost portrait and held it near the glimmering lantern. The mice had pretty much ignored it; it had not warped or split. Because Edryd had preferred to work on sawn wooden panels, the portraits were all small, no more than heads and necks, not quite life-size. The first was of the artist himself, eyes fixedly staring out of the mirror he had used. And young! Of course Edryd could not have been much older then than Badger was now. That was an unwelcome surprise. He propped the panel against the wall and reached for the next, unable to remember the order in which he had left them, twelve long years ago.

The second picture was of Bevan himself, a grinning imp of a child with his silver lock prominent. No need to linger over that one.

The third was Aneirin. Poor, tortured Aneirin! Even then, in the golden days of youth before the uprising, life had never been easy for Aneirin. There had been voices and inexplicable changes of mood. Edryd had caught some of that agony in the lowered glance, the hint of sunken cheek.

Then Lloyd, the scholar, with chin cupped in ink-stained fingers, staring down at something not shown—a book, perhaps. Lloyd himself had long since returned to the elements, and only this likeness remained to show that he had ever existed.

Ceri was fifth. Again—how *young*! How very, astonishingly, young! Ceri looked no older than an Ironhall senior, but perhaps he had been only nineteen or twenty when he posed for his brother. Yet how magnificent, even then! The dark curls lapping the forehead, the line of jaw, eyes raised to horizons unseen by lesser mortals. The silver lock had been most marked on him—Ceri had excelled at everything, always. Even Edryd had been inspired to create a masterpiece when he painted that wonderful head, those shiny eyes, those lips about to speak.

How young! And how...How *what*? For a long time Badger held the panel, staring at it, teasing out every detail, analyzing it with the experience gained in the past twelve years—adolescence, the longest and most vital years in any man's life.... How *what*? What exactly was it he was seeing there that he had not expected? A dreamer? Yes, but he had always known Ceri was a dreamer. Leadership, of course. Intelligence. Courage. What else? Ruthlessness? Rather call it ambition. He had known his rebellion would cost many men's lives. He had known that his own chances must be least of all, and he had been willing to take that chance.

No, that still wasn't it. *Idealism*? Badger had never thought of Ceri as an idealist. He himself certainly wasn't. Childhood poverty as a foreigner in Isilond had wiped the stars from his eyes. Years of grind in Ironhall under selfimposed sentence of death had toughened him even further. Ceri had been a nobleman's son, raised in luxury. Maybe Ceri had really expected to find justice and liberty and kindness in this world. Amazing!

Time was up. They would be starting soon.

Badger left the hatch open and everything else where it lay. Only the dagger he tucked out of sight under his robe. Taking up the lantern, he headed back to the stair.

22

Point of View

LEAVING poor Wart in his cell was the hardest thing Emerald had ever done. Since Quagmarsh she could never doubt his courage, yet he had not quite managed to suppress the quaver of dread in his voice. His arguments made sense—she could do no good there, and it was her duty now to see that the traitors were brought to justice. Sick at heart, she wriggled off through the weeds until she was far enough from the watchers' fire to risk standing up; then she picked her way through the dark behind the hay shed, waving the rapier in front of her as she had before.

She had promised Wart very faithfully that she would make her own escape now and wait for the promised rescue that would come too late to save him. Or save the King! As she made her stumbling way around the complex of buildings, she realized that Wart had been wrong. Justice must wait. Her first duty was to save the King, who was also destined to die before dawn. And it was then that she sensed again the magic aura of the octogram.

The big building had changed. Earlier it had been dark and deserted. Now a faint flicker of firelight showed through the open door. The elementary was being made ready for the conjuration. She went closer, trying to ignore that cloying stench of sorcery. Standing on tiptoe, she peered through a window slit. The thickness of the wall restricted her view to a fire burning in an open hearth near the center and colored banners hung on the wall opposite. Nothing more.

She hurried around the back, stubbing her toes and shins several times in the process. There the ground was a little higher, and the window holes were dark, so there must be a separate room back there. She found one slit a little wider than the others, where the logs had rotted. It was a very tight squeeze, and the sword hindered her, but she managed to scramble through.

The rear chamber was an afterthought, cut off from the main hall by a jerry-built partition of rotting planks. At the cost of a few more bruises, she established that it was furnished with benches; she concluded that the Fellowship used it as a classroom. That might not be its only purpose, though. If it also served as storage or a dressing room, then the adepts were liable to walk in on her at any minute. She put an eye to a chink in the wall and inspected the main room again.

The fire wafted white smoke upward. Now she could see the octogram outlined on the flagstones, but the building was clearly a heroes' mead hall left over from days of yore. A sort of cloister along one side puzzled her until she realized that it was another addition, a gallery for spectators or musicians. It sagged in places and some of the posts supporting it were canted at odd angles, so obviously it was no longer in use. The stair to it began right outside the door beside her. If she could hide up there, she decided, she would be safer and see better. She would be almost directly above the conjuration. Even if she could not find a way to stop the evil, it would be a good place to hide until the Sheriff's men arrived.

Too late! Voices came drifting in the main doorway, followed by the speakers themselves, two male novices in white robes. One of them carried a sledgehammer, and had probably been chosen for the breadth of his shoulders. They were grumbling in the manner of prideful young men set to do servants' work. When they reached the center of the octogram, the smaller man crouched and positioned something he had brought with him. He steadied it while his companion tapped it down with the hammer. Once it was secure, the little man stepped back and Shoulders swung his hammer in earnest. The hall shuddered. Dust cascaded down from the roof; a cloud of bats whirled in squeaks of protest and drained out the windows. The two men walked away, still grousing. Where they had been working stood a shiny metal staple.

Emerald was again alone. Moving as fast as those frightened bats had, she slipped out of the smaller room and scrambled up the stairs to the gallery. As she reached the top, a lurch and loud creaks warned her that she had made a foolhardy move. Under an ancient layer of bat guano, the planks were worm-eaten and rotted. One gave way, her right foot went through, and she sprawled headlong on the filth. The platform swayed, then steadied.

Bearing lighted lanterns, a line of sorcerers and swordsmen came trooping into the elementary. She was trapped on a most precarious perch.

23

Change of Heart

THE night had turned frosty, but there was no wind. The waning moon floated like a boat above the cliffs. Hurrying across to the elementary, Badger could see the window slits drooling ribbons of white smoke upward, and another cloud rising from the watch fire outside Wart's prison. Despite the fire, the interior of the elementary was still quite dark; the lanterns hung around the walls glowed like stars in the miasma of woodsmoke. He saw seventeen swordsmen—Ironhall training made him count them—and three novices in white robes plus a dozen adepts, barely visible in their black. One of those was Owen, scrutinizing every face that came in the doorway and issuing orders to Eilir at the same time.

"...and leave no more than six in here," he concluded.

"I thought you had the whole complex warded?" the Sergeant grumbled.

"There are ways they can bypass the warding if they bring sorcerers with them."

"Do you ever worry about wolves in the woods 'round here?"

"There have been no wolves in Chivial for a hundred years," Owen snapped. "Nor in Nythia either."

"No one's *seen* any, you mean. Who's to say they haven't just learned how to look like squirrels?"

"Do as you're told!"

"Yes, Your Malevolence." Eilir raised his voice in a bellow. "Gruffydd, boy! Stay you here with all your troop. The rest of you fine lads come with me. Going to freeze the buttons off your britches, we are." He strode out and the men-at-arms reluctantly followed him, all but five. It was a chilly night for picket duty.

Owen scowled at his brother.

Badger scowled back. "How long will this take?"

"An hour or more, once we get started. It's a very complex conjuration. Maybe longer."

It would be almost dawn.

"Well, you don't need me. I'll go and feed the bedbugs for a while." Badger was out on his feet. He had not slept for two nights, and had not slept *well* for two weeks before that. Owen expected him to set out for Buran at first light and keep going until he arrived at Grandon—and then he would need all his wits about him whether the King was alive or dead. Yet he saw the instant veil of distrust fall over his brother's face.

"Why? Is your conscience troubling you?"

"Of course not."

"You should be here to witness our triumph. I want you here."

"As you wish." Badger sighed and added under his breath, "I see why Eilir called you Malevolence." He strode off across the hall with his absurd gown swishing around his ankles.

The adepts stood around under lanterns, alone or in small groups, reviewing sheafs of paper, which he assumed spelled out their spells for them. He had not seen the hall in use since the great day of Ceri's proclamation. For no better reason than that he wandered all the way to the corner by the gallery stair and placed himself directly below the spot where he had hidden that night to watch the birth of the revolution. The crowd then had been bigger, noisier, infinitely drunker—several hundred armed men on benches swilling mead and ale, singing patriotic songs, cheering every word of the speeches. Especially Ceri's speech. *Liberty*! he had declaimed. *Justice! Down with foreign overlords, and foreign taxes. Ancient rights. Ancestral freedoms...*The applause had echoed from the hills and shaken the old ruin to its foundations.

Crazy youthful idealism! With childish trust, young Bevan had believed every word of it. The older, cynical Badger did not and was quite shocked to realize that Ceri might have believed it himself.

Ironhall lectures about Nythia had been straight Chivian propaganda, but some of the ancient knights who moldered in unneeded corners had been knowledgeable and willing to speak out in private conversations. Although he had needed to be cautious in what he admitted knowing, he had enjoyed a talk or two with old Sir Clovis. The snarly old veteran had insisted that Ceri's worst mistake had been his tolerance of those who refused to support him. "Should have chopped off some heads," the old tiger had claimed. "Wiped out the fence-sitters. Gotten everyone behind him."

Ceri would never have done that.

And Ceri would never have done what Owen was doing tonight.

Badger's reverie was interrupted by the arrival of four men-at-arms and the prisoner. Wart was invisible inside a black gown comically too large for him, trailing on the ground. He tripped frequently, but two of the bull-size guards had hold of his arms, almost carrying him. Another led him by a tether, like an animal.

Owen followed them to the octogram, where they pushed the captive down on his knees and tied his leash to the staple. The Prior inspected the knots and then sent the guards out to join Eilir and his pickets. He glanced around the elementary to see who remained.

"Adepts take your places. The rest of you will remain absolutely silent. And do not wander around. This is a long enchantment. If you want to sit, do so now."

Four men and four women took up position within the

octogram, one at each point, all clutching their scripts. Four more adepts, three novices, and five swordsmen remained standing around the walls in ones or twos. No one sat down.

A small fragment of wood bounced off Badger's shoulder and dropped at his feet. Surprised, he looked down and saw others, plus a few larger splinters, a small heap of guano. The old gallery must be about ready to collapse, which would not be unexpected. There might be mice at work....

Was that a very faint *creak*?

How big a mouse did it take to make a floor creak?

There was someone up there.

"Ready?" Owen proclaimed, and cleared his throat. "In your incantations you should find that the words 'the donor, Lord Digby' have been corrected in all cases to 'the donor, King Ambrose.' We think we have caught every instance, but please watch in case we—"

"Wait!" Badger shouted.

He strode over toward Wart without thinking. Or thinking, rather, of so many things at one time that he didn't know which was which. He needed time to work it all out. Owen had been right—there was an ambush, whether Wart knew of it or not. There had to be. *Snake already had men hidden up there in the gallery*! They had bypassed the wards; they were in the compound. Eilir and his men outside were probably under arrest already or just plain dead, if the Old Blades were capable of cutting throats by night. As soon as the adepts began their conjuration, the tigers would pounce on them also.

The cause was already lost. That was an astonishing relief.

"What do think you're doing?" Owen roared.

"You swore there would be no torture!" Badger roared back. "You've left his hands tied. I've seen Ambrose's wrists and they're fat as hams. And the boy still has boots on—they'll crush his feet."

He reached the prisoner and bent to look at him. Wart was obviously uncomfortable, doubled over on his knees with his hands behind his back, folded like a trussed chicken. The jeweled star was pinned on his shoulder.

"Flames!" Owen shouted. "Take off his cursed boots if you want. Leave him tied there, though! And hurry up!"

Badger checked the noose to make sure it was wide enough not to strangle Wart when the sorcery made his neck larger. He drew Ceri's dagger and bent to cut the bonds around the slender, boyish wrists. Remembering Ambrose's, he winced when he saw how the binding had already dug into the flesh.

"Thanks," Wart mumbled. He put his hands on the floor to ease the strain on his back.

Badger went down on one knee to remove Wart's boots. "I'll leave you the knife," he whispered. "Make a break for it when you get the chance." He pulled off the boots and threw them out of the octogram. Then he rose and stalked back to his former place. In the darkness no one had seen him slide the dagger in under the folds of the prisoner's gown.

"If we may now proceed?" Owen said sarcastically. "The words, 'the gifted horn' should have been changed throughout the incantations to 'the gifted star.' Otherwise there are no changes. First canto begins with fire and air in unison. Ready? One, two—"

Badger felt better. Ceri would have applauded what he had just done. Ceri would have detested this perverted, sorcerous vengeance. True, by giving Wart at least a sporting chance in the coming fight, Badger was following the family tradition of treachery, betraying his brother and his oath, but he took comfort in knowing that the cause was hopeless now. He waited tensely for the Blades hiding in the gallery to make their move.

24

Stalwart Stalwart

EMERALD had known some bad moments in her life, especially in the last two weeks, but this had to be the worst ever. She lay facedown in filth whose dust stung her eyes and tickled her nose, so she perpetually needed to sneeze. As a witness to treason, she was in fearful danger. She was already developing cramps, but any attempt to find a more comfortable position wrung squeaks and protests out of the dilapidated structure. Mere breathing seemed almost enough to shake it and send showers of dirt dribbling down through the rotten planks. Now she faced the horrors of the conjuration itself. After spending four years becoming attuned to the subtlest variations in the elements, she would find interrogation on the rack mere child's play compared to witnessing a major enchantment at close quarters.

As the adepts began their invocations, she gingerly raised her head to look. She could not see Badger, but she knew he was standing right below her, because she had almost died of fright when he called out. There were half a dozen men-at-arms scattered around the hall, plus a dozen or so male and female sorcerers. Wart was helpless, a huddled heap in the center of the octogram. That left only her to fight for the right. Bad odds!

Wart was facing toward her, his face invisible under the hood of his robe. She could think of no way to free him and pass him his sword, and even if she could, the odds were impossible, even for him. Light flashed.... What?

Then again.

Apparently no one but Emerald noticed anything—everyone else was intent on the enchantment, and she was looking down, at a very different angle. *Again*! Wart, she realized, was surreptitiously cutting through his tether and the light she was seeing was torchlight reflected from the blade of his knife. How had he gotten hold of a knife? That could have happened only in the few minutes between the time Emerald left him in his cell and the guards' coming to fetch him. His rapier had been too wide for the air hole, but a knife or dagger could have been passed in easily enough.

Who? It could only be Mervyn and his men, no one else. They had arrived already! Perhaps not all of them, just an advance scout or two. She could not imagine how they had passed by the warding spells unnoticed, but if anyone could do it, who else but foresters? So the rest of them would be on their way. Rescue was coming!

By the time she had worked that out, the elementals had begun to answer the enchanters' call and the resulting spirituality drove every other thought from her head. Owen and his accomplices were ripping apart the fabric of the world. The discordance assaulted her senses, blinding, deafening, choking. It skewed all eight elements, violating every principle of balance and harmony, but its main components were love and fire, as the Sisters in the court had reported. Love was elemental in all relationships between people, and forcing one man into an exact replica of another was to forge the closest relationship imaginable. Fire included light and hence vision, and so was required to change his appearance. Air elementals could make him sound like the King, water would reflect his likeness...and so on. As an example of the art of conjury it was a masterpiece, but it was also utter evil.

She felt as if she were being spun around, beaten with iron rods, choked, burned, and frozen, all at the same

time. She needed to scream for them to stop, yet she must
not move a finger. She had never heard of a conjuration so
long and complicated. A single performance would have
taken a couple of hours. But, like all spells, it had to be
recited perfectly, and three times one of the chanters made
a mistake. Each time the Prior cursed and ordered them to
begin again at the beginning.

Where were the foresters? Why didn't they hurry?

By the time Emerald's ordeal ended, a dim light beyond
the windows told of the first tremors of dawn. Even the
sorcerers seemed to welcome the release, for they lapsed
into total silence. In that blissful stillness, she heard birds
tuning up their morning chorus.

Fighting giddiness and nausea, she dared to raise her head
and look. Wart had gone. A much larger man had taken his
place, for the black gown that had flopped so loose around
him now strained across a massively rounded back. A thin
cheer from the sorcerers confirmed that the conjuration had
succeeded.

"Magnificent, brothers and sisters!" the Prior shouted,
hoarse from long chanting. "Gruffydd, go and bring Eilir
and the others so that they may witness this historic justice.
Gather 'round, all of you, and watch the tyrant's execution."
Carrying a huge two-handed broadsword, he marched
forward to the helpless prisoner. The others drew close also.
Man-at-arms Gruffydd headed for the door.

Why were Mervyn's foresters not doing something?
Very gently, trying not to make the gallery shake, Emerald
drew Wart's sword from its scabbard. If somebody did not
do something to save him soon, she would have to watch
him die. Do what, though? All she could think of was to
throw him the rapier. Thoughts of hurling it like a javelin
and impaling the odious Owen were pure wishful thinking.
Having never fenced in her life, she could not hope to rush
down and slaughter five men-at-arms. Most of the adepts
wore swords, as well. Mervyn and his men were going to be
too late, for Wart's life would end as soon as the Prior tired
of gloating. He set the monstrous sword vertically on its

point right in front of the prisoner's eyes. Resting his arms on the wide quillons, he gazed down, feasting his eyes on his victim.

In spite of his wretchedly cramped position, Stalwart had not been idle during the conjuration. Badger's gift of the dagger had put new life into him, or at least some hope of extending his present life. It was wonderful to realize that he had *not* been wrong to trust his friend! Whatever reasons had led Badger to return to Smealey Hole instead of going back to Buran, he was one of the good guys after all. His whispered remark about making a break for it meant that there was going to be a rescue attempt. After some thought, Stalwart had remembered the hints that not all the inhabitants of the Hole were traitors. So Badger had somehow organized a revolt. When the time was ripe, he would give the signal for the loyalists to rise and overthrow mad Owen.

The time did not ripen quickly. While the sorcerers wailed their enchantment, Stalwart surreptitiously sawed through his tether, leaving a few threads intact so it would look right. After a while he began to feel giddy—heart pounding, arms and legs twitching. He thought he was just having cramps until a tightening of his robe warned him that the magic was changing him. He was growing! For years he had been wanting to grow—but not like this. He could feel his belly expanding like a wineskin being filled.

When the chanting stopped, the first light of morning was creeping into the elementary. His head had cleared, but now his cramps were real. He was not at all sure he could stand up without help, or at least a few minutes to stretch his muscles, and the traitors would never allow that. Soon they would notice the almost-severed rope. Why were Badger and his friends not doing something?

He heard Owen summon Eilir and his men. Then a broadsword touched the flagstones in front of him.

"Well, Sir Stalwart?" said the Prior's odious voice. "How does it feel to be a king, mm? I fear we cannot allow you long to enjoy your new status, because we must flush your remains down the Hole before sunup. You did swear to die for your King, didn't you? Aren't you happy to have the chance?"

Chuckling, steadying the sword with one hand, he bent to peer in his victim's face.

With a roar that astonished even him—and was partly a scream of pain—Stalwart sprang up, snapping the last threads of his tether. He grabbed the hilt of the broadsword and simultaneously slashed the dagger at the sorcerer. He would have killed him had his limbs not cramped up on him so much, or had Owen not turned out to be so much *smaller* than he expected. Nevertheless, the Prior squealed and fell back with blood spurting from a gashed arm. Onlookers howled in horror.

"Execution?" King Ambrose's voice thundered through the hall. "If there's to be executions, I'll do the executing." Two-handed, Stalwart swung the broadsword at the conjurer, but again his stiff limbs betrayed him. He stumbled and missed. Owen was already backing away, fumbling to draw the sword that hung at his side.

Boots hammered on the stairs at Emerald's back. The gallery groaned, rocking like a cockleshell in a tidal bore.

Seeing another scythe stroke coming, the Prior dodged, dropped his sword, and fled. The King lumbered after him, swinging the broad-sword around as if it weighed no more than a riding crop.

Man-at-arms Gruffydd bellowed, "Kill him!" and charged. His followers and the armed adepts drew their swords also, but with less enthusiasm.

Emerald turned and saw Badger's horrified face staring at her. The platform began to shift one way and the stair another.

Gruffydd closed with Stalwart and stopped a killer swipe that brushed aside his attempt to parry and practically cut him in half. "One!" roared the King.

Badger howled, "The sword!"

Emerald hurled the rapier to him an instant before the

gallery collapsed. She slid, yelled, clutched at the teetering railing, and then shot down in an avalanche of rotten timber and filth. An explosion of dust shot out, filling the entire elementary with foul and acrid fog.

That saved the day.

For a few minutes everybody was blinded. Badger began yelling a war cry of, "Starkmoor! Starkmoor!" between coughs, and the King took it up. Everyone else was enemy, so the two of them laid about them at will, hunting down and striking every blurred shape. A few voices countered with, "Nythia! Nythia!" but those were rapidly silenced or turned into screams.

Emerald felt safest just lying where she had fallen. Only when she was sure she had not broken any bones did she stand up, choking and weeping. By that time, the battle was over. The last fugitive sorcerers had vanished, taking their wounded. Badger and the King stood in the doorway, howling derision after them.

Three adepts, one novice, and five men-at-arms lay dead on the floor. She noticed that none of the adepts wore the Prior's gold belt. The victims of Wart's butchering broadsword were easily distinguished by their gaping wounds and the pools of blood around them. It seemed only three of the nine had been felled by Badger's surgically precise rapier. The two victors lowered their blades, looked at each other, and then whooped louder than ever. They crashed together in an embrace and a dance of triumph. The King lifted Badger off his feet and swung him around.

Ignoring her bruises, Emerald hobbled over to the capering lunatics at the door. "Wart?"

"Em! Are you all right?"

"Are you Wart?"

"Of course I'm Stalwart." He thumped his prominent belly. "*Exceedingly* stalwart!"

He might think he was Wart. To look at he was King Ambrose—huge and fat and loud, but capable of twirling Badger around like a child without even laying down that broadsword. He filled the sorcerer's gown beyond capacity, for it had split at the shoulders and barely met across his bulging belly, exposing a tangle of reddish fur on his chest. Although he seemed to be unwounded, he was splattered with other men's blood from his bare feet to his bronze beard. His globular face was coated with the foul gray dust, showing red streaks where sweat had run down it. He was gasping and panting, but his piggy little eyes gleamed with triumph. He reeked of the evil sorcery.

"Whoever he is," Badger said, "he wields a broadsword like a rapier. Very nice counter-disengagement on that last exchange, Your Grace."

The King beamed down at him. "Thank you, my boy. You're a deft hand with a rapier when you have to be. We hereby appoint you commander of our personal—"

"Idiots!" she shouted. "There's another dozen swordsmen around somewhere!"

"Well? The lady has a point. Will they fight or run?"

Badger sighed. "Now they have friends to avenge. Owen won't give up."

"I'd hate to think we just won a battle only to lose the war." The voice was the King's, but the note of worry in it was Wart's. "It's not light yet, so we—"

"Look out!" Emerald yelled.

Sergeant Eilir and another man charged out of the twilight. They had donned proper battle gear—breastplates and steel helmets—and they carried shields. With that advantage, those seasoned veterans must have expected to dispose of untried, unarmored boys before they could work up a decent sweat. But their opponents were fresh from four years' training in the world's finest swordsmanship. They jumped forward to confine the attackers in the narrow doorway.

Eilir had put himself on the left so his blind side would be partly covered by his companion's shield. He was a large and powerful man, but he did not compare to King Ambrose. He tried to block Wart's broadsword stroke with his buckler, but the sheer power of the blow sliced it open from the top edge down almost to his arm and made him stagger. The other man parried Badger's rapier successfully, but before he could riposte it flashed back again, stabbing at his groin. While he blocked that stroke, his shield caught on Eilir's shoulder. Badger's next lunge poked deep into his eye. The falling body fouled the Sergeant, who stumbled and was chopped down by Wart.

"Eleven!" roared Wart. "Who's next?"

Emerald grabbed him with both hands and pulled him back into the shadows—the hall was now darker than the yard outside.

"That should slow them down a little," he said, puffing hard.

"Some, but not Owen," Badger said. "Come on!" He ran toward the far end of the hall.

Stalwart lumbered after him, feeling like a moving haystack. Size and strength were an enjoyable novelty, but he had lost his speed and that was not a good exchange. He was in very real danger still, which meant that the King was.

The elementary was too enormous to be defended by only two. Men with axes could easily chop away the rotten logs to enlarge the window slits and make a dozen extra doors. If the traitors just tossed a flaming torch in on the ruins of the gallery and turned the place into a furnace, it would burn like tinder. Would anyone in Waterby have listened to old Mervyn's story? His rescue was not due until dawn, if it came at all. Dawn at the cliff top. It would take him and his companions time to reach the Hall, and Owen might have set guards on the path.

Stalwart followed Emerald into the back room. Badger was already hauling on a brass ring set in the floor, lifting one of the slabs to reveal empty darkness below.

25

Secret Passage

THE hatch thudded shut overhead and cut off all traces of light. Standing at the bottom of the steps, Emerald could not even see Wart right beside her.

"I don't like this!" growled the King's voice. "We're trapped!"

"There's a bolt here," Badger's voice said from the top, "so they can't follow us." His boots tapped softly as he felt his way down. "This is an escape hole; it locks on this side."

"Where does it go?"

"Just out to the riverbank, not far. Give your eyes a moment and you'll see some light, I think."

The air was dank, as if somehow dusty and moldy at the same time. Somewhere water dripped steadily. Emerald enjoyed the solid, safe feeling of a cave. So would Badger, but it would be torture to an air person like Wart.

"This is the secret passage you told us about? And who else knows of it?"

"Only us and one other in the world, I expect," Badger said sadly. "I think this is why the old elementary was never pulled down—the owners, whoever they were, always liked to keep their back door a secret."

"Owen knows of it, you mean. So he'll cut us off."

"He may have forgotten."

"Nonsense!" Wart snarled, and Emerald agreed with him. Owen Smealey would never forget a secret back door.

"Hold on to me," Badger said, "and watch you don't bang your crowned head, Your Grace."

Emerald laid a hand on Wart's shoulder to complete the chain. She thought the cave must be natural originally, but its floor had been smoothed, perhaps paved. The walls felt rough to her touch as she felt her way with her free hand.

"It'll be too light outside to make a run for the hills," Badger murmured, his voice echoing eerily. "We'll have to wait for Mervyn."

"If he ever shows up."

When they rounded a bend and saw a gray shimmer of light on the floor, Stalwart felt a huge rush of relief. He hated this rabbiting around underground.

"Let's sit down and wait," Badger suggested. "We can hold this place against an army."

"No!" Stalwart said. "If I were your sweet brother I'd smoke us out like wasps or bury us alive. I'm going out to have a look." The exit was a narrow shaft sloping steeply upward. He was not even sure he could get his bloated body through that crevice. Ignoring the others' protests, he laid down his broadsword and made the attempt.

It was a very tight squeeze. He had to put his arms ahead of him and wriggle on his belly, but in a moment he scrambled out into a natural alcove in the rocky riverbank. Black and deadly, the swift-flowing Smealey ran twenty feet or so below him. The sky was blue, close to sunrise. To his left he could see upriver, across a wide meadow to distant hills. He assumed the foresters would be coming from the opposite direction if they came at all. His view that way was blocked by a spur of the cliff, but there was a sort of path around it, a very narrow ledge. Normally he could cheerfully have run along that while juggling flaming torches, but at the moment he was a very fat man, made unsteady by an unfamiliar body.

So he went slowly and carefully, watching where he placed his bare feet. He had hardly started when Owen screamed in triumph and jumped him.

He had been waiting just around the corner. As Stalwart staggered under the impact, the madman crushed him in his massive, horseshoe-bending arms. He laughed, hatred burning in his eyes.

"Die, King Ambrose! They'll find you drowned in your bed. Take me with you if you can—I won't care." Owen made to hurl King Ambrose off the ledge.

"I care!" Stalwart bellowed. He twisted and slammed them both against the rocky wall. He was on the outside, of course.

Owen uttered a choking gasp of dismay. He pushed them both away from the jagged surface. Stalwart smashed him back into it again. Panic flickered in the sorcerer's eyes— obviously he had no experience at wrestling bulls. He should have stamped on Stalwart's vulnerable bare feet, but he didn't. When his head and kidneys were ground against the rocks a third time, his grip weakened. Ambrose pounded him bodily against the cliff a fourth time for luck, then prized him loose. He held Owen out over the river and let go. The sorcerer vanished in silence, with barely a splash. Smealey River swallowed another Smealey and flowed on as if nothing had happened.

Alone again, Stalwart leaned back against the rock to catch his breath and wipe the sweat off his face. Even though he was due for a little good luck for a change, that had been an unpleasantly close call. Owen had been in too much of a hurry to reach the exit and block the fugitives' escape, he assumed, and had not waited to round up help, or even a replacement sword.

Meanwhile he hoped the King was not about to have a heart attack. There were certainly advantages in having some weight to throw around. Owen ought to be going over the falls just about now....

But he had won! With Eilir and Owen and so many others dead, the traitors would surely flee now. He must keep himself safe for the King's sake, but surely he could send Badger to rally the loyalists and take over the Hall.

"What are you doing?" Emerald emerged from the cave.

"Just admiring a sunrise I had not expected to—what's that?" He turned to peer upstream. It was not a hunting horn, it was a bugle. Dawn sun flashed off shiny breastplates and helmets; it blazed on flying banners and rainbow plumes. Hooves thundered. A troop of about fifty lancers came galloping across the meadow.

"Rescue!" Emerald yelled. "The King's men!"

"Oh, *pus*!" Wart said. "Pus and *puke*! Yeomen! Household Yeomen!"

Why did *this* have to happen, just when things were going so well?

Ten minutes later, the cavalry was milling around in the yard. The leader, who swung nimbly down from his foaming charger, was not clad in the armor of the Household Yeomen. Nor was he wearing his customary scarlet robes and golden chain, but there was no mistaking his air of authority. He looked around the complex, then strode over to the corpses lying in the door of the elementary. He stopped and stared incredulously as Emerald emerged, stepping over Eilir's body.

"Sister!" Durendal bowed.

Remembering that the filthy rags she was wearing were the remains of a man's costume, not a woman's, she bowed in return. "Welcome to Smealey Hole, Lord Chancellor!"

"Have I arrived too late for the excitement?"

"A few hours earlier would have been preferable." She forced a smile, but she knew that she was on the brink of collapse. "You are a most welcome sight all the same, my lord."

Why and how he came to be leading this troop of lancers did not matter. He was in control now, and all would be well.

Badger stepped out of the shadowed doorway and raised *Sleight* in salute.

It was an article of faith around court in Chivial that

no face was more inscrutable then the Lord Chancellor's. Negotiators from a score of countries and factions could testify that the only emotions he ever displayed were those he chose to display. But his eyebrows did rise as he noted the bloodstains and that tell-tale silver curl. He would certainly recall the long-ago battle outside Waterby that had established his reputation as the greatest Blade of them all. He scowled at the cat's-eye on the hilt of the rapier. He frowned at the blood-smeared face.

"I've seen you before...not Guard..."

"In Ironhall, Lord Chancellor," Emerald said. "May I have the honor of presenting Prime Candidate Badger?"

Badger nodded ironically. "Formerly Bevan Smealey of Smealey Hole. You met some of my brothers once."

Lord Roland definitely let slip a blink of surprise at that news. Then he looked up at the third figure emerging.

History was made. He paled. His eyes bulged. His jaw dropped.

"About time, Chancellor!" boomed King Ambrose. "What kept you, man? We have been seriously inconvenienced by your tardiness. No, don't bother to kneel."

26

The Fall of the House of Smealey

WHEN the story had been told, two lancers the size of fir trees conducted Badger over to a bunkhouse. He fell on the first bed he saw and slept until nightfall, and even then it was only hunger that woke him. Washed, changed, and fed, he began to feel alive again. He hoped that this condition would not be too transient.

Still under guard, he was taken to the office in the residence to face Lord Roland, and on the way there he met a second procession, comprising King Ambrose and another four troopers, although in his case they would be more bodyguards than jailers. Bewilderingly, the King flashed Wart's smile at him. He was still dressed as an adept, in a cowled robe far too small for him. Perhaps there were no clothes in Nythia large enough to fit that king-sized bulk, or perhaps Lord Roland just wanted to keep the famous face concealed as much as possible. Badger was comforted to know that there would be a witness present, because he was well aware that his troubles were far from over. A lot of difficult questions need never be asked if the last of the Smealeys just accidentally fell in the river.

Sister Emerald was already present, seated on a stool,

chatting with the Chancellor across the table. Her baggage must have arrived from Waterby, for she was decked out in the snowy robes and tall hennin of the Sisterhood. She had seemed wrong as a boy, too diffident, although certainly stubborn enough. As a young woman she conveyed confidence and determination, without being in any way unfeminine. Not every bachelor at court was going to crash at her feet, Badger thought, but the toll would be heavy.

The weary, red-eyed Chancellor had certainly not lain abed all day like his visitors. The table's snowdrift of papers had been sorted into piles; the candles were well burned down already. He did not rise when the two men were ushered in; for a moment it seemed they would be left standing. Then two more stools arrived and the door was closed. Four occupants crowded the poky chamber like a beehive.

Roland looked them over. "I was just congratulating Sister Emerald on her courage and loyalty. She is absolutely the only person who comes out of this affair with credit." He shot a pointed glance at Sir Stalwart. "My lady, I have ordered a carriage to take you into Lomouth in the morning, where the Sisters can provide hospitality and further transportation."

"That is very kind of you, my lord." She was not blushing or preening. She had accepted the praise as her due, but she would not let success go to her head—unlike a certain Blade currently present.

"I left strict orders that the transfer of Peachyard to your mother be treated as a matter of urgency. The deeds will be ready by the time you reach Grandon. You do understand that this Smealey affair and your part in it must never become public knowledge?"

Durendal turned to Badger and the smiles ended. "I have more questions for you, Master Smealey."

Badger made himself hold that dark gaze without flinching. "I shall answer them if I can, Your Excellency."

"By accompanying Stalwart from Ironhall, you tacitly put yourself under his command. If you found the situation intolerable, you should have told him so and returned at once to Ironhall. Instead, you accepted his instructions to go and report to Sir Snake. Then you disobeyed. You came here, to Smealey Hole."

Badger nodded. He was determined not to beg for his life. If he had to die on the block like Ceri, he would do it proudly. Honor and duty and loyalty had failed him. Courage was all he had left.

Never changing his piercing stare, Roland continued, "You must have betrayed him to the sorcerers, since they knew the significance of the brooch. But then you gave him a knife so he could free himself. You fought at his side. Will you explain your purposes, when and why you changed your loyalties, and where they lie now?"

Badger shrugged. "Who can say exactly why he does anything? Motives may be very complex, Lord Chancellor."

The great Durendal did not like that answer. "You are a cynic. I have always found duty to be adequate motive."

"Duty? I was brought up to believe that my duty was to kill King Ambrose by any means whatsoever, even at the cost of my own life. My mother made me swear to it on her deathbed."

There was a silence.

"I see," Lord Roland said coldly. "And where lies your duty now?"

Badger had not thought about it. He took a moment to do so. "I cannot see that I have any duty or prospects in Chivial, my lord, so I suppose I must seek those elsewhere— if that option is available to me." That was as close as he would go to asking for mercy.

The Chancellor lifted a paper from a pile and passed it across. It was a declaration by Bevan Smealey, son of the late Baron Modred of Smealey, that he waived all claim to the lands and defunct baronetcy of Smealey, and also any claim that any member of his family had formerly advanced to royal status or the overlordship of Nythia; that he would now quit the realm of Chivial and Nythia with all possible dispatch; that he would never return, nor ever take up arms against the King of Chivial, Prince of Nythia; and that he signed under no duress or compulsion. That last bit was probably only true so long as he did not ask what the alternative was, but it was a shrewdly worded document.

He reached across for a quill, dipped it in the inkwell, and signed.

"Sister," said the Chancellor, "would you be so kind as to sign also, as witness? Thank you." He sifted sand on the ink. "And would you graciously allow Master Smealey to ride in your coach to Lomouth tomorrow? Now the Baelish treaty has been agreed, he should have no trouble finding a ship."

He tossed a purse. Badger caught it and knew by the weight that it held gold. The clouds were lifting faster than he had believed possible. He would live! He was going free! Just for a moment—and because he was a Smealey in Smealey Hole—he wondered if all this might be some sort of trap. But when he looked again at Durendal, even he could not believe that. The man's integrity almost glowed. No one could doubt that he deserved his reputation, or that nine tenths of the government of Chivial was present on the far side of the table.

"Your Excellency is most generous."

Astonishingly, Sister Emerald demurred. She was a very determined young lady. "Surely he may be given a little time to arrange his affairs, Lord Chancellor? Whatever his actions yesterday, Chivial owes him a considerable debt for what he did this morning."

"I have no affairs to settle, my lady," Badger said quickly. "I speak fluent Isilondian; I am an Ironhall-trained swordsman. I shall not starve." And tomorrow he would ask her to halt the coach for a moment beside the hollow tree. He would go forth to seek his fortune with a good sword at his side.

"Then I shall be happy to see you to the docks."

Roland's manner had thawed a little. "Of course you will have a mounted escort tomorrow, Sister, and it will make sure that he does as he has promised. If I may presume to ask one last favor? When you see Master Smealey embark, would you then—and only then—give him this package?"

It was anonymous, wrapped in cloth, but just the right size to be a dagger with a green dragon worked into the hilt.

"You are more than generous, my lord," Badger said thickly. He had hoped for leniency. He had not expected generosity. He had never met it before. He did not know how to deal with it.

Roland's dark stare suggested that he had guessed as much. "As Sister Emerald says, we owe you a debt in the end. I warn you that I will burn this place to the ground before I leave. Not a stone will remain standing, and the land will be included in the royal forest of Brakwood. If there is anything else you wish to take from here, ask now."

He had found the paintings.

Badger hesitated, then said, "Nothing. Burn it all."

The door closed behind Badger and Emerald. Stalwart stayed where he was because he had been told to do so. The next few minutes were going to be tricky and his temporary resemblance to King Ambrose was not going to help him one little bit. Durendal was giving him the basilisk stare treatment. When in doubt, attack...

"May I inquire, my lord, how you managed to arrive so opportunely this morning?"

"No. Do you recognize my authority to give you orders?"

Technically a government minister had absolutely no authority over a Blade in the Royal Guard. This was no time to be technical.

"I will do whatever you say, my lord." There were three, and only three, Blades in the Order he must not address as "brother"—Leader, Grand Master, and the present Lord Chancellor, and he only because he was Durendal, not because of his office.

"Tomorrow," the great man said, "you and your escort will move to one of the royal hunting lodges, and there you will remain until you are yourself again—a matter of a week or so, according to the prisoners. During that time, you will be subject to the orders of Ensign Rolf. You will obey him in every respect, without argument or reservation. Is that clear, Sir Stalwart?"

Stalwart cringed. "A Yeoman?" If the Guard ever heard about this he would be ruined.

Roland's stare had grown even more menacing. "Have I your word on it?"

Sigh! "Yes, my lord."

"Three nights ago I congratulated you on the success of your first mission. I am considerably less impressed by your second."

Stalwart wiped his streaming forehead. His current body did sweat a lot. It was also perpetually hungry. He had eaten two enormous meals and was still starving.

"I may have let my earlier success make me a little overconfident."

"A *little*?"

In Stalwart's considered opinion, he had met with a lot of bad luck, but only a ninny blamed his luck. "I should have listened to Sister Emerald. And yet, in the end, I was right about Badger and she was wrong. I was right to trust him with the message, because I had good reason to think a conventional letter might not arrive. I meant to send a backup letter in the morning, I really did. If we hadn't found the body, I wouldn't have been captured." He waited, hoping to be dismissed.

Roland was not finished. "Before leaving here, you will write a detailed letter of apology to Grand Master."

That was too much! "Grand Master is an incompetent oaf!"

The Chancellor stiffened. "Guardsman, watch your tongue! You are speaking of the senior officer of the Order to which I also have the honor of belonging. If you refuse to apologize to him, then you will write a detailed letter to the King explaining what you just said!"

"Very well!" Wart said recklessly. He was flying now. "I'll do that. I will point out that if Grand Master had bothered to investigate Badger's erratic behavior, he would have realized it was caused by more than a normal dose of seniors' nerves. Then he would have uncovered a conspiracy that would have taken the King's life at the next binding. By removing Badger from Ironhall, I undoubtedly saved—"

"*That was pure luck!*"

Stalwart pulled himself back to ground level. He was the most junior Blade in the kingdom. Who was he to bad-mouth Grand Master? "True! You are quite right, my lord. It was luck."

"If you will promise to keep your opinions to yourself," the great man said warily, "I will waive the letter of apology. His Majesty will be informed of events, of course."

"Thank you, my lord. Have I your permission to withdraw?" Stalwart began to heave his bulk off the stool, planning another trip to the kitchens.

"No. Wait a minute." Lord Roland reached out finger and thumb to snuff a guttering candle. "This affair will never be made public. The ringleaders will be tried in secret and I'm sure many will be executed in secret, too. The rest will be locked up forever. We were all very lucky that His Grace survived this conspiracy. Digby did write a letter."

"And the traitors intercepted it, Badger said."

"He wrote *two* letters. The second one he sent from Buran, on his way home. He was a Blade, after all; not quite the blockhead many people thought him." The great man looked inquiringly at Stalwart.

"Certainly." Stalwart wondered uneasily what had happened to Digby's sword. Better not to mention it.

"You will find...You will learn, as I have, that conspiracy is much less common in this world than plain, brainless incompetence."

"Er...my lord?"

"About two hours after you and Emerald left the palace, I arrived at my office to start a long day's work. I found Lord Digby's name in my appointment book. I made inquiries, of course. I learned that he had tried to see me the day he returned, the day before his death, but I was occupied with arrangements for the reception."

Was it possible that the notoriously impassive Lord Roland was actually looking a little embarrassed?

"Digby did not send his letters to Sir Snake, because he knew the King would disapprove. Having discovered an incompetent sheriff, he wrote posthaste to me. It was absolutely his duty to do that. He also mentioned a curious coincidence about the silver streak in the Prior's hair. That was enough to set my britches on fire, I can tell you!"

Wart stared blankly. "But...?"

"My clerks," the Chancellor said ruefully, "had treated the letter as entirely routine. It was put away for consideration at the regular meeting of the Council next month."

"Ah!" He had good reason to feel embarrassed!

"I sent a courier after you—he missed you, obviously, probably because you went around by Ironhall. Snake and the Old Blades had been chasing their tails looking for octograms until they were all exhausted. I dragged the King out of bed to appoint a new sheriff, commandeered the Yeomen Lancers, and came boiling out here to Nythia to rescue you. As it happened, you didn't really need all that much rescuing..."

Lord Roland broke off to glare at his listener. His fist slammed down on the desk. "I have to put up with that supercilious smirk when the King's behind it. *I don't need to take it from you!*"

"No! No, of course not, my lord!" Stalwart said hastily.

Durendal sighed. "Sometimes even the best of us have to fall back on luck—*brother.*" He smiled as if he meant it.

BOOK THREE

SILVERCLOAK

"Will you walk into my parlor?" said the Spider to the Fly,
"'Tis the prettiest little parlor that ever you did spy.
The way into my parlor is up a winding stair,
And I have many curious things to show when you are there."
"Oh, no, no," said the little Fly, "to ask me is in vain,
"For who goes up your winding stair can ne'er come down again."

—MARY HOWITT
"The Spider and the Fly"

1

The Snakepit

HAVING SPENT A FEW DAYS WITH HER MOTHER at Peachyard, Emerald headed back to her duties in Greymere Palace in the heart of Grandon. Old Wilf, her mother's coachman, was unfamiliar with the city and took a wrong turning in the maze of narrow streets. Thus he found himself in a shabby alley where there was barely room for the horses to pass and he was in danger of banging his head against upper stories projecting out over the roadway. Street urchins jeered at the rich folks going by; hawkers with barrows cursed as they cleared a path for him. Then his passenger slid open the speaking panel in the roof behind him.

"What's this street called?"

"Sorry, miss—er, Sister I mean. Have you out of here in a jiffy."

"I don't want out of here!" she snapped. She had her mother's temper. "I want you to turn around somewhere and drive back along this exact same street again. And I want to know what its name is."

There was no accounting for the lass, and she would bite his ears off if he argued. Seeing a woman leaning out of an upper window just ahead, Wilf tipped his hat to her and inquired the name of the alley as he went by underneath. "Quirk Row," she said, grinning at his predicament.

He made several right turns and eventually managed to retrace his path along Quirk Row. This time the jeering was louder and some of the gutter brats threw squelchy stuff at him and his highly polished paintwork. He cracked his whip at them, but it did no good.

Another edict from the panel: "Go to Ranulf Square."

The coachman sighed. "Yes, miss, er, Sister." Why couldn't she make her mind up?

He had no trouble finding Ranulf Square, for it was one of the more prestigious parts of Grandon, close by Greymere Palace itself. He enjoyed driving along such wide streets, under the great trees, admiring the fine buildings. His pleasure was short-lived.

"Turn right at this corner!" said the voice of doom at his back. "And right again. Slower...Stop here."

"But, Sister!" This street looked very nearly as unsavory as Quirk Row. The windows were both barred and shuttered, the doors iron studded, and the few people in evidence all looked as if they had just escaped from a jail, or even a tomb. "This is not a good area, miss!"

His protests were ignored. Before he could even dismount to lower the steps for her, Sister Emerald threw open the door. Holding up her skirts, she jumped down. Her white robes looked absurdly out of place in this pesthole. She reached back inside for her steeple hat, which was too tall to be worn in a coach, and settled it expertly on her head.

"Go and wait for me back in Ranulf Square," she called up to him, slamming the coach door. "Er...once you've made sure I can get in."

Why would she even want to get in? Spirits knew what might go on behind that sinister façade! But Wilf did as he was bid, watching her run up the steps, waiting until her vigorous pounding of the knocker brought a response. The man who opened the door could not be a servant, for he wore a sword—which usually indicated a gentleman but might not in this neighborhood. He evidently recognized

Emerald, for he bowed gracefully and stepped aside to let her vanish into the darkness of the interior.

Whatever would her mother say? Sighing, Wilf cracked his whip over the team and drove off. He did note the number 10 on the door, and he inquired the name of the road, which turned out to be Amber Street. It meant nothing to him.

It meant nothing to most people.

Most people would not even have realized that these rundown barns backed onto the fine mansions of Ranulf Square. Number 10 Amber Street, for example, was directly behind 17 Ranulf Square, which contained government offices. The brass plates listing these bureaucracies included one saying simply HIS MAJESTY'S COURT OF CONJURY. It was to 17 Ranulf Square that people went to lodge complaints about illegal magic—someone selling curses or love potions or other evils. There the visitors would be interviewed by flunkies whose glassy, fishy stares showed that they were inquisitors, with an enchanted ability to detect falsehoods.

Then files would be opened, depositions taken, reports written. Eventually, if the case seemed worthwhile, a warrant would be issued and the commissioners themselves would raid the elementary. That was when things became exciting. Elementaries might be guarded by watchdogs the size of ponies, doormats that burst into flames underfoot, or other horrors. The commissioners were all knights in the Loyal and Ancient Order of the King's Blades, former members of the Royal Guard and therefore supremely skilled swordsmen.

In her brief career in the palace, Emerald had learned to avoid red tape at all costs. She knew about 10 Amber Street because she had heard the Blades of the Guard refer to it; they called it the Snakepit. Whatever the brass plates of Ranulf Square might say, the Old Blades' real headquarters was here.

The man who let her in said, "Sister Emerald, this is a wonderful surprise," as if he meant it.

She curtseyed. "My pleasure, Sir Chefney." Chefney was Snake's deputy and had been partly responsible for her hair-raising adventures at Quagmarsh. In spite of that, she liked Chefney. He was unfailingly polite and good-humored.

"What brings you to our humble abode, Sister?" "Humble" was pure flattery. The hallway reeked of mildew and dust, the floors were scuffed and splintery, much of the paneling had warped away from the walls, but originally this had been a gracious, rich-person's residence. Somewhere upstairs feet were stamping and metal clinking as swordsmen kept up their fencing skills.

"Someone is performing an enchantment not three streets from here. I detected it as my coach went along Quirk Row."

Anyone else except possibly Mother Superior would have countered with, "Are you *sure?*" Emerald might then have made a snippy retort.

Chefney did not ask if Emerald was sure. He did not produce a form for her to fill in nor summon an inquisitor to interrogate her or a notary to witness her testimony. He did not even inquire what a lady was doing driving along Quirk Row. He just said, "In here, please, Sister," very brusquely. As she stepped through the doorway he shouted, "Put away the dice, lads. We've got work to do."

The long room was almost filled by a very large table. The half dozen men standing around it had not been playing dice. They had been rummaging through a wagonload of books and paper, and there were mutters of relief as they turned to greet her. She recognized Sir Snake and Sir Bram and Sir Demise. She was introduced to Sir Rodden, Sir Raptor, Sir Felix...and so on.

They were all very much alike, men in their thirties, still trim and athletic, neither very tall nor very short; they all moved like hot oil and their eyes were quick. They looked like older brothers of the Blades of the Royal Guard who strutted around the palace in blue and silver livery and were ever eager to squire a young lady to masques, balls, hay rides, fairs, or a dozen other festivities. The main difference to Emerald was that the Old Blades did not reek of hot iron, which was how she perceived the binding spell on the guardsmen.

The formalities were brief, and then Snake did not even ask her to state her business. He just raised his eyebrows. She knew she might be about to make an epochal fool of herself. What she had sensed might have a very innocent explanation. Then these men would all smile politely and thank her and go back to the important work she had just interrupted.

"My coachman took a wrong turning, into Quirk Row. I detected someone conjuring. I made him go back the same way and noted the house, number 25. There shouldn't be an elementary operating this close to the palace, should there?"

She was meddling in matters that did not directly concern her. Her business was watching over the King in whichever palace happened to be his residence at the time. Correct procedure probably required her to report her suspicions to her supervisor, Mother Petal, who would inform Prioress Alder, who would then write a note to Mother Superior herself, who would pass the word down to old Mother Spinel, who handled relations between the Sisters and the Old Blades—red tape!

Snake did not say, "Oh, that's just the so-and-so Sisters of Healing. They mend peoples' teeth." Or, "That's the Brethren of the Occult Word, where courtiers go for their good-luck charms—they're harmless, so we ignore them."

No, Snake's stringy mustache curled in a leer of great delight. "Absolutely not, my lady!" He was as thin as his namesake and about as trustworthy—utterly loyal to the King, of course. Almost too loyal, because he had been known to use very sneaky-snaky means to achieve his ends, as Emerald well knew. "Bram, the map! Raptor, ring the bell!"

The swordsman nearest the fireplace hauled on a rope. Instead of discreet tinkle in a distant kitchen, this produced a startling clangor out in the hallway, like a fire alarm. The muffled tap of fencers' feet overhead was replaced by sounds of an avalanche on the staircase.

By the time another dozen or so men poured in the door, Emerald was bent over a very grubby and dog-eared chart that Sir Bram had spread out over the table litter. Thick swordsmen's fingers pointed for her.

"Ranulf Square."

"We're here."

"That's Quirk Row."

"What does 'seventy-five' mean?"

"It was about here," she said, when they let her do some pointing of her own. "We came along here and then back this way...the elementary's in this building...a green door next to an archway...about here."

"Aha!" said Snake, and spread himself full-length across the table so he could hold a lens over the tiny scribbles. "Number twenty-five. There's the archway, *there*. Hand me a crayon, someone. Leads through to a mews, or a pump court. So one gets you a thousand there's a back door, even if there aren't any secret passages through the cellars. And there's four ways out of the court, see? That's a fine location for a nest of traitors. What's this 'seventy-five' written here for?"

"Sighting report," said a man in the background, rustling paper. "Must have been recent. Someone claimed he—"

"That was me," said a familiar voice. Stalwart squirmed in through the crowd. "I saw Skuldigger."

Snake sat up on the table and crossed his bony legs. "So you said." He had collected ink stains on his silk hose.

Everyone else made eager *go on*! noises. Skuldigger was the maniac sorcerer genius who had created the chimera monsters. Those had killed many Blades, and more than once endangered the King himself. Skuldigger had escaped at Quagmarsh, but every Blade dreamed of adding Skuldigger's head to the trophies above his fire-place.

"Good chance, Em." Stalwart flashed Emerald a joyful smile. They had not seen each other for several weeks and she had forgotten how boyish he looked, especially when surrounded by men twice his age. If he had grown in the last month, she couldn't detect it. His straw-colored hair was not quite as tumbledown shaggy as before, but still absurdly short.

"Good chance to you, Wart. I hear you're still collecting sorcerers' heads to hang on your wall."

"Oh?" he said casually. "Who told you that?"

"The King. He praised you highly."

His face reddened in anger. "Fat Man has a funny way of showing his gratitude."

She had intended to flatter him in front of the others. She had forgotten how much he wanted to be a *real* Blade, a member of the Royal Guard. Valuable though it was, the undercover work he was doing for Snake seemed to him like cheating, and unworthy.

"*Skuldigger*, guardsman!" Snake snarled. "We're waiting!"

"Er, yes, brother. If I'd had my sword with me, I'd have nailed him to a post and called the watch." Wart was not joking; he was deadly when he had to be. "But I didn't. Saw him on Cupmaker Street, heading toward the palace. Two days ago. I followed him. He turned into Long Bacon Road and I lost him near the Silk Traders' Guildhall." Snake started to speak, but Wart drowned him out. "I'm *certain* he didn't see me. And look on the map— There's an alley there leads into that same pump court!"

"So that was a shortcut for him." Snake leaned over to thump Wart on the shoulder. "He was just going the best way home. Well done!"

"So now do you believe me?"

"Do you think I ever doubted you?" Snake asked in outraged tones, scrambling down off the table in a shower of paper and a couple of writing slates.

"Yes."

"What sort of conjuration?" asked a new voice.

The men cleared a way for a tall, elderly lady in White Sister robes and high hennin. Emerald had met Mother Spinel only once, but knew her reputation as a battleaxe second only to Mother Superior herself. Behind her very upright back she was known as "Sister Spinal."

Emerald struggled to recall the elemental spirits she had detected. "Mostly air, my lady, a trace of fire, I think, and maybe some earth, too...I was in a moving carriage...."

Sister Spinal's face had more wrinkles than a basket of walnuts and they all seemed to deepen in disapproval. "Not threatening, then?"

"Um, no, Mother. It gave me no sense of evil."

"Doesn't matter!" Snake snapped. "Unlicensed conjuring near the palace is forbidden and we have a Skuldigger sighting. That's enough. We'll do this the way we did Brandford Priory last week. Sir Dagger, you'll handle the door for us again."

Wart pulled an angry face. "Yes, brother."

"By the time you get there, we'll be in place. If there's no back door, use the front." Snake smirked. "Don't get stepped on!"

Scowling, Wart headed for the door. Emerald noticed grins following him. His earlier exploits had made him a hero, but now the others were treating him as their mascot or water boy. He must hate that.

Snake was barking orders. "Head over there in twos and threes—leisurely stroll, don't hurry, don't dawdle. I want everyone in position when the palace clock chimes three. Chefney, you and Demise take the Quirk archway next to the house itself. Blow your whistle when the kid gets in. They may make a break out the front. Felix and Bram, take Quirk Row on the palace side. Raptor and Grady..." When he had assigned everyone he grinned. "Any questions?"

"What if the kid doesn't force the door?"

"I'll bring a pry bar. Two whistles for that, Chef. Any more questions? No? Then go and get your swords wet!"

Laughing, the men began pouring out of the room, almost jamming up in the corridor.

Snake himself paused in the doorway to look back. "Mother, would you be so kind as to alert Master Nicely— soon but not too soon?"

The old lady seemed to draw herself up even taller. "I certainly will do no such thing. You think we Sisters are kitchen scullions to be sent on errands?"

"Ah, well I did try to keep him informed." Snake vanished. Emerald heard him laughing as the outer door slammed.

"Don't they need a search warrant?"

Mother Spinel coughed disapprovingly. "Not if they can catch them red-handed, and your evidence is good enough for that. Besides, if Sir Snake can just nab Skuldigger, he can count on a royal pardon, no matter what he does. The enchantment you detected—could it have been a language spell?"

"Um, yes! Yes, it could." It could have been several other things, too.

"Interesting." The old lady frowned without explaining why that should be interesting or why she had made such a guess. "And you came straight here, to the Snakepit?"

Emerald braced herself for an ear-roasting tirade on the Importance of Going Through Proper Channels. "Well... yes, my lady. I, er...Yes."

"Very quick thinking! I commend you. Too many young people today just never seem to use their brains. They have *no* initiative! Where did you leave your coach?"

"Oh! I told the man to wait in Ranulf Square."

Mother Spinel rearranged some wrinkles into what was apparently a smile. "I have to go through to the front office and alert the inquisitors. I don't like Master Nicely any better than Snake does, but he should be told. And also the healers, whom Sir Snake tends to forget until it is too late. I expect you want to see the end of this affair? Why don't we ride over to Quirk Row together and help pick up the pieces?"

"That is most kind of you, my lady." This was turning out to be very interesting afternoon.

2

All the King's Men

SIR DAGGER? SPURRED BY FURY, STALWART
bounded up two flights of stairs without drawing breath.
He was unlucky with names. When he was admitted
to Ironhall four years ago, he had chosen to call himself
"Stalwart" and promptly been labeled "Wart." That had not
bothered him too much, it being so like his original name
of Wat, but "stalwart" did not only mean "brave," it also
meant "big and strong" and here he was, four years later,
just turned seventeen and still a *runt*! Understandably, the
Guard had no use for a Sir Stalwart who looked like a puny
kid. Now Snake had picked up Ambrose's infantile joke
about the King's Daggers, so Stalwart was "*Sir Dagger*" all
the time. Big bellylaugh!

He charged into the hot little cubicle that was his personal
piece of the world just now. His precious lute stood in a
corner and a rickety wicker hamper held all the rest of his
worldly goods. He pulled off his baldric and his sword,
Sleight. He laid her carefully under the bed, then began
tearing off his clothes, willfully spraying buttons that he
would have to find and sew on again tonight. *What use was
a swordsman without a sword?*

Spirits, he was a *good* swordsman! He'd been the best in

Ironhall when he was sworn in to the Guard—better than Panther or Orvil or Rufus or Dragon, who had all been senior to him and had been bound that day. It was not because of his swordsmanship that the King had refused to bind him. It was because of his stupid *looks*! He was a better swordsman than most of the Old Blades, even—he could beat Snake with his eyes shut (well, almost). The only men who could outscore him consistently were Chefney and Demise, and they'd both won the King's Cup in their day. Now they were coaching him for next year's tournament, swearing that he was going to come out of nowhere and beat even Deputy Commander Dreadnought, who'd won it for the past two years. One thing Stalwart would not complain about was the fencing instruction he was getting. They worked him to bare bones, day in and day out, but they were making a crack Blade out of him. Chefney said he was already one of the top dozen swordsmen in the *whole world.*

Yet Snake wouldn't let him use his sword in the real fights!

He'd *killed* men, and still they gave him jobs where he couldn't wear his sword.

He threw open the hamper and pulled out a greasy smock, a stinky, tattered thing that left his arms bare and covered the rest of him to the knees. *This* was what he wore these days to serve his King. He'd worn it when the Old Blades raided Brandford Priory, and he'd worn it for three awful days at the Darland Brethren place, working as a kitchen scullion to gather evidence—and bloodcurdling horrible evidence, too. He'd begun his Blade career disguised as a wagon driver, in the Quagmarsh affair, so how could he start complaining now?

It was important work and he'd helped destroy a lot of the King's enemies in the last three months, but he still felt jealous of Orvil and the rest strutting around the palace in their fancy livery. A man needed friends of his own age. All of his were either in the Royal Guard or still back in Ironhall.

He jammed a shapeless cloth hat on his head and slid his feet into wooden shoes. They were surprisingly comfortable and ideal for working in filthy streets and courtyards, but a man couldn't fence in them. He scowled at himself in the mirror. Something wrong? Yes, he was too clean. He ran his fingers along the top of the door and collected a century of dust to smear on his face. He gave his upper lip a double dose and peered closer. There was some faint blond fuzz there, but the dirt didn't really make it any more visible. And now all the world would smell of mouse. Sigh!

Lastly, he took up the feather-stuffed sack he kept in the corner and slung it over his shoulder. It weighed nothing, but back in his days as a minstrel's helper he had learned some miming, so he knew how to make it look heavy. Indistinguishable from hundreds of boys who earned a skimpy living running errands around Grandon, he clattered off down the stairs in his wooden shoes.

Sir Stalwart, member of the Order of the White Star, companion in the Loyal and Ancient Order of the King's Blades, guardsman in the Royal Guard on temporary assignment to the Old Blades, Commissioner of His Majesty's Court of Conjury...reporting for duty, SIR!

As Emerald accompanied Mother Spinel through the bewildering interior maze of the Snakepit, she suddenly detected a strong odor of rotting fish. A moment later their way was blocked by a roly-poly man in unusually gaudy clothes—purple hose, silver boots, gold-striped velvet cloak, and a green-and-scarlet jerkin all puffed and piped and slashed. His smile did not go up to his eyes. His bow barely reached down to his shoulders.

"Sister Emerald! I am delighted to make your acquaintance at last, having heard so much about your exploits."

Having never met the man before, Emerald found herself at a loss for words, an unfamiliar sensation. Although he was not wearing the usual black robes and biretta, she knew he was an inquisitor by the stench of the Dark Chamber's conjuration. And there was no mistaking the unwinking fishy stare.

"Senior Inquisitor Nicely," Mother Spinel explained drily,

"seeks to impress you with his all-seeing wisdom, but in fact his minions keep watch on the door of the Snakepit. I expect your arms are emblazoned on your coach?"

"My lady," Nicely protested, "you will corrupt the fair damsel with your cynicism." He was not merely hatless but also totally hairless, so that his head resembled a polished wooden ball. His eyes had been painted on as an afterthought.

"There are worse ways of being corrupted," Sister Spinal retorted. "I am surprised that you are not taking part in the raid."

"*Raid?*" That was the first time Emerald had seen an inquisitor startled.

"Sir Snake and his merry men are presently storming the illegal elementary at twenty-five Quirk Row."

"I was not informed that there were premises under surveillance at that address."

"Perhaps," Mother Spinel said, with one of her gruesome little smiles, "you should keep closer watch on the enemy and less on your friends."

"Perhaps," Nicely said coldly. He spun around and waddled off the way he had come.

"What is it about inquisitors?" Emerald muttered as they followed.

"They like to make us feel guilty."

"But I have nothing to feel guilty about!"

"To an inquisitor," Mother Spinel said blandly, "that would seem highly suspicious."

The old lady was very effective at getting her way. When they arrived at the musty but grandiose offices of the Court of Conjury, she said, "Why don't you summon your carriage, child, while I roust up a bevy of healers?" and Emerald promptly found herself out on the steps.

There were coaches parked all around Ranulf Square and it took her a moment or two to recognize her mother's on the far side. That was not Wilf's fault, since she had not told him exactly where to wait for her, but now he was deep in gossip with two other coachmen. Street cleaning being a service unknown to the civic fathers of Grandon, and ladies' shoes not being made for walking in mire, Emerald was still frantically waving when Mother Spinel came out to join her on the doorstep.

"Tsk!" the old lady said. She put her head back inside and shouted, "You! Boy!" When an alarmed apprentice appeared, she had Emerald identify her carriage and sent the lad off at a run. Emerald wondered wistfully what would have happened if she had tried that.

But it was fun to see the expression on Wilf's face when he saw the imposing Mother he was to transport, and even more when Emerald ordered him to take them back to 25 Quirk Row.

3

Defeat Snatched from the Jaws of Victory

O NE OF IRONHALL'S BASIC LESSONS, POUNDED into every candidate, was *Know your ground.* Wherever a Blade found himself, he owed it to his ward to be familiar with every bush, puddle, and tree—or street, square, and alley, as the case might be. That, the masters said grimly, was often half the battle. Stalwart had spent many hours walking the streets of Grandon. He knew the archway Emerald had mentioned, leading from Quirk Way to the fetid, gloomy courtyard where the locals pumped their water. He even had a vague recollection of the green door she had pinpointed. As Snake had said, there would be a kitchen exit at the rear of the house.

The map had showed four ways into the yard. He went past the Pepper Street entrance, where Sir Julius and Sir Rodden stood, chatting as if they had just met by chance. Julius flashed him a wink. He turned into Nethergate and went along seven houses until he came to Sir Terror and Sir Torquil in a ferocious argument about some fictitious gambling debt. The entrance beside them would do well, because he would cross the full width of the court to reach his destination. If there happened to be guards watching from a rear window—possible, but not probable—they would note the "errand boy's" approach and not be taken by surprise.

Stalwart trudged through the tunnel and across the cobbles, tilted over as if the sack on his shoulder weighed as much as he did. Buildings four or five stories beetled all around, shutting out the light. The air stank of garbage and urine. Two women gossiping beside the pump ignored him, as did some grubby toddlers stalking pigeons, but excitement was drying his throat and twisting knots in his belly. Chefney and Demise stood in the Quirk Row archway ahead of him; neither seemed to look his way, but a casual gesture from Chefney confirmed that the door Stalwart needed was the one next to the corner. It was comforting to know that two of the world's best swordsmen were close at hand to back him up.

The easiest way to open a locked door, of course, was to arm a husky blacksmith or woodcutter with a sledgehammer and say, "Now!" and then, "Thank you!" For obscure legal reasons, the Crown's lawyers preferred that the door be opened voluntarily. They liked the occupants themselves to admit the King's men, even if the first one in did happen to look like an errand boy.

It had worked at Brandford. A servant girl had opened the door and Stalwart had pushed past her with a shout of "Open in the King's name!" The Old Blades had poured in at his back and most of the enchanters in residence had been arrested while they were still asleep in bed.

If he failed, there were other methods. The inquisitors had a sorcery that would open any door, but the Old Blades did not ask favors of the Dark Chamber unless they absolutely had to. Give those fishy-eyed scorpions an inch and they'd hang you, Snake said. The King had put the Old Blades, not the inquisitors, in charge of the Monster War. Master Nicely and his team were welcome to tidy up later—interrogate prisoners and handle the paperwork.

The door was set back in a shallow alcove. It was made of massive timbers, with a small grille set in it at eye level, and it opened inward, which was good. Still aware that he might be observed, reminding himself that the sack was full of rocks, Stalwart rapped hard with his shoe. He leaned his burden against the wall, to help support it, but in a position where it could be seen through the peephole.

He was just going to kick again when a face peered through the grille...a man's face...quite young, oddly familiar....

"Carrots!" Stalwart yelled. "Brought your carrots."

"You got the wrong house." Even the voice sounded familiar.

"Twenty-five Quirk Row? Bag o' carrots," Stalwart insisted, speaking as if he were straining to hold up the bag. "Someone here paid five groats for these carrots."

"Well, if they're paid for..." A bolt clattered. The door squeaked.

This was the tricky bit. All it needed was one wooden shoe in the door. That mythical blacksmith or woodcutter could have just straight-armed the man out of the way, door and all. Stalwart sorely lacked weight, but what counted was not so much weight itself as how you used it. Most people would throw themselves at the middle of a door, which was useless. The trick was to hit the edge, as far from the hinges as possible. He did have surprise on his side.

He leapt. "*Open in the King's—*"

The door slammed shut, flipping him bodily out into the courtyard. He sprawled flat on his back and his head hit the cobbles with a star-spangled crack.

The blacksmith had been on the wrong side....

A whistle shrilled. Boots splattered in the filth as Chefney and Demise came charging past. Demise jumped right over him. "Open in the King's name!"

Clang! Clink! Clang! The sound of swords clashing jerked Stalwart out of his daze. He was in a sword fight, flat on his back with boots dancing all around him. He scrambled to his feet. Someone screamed. Someone fell. Someone dodged around him and ran. He grabbed Chefney's fallen sword and reeled a few steps after the fugitive. Old Blades came streaming in from all directions. Everything started to spin. Voices...shouting...

Stalwart's knees melted under him and then there were three bodies on the ground.

Hooves clumped, harness jingled, axles squeaked....

"Almost there!" Emerald tried not to sound excited, which she was. Respectable White Sisters must certainly not bounce up and down, either. "I can't detect any sorcery yet, can you, Mother?"

Her companion sniffed disapprovingly. "I detect old meat and fresh sewage. Cats and garlic. But no sorcery."

The coach rattled slowly along as pedestrians grudgingly cleared out of the horses' way. A surprising number of well-dressed young gentlemen had come slumming today, in among the usual shabby residents—Sir Jarvis standing in a shaded doorway, Sir Bram apparently haggling with a pedlar over a string of beads, Sir Raptor and Sir Grady strolling alongside Emerald's carriage. None of them would be visible from number 25.

The coach passed an arch, and Emerald caught a glimpse of a covered walkway and a courtyard beyond. The high note of a whistle stabbed at her ears. Sir Snake appeared from nowhere with Sir Savary and Sir Vermandois beside him, all throwing themselves at the now-familiar green door, beating on it and yelling, "Open in the King's name!"

"Oh, excuse me!" Caught up in the excitement, Emerald grabbed her hat, threw open the carriage door, and jumped out.

Holding up her skirts, ignoring what she might do to her shoes, she ran back to the archway and was almost bowled over by a man who darted out, dodged by her, and vanished into the startled crowd. She caught a whiff of unfamiliar magic, then he was gone.

Snake and four or five others were noisily forcing the green door, while two more Blades went swarming up the front of the building like cats, already past the overhang of the second story. She raced along the alley, footsteps echoing, into the courtyard where two women and a gang of small children were having screaming hysterics.

The backdoor stood open, emitting sounds of shouting. Two men lay facedown. Sir Torquil was helping Wart to his feet. He was filthy, dazed, unsteady on his feet.

"Take him, Sister!" Torquil said, and she grabbed Wart before he fell. "He's banged his head." Torquil ran into the house after the others.

"...'m a'wright," Wart mumbled.

"You're hurt." She tucked her shoulder under his arm to steady him.

He blinked tears. "Chefney's dead. And Demise."

She glanced down at the two corpses and quickly looked away again. There was very little blood. She had seen dead men before, but this was different; she had liked Chefney— he had regretted the need to be devious, unlike Snake, who enjoyed deception. Demise she had barely known.

It was her fault. She should have minded her own business. She had sent these men here to die. "Let's go inside."

"Couldn't help it," Wart muttered. He walked unsteadily, leaning on her; his face was crumpled with grief. "Unarmed! If I'd had *Sleight* with me I could have helped them." He swallowed hard, as if to banish the quaver in his voice. "Em, Chef and Demise were the best we had!"

"How many traitors were there?"

"Just one." His eyes widened. "*Em, there was only one man!*"

"That's impossible," she said, and realized that that was exactly what he was trying to tell her.

"There isn't a swordsman in the world who could best these two together!...'s impossible.... I *saw* it!"

The horror in his face frightened her.

The man running... "He had magic on him," she said. "I didn't see his face, but I'd know the magic again."

The Old Blades had caught the hated Doctor Skuldigger and his horrible wife, Carmine, the renegade White Sister, who was almost as valuable a catch. They and another dozen men and women were sitting on the floor in a front room in glum silence, their hands on their heads. Sir Bram and Sir Grady stood over them holding swords as if they dearly wanted an excuse to use them. Sounds of boots upstairs suggested that the Blades were still completing their search of the house.

Emerald sat Wart down on a stool to recover. She went off, tracking an odor of sorcery into what was normally a kitchen, where an eight-pointed star had been outlined on the flagstones in red paint. No surprise—an octogram must always be on the ground floor. Earth spirits would ignore the summons if it were upstairs, and air elementals would not go underground.

There she found Sir Snake and Mother Spinel, together with Raptor, Felix, and Julius, who were thumbing through papers on a dresser. The ceiling was so low that Mother Spinel had to stoop, so she was not being Sister Spinal at the moment. She favored Emerald with one of her grim little smiles.

"There you are. A second opinion for the commissioners, if you please, Sister. What was the last enchantment performed in here?"

Emerald closed her eyes for a moment to consider the residual taint of enchantment. Air, fire...just what she had sensed in the coach, and there had not been time to perform another conjuration since. "It could have been a memory enhancement, but in that case I'd expect more earth elementals. A language spell does seem most likely, my lady."

"Are you just saying that because I suggested it earlier?"

"No, Mother. But I am not absolutely certain, because this is a very recent octogram, not well seasoned."

Spinel pouted. "Any fool can see that the paint is new." She turned triumphantly to Snake. "A language enchantment has been performed here very recently, within the hour. You see?"

"I don't doubt you, my lady." He had lost his usual cheerful aplomb. He continued to thumb listlessly through a bundle of papers. "So now he can speak perfect Chivian? It doesn't make me feel any better."

The old lady shrugged her narrow shoulders. "Well, you lost him. I'm sure the prisoners have a fair idea of where he's gone and what he looks like. Master Nicely will get the information out of them in short order. You collared Skuldigger! That's what matters."

"What matters is that I lost my two best men! Two very close friends."

The old lady flinched. "I did not know that. I'm sorry."

"No." Snake swung around to peer at Emerald. "What matters is that we almost had Silvercloak and we lost him. And we never even got a decent look at him! Did you?"

Who was Silvercloak? "A man ran past me, coming out of the alley.... He was sheathing his sword as he ran, so he had his head turned away from me. I caught a whiff of sorcery on him, but not strong. I did not get a good look at him."

"I did!" Wart said. He was leaning against the doorjamb, clearly still groggy, although now his pallor suggested fury more than dizziness.

"What did he look like?" Snake demanded.

Wart shrugged. "Very ordinary. Young. Fairish. He seemed familiar, somehow. But I'll know him again when I see him. Who was he?"

Snake threw the papers back on the dresser. "No one knows his real name or where he comes from. He's been called Argènteo or Silbernmantel—Silvercloak."

"A sword for hire," pronounced Master Nicely, mincing in. "The most dangerous assassin in all Eurania, the man who killed the last King of Gevily and the Duke of Doemund. And numerous others. He is deadly, greatly feared, a master of disguise. We at the Office of General Inquiry issued a warning that he was heading for Chivial. In spite of that, you lost him, Sir Snake. His Majesty will not be pleased." Master Nicely was, though.

Snake shot him a look that should have melted all the fat off his bones. "You can have the pleasure of squeezing his plans out of the prisoners. We got Skuldigger."

"A poor second best. You missed the big fish."

"I'd have got him!" Wart shouted. "If I'd had my sword."

"You?" the inquisitor sneered. "When he can take on

Chefney and Demise and kill both of them, you think you would have had a chance, boy?"

"He's right, Wart," Snake said. "Not having your sword with you today was probably the luckiest thing that ever happened to you."

4

Hidden Agenda

NIGHT CAME EARLY IN TENTHMOON AND SUNSET brought a dreary rain that did nothing to brighten the grim mood in the Snakepit. The Old Blades mourned their dead and wondered what sort of foe could slay their two best single-handed. Magically enhanced swordsmen were not unknown, but the Blades had always held them in contempt. The King's Cup was open to all comers, but only Blades had ever won it.

As miserable as anyone, Stalwart decided to take his throbbing head off to bed right after the evening meal. Then Snake informed him tersely that Lord Roland wanted to see him.

This news raised such interesting possibilities that he went up the stairs three at a time, headache forgotten. He had never been inside Greymere Palace, but he was certain that no visitor could reach the Lord Chancellor's office without being seen by the Royal Guard. Hastily he donned the uniform he had kept so carefully pressed and stored for just such an occasion. It had been made for him on his one and only visit to Nocare, another palace, and he had worn it only once, at a private supper with the King. He was delighted to discover that the jerkin had become tight across the shoulders. The sleeves were too short, the hose too tight. He was making progress! He added the four-pointed diamond brooch that marked him as a member of the White Star, the senior order of chivalry in the land. He had never had a chance to flaunt that in public, either. Just wait until Orvil and the rest of the lads saw that!

When he trotted back downstairs, Snake's only comment was a sardonically raised eyebrow. Under his arm he carried two sheathed swords, undoubtedly Chefney's *Pacifier* and Demise's *Chill.* He was wearing full court dress—resplendent, grandiose, and enormously expensive—and notably a star whose *six* points meant he was an officer in the order. Everyone knew about that, but even Felix, who was with him, obviously had not known that Stalwart was a member. His eyes widened.

"When did you collect *that* bauble, brother?"

Wart shrugged. "Couple of months ago." What use was an honor nobody ever saw?

"Congratulations! I couldn't keep quiet about it that long if it were mine."

"King's orders," Stalwart said glumly. He had guessed from Snake's reaction that his hopes of parading star and livery where the Guard would see him were about to be dashed, and he was right. Instead of setting off for the palace, Snake led the way into the back corridors that led through to 17 Ranulf Square. He had not mentioned earlier that this was to be a *secret* meeting.

Emerald, meanwhile, had been hustled back to Greymere to report the afternoon's events directly to Mother Superior, whose obvious displeasure made even the formidable Mother Spinel seem mild and benign.

"*Very* bad news!" she barked. "I cannot assign much of the blame to you, but the consequences may be dire indeed."

The two old ladies then proceeded to cross-examine Emerald at great length on the enchantment she had detected on the killer— mostly fire, some water, and traces of earth and death. There were no greater experts in the

Sisterhood than that pair, but neither of them could recall encountering such a spell in the past or guess what it might accomplish. She suspected they did not believe her analysis of the elements involved.

"*Well!*" Mother Superior concluded, obviously meaning *not well!* "By all accounts, this Silvercloak man is utterly deadly. Inform Mother Petal that from now on you are to be posted in close attendance on His Majesty whenever possible. And if you catch even the *slightest* hint of that sorcery *ever, anywhere*, you are to give the alarm *at once!* Do you understand? Even if you have to scream at the top of your voice in the middle of an ambassadorial reception, you will alert the Blades *instantly!*"

From Emerald's point of view, this was very bad news indeed. Close attendance on the King was always wearing and frequently boring. It involved endless traveling. At this time of year he spent days on end chasing game in the royal forests. Courtiers muttered darkly of cramped and drafty hunting lodges.

Besides, tonight Sir Fury had been going to take her to see a play being acted by the King's Men. Duty came first.

She thanked Mother Superior, curtseyed, and hurried off to assume her new duties.

But that was not to be. She had just changed out of her travel-soiled clothes when she was informed that Lord Chancellor Roland required her presence. She had barely time to write a hasty note to Sir Fury before she and Mother Spinel were rushed away in a carriage, escorted through the rain-filled streets by a dozen Yeomen lancers on white horses. Night was falling.

All the clerks and flunkies had gone home, leaving the offices of the Court of Conjury dark and echoing. The meeting room was a gloomy, deeply shadowed chamber, lit only by the dancing light of candles set on a small table in the center. Two naked swords gleamed there beside them. There were no chairs, because the King believed people sitting down talked too much.

Sir Snake and Sir Felix were already present. Beside them stood a blond young man in Royal Guard livery—Sir Stalwart as Sir Stalwart wanted to be, flaunting his diamond star, a cat's-eye sword slung at his thigh. Emerald smiled at him; he winked and grinned back proudly. Honestly, though, he still looked like a boy dressed up.

A familiar stench of rot warned her who was coming before Master Nicely rolled in, wearing formal black robes and biretta. With him stalked Grand Inquisitor himself, like a gallows taking a stroll. The two of them made an unlikely pair—the squat, tubby Nicely and his enormously tall, elderly superior. The only good thing to be said about Grand Inquisitor was that he made even Nicely seem human.

No one spoke. Inquisitors stared fishily across at Old Blades; Old Blades sneered back at inquisitors. Why was Emerald needed? Her report could hardly be simpler and she could add nothing more to it. She was starting to suspect that there might even be worse things in store than "close attendance upon His Majesty."

The familiar dry odor of hot iron announced the arrival of Blades, in this case Sir Bandit and Sir Dreadnought, who were, respectively, Commander and Deputy Commander of the Guard. Bandit concealed warmth and courtesy behind the bushiest, blackest eyebrows in the realm; Dreadnought was blond and usually brusque. They bowed to the ladies, nodded coldly to the inquisitors, and strolled over to join Snake and his men. Stalwart slapped the pommel of his sword in salute.

"Fiery serpents!" Dreadnought said. "No wonder I can't make the payroll accounts come out even! When were you bound, brother?"

"I'm not." Wart's face had gone wooden in an effort to hide his feelings, but he must be deeply hurt that even the Deputy Commander had not known about the secret guardsman.

"Admitted by special royal edict," Bandit explained.

"I didn't know that was possible!"

"First time for everything. Brother Stalwart has proved

amply worthy. He won that ornament at Quagmarsh, which was his doing—and Sister Emerald's."

Dreadnought saluted each of them in turn. "I am impressed!" He was flaunting a diamond star of his own, which he had won by saving the King from a chimera monster. Very few Blades in history had ever been appointed to the White Star—as Wart had explained to Emerald more than once—and all three of those still living were here in the room: Snake, Stalwart, Dreadnought.

"So am I," Bandit said. "That uniform looks a little snug, guardsman!"

Wart lit up like a tree struck by lightning. "Yes, Leader! I'll order another tomorrow."

The Commander laughed, not unkindly. "Don't be too hasty. His Majesty is very impressed by the work you're doing with the Old Blades. He wants to keep you under wraps a little longer."

Wart deflated with a sigh. "Yes, Leader."

A click as the door closed turned all eyes to the impressive figure in crimson robes standing there, looking over the company as if counting. When he headed for the table, everyone else bowed, curtseyed, or saluted, as appropriate. Lord Chancellor Roland was another knight in the Loyal and Ancient Order of the King's Blades, the former Sir Durendal. He wore a cat's-eye sword and a diamond-studded brooch alongside his gold chain of office—an *eight*-pointed star. Emerald had forgotten to count him. He was a full companion in the White Star, the highest rank possible. It went with the job of being the King's first minister, head of the government.

For a moment he stared down in silence at the two swords, shaking his head sadly. No one spoke—Roland had the knack of being the center of any room he was in. Everyone else had become pupils before a teacher.

"I hereby give notice," the Lord Chancellor said, "that these proceedings are Deep Counsel as defined in the Offences Against the Crown Act. That means that any mention of them after the meeting ends is automatically classed as high treason unless you can prove that His Majesty's safety required you to speak. That includes mention to anyone else who was present."

He allowed a moment for that dread pronouncement to sink in.

"Let us begin with a quick review of the facts. Sir Snake, will you outline this afternoon's events?"

Snake spoke swiftly, tersely. He began with Emerald's arrival at the Snakepit, went through to the prisoners being formally assigned to the inquisitors, and then doubled back. "The door was magically booby-trapped. Stalwart is no ox, but none of us could throw him around like a pinch of salt. The felon then slew Demise and Chefney and escaped into Quirk Row. Unfortunately Sir Torquil and Sir—"

"Who saw the killer?" Roland must know the answer; he wanted it to be a matter of record. It was soon established that Stalwart was the only one who would be able to recognize the man again. Torquil, Julius, and the rest had seen only his back as he fled and could not even agree whether he had been left-handed or right-handed—a matter of much concern to swordsmen. Even Emerald, who was now called upon to describe her encounter, had not seen his face.

"Just a young man in a pale-colored cloak and a floppy hat. I would know his magic, again, though. It was unusual—fire and water, mostly."

"A disguise spell?"

"Not like any that I was taught to recognize at Oakendown."

"Young, you said. He moved nimbly, I assume, like a swordsman?"

Emerald hesitated.

"Take your time, Sister," Lord Roland prompted gently. "If you have more to contribute, we are anxious to hear it."

"There *was* something…odd about the way he moved, my lord." She could not place it. "Sir Stalwart said he seemed familiar, and I felt the same."

"Interesting! It might be helpful if you two prepared a list of all the people you have both met on your adventures. That might trigger memories."

The Lord Chancellor paused, and the room waited. Emerald wondered why Wart was looking so almighty pleased with himself all of a sudden. Eventually she worked it out. She was the only Sister who might hope to recognize the notorious assassin by the enchantment he used, and only Wart had glimpsed his face. So Wart, too, was going to be posted in close attendance on the King from now on. His days of undercover work were over and he would be moving his lute to the palace at the close of this meeting.

Roland sighed. "We are dealing with most potent sorcery! I am not without knowledge of fencing myself"—the Blades grinned widely—"and I assure all of you that, even years ago, when I was in my prime, I could not have disposed of Demise and Chefney together like that. So we have two of the King's men slain and an illegal octogram. We can be certain that heads will roll or necks stretch."

"Let us hope that royal blood does not flow!" Master Nicely said. "Had Snake followed proper procedures instead of rushing off in the pursuit of personal reputation, this catastrophe would never have happened."

The temperature in the room shot upward. Snake's bony features flamed red. His hand went to his sword. "It was not my reputation that concerned me, Inquisitor. That is safe enough. It was security."

"You need not shout," Nicely retorted, although Snake had barely raised his voice. "You are accusing someone of treason?"

"Keep personalities out of this!" Lord Roland said. "But if you have charges to bring, Sir Snake, we'd better hear them."

Snake must be in considerable trouble if even his friend Roland was taking that tone with him. Emerald wondered just how angry the King was over the day's events. Oh, *why* had she not minded her own business?

"We know the conspirators have spies at court," Snake growled, glaring at Nicely. "We also know that the Dark Chamber employs more sorcerers than even the Royal College of Conjury. I suspect that some are not above doing favors for old school friends. Or accepting some of their ill-gotten gold. If we had followed the rule book as you suggest, I'm sure we would have found twenty-five Quirk Row an empty shell."

"You may be sure, but have you evidence to persuade others of your lies and slanders?"

"Yes I do. You take charge of all prisoners. Explain to me why three of the men we arrested today are men we have arrested before? Did they receive royal pardons? Or did they *buy* their release from their jailers?"

The inquisitors' fishy stares gave no clue to what they were thinking. No one liked inquisitors, but very few people dared quarrel with them openly like this. The idea that the Dark Chamber might betray the King was terrifying—who could call it to account?

"Is this true, Grand Inquisitor?" the Chancellor demanded.

The gaunt old man displayed long yellow teeth in what could only loosely be termed a smile. "Five days ago we released several suspects—two who had been arrested at Quagmarsh and three from Bosely Down. There was, in the justices' opinion, insufficient evidence to proceed with their cases."

"*Insufficient evidence?*" Snake howled. "That is the most—"

"Wait! Continue, Grand Inquisitor."

"Thank you, Excellency. Two of them had agreed to turn King's evidence and we believed they would be reliable informants, since we still have their families in custody...for their own safety, of course. The other men were being most carefully tracked."

"You are telling me that you had this nest of traitors under surveillance? You had not informed me of this, nor Sir Snake, apparently. Is His Majesty aware of these double agents of yours?"

After the slightest of hesitations..."I did inform him, yes. Verbally. Perhaps hastily, as he was occupied at the time in—"

"I have warned you before, Grand Inquisitor," Lord

Roland said sharply, "that your reports are to be made in writing and passed through me. Anything you tell His Grace in conversation you are to write down promptly and submit to me. We shall pursue this matter further tomorrow. If you have been subverting criminals with promises of royal pardons, I shall expect to see your authority to do so. Meanwhile, what have you learned from the prisoners taken today?"

"Little so far. The persons apprehended..." Inquisitors' memories were magically enhanced, and the gaunt old man rattled off a score of names without hesitation. Emerald recognized only those of Skuldigger and his wife. "Of course it took us some time to locate His Majesty and obtain the royal seal on the necessary warrant. And the Question is a lengthy conjuration." He glanced around the circle, peering down at everyone as if curious to know who shuddered or grimaced at this mention of the most horrible of sorceries.

"So far we have used it only on the prisoner Skuldigger. He had just begun talking when I left to come here. It will be many days before he can *stop* talking, of course."

"And what was he saying?" the Chancellor asked with distaste.

"Much as we surmised, Excellency. The traitor sorcerers, having decided that their efforts to kill the King by magic were meeting with little success, banded together to hire the notorious assassin Silvercloak. He arrived in Grandon in an Isilondian ship this morning. He was taken to the hideaway on Quirk Row and made fluent in Chivian; that was the sorcery the girl detected. He probably answered the boy's knock on the door just to practice his new skill."

"And what of his plans?"

"Skuldigger knows nothing of them. Silvercloak works alone and keeps his methods secret."

"But he works for money," the Chancellor said. "Now we have captured those who hired him, he cannot hope to collect whatever fee he was promised. Surely he will simply give up and go home, back to wherever he came from?"

Again Emerald had the odd impression that Lord Roland

was asking questions to which he already knew the answer. So who was he trying to impress?

Again she wondered what she was doing here—and Wart also. They did not belong in an emergency meeting of senior ministers.

Then she wondered if those two questions were somehow related.

Inquisitor Nicely replied. "Only two things are generally known about Silvercloak. One is his reputation. He has never failed. None of his chosen victims has ever survived, and he will not want to make an exception in this case. That would be bad for business. The other open secret is that his agents are the notorious House of Mendaccia in Porta Riacha, the most secretive of bankers. Skuldigger and his fellow conspirators deposited an immense sum of money— two hundred thousand Hyrian ducats—with the Mendaccia. It will be paid to Silvercloak if His Majesty dies by Long Night."

Emerald calculated, and no doubt everyone else did so also. This was a thirteen-moon year, so there were still almost ten weeks left in it for the killer to earn his blood money.

Lord Roland nodded as if satisfied with the way the script was being followed. "Leader, we must assume that His Grace is in grave peril."

"His Grace is spitting fire!" Bandit said glumly.

"You are taking all possible precautions?"

"All *reasonable* precautions, my lord."

There were persistent rumors that when the monsters started coming in the windows of the royal bedroom on the Night of Dogs, Roland, who had then been Commander Durendal, had locked his sovereign lord in the toilet. But Roland was exceptional; if Bandit tried that he would be beheaded. Emerald knew how disinclined Ambrose was to take precautions or put up with restrictions on his movements. Kings did not hide, he insisted. The Blades grumbled that he had more courage than brains and made their work much harder than it should be, but they loved him for it.

"Are there any additional measures we could take to increase the King's safety?"

"Certainly," said Master Nicely. "The Royal Guard may be adequate protection under normal circumstances, but it is obviously not capable of dealing with the world's most deadly assassin. Today Silvercloak showed he could dispose of two of the highest-ranked Blades with no difficulty whatsoever."

Lord Roland frowned. "What are you suggesting?"

"Dogs. As I have previously informed Your Excellency, we can provide a pack of trained and magically enhanced hounds guaranteed to stop any swordsman. Much more effective guardians."

The Blades and Old Blades all growled angrily. Nicely smirked.

"And the answer remains the same," said the Chancellor sharply. "His Majesty refuses to consider the idea. He will not have monsters eating his Blades, he says."

"Or his inquisitors?" said Felix. "Hard to keep a dog away from carrion."

"Snake, if you cannot keep your man quiet, send him home!"

Coming from the great Durendal, that rebuke was enough to turn Felix's face bone white. The Chancellor went back to business.

"Leader, I hope you are taking especial care that His Grace's plans are never announced in advance?"

"Standard procedure, my lord. Our best defense against assassins is always to prevent them from knowing where His Majesty will be or when he—"

"*Ironhall?*"

This time the interruption came from Wart. Perhaps he had not meant to speak aloud, because he blushed when everyone turned to stare at him.

"You have a comment, guardsman?" The Chancellor's voice was a stiletto dipped in honey, but even he could not intimidate Wart when he had a bright idea to suggest.

"Ironhall, my lord. Fat M— His Grace has been going

down to Ironhall to harvest seniors every two months ever since the Night of Dogs, and he's overdue. It's almost three months since I was, er, not bound." His eyes gleamed. Ironhall rules said that candidates must be bound in order of seniority, so the next man up should still be Wart— assuming the King chose to play by the rules, which kings did not always do.

"An interesting point, brother. It is indeed likely that the King will choose to go to Ironhall in the near future. Right, Leader?"

Frowning, Bandit nodded. "Grand Master reports a good crop ready, and spirits know I can use the men!"

"But if his visit is so predictable—no offense intended, Brother Stalwart—then we must take extra care that his enemies do not take advantage of it."

"My lord!" Sir Dreadnought protested. "*Ironhall?* Surely the King is safer there than anywhere?"

"Mm? What do you think, Master Nicely? You've studied Silvercloak's methods."

The tubby inquisitor pursed his fat lips. "How many people live there?" No inquisitors, of course. Probably no inquisitor had ever set foot in the school.

"It varies. Do you know the present tally, Sir Bandit?"

"One hundred and ten boys just now, my lord. Fifteen masters and about a score of other knights—several of them in their dotage—and roughly as many servants. But everyone there knows everyone else. A stranger would stand out like a full-grown lion. And it's all alone on Starkmoor, leagues from anywhere; an assassin could not hope to escape afterward."

"And the Guard goes there when the King does," Dreadnought added.

"True." The Chancellor turned. "You want to continue this argument, Sir Stalwart?"

Wart blushed even redder. "I apologize, my lord. I spoke without thinking."

Emerald knew that Wart knew there had already been a plot—another plot altogether—to kill King Ambrose on his next visit to Ironhall. He had uncovered it by accident and thwarted it, but only the two of them and Lord Roland were aware of it. Perhaps the King had been told, but almost certainly no one else, even the most important people in this room. Apparently Lord Roland did not consider the information relevant.

"If no one has any other suggestions," he said, "we can adjourn. I remind you again how secret these proceedings are; I charge you all to be especially vigilant in the face of this terrible threat to His Majesty. If you have any suspicions at all, pray do not hesitate to inform me or Commander Bandit."

Emerald glanced around the room and saw her surprise reflected everywhere. Why had this secret meeting been called? It seemed to have achieved nothing. Lord Roland was a very clever man, not the sort to waste people's time to no purpose.

What was he up to?

5

Stalwart to the Fore

THE FOLLOWING AFTERNOON STALWART WENT to the Snakepit fencing room for his usual workout, but it wasn't the same without Chefney or Demise. No one else could give him a fair match. Only Dreadnought and some of the other crackerjacks in the Royal Guard were in his class now, and they were off-limits for him. He had just put away his foil in disgust when Snake appeared in the doorway and beckoned him out.

His hat and cloak were damp; he smelled of wet horse. "I want your warrant, Wart," he said brusquely.

Stalwart almost said, *What?* like a dummy, but remembered in time that Blades did not question orders. "Yes, brother."

He scampered up the stairs. His commission in the Court of Conjury was an imposing piece of paper bearing the royal seal. It gave him enormous authority. Why was he losing it now? Was he being discharged from the Old Blades at last?

The attics were silent and deserted—but there was a faint odor of wet horse up there, too. The door to his cubicle was ajar. He had left it closed. Warily, wishing he had a sword with him, he stood back and kicked it wide. A man in nondescript, drab-colored clothes was sitting on his bed. Astonished, Stalwart opened his mouth—

Lord Chancellor Roland said, "Sh! Come in. Leave it open a little so I can keep an eye on the stairs. Sit down."

Bewildered, Stalwart perched on the clothes hamper, hoping it would not collapse under him. The great man was smiling, which was a good sign.

"At a recent meeting I mustn't mention, you made a suggestion I won't describe."

"And was shown my folly in speaking out of turn, my lord."

"No." Lord Chancellors could even grin, apparently. "I apologize for snubbing you. Your idea was brilliant. I didn't expect anyone to see that opportunity. I stamped on you because I didn't want it taken seriously."

Again Stalwart swallowed a *What*!? "Thank you, my lord." Then he realized the implications. "You think there were *traitors*—"

"No." Durendal turned serious. "But the danger to His Majesty is so extreme that I do not intend to take *anyone* into my full confidence. Even honest people can be overheard or speak without thinking. I have a job for you if you think you can handle it."

Stalwart could feel a smile creeping over his face, despite his best efforts to remain solemn. "Identify the killer, my lord?" He was going into the Guard at last!

"No." The Chancellor frowned. "You expect me to set you at the King's elbow to shout if the assassin approaches? You haven't thought it through, Stalwart. Put yourself in Silvercloak's place. He has only nine weeks or so to fulfill his contract. He may have some accomplices we don't know about, but in the end he will act alone, because he always does. Now do you see what you missed?"

"Er…" It was very flattering to be asked to give an opinion, and very humiliating to feel so stupid. Lord Roland had the reputation of being as fast with his wits as he was with a sword.

"Where does he begin?" the Chancellor prompted.

"Ah!" *Got it*! "He scouts the ground, of course! He'll watch what the King does, where he goes, how he rides out in public, how he leaves the palace. And if he sees *me* with him all the time—"

"Then he kills you first. Or he finds a way around you. You know his face, but he knows yours, too. Not many errand boys issue commands in the King's name."

"So what do I do instead, my lord?" The hamper under him seemed to sense his excitement, for it creaked alarmingly.

"I want to put you in the front line. No one—absolutely no one, not even Leader or the King—knows about this. You are to turn in your present commission to Snake, but Commander Bandit has agreed to assign you to Chancery for a special duty. Will you take my word for that? We haven't had time to do the paperwork and there probably isn't a proper procedure anyway."

"I am honored to be under your command, Your Excellency." Confidential aide to the great Durendal? This was trust indeed. What man could possibly refuse such an adventure?

"Glad to have you." Roland flipped a leather purse at him. "Expenses."

Stalwart caught it; it was heavy and clinked. He felt the belly thrill of excitement that came at the beginning of a new quest. "For?"

"Hasten over to Sycamore Market and dress yourself as a stableman."

"A gentleman's hand or just a churl?"

The Chancellor chuckled. "How about a well-paid, well-tipped, assistant hostler who sells his employer's oats out the back door and short-changes the customers? Throw in an extra shirt. You may be gone some time."

At least Stalwart would not be shivering in rags, but he still wasn't going to be a Blade. His disappointment must have shown, because his visitor snapped, "You *do* want to see Chef and Demise avenged, don't you?"

"*Yes*, my lord!"

"I'm offering you first shot at the killer. I want you to

catch Silvercloak for me. Do that, my lad—" Lord Roland smiled "—and you'll be a hero to the Blades for the rest of your born days. Now, do you want the job?"

"*Yes, my lord!*"

"Then head out as soon as you've collected your gear. You can make a few leagues before dark."

"Can I wear my sword?"

"On the journey, yes. Now listen. The King will be going to Ironhall very soon, as you guessed. And despite what Leader and Grand Inquisitor and the King and everyone except you and me think, my guess is that Silvercloak will follow—or even be there waiting."

He paused, waiting for comment. Testing.

"He may go by stagecoach, or he may ride," Stalwart said cautiously. "It's too far for a single horse, so if he rides, he will need fresh mounts on the way. And if he goes by coach… *Yes!* Either way he'll have to visit posting houses."

The Chancellor was smiling and nodding. "But which posting houses?"

"He's a foreigner. He doesn't know the roads. He may go by coach as far as he can, which means…The nearest the stage would take him is…Holmgarth? And if he's riding, he'll need a remount after that long stretch from Flaskbury….
Yes! Holmgarth, my lord?"

"Very well done! You worked it out faster than I did. It's not quite certain. He may see the danger and take a roundabout route. Because, Brother Stalwart—and remember this always—*Silvercloak is the smartest person you have ever met*! Repeat that to yourself once every hour, twice when you go to bed, and three times when you get up in the morning. *Never* underestimate him! Your life will depend on it. If he does slip up and go by way of Holmgarth—"

"I'll be there?"

Durendal nodded. "You'll be there."

The hamper creaked as Stalwart scrambled to his feet, too excited to stay seated. "When I see him I challenge?"

"No. You're too precious and he's too deadly."

"But—" *Wait for the rest of your orders, stupid.*

"But you won't have the Old Blades to back you up this time. No Royal Guard, no Household Yeomen. I could give you any of those, Stalwart, but if I try hiding a dozen armed men behind hay bales in the stables, the whole town will know. Sure as death, Silvercloak will get word of it somehow. I don't want to scare him away! If he takes fright we'll lose him, and he'll strike at some other time and place."

Stalwart nodded doubtfully. He thought the Chancellor was carrying respect for his enemy to absurd lengths.

"We are laying a trap for the smartest man, remember?"

"Yes, my lord. And the deadliest swordsman. So what do I do if I see him?" *Hit him with a shovel?*

The Chancellor shrugged. "That's up to you. A long time ago the King taught me that when you send a man to do a job, you tell him what you want done and let him work out how to do it. If I try to direct you at this distance I'll get it all wrong. You'll be the man on the spot—you decide what to do."

"I appreciate the trust you place in me, my lord." Unless there was more to come, Stalwart was hopelessly out of his depth.

The great man chuckled and produced a sealed packet. "Take this letter to Sir Tancred in Holmgarth. He's a knight in our order but an old man now—he was Leader back in the reign of Ambrose III. After his stint in the Guard he ran the Holmgarth posting house for many years. His sons and grandsons run it now. He was also the county sheriff until his health began to fail this summer. I'm letting his son try out for the job, so he ought to be eager to show his mettle by helping you."

Sheriffs could call out militia. Stalwart would not be alone.

"Without mentioning Silvercloak by name, I've told Tancred about Chefney and Demise and the danger to the King. I've ordered him to give you any help you want. Work out a plan—and let me know what it is. I want a detailed report from you every day by the eastbound stage, understand? Even if you have nothing new to report."

"Yes, my lord."

"Are you familiar with that posting house?"

"I've been through there a couple of times."

"Very solidly built." Lord Roland smiled. "You'll see what I mean. And stablemen are a tough lot. Organize your reception for Silvercloak so that the moment you see him— snap! Just don't let him see you first, or you'll be one more name in the *Litany of Heroes*. And I don't want a dozen dead stableboys, either."

"No, my lord."

"Any questions?"

There must be a million questions. "He may have magic tricks?"

"I'm certain he does."

"I have authority to kill him if necessary?"

"Certainly." Then Lord Roland sighed. "But if you do, for spirits' sake be sure you've got the right man! You can't say 'sorry' if you haven't." He waited for the next question.

Stalwart could not think of a single one, which was frightening. He was probably too stupid to see the difficulties until they were on top of him.

Lord Roland said softly, "This may be the toughest assignment I've ever given anyone. Your record is so impressive that you've earned the right to be lead horse on this one, but if you want me to put an older man in charge to take the heat off you, I'll do that. I won't think any less of you for asking. Knowing your own limitations is not cowardice. And sending a boy to do a man's job isn't smart. Is that what I'm doing?"

Stalwart squared his shoulders, wishing they were just a little broader. "No, my lord. I can handle this. If the killer comes through Holmgarth, I'll get him for you."

6

Stalmart at His Post

*Done by my hand at Holmgarth Posthouse,
this 22nd day of Tenthmoon, in the year of
Ranulf, 368.*

With humble salutations...
Stalwart dipped his quill in the inkwell and sighed. He
had barely begun his job and the eastbound stage left in an
hour. He was writing his first report. He would rather duel
to the death any day.

*Pursuant to Your Excellency's instructions, I made haste
to Holmgarth. I arrived late last night. I gave your warrant
to Sir Tancred. The noble knight offered most gracious aid.*

The old man was frail now, but his mind was still sharp.
He had already retired, for the hour had been late, and he
had looked with deep suspicion on the exhausted juvenile
vagabond who came staggering into his bedchamber,
dripping mud and flaunting a cat's-eye sword. The moment
he finished reading the Chancellor's letter, though, he had
ordered food and drink for his visitor. He had summoned
his two sons and directed them to do anything the stranger
said, without argument or delay. The elder, Elred, was
courteous and silver-haired, keeper of the inn adjoining the

stable. Sherwin was a rougher character; he ran the livery business and was also the county sheriff. Stalwart would be dealing more with him.

After a solid night's sleep, he was just starting work, so what more could he possibly put in his report?

I can easily observe horsemen arriving in the stables. But the stagecoach and private carriages usually stop at the post inn to disembark passengers before entering the yard.

Perhaps he should not whine about his problems, but he was proud of the solution he had discovered for this one, and it would show Lord Roland that he had achieved something already.

I asked the innkeeper to hire workmen to tear down and rebuild his porch. This construction blocks the front entrance to the inn. Now all traffic will come first into the yard and stop at the rear door. I most humbly request that your lordship will approve the expense.

A simple two-day carpentry job might have to be dragged out for weeks. If they made Stalwart pay for it out of his Guard wages, he would be poverty-stricken for the next hundred years.

Another clatter of hooves brought his head up as a two-horse gig clattered and squeaked past his window. The passenger was an elderly, plump woman, but he kept watching until he had a clear view of her driver—Silvercloak would not sneak past *him* disguised as a servant!

Two horsemen rode in, three departed. Another carriage... The post yard was still shadowed but starting to bustle as the sun came over the walls. Men and boys were walking horses, feeding them, currying them, mucking out stables, wheeling barrows, saddling, harnessing. Their breath showed white in the morning chill, and fresh dung on the paving stones steamed. There had been ice on the water troughs at dawn. A farrier's hammer clinked.

Standing at an important crossroads, Holmgarth was one of the busiest posthouses in all Chivial, employing scores of people. Every day hundreds of horsemen hired remounts there and a dozen coaches changed teams. The

King boarded horses there for his couriers and the Blades. As if to demonstrate, a horn blew in the distance and men started running. Moments later a royal courier thundered in past Stalwart's window. By then a horse had been led out and was being saddled up for him. In moments he went galloping out through the archway again. *Show-off!*

Could Silvercloak disguise himself as a courier—or even a *Blade?*

The yard was large enough to hold two stagecoaches and their eight-horse teams. It was shaped like a letter *E*, its east side the back of the inn, and three long alleys leading off to the west, flanked by rows of stalls. There was only one gate and the walls were high, because valuable horses must be well guarded.

In tomorrow's report, I shall describe to your lordship my arrangements for catching the

Sir Stalwart pondered a good way to spell "malefactor" and wrote "felon" instead. He had no idea yet what those arrangements were going to be. The iron-barred window of the cashier's office was right by the yard entrance, designed to give a clear view of anyone trying to sneak a horse out without paying. The cashier on duty was Mistress Gleda, Sherwin's wife—a plump, ferocious-looking woman with a visible mustache and a deep distrust of this upstart boy who had taken over half her worktable. Fortunately she was kept busy handling money and tokens brought to the window. Keeping track of all the horses going in and out must be a huge job.

If she was asked, Stalwart was her nephew, visiting dear Aunt Gleda.

This seat gave him a clear view of anyone arriving. So far so good. He would certainly see Silvercloak if he came, but putting a collar on him was going to be a lot harder. To sound an alarm—ring a bell, say—would alert the quarry as much as the posse. Then the quarry would either escape again or cause a bloodbath.

Roland had dropped a hint—

As your lordship graciously advised, these stables are built of solid masonry. Any stall could serve as a cell.

But if Silvercloak was so smart, how could he be lured inside and locked in—alone, with no hostage to threaten? The answers would have to wait for tomorrow's report. Lord Roland would understand that there had been no time to write more in this one. Now to sign it and then seal it. Blades used the inscription on their swords as their seals. Stalwart's was ꜱⱭⱢⱯⱭ— in mirrorwriting, of course.

The door at his back creaked open, and the office was suddenly full of Sherwin. The Sheriff's well-worn leathers bulged over the largest barrel belly Stalwart had ever met, even larger than the King's. He had the biggest hands, too, and a jet-black beard fit to stuff a pillow. At his back came a rangy man, younger and clean-shaven.

"This here's Norton," the big man growled. "Nephew. Can't find me, talk to him. He'll be your sergeant, like. *This* is Sir Stalwart, Norton." He made that last remark seem surprising.

Stalwart rose and offered a hand to the newcomer, whose horny grip did not crush as it might have done. "Please don't use that title, not ever. My friends call me Wart."

"'Pimple' would be better," said Sherwin, looming over him like a thunderstorm. He had very dark, very glittery eyes. His face—the part visible above the undergrowth— was deeply pitted with old acne scars.

"Looks like you know more about pimples than I do. Glad to have your help, Master Norton."

Norton just nodded, but he had not disapproved of the pimple riposte. Sherwin's wife sniffed in an amused sort of way, and Sherwin showed no offense. Perhaps he had just been testing a little.

"We picked out seventeen men for you," he said, "all good lads in a roughhouse."

"Not outsiders?" Stalwart sat down to show that he was in charge.

"You already said you didn't want outsiders. They all

work here. Some all the time, some sometimes. I'm not stupid, sonny."

"Will they keep the secret?"

"I don't *hire* stupids, either. You want all of us on duty every day, all day? King'll pay for that?"

Oh, why, why, why had Stalwart not asked Lord Roland how much money he could spend?

"We'll work something out."

"Work it out with Gleda there. You won't cheat her."

Stalwart held fast to his temper as the fat man sneered down at him over his jungle of beard and mountain of lard.

"I don't cheat anyone."

"And if this killer you want is so dangerous, how much danger money will you pay them?"

"How much do you usually pay them? You're the sheriff, so I'm told. We'll cover costs the way you usually do."

Mistress Gleda uttered a disagreeable snort behind Stalwart's back.

"You want me call the lads in so's you can tell 'em what this outlaw looks like?" her husband demanded. "How're you goin' to tip us off when you see him? What d'we do then?"

These were exactly the questions baffling Stalwart, but he was not about to admit this to his troops. "I'll explain all that later. I must finish this letter first. Then I want to take another walk around."

If he was still stymied at noon, he would have to ask for help.

"Why'd Lord Roland send a boy to catch a dangerous killer?"

Stalwart gave the fat man what he hoped was a cold stare. "Because it takes one to know one, I suppose."

"*You*, Pimple?"

"Me. But I only kill traitors, so you should be safe, shouldn't you?"

Before Sherwin could counter, another coach rumbled past the window and headed for the inn door. But the inn door was some way off, and now there were men and boys and horses everywhere, blocking the view. With a yelp of panic, Stalwart jumped for the door, ran outside, and dodged through the crowd. When he got close enough to see the heraldry on the carriage, he almost fell over a wheelbarrow of horse dung being pushed by a skinny, chilled-looking boy.

An octogram and a waterfall? Those were the arms the King had granted to Emerald after the Nythia adventure—a very rare honor for a woman.

He didn't trip. He just stood and stared with his mouth open as the porter opened the coach door, lowered the steps, and stepped back to let the occupants emerge.

Stalwart had never met Emerald's mother, but he did recognize the woman descending. She was not Emerald's mother.

She was not Silvercloak, either.

Silvercloak would have been less surprising.

And the youth in shabby, ill-fitting clothes shuffling along behind her? Yes, Stalwart knew that face also, although the close-cropped hairstyle was new. Fortunately both newcomers disappeared into the inn without noticing him standing there like a lummox.

How many unexpected tricks did Lord Roland have up his sleeve?

This one was almost unthinkable. She was crazy! Why had she ever let him talk her into *that*?

He wandered back into the cashier's office and flopped down on his stool. Norton and Sherwin had left, fortunately, and Mistress Gleda was dealing with a procession of grooms and customers. Stalwart's report, which he had stupidly left lying there, had been moved and therefore read.

More horsemen trotted into the yard and he craned his neck to watch them go by. He had not, as he had thought earlier, solved even the first of his problems. This window would not let him see everyone who arrived, because the coaches unloaded too far away and the crowd would often block his view. So he was right back at the beginning again.

Except he now owed someone for the cost of the inn's new porch.

He must close his report to Lord Roland. He added one more paragraph.

I respectfully advise your lordship that your gracious lady wife passed through Holmgarth this morning with a companion known to me. I judged it fitting that I not address them.

I have the honor to be, etc., your lordship's most humble and obedient servant, Stalwart, companion.

7

The Meat Wagon

EMERALD'S PREVIOUS VISIT TO IRONHALL HAD
been made in rain and pitch darkness. She had missed
nothing in the way of scenery, for Starkmoor was well
named. Under a leaden winter sky the rocky crests of the
tors were streaked with snow; thorn and scrub tinted their
slopes drab brown; and the tarns in the hollows shone a
frigid, rippled gray. The only color anywhere was the sinister,
lurid green of bogs. Even cattle were rare, and she had seen
no houses for hours. As the coach limped and lurched along
the track, with wind whistling through every tiny gap, she
huddled her blanket more tightly around her.

Lady Kate noticed the move and pulled a face. "There
is snow in the air. I have been expecting it ever since we
stopped at Holmgarth. This cold is very unseasonable!"

Why was she complaining? She was muffled all over in
a reddish-brown fur robe with matching hat and muffs, so
that only her face and boots were visible. She looked as
warm as a roasting chestnut, while Emerald felt half naked.
Cold drafts played on parts of her that were usually covered:
ears, neck, legs.

"I hope Wilf is all right." She had volunteered her mother's
coach for the journey because her companion's would

certainly be recognized by its heraldry. The old man out there on the box had never been this far from Peachyard in his life before, and he might not have thought to bring warm clothes.

"We're almost there."

Ironhall loomed closer now, grim and black. From this angle it seemed to stand atop a low cliff. It sported a few towers and fake battlements, but it was less like a castle than she had expected. The hard knot of nerves inside her twisted.

"This is absolutely your last chance to back out, Sister." Lord Roland's wife was petite and seemed almost fragile, her golden hair and corn-flower-blue eyes as bright as glaze on fine porcelain. Nor did she look old enough to be the mother of two children, one of them a son as tall as herself. Appearances were deceptive, though. Lady Kate was most certainly not fragile. A former White Sister, she thoroughly disapproved of the devious scheme her husband had devised. For three days she had been trying to talk Emerald out of it.

"I will not sacrifice all that hair for nothing, my lady."

Lady Kate pouted her rosebud lips. "You may lose more than that. Blood and teeth, perhaps. A great deal of dignity, certainly." Receiving no answer, she asked suspiciously, "Mother Superior did approve this charade, did she not?"

Three nights ago, after the meeting in Ranulf Square, Lord Roland had offered Emerald a ride back to the palace in his carriage—greatly shocking and offending Mother Spinel by not including her in the invitation. But the hasty private discussion that had followed, as the carriage rattled through the rainy streets, had been his chance to explain his Ironhall plan. Emerald had agreed to play her part. Mother Superior...?

"I'm sure your husband said so."

Kate's eyebrows rose as a warning that Emerald was not the only White Sister who could detect falsehood. "Ha! I'll bet he forgot to tell her until after we'd left Grandon and it was too late for her to object. This is an outrage."

Her efforts to dissuade Emerald were self-defeating,

for the dominant elements in Emerald's personality were earth and time, a combination that produced extreme stubbornness. Often in the last three days she had almost lost her nerve; left alone, she would probably have backed out by now. Kate's opposition had helped stiffen her resolve.

"I cannot imagine how even my glib-tongued husband ever persuaded you to make such a fool of yourself, Sister."

"He did find me a challenge, I think. Until he offered me a chance to avenge a man I greatly admired."

"Who?" Kate demanded sharply. "Not more deaths in the Order, I hope!"

Sir Chefney's death was still a state secret, not to be discussed. Fortunately the conversation was interrupted by shouting outside.

"Meat wagon!"

"Make way for the meat wagon!"

"Raw meat coming!"

A dozen or so boys on horses pounded past the coach and took up station ahead of it as a ragged guard of honor, laughing and shouting in a mix of treble and baritone. A carriage arriving at Ironhall could be bringing only one cargo.

These were young, feral males—unpredictable and potentially violent. Emerald had met no boys during her years at Oakendown, and her subsequent life at court could be no preparation for Ironhall. She must expect some unpleasant experiences.

Kate said, "Ha! Some of your new friends. Wanting you to come out and play, no doubt."

Again Emerald was saved from having to answer. As the trail bent close to the compound wall, a surge of elementary power made them both wince.

"Spirits!" Kate cried. "You cannot endure that!"

"It is only the Forge, very local." Already the effect was fading.

"I still think you are completely insane. You met Sir Saxon, you said?"

"Grand Master? Once, my lady."

"What did you think of him?"

"I was not much impressed. To be fair, he was in a difficult position that night. Stalwart was there, baiting him mercilessly. He was armed with his commission from the Court of Conjury and eager to pay off four years' resentment."

"That Stalwart wanted to do so says a lot about the man. Durendal never mentions Saxon at all, and I am sure that is because he dislikes speaking ill of people. A mean little politico. Water and chance, I thought."

That was a question, one White Sister to another.

"I thought so too, my lady."

"An awkward mixture. Makes him moody and capricious."

And untrustworthy. "You know him well?"

"No. He came to court briefly a couple of years ago. I don't expect he will remember me."

Nonsense! More than just an important man's wife, Kate was memorable in her own right. Her dominant virtual element was love, and everyone at court approved of her or even adored her, from King Ambrose down to the lowliest flunky. In the rat-eat-rat world of a palace, that was highly unusual. Nevertheless, her manifest element was fire, and there were tales of people who had crossed her and discovered that the kitten had claws.

More hooves thundered past the carriage window and a man's voice bellowed at the self-appointed honor guard, uttering dire threats of extra hours of stable duties. Screaming with laughter, the boys cantered off and vanished like a cloud of gnats.

"Follow me, master coachman!" the horseman shouted.

The trail divided, the left branch curving around the compound to an arched gateway. In the paved quadrangle within, several dozen boys and men were paired off, jumping back and forth and clattering swords. Voices were calling out comments and instructions. The guide led Wilf and the team around the perimeter, to an archaic building with towers and battlements. There he reined in and dismounted. He wore a sword, but was probably no older than Emerald.

He shouted angrily at some of the younger fencers who

had broken off their lessons and come running to inspect the new arrival. "Back to work! All of you! If he's admitted you've got lots of time to pick on him. If he isn't, then he's none of your business. Go, or I report you all to Second!"

They retreated, but not far. Clutching foils and fencing masks, they waited to inspect the visitors. Stray snowflakes swirled in the air.

The boy with the sword called to someone named Lindore to look after the horses. Then he dropped the steps, opened the door, and handed Kate down. "Good chance, mistress." He had recognized that the arms on the coach included no crown or coronet and therefore did not belong to a noble. "Prime Candidate Marlon at your service."

About to make a dignified, ladylike descent after Kate, Emerald recalled her new role and jumped instead. Her overlarge shoes almost betrayed her; she stumbled and recovered. The watching boys hooted and jeered. An applicant who fell flat on his face on the doorstep would not go far in Ironhall.

Marlon smiled doubtfully at her and said, "Good chance," again in a kindly tone. Then he offered his arm to Kate. In an all-male world, a lady was *much* more interesting than yet another boy. "If you would be so kind as to let me guide you, mistress, I'll find Grand Master for you. What name should I tell him?" He was trying out the courtly manners he had been taught.

"Mistress Dragonwife," Kate said sweetly.

"Dragonwife?"

"Exactly."

His eyes gleamed with amusement. "I am sure he will be eager to meet you, Mistress Dragon-wife."

Emerald slouched along behind, trying to look surly and dangerous, but feeling a freak. This was not her first experience of wearing male clothing, a ruse the White Sisters found expedient on long journeys. They usually did it in groups, though, and Emerald was very much on her own. She was hoping to masquerade as a teenage boy for several days in a jungle of teenage boys. Neither Oakendown nor royal palaces were adequate preparation for that. What did boys talk about among themselves? What sort of table manners did they have? What did they wear in bed and where did they change? And so on.

Although Kate thoroughly disapproved of Emerald's mission, it was typical of her that she had been unstinting in her help—help with hair, with clothes, and with rehearsing the fictitious life story an imposter must have ready at all times. Emerald's breasts were tightly bound inside a coarse linen shirt and stiff leather doublet. Her jerkin and britches were shabby and several sizes too large for her, like hand-me-downs. She had been impressed with her first sight of herself in a mirror, but now fright and the critical stares of the audience made her feel desperately unconvincing.

"Spirits!" said a childish voice from the gallery. "What's he got in those pants?"

"Blubber!"

"Ham? Two hams?"

Emerald was *not* fat! Although her dominant earth element did make her large boned, her mother kept telling her she was too skinny. But she was female and fully grown. Ironhall would not accept boys older than fifteen and preferred them younger, so few newcomers would be her height yet. Those that were would be built like fishing rods. She was not. She needed a bonier face, more chin, and the hips of an eel.

"Hasn't got a hope," said another.

"Grand Master can't be that desperate."

"Have to keep that one away from the swill."

"Run him up Black Tor and back every morning...."

"Aw, the sopranos will soon sweat it off him...."

Emerald's feet froze to the ground, a giant hand of terror crushed her insides to rock, and a voice that sounded very much like Mother Superior's screamed silently in her ear: *Stop! This is madness! You are crazy!* She stood there, watching Kate's back disappearing through the doorway. The urge to turn and race back to the carriage made her quiver like a violin string. What was she dreaming of? Why was she doing this? Not for fat, blowhard King Ambrose, certainly. No, for Sir Chefney—for his gracious bow, his smile of welcome when she turned up at the Snakepit. She had sent him to Quirk Row to die. *That* was why she was doing this! Revenge, justice!

She stuck out her tongue defiantly at the jeering gutter trash, raised her chin, and marched after Lady Kate and young Marlon into Ironhall.

8

The Prettiest Little Parlor

L OW CEILINGS AND TINY WINDOWS MADE THE old building dark and uninviting. Prime escorted the visitors along a corridor and up a stair to a gloomy passage furnished with a single crude bench. He threw open a door.

"If you would be so kind as to wait in here, mistress, I will inform Grand Master of your arrival." He stepped back for Kate. Emerald almost made a serious blunder, but remembered in time to let Marlon precede her. As she shut the door, he gave her a wink and a whispered, "Cheer up. It's not as bad as it looks." He crossed the room and left by another door. She decided she approved of Marlon.

The room was grim enough. Snowflakes drifted in through two windows, barred but unglazed, and the hearth was cold and bare. The only furnishings were a table, two hard chairs, and a bookshelf. Lady Kate inspected one of the chairs carefully for cleanliness before trusting her furs to it. Emerald headed for the other.

"I don't think that one's meant for you, boy."

"Oh, probably not." Emerald went to a window instead, clumping in her absurd shoes. The moor was barely visible through flying snow.

A few moments later, Grand Master entered by the second

door. He shut it and advanced, rubbing his hands. "I am Grand—" He stopped. "Lady Kate!" He spared Emerald only a brief glance before twisting his beard into a smile. "By the eight, what brings you to Ironhall, my lady? You come incognito?"

Kate offered a hand to be kissed. "Royal business, Grand Master. Royal monkey business in my opinion. My husband is behind it."

"The Chancellor's skill at politics is as admired as his swordsmanship." His words were not quite a lie, but they were so close that Emerald felt the chill of death elementals. Grand Master was jealous of men more successful than himself. Like all Blades, he was of average height and slender build, yet somehow he seemed small. His cloak, jerkin, and britches were shabby. He bore a cat's-eye sword.

In a sudden flash of memory, he swung around to look at his other visitor. "I know you!"

"I was presented to you as Luke of Peachyard, Grand Master." Emerald did not want to antagonize him, but she had already roused painful memories.

"You were with Stalwart that night!"

"I was traveling with him, but I was present here as an unwilling witness only."

That was not the speech of an adolescent male hellion. Grand Master sat down, looking suspiciously from one visitor to the other. In a typical sudden change of mood, he turned a mawkish smile on Kate. "And now you want to enroll him in Ironhall? Or has Lord Roland some more devious prospect in mind?"

"Much more devious, I fear." She handed him a packet she had been hiding in her muff. "And he has won a free hand from His Majesty."

Grand Master scowled as he recognized the King's privy seal. He broke it to read the letter. Emerald knew it contained a blanket command to follow Lord Roland's instructions. Without that royal edict he would not be bound to do so. Chivalrous orders were under the direct rule of the monarch and no one else.

Sir Saxon folded the paper, his lips pale with anger. "And what instructions does his lordship have for me?"

In silence Kate handed him a second letter, this one bulkier. As he read it, the women exchanged glances. More than the premature winter weather was causing the icy chill in that room. Once he looked up briefly to stare at Emerald. By the time he had finished reading, he was livid with fury.

"*Sister* Emerald?"

"I am."

He threw the letter on the floor. "This is madness! You cannot hope to get away with this deception."

"Of course she can," said Kate, who had been arguing the contrary case for the last three days. "She has fooled you twice."

"For minutes only! Your husband talks of days, perhaps two weeks." He returned his glare to Emerald. "You cannot have the slightest idea what you are letting yourself in for! Ironhall collects sweepings of the gutter—thieves, outlaws, arsonists, even killers. These boys are wild and brutal, rejected by their families, often convicted felons whose only hope of escaping the gallows is to be bound as a Blade. That brings an automatic pardon, because by then we have civilized them."

"I know," Emerald said hoarsely, although what he said was not true of all Blades. Marlon's studied manners might hide a seamy past, but Wart had been a minstrel and tumbler, not a criminal.

"Do you know what happens first?" Grand Master thumped the table. "The newest boy is always just the Brat, without a name, without a friend, fair game for anyone. The juniors' recreation is tormenting and hazing him, because they all had to put up with that in their day, so they think they are entitled to do it to others. It weeds out the weaklings, and often it shocks the others into making a fresh start. They can take pride in having survived the worst the rest can do to them. A girl cannot possibly expect to—"

"Sister Emerald," Kate snapped, "is a courageous and resourceful young woman, who has several times performed incredible feats of clandestine investigation in His Majesty's service."

Grand Master swallowed as if at a loss for words.

"I am not without experience of roughhousing," Emerald protested. "I did have two older brothers."

"*Roughhousing*, girl? Even the smallest of these young thugs is probably stronger than you. When your brothers were adolescents did they ever give their sister a thorough pounding? Get you in a corner and pummel you black and blue, throw you on the ground to kick and stamp you?"

"You permit that?" Kate demanded.

"No, but it happens, my lady. Master of Rituals has to perform a healing on almost every Brat at least once, mending flattened noses or broken ribs. I always understood that White Sisters were unable to tolerate healing magic?"

Kate's eyes widened, as if she had not foreseen that problem. Emerald shivered. She thought she could endure a healing if her injuries were serious enough, but she was not sure.

"Some of us can."

Grand Master bent to snatch up the Chancellor's letter again. "Sister, you *cannot* get away with this hoax! In the bath house? The latrines? You are tall, so you will certainly be challenged to fights. Throwing the Brat in a horse trough is a good start to an evening. Then what? And if the juniors ever have the slightest suspicion, they will have the clothes off you in no time."

"Then what?" Emerald barked, louder than she had intended. As usual, opposition was making her dig in her heels. "Will I be assaulted further?"

He stared down at the letter for a few moments, crackling it, while his face turned red and redder yet. At last he muttered, "I don't know. I think and hope that that will be the end of it. I am guessing, because this has never happened."

"Well, then." She rejected her last chance to escape. "If extreme embarrassment and some bruises are the worst I have to fear, I consider the importance of my duties justifies the risk. Does the Chancellor not explain? I must begin by making sure that no sorcerous devices have been smuggled onto the premises and that no residents have been enchanted."

Kate said, "My husband would not be proposing such drastic measures if he did not have real grounds for concern. How long do you suppose that will take you, Sister?"

"A few hours."

"Till sunset, say? Surely you can guarantee her safety that long, Grand Master! If she is willing to continue the deception after she has been shown around, can you not support her for a few days? Then His Majesty will arrive, and you can present your objections to him in person."

This cunning mention of the King made him scowl. He began reading Lord Roland's letter again. Kate shot a triumphant smile at Emerald, who returned it as best she could.

He soon discovered another grievance. "I am instructed to expect Princess Vasar of Lukirk. Who's she?"

Good question. The name meant nothing to Emerald.

"I have no idea," Kate said airily. "Some foreign royalty the King wants to impress? Possibly a relative of his betrothed, Princess Dierda of Gevily."

The explanation rang like a tin gong to Emerald. Kate was not good at lying.

Grand Master sighed deeply and folded up the letter. He took a moment to become fatherly, then spoke in sorrow. "Sister Emerald, I beg you to reconsider. Believe me, I have only your own good at heart. I am much older than you are. I have known Ironhall since long before you were born, child, and I assure you that what you propose cannot succeed and will cause you terrible heartache. Consider the inevitable scandal, which may ruin your reputation and standing forever. Even if the urgency of the crisis is as great as Lord Roland believes—which I find hard to credit—why cannot you perform your duties in female clothing? Why this playacting, this mummery?"

"To keep my presence here a complete secret." The Chancellor was certainly carrying security to extremes, but he had explained to Emerald that other governments had set every trap imaginable for the notorious Silvercloak. They had all failed.

"I did not say you must wear the habit of your Sisterhood. Why not be…oh…my niece, come visiting?"

Emerald returned the answer Lord Roland had given her. "Because a stranger would be noticed. I would not have easy access to every part of the complex, and because traitors, if any, would either take precautions or simply flee."

"But—"

"Cases of treason may require extraordinary measures," Kate said sharply.

Grand Master flinched. When treason was in the air, no one was safe. He shrugged. "Very well, my lady, Sister… under protest, I will do as I am ordered. If we are to keep your identity a secret we must follow the normal procedures exactly, yes?"

"As much as possible, please."

He pulled a bag from a pocket. "Lady Kate, please wait outside while I test the 'boy' for agility."

The test consisted of throwing coins for Emerald to catch. It did not take long. Then she had to crawl around on hands and knees to pick up the ones she had missed, which was all of them.

"If asked," Grand Master said smugly from his chair, "you had better say you caught six. That is the minimum we ever accept."

"Becoming a Blade is not my ambition, I assure you," Emerald remarked from under the table.

"How fortunate! We rarely waste time teaching the Brat anything until we are sure he will be staying. But some time in the next few days Master of Rapiers will undoubtedly give you a foil and check to see whether you have any native ability."

"Which I don't."

"Not a shred. If you were genuine you would be on your way back over the moor already."

She scrambled to her feet. "Then I will have to twist an

ankle, won't I? As an excuse not to fight or play with foils, but nothing so serious that you need perform a healing on me."

His eyes flashed. "Use that tone to a master, boy, and you will regret it."

She reined in her temper. He was in the right, which did not excuse his obvious enjoyment. "I am sorry, Grand Master. It will not occur again." Not until the next time.

"You still wish to proceed with this farce?"

"I do."

"Very well. On your own head be it." He rose and frowned out the window. Snow was still falling, starting to settle. "Mistress Dragonwife had better make haste. I will send a couple of seniors on horses to make sure her driver finds his way off the moor. Wait here."

9

Intrepid

EMERALD SHUFFLED BACK TO THE WINDOW. SNOW hid the tors. Close at hand, though, three boys were running—not running *to* anywhere, just running, going in circles, clowning, laughing, shouting as they rejoiced in being young in snow. She could not hope to imitate that behavior.

Kate had fussed a lot about shoes, insisting that a boy of Emerald's height would have feet twice as big, which was why she was now wearing flippers, their toes padded with wool.

"I can't wear these," she had protested. "I will trip over them!"

"Nonsense. You just need practice. And they will remind you never to run unless you absolutely must. Women don't run the way men do."

Behind her a door squeaked. A face peered around it.

It was not a conventional sort of face. It possessed a very snub nose; a huge number of sandy freckles; two large blue eyes encircled by fading yellow and purple bruises; and a puffed, inflamed lip. It had one eyebrow, which was the same coppery red as the tangled hair on the right half of its scalp. The other side had been shaved bald and bore the word "SCUM" in black ink.

"You're *staying*?" he asked squeakily.

"Yes."

He yelled approval: "Yea! *Fiery!*" And walked in. He was about twelve, about shoulder height. His threadbare jerkin and britches were squalid, as if they had been used to wipe out half-empty cook pots. "They said you didn't look very promising material."

"You don't look so hot yourself at the moment."

He scowled. "Watch your mouth! You're the Brat now."

Emerald cursed under her breath. "I'm sorry. I forgot!"

"Call me, 'sir'!"

"Yes, sir." Boxing his ears would have to wait.

"The first thing—" Grand Master said, striding in. He glared when he saw she had company.

"Ah, Brat..."

Emerald said, "Yes, Grand Master?"

He pointed. "You are still the Brat."

"*I am?*" the boy howled.

"Until Master of Archives signs you in. Go and find him and choose your name. *Then* the new boy takes over."

The Brat shot Emerald a predatory leer, made even more sinister by his swollen lip. "So he does."

She was sure she could outpummel this one if she had to. If he was alone.

"But you have one more duty. You have to tell him all the rules and show him around."

The kid shrugged offhandedly. "Mm..."

"Boy!" Grand Master barked. "I recall twice in the last two weeks when you couldn't find a place I sent you to, and once you gave a note to the wrong master. That really was Wilde's fault, for not training you better, wasn't it?"

"Yes, Grand Master," the Brat agreed, stepping right into the trap.

"So if this new boy can't find his way around, that will be your fault!"

The freak face fell. "But—"

"You arguing, candidate?"

"*No*, Grand Master."

"Very well. I want you to show the new Brat *everything*, understand? Not upstairs in King Everard House, of course; not the servants' quarters, and not the Seniors' Tower, or they'll skin you. But everywhere not off-limits. And see he knows all the masters by sight."

"Yes, Grand Master!"

"And if he gets lost tomorrow, then it will be your fault, and you will be punished!"

"B-but...me? I mean, I can take him, but most places I don't know what they're *called*. How do I tell the names?"

"Ask someone, stupid." Grand Master smirked at Emerald. "When you're done, come back here. I will announce your admittance in the hall tonight."

"Yes, Grand Master."

"Off you go, then, *boys*."

Emerald did not like Grand Master's smirk.

"The Brat can go almost anywhere," Lord Roland had told her, "because he is errand boy. He attends no classes, has no other duties. If I send you there as a visitor, you will attract attention and your movements will be restricted. No one really notices the Brat. Other boys haze him, but Grand Master will be able to protect you from most of that without raising any eyebrows. You'll have to put up with a lot of impudent heckling, I admit. You may find yourself dancing like a chicken or turning a dozen somersaults to order. Can I beg you to endure a few days' humiliation for your King?"

But supposing he had been wrong? Supposing this water-and-chance Grand Master resented the Chancellor's orders so much that he would not defend her? He had told her what she intended was impossible. He could make his own prophecy come true. Now he was pouting down at the Brat, who was holding out a hand to him. Grand Master fumbled in pockets until he found a small brass disk, which he passed over.

The boy showed it to Emerald as he opened the door. "The token, see? When a master sends you on an errand, get his token. Then you're on business and can't be jostled. Come on!" He went downstairs at a run.

Emerald followed as fast as her shoes would allow. She did not understand Grand Master, but she could guess what the Brat meant by "jostle." "So you're safe as long as you have a token?"

"More or less." He ran along the corridor. There were no witnesses, so she ran after him, grinning down at his absurd, half-bald head. "This is First House," he explained over his shoulder. "The oldest. That room we was in is the flea room. We go up here."

First House was a maze, a warren of stairs and passages. She was never going to learn her way around, but judged it wiser not to say so. The Brat plunged around another corner...*Yelp! Curse! Thump! Much louder yelp....* Emerald, following cautiously, discovered her guide sitting on the floor in a litter of books, rubbing a pink, freshly slapped cheek. An older, larger boy loomed over him.

"Stupid brainless swamp thing!" The other boy had a possible mustache on his lip. He wore no sword, but the size of his fists and shoulders said he could be dangerous enough without one. "Pick them up!"

The Brat scrabbled around, collecting the books. He knelt to offer them. "I am truly sorry, Most Exalted and Glorious Candidate Vere."

The other took them. "Give me ten!" He watched as the Brat hastily stretched out and performed ten push-ups, then returned to his knees. "And what is this rubbish?"

Emerald could explain that she was not the Brat yet, but such technicalities were not likely to prove helpful. She knelt beside her guide. "I am to be the next Brat, sir."

"*Sir*? You weren't listening, trash."

"I beg pardon, Most Exalted and Glorious Candidate Vere."

"Better. But I'm tired of that name. *You* will address me as Supreme and Mighty Speaker of Wisdom Vere."

"Yes, Supreme and Mighty Speaker of Wisdom Vere."

"And don't forget it." Vere stalked away around the corner.

The Brat rose and slouched off the opposite way, rubbing his face, muttering words Emerald preferred not to hear. "The rest of the fuzzies are all right," he said. "Vere and Hunter are the only real cesspits. Most of the beardless don't jostle much either."

"Sopranos, fuzzies...?"

"Sopranos, beansprouts, beardless, fuzzies, seniors. Seniors wear swords and don't bother you. The rest you just get to know ranks by seeing where they sit in the hall."

"Does it matter?"

"You call me 'sir'!"

"Yes, sir."

"Until I get my name. Then I'll tell you how to address me."

"Thank you, sir," Emerald said, mentally chalking a scoreboard. "The fuzzies are the ones who shave?"

"Naw! Tremayne shaves, and he's just a soprano. It's fencing that counts. That's why there's so many sopranos just now—Tremayne's such a woodchopper that they won't promote him to beansprout and he's holding up a half dozen." The Brat chuckled. "They make him practice all day and all night!"

"Does Brat-hazing go on all the time, too?"

He shrugged. It was no longer his problem. "Jostling? In the day they're usually kept too busy. It's evenings you need to look out. Good, he's in." He walked through an open door and squeaked, "Sir?"

Without question, this was the archive room, stuffed with scrolls and gigantic books, smelling of dust and leather. The man standing at the writing desk under the window was suitably bookish, with ink stains on his fingers and spectacles perched on the tip of his nose. His mousy hair was almost as untidy as the Brat's half thatch. Had he not been wearing a cat's-eye sword, he could have been a clerk or librarian anywhere. He turned and pouted at his visitors.

"Brat? Ah, two brats! One brat, one candidate. Come to choose your name?"

"Yes, sir, please, sir." Recalling his duties to Emerald

the boy added, "This's the record office. He's Master of Archives." He was relaxed now, and excited.

"Where *did* I put the book?" The archivist peered around, muttering. "Oh, *where* did I put the book?" He meant some special book, for books were piled everywhere—on shelves, on the floor, on both stools, along with boxes and heaps of paper. "...did I put the *book*?"

"Ah!" He retrieved a very slim volume and handed it to the boy. "Here is every name ever approved. The ones marked with a cross are in use. Those with triangles are available. You can choose any of those. Any other name must be approved by Grand Master and you stay the Brat until it's settled. Take your time. You'll be stuck with it for the rest of your life." He turned to blink doubtfully at Emerald. "How old are you, lad?"

"Fourteen, sir."

"Can you read?"

"Yes, sir."

It was obvious from the Brat's dismay that he could not.

"Good.... Anytime you have a spare moment and I'm here you can drop in and start going through the book. They can't jostle you in here."

"Thank you, sir."

"It saves my time in the end. Of course they can wait outside for you." He turned to the Brat. "What sort of name? You want to take a hero's name? Some boys prefer one they can make famous themselves. Or a descriptive name, like 'Vicious,' or 'Lyon'? Trouble with those is that they can get you laughed at or start fights. The King doesn't like them, so you may end up a private Blade and not in the Guard. There's lots of names that don't commit you to anything but sound good—'Walton,' 'Hawley,' or 'Ferrand.'"

"Wanna hero's name," the Brat said firmly. "A Blade in the *Litany*. And a name that means 'brave'!"

"Mm. Well, there's 'Valorous.'"

"Or 'Stalwart'?" Emerald murmured.

Master of Archives coughed. "That one would not be approved.... I recall no 'Stalwart' in the *Litany*. We had the story of a Sir Valorous the other night. The one who was tortured to death, remember, but did not betray his ward?"

The Brat seemed unimpressed by that as a way to die. "Have any Sir Viciouses been heroes?"

"Don't believe so. The only Sir Vicious I can recall is the last Grand Master. 'Brave'...?" He fumbled pages. "Yes, there's still a Sir Brave somewhere, although from the look of this ink he must be ancient. I could confirm that.... I think 'Gallant' is permitted. Yes. 'Gallant'?"

"Don't like it."

"'Doughty'?" Emerald suggested. She was anxious to begin her guided tour. "'Audacious'? 'Dauntless'? 'Pertinacious'?"

The archivist frowned. She was not behaving like the average fourteen-year-old fiend.

"How about 'Intrepid'?" he said impatiently. "Sir Intrepid is in the *Litany*. A fine lad. He died last spring saving King Ambrose from a chimera monster. Sir Dreadnought killed it. 'Intrepid' means 'without fear.'"

"Intrepid?" The boy tried the sound of it doubtfully.

"It would be a very clever choice. When you're ready to be bound, the King will remember what he owes to the last Sir Intrepid and will want to put you in the Guard." He was looking ahead five years. Emerald would be quite content if King Ambrose were still alive five *days* from now, able to leave Ironhall and take her with him.

The boy hesitated, muttering the word as if frightened he might forget it. "There's really chimera monsters? I thought they was just joshing me."

Emerald had firsthand experience of the horrors, but she let the Blade answer. He told of the giant man-cat attacking the King in the forest, of his three Blades jumping to his defense, of Sir Knollys being disemboweled, of young Sir Intrepid closing with the monster so Sir Dreadnought could get behind it and kill it while it was breaking Intrepid's neck. The Brat was convinced, his eyes stretching ever wider inside their bruises.

"Yea! Wannabe *Intrepid*!"

"Good! Now where did I put the current journal...?"

The name was entered in three different volumes, in one of which the new Intrepid made his mark. It turned out that there had been three Sir Intrepids in the Order and two of them had achieved immortality in the *Litany*.

"There!" Master of Archives said, putting away the quill. "Welcome to the Order, Candidate Intrepid! Report here for reading lessons at first bell tomorrow."

"Reading? But I wanna use a sword!"

"No. No fencing and no horses until you can read and write. Off with you."

The new candidate stamped grumpily out into the corridor, his lopsided mane waving.

"You can give me the token now," Emerald said, following him. "Sir."

He fumbled in his pocket and suddenly remembered. "Kneel when you speak to me, Brat!" He beamed as she obeyed. His eyes were not much above hers, even then. "What were those other 'brave' words you said?"

"'Dauntless'? 'Audacious'? er...'Presumptuous'?"

"Then you address me as Dauntless, Dacious, Presumchus Intrepid." He handed her the token.

10

The Soprano Jungle

IN SPITE OF HIS IGNORANCE AND BRUTAL intentions, there was something likable about Dauntless-Audacious-Presumptuous Intrepid. He had panache, and five years of Ironhall might well turn the snotty little horror into a fine young man. At the moment he was a blatant liar. He lied when he claimed to be thirteen. He lied when he told how he had killed people and reached Ironhall a step ahead of a posse wanting to hang him. When he said that the Brat was supposed to sleep in the sopranos' dorm but would be utterly crazy to try, he was telling the truth. But he lied again when he retrieved his blanket from a spidery nook under a cellar stair and told Emerald that this was a safe place to sleep. Obviously he would lead the rat pack there in search of her that very night—he couldn't wait to start getting his own back for everything he had suffered in the past eleven days. Wise Brats, she concluded, found their own hidey-holes and kept their blankets hidden elsewhere by day.

Intrepid lied about the hazing he had endured, exaggerating it to frighten her. He did admit that he might have brought the worst upon himself by losing his redhead's temper and trying to fight back. He had not yet seen that controlling that temper might be the most important thing he could ever learn and Ironhall had already begun to teach him.

She enjoyed his bubbling happiness. He had been brought to the school as a reject, a failure, but now he had run the gauntlet of Bratdom and would be one of the boys. As Grand Master had said, a little pride could work wonders.

After he had run her all up and down and through the labyrinth of First House—flea room, library, Grand Master's study, record office, guardroom, Observatory, and a dozen other places she might never find again—they went out into the courtyard. Snow was still falling. Treacherous footing had driven the fencers indoors. The only people in sight were boys saddling horses near the gate.

"Them's the stables," Intrepid chirped, pointing that way. "Servant barns, West House, King Everard House. That's the bath house and rose garden. That's the gym. We'll go that way and do Main House last. Come on." He ran. Emerald did not bother asking what the rose garden was. She could guess.

The school had grown haphazardly over the centuries, in a mishmash of styles. The oldest parts, on the east side, were First House and the one Intrepid had called the bath house, both of which sported corner towers. They, and the curtain wall connecting them, were topped with battlements, so any invading army advancing from that direction would be stopped in its tracks.

Main House was an imposing stone-built edifice, built after fake fortifications had gone out of fashion. The gym was more recent still, and brick. The dormitories to the north and west could have been modern timber-and-plaster tenements stolen off any street in Grandon. The stables and servants' quarters had an ageless rustic look.

Forge and gym were freestanding. The rest of the buildings formed a chain around them, those not actually in contact being linked by stone walls. Other than the stage scenery on the east, none of those were high enough to stop agile youths.

Intrepid did not bother taking her to the bath house. He ran straight to the gym, which was a madhouse of noisy sword practice, much too small for the number of people leaping about in it. He hung around for a few minutes, hoping to be noticed, but everyone was too busy.

"King Everard House!" he said, and took off at a sprint again. He had overlooked the Forge, which was hidden behind the gym. Emerald could hear faint clinking of armorers' hammers. Even more, she could sense its surging elemental power and so was glad to avoid it.

She also wanted to avoid running, and chance smiled on her again before they reached the next building—Intrepid slipped on the snow and sprawled flat. She tried to help him up, but he was too furious to accept aid.

"Let's walk," she said. "A broken wrist wouldn't be a very good way to celebrate your admission."

He snarled at her and marched away, trying to hide a limp.

As they reached King Everard House, a young man trotted out. He stopped and grinned and held out a hand to shake. "Well done! I'm Loring. Who're you?"

Intrepid puffed out his chest. "I'm Candidate *Intrepid*! That means 'without fear.'"

"Fine choice! A great name to live up to. About two weeks?"

"Eleven days."

"Average." He flashed Emerald a stunning smile. "You'll hear of Brats having to stick it out for months, but that's rare. And someone else may turn up tomorrow. Good chance to you!" He strolled off, whistling.

Emerald *definitely* approved of Loring.

"A fuzzy," Intrepid said. "Not much of a swordsman."

"Oh?" she said. Who cared? With that profile he was going to break a thousand hearts when he came to court.

They passed by the lecture rooms in King Everard House. Upstairs was where knights and masters slept, and off-limits. Emerald detected no sorcery, other than a faint, pervasive hint of the binding spell everywhere. West House contained the candidates' dormitories, all suitably named, from "Rabbit" and "Mouse" for the sopranos up to "Lion" for the exalted seniors. They all passed her inspection for magic, if not for housekeeping.

The stables, likewise, were free of sorcery. By the time she and her guide emerged from them, the light was starting to fail and the snow had turned to slush. She learned that her shoes leaked. Three boys came running out of the dusk, pink and sweaty, fresh from the gym, seeing a new Brat as future sport.

First they slapped Intrepid on the back, wrung his hand, and introduced themselves as if they had never met him before—Wilde, Castelaine, and Servian. They praised his choice of name. A couple of hours ago they would have insulted and bullied him. Then they turned to study Emerald. They were all tall enough to make Intrepid look like a child, and Servian was full man-size.

"Oh, yucky!" said one.

"They get worse and worse."

"We'll really have to work hard on this one." Servian was heavyset for a future Blade, and obviously the ringleader. If it came to pummeling, he would flatten her, for the sisters at Oakendown did not teach pugilism. "Brat, I am the Most Magnificent and Glorious and Heroic Candidate Servian. You kneel when I deign to notice you."

"I am extremely sorry, Candidate Servian, but I carry Grand Master's token and must hurry. Some other time."

Servian's dark eyes narrowed and yet gleamed brighter. "We really cannot tolerate this insolence. Since you're new, I'll let you off with six somersaults for calling me by the wrong name and six for not kneeling."

"It's not playtime now. Come, Intrepid."

Intrepid was staring at her openmouthed, uncertain whether to be impressed by her courage or delighted by the prospects. Fortunately she was not the adolescent boy they all thought she was; she was a grown woman of very nearly seventeen, highly trained in her craft, and a veteran of hair-raising adventures with Wart. Her confidence threw them off balance long enough for her to slip past them and walk away. She was shaking—from rage or relief or fright or possibly all of those.

The boys followed—Intrepid almost at her side, but not quite, the other three close behind, kicking slush at her bare legs with every step.

"He gave you orders, Intrepid!" Servian said. "Candidate Intrepid takes orders from the Brat!"

Intrepid squealed in horror. "Do not! I'm doing what Grand Master said!"

"Candidate Intrepid takes orders from the Brat!"

Wilde and Castelaine joined in the chorus.

"Candidate Intrepid takes orders from the Brat!"

"Candidate Intrepid takes orders from the Brat!"

More boys came running.

"Candidate Intrepid takes—"

"*I do not*!" Intrepid screamed, dancing in agony, splashing slush.

"Then you'll have to fight him!" Servian crowed.

Emerald strode on, fists clenched, ears burning.

Intrepid looked up—way up—at the Brat beside him. His face was crumpled in misery. "He don't give me orders! Grand Master said I hadda show him around."

"Candidate Insipid takes orders from the Brat!"

"That's *Intrepid*!"

"Insipid! Insipid! Insipid!"

"Invalid! Invalid! Invalid!" yelled one of the others.

Intrepid howled. "Awright, awright, awright! I'll fight him tonight!"

"Fight tonight!" yelled Servian.

Emerald continued to stride ahead, half soaked now. A dozen chanting tormentors marched behind her, pelting her with soggy snowballs. They were passing the servants' quarters, which were off-limits, heading for Main House, but it seemed a fearfully long way away. She felt a desperate need to run but dared not trust her shoes on the slippery paving.

"Faster!" Servian roared, thumping her in the middle of her back hard enough to make her stumble. "You're serving Grand Master! Faster!"

Thump! again, but she was ready for it and kept her balance. Forget the risk of falling, he was hurting more! Dared she run with so many witnesses behind her? "Women don't run the way men do," Lady Kate had warned her.

Inspiration exploded inside Emerald's head. ("Faster for Grand Master!" *Thump*!) Lord Roland had asked, "He moved nimbly, I assume, like a swordsman?"

("Faster for Grand Master!" *Thump*!)

She barely noticed the pain. She recalled her answer: "There *was* something odd about the way he moved."

"Faster for Grand Master!"

Thump!

They were all shouting it now: "Faster for Grand Master!"

Thump! Servian's punches were growing steadily harder, all on the same place between her shoulder blades.

And still her mind was far away, remembering the encounter in Quirk Row. Was it possible? Could the deadly Silvercloak be playing the same deception she was? Could the killer actually be a woman? That could explain "his" skill at disguise—she committed her crimes in disguise, and the rest of time everyone looked for the wrong sort of person. It meant Lord Roland was looking for the wrong sort of person right now! So were Wart and Sir Bandit. They must all be warned—

"Faster for Grand Master!" *Thump*!

Emerald spun and swung a haymaker blow at her tormentor. "Shut up, you great lout! I'm trying to think."

Her wild swipe missed, of course—Servian was a hundred times faster than she was. She would never, ever, lay a hand on Servian. But in evading her he stepped on another boy's toe and lost his footing. His legs shot out from under him and he sat down hard, perhaps harder than he ever had.

Splat!

Shower of slush.

The audience howled with joy. Servian came up screaming,

intent on massacring the Brat who had so humiliated him. Others grabbed him. It took four of them to force him along as they marched off into the dusk, happily chanting.

"Two fights tonight! Two fights tonight! Two fights…"

11

At the End of the Day (1)

IT WAS SUNSET BEFORE BUSINESS SLACKENED IN the posthouse yard. Travelers stopped arriving. Weary grooms were settling the last horses in their stalls.

Stalwart had spent all day chasing around in search of a viewpoint from which he could see everyone arriving without being seen himself. He had not found one. If he stayed at the gate, he could not see the coach passengers; at the inn door he might miss solitary horsemen. He was *almost* certain that Silvercloak had not passed through there that day, but could have done nothing to stop him if he had. Baffled, he trudged into the cashier's office and sank wearily onto his stool. Gleda had been sent home to make supper. Sherwin himself was counting the day's take, clinking coins into bags.

"Still no prisoners, Pimple?"

Stalwart shook his head. "I need some advice."

The sheriff looked up mockingly. "Spirits! You mean you're actually asking for help?"

Stalwart swallowed his pride, like a brick. "Yes, sir."

"Well! About time." The fat man leaned back against the wall. "What do you need to know?"

"Lots of things. Like how to apprehend an armed and

extremely dangerous swordsman after I spot him." A sheriff ought to know that much. "I don't want men killed. I'm trying to think of some way of luring him into a horse stall and then—"

Sherwin said a word never heard around court, except sometimes from the King himself. "How good are you with that sword of yours?"

"I'm a Blade."

"How good a Blade?"

"Better than most," Wart said defiantly.

"Are you so?" The Sheriff scratched his great beard. "Why don't I get my trusty quarterstaff and we'll go outside and try a round or two?"

A man his size would move like a pudding, and Stalwart was lightning on wheels. But a rapier was not the best weapon against a quarterstaff, and he lacked the muscle to swing a broadsword. Ironhall warned against quarterstaffs. They were peasants' weapons, not romantic, not impressive. But out-of-doors or wherever there was space, an agile man with a six-foot ash pole was a dangerous opponent, even for a Blade.

"I think it'd be a standoff. I'd stay out of your reach, but you'd be out of mine." Flesh wound versus cracked head.

"And if I had Norton to help? Him and another ten, say?"

Stalwart laughed, feeling one of his clouds lift. "Your men are trained in quarterstaff?"

The dark eyes glinted sardonically. "Every one, sonny. And no one notices a pole or two stacked around a stable yard. You point out your killer to us and he'll have a broken shoulder before he knows what's happening. And a broken leg if he tries to run."

"Well, that helps! Helps lots! Thank you. But that's another problem. When I see him, how *do* I sound the alarm? How do I bring your men running without alerting him too? If he grabs a hostage—"

Sherwin tossed something. It was a clumsy throw, perhaps deliberately, but Stalwart's hand flashed out and snatched it from the air—a roughly carved piece of wood, about the length of a finger.

"A whistle?" He put it to his lips and blew, but nothing happened.

A noise in the yard caught his attention, but it was not late arrivals riding, just barking dogs upsetting a couple of horses, which were giving their grooms trouble. He turned back to Sherwin and saw teeth grinning in the black jungle.

"You did that, Pimple! Yes, it looks like a whistle. I made that when I was a lot younger than you are. Every boy whittles a whistle or two when he's naught better to do. Well, most of mine worked right, but that one...I must have gotten a piece of magic wood, or something, because that's a magic whistle. You can't hear it. I can't hear it. But dogs and horses can! You blow that in a yard full o' horses, boy, and they'll all at least twitch their ears. The closest ones'll jump. All the stable dogs'll start barking."

The second cloud had gone. "And the killer won't know what's happening! Thank you, Sheriff!" Suddenly Stalwart's quest looked possible again. "Thank you *very* much!"

"I want that whistle back, mind! Any more problems?"

"No, I don't think so. You give your men their orders, please? Introduce me as the witness who knows what he looks like, that's all, and I'll describe him."

The fat man regarded him curiously for a moment, chinking coins in his hand. "He knows you, too?"

"Yes, but he won't be looking for me the way I'll be looking for him."

Again the dark eyes measured. "Where're you going to be? How're you going to make sure you see this villain of yours before he sees you?"

Stalwart swallowed more pride—all of it, every last bit. "You just hired a new yard boy, Master Sherwin."

"Go on, son," the fat man said softly.

Wart explained the conclusion he had so reluctantly reached. "I could be a groom. I know horses. Horses like me. But if a boy keeps walking a horse around all the time, people may notice. No one sees the boys with the barrows or wonders what they're doing."

"You're a *Blade*, you say? You bring warrants from the Lord *Chancellor*? And you're going to shovel *dung* in my stable yard?"

Stalwart nodded miserably. "I shoveled plenty at Ironhall."

"And here I thought you were a gentleman!"

"I have friends to avenge, Sheriff. This is the only way I can be sure of getting near him to mark him for you and your men. And he may not be too dangerous by then. When I blow this magic whistle of yours, I want you to arrest the man who's just had a shovelful of the stuff slammed right in his face!"

"*Flames and death!*" Sherwin uttered a bellow of laughter that should have startled every horse in the county. "Good for you! I see the Chancellor did know what he was about. Me and the boys'll be happy to help you, Sir Stalwart." He leaned across the table, extending a hand as big as a cat. "Sorry if I gave offense, sir. Like to judge a man by his melting point. I didn't find yours."

"You came close, Sheriff."

Not really. Stalwart's stint as the Brat in Ironhall had lasted six whole, horrible weeks. Nothing thickened a man's skin like that did.

12

At the End of the Day (2)

THE BRAT ALWAYS ATE IN THE KITCHEN WITH
the servants—so Intrepid had told Emerald in an unusual
fit of accuracy. That was while he had been showing her the
dining hall, with its famous sky of swords. Five thousand of
them dangled overhead, point down, flickering reflections
of the candles, ever softly tinkling. Each was the weapon of
a former Blade.

"Sometimes the chains *break*—" In tones of horror,
Intrepid had described the resulting carnage. He had not
been lying, just deceived by lies others had fed him. Wart
had told her about the swords weeks ago, so she was not
worried about them. She was worried about the King's
safety, because she could not give Ironhall a clean bill of
health. Intrepid had shown her as much of it as the Brat
would ever need to know, but not enough to satisfy Lord
Roland's spy. She had questions needing answers.

She was worried about her insight into Silvercloak's
identity. Her suspicions might be wrong, but somehow she
must inform Lord Roland of them as soon as possible.

She was also worried about Servian. Servian was
the worst of all possible enemies, Intrepid had told her—
truthfully. Grand Master favored him because he was a

good swordsman. When the previous Prime had publicly told Grand Master to dump Servian, Grand Master had expelled Prime instead. That had been Candidate Badger, of course, and Emerald knew things about Badger she was sworn never to reveal. She could certainly use him at her side right then to defend her against Servian and his cronies.

Common sense insisted she go straight to Grand Master and admit that he had been right and she could not carry off this imposture. What could it achieve? If Silvercloak really was a woman, Ironhall was absolutely the last place she would attempt to strike at the King. Alas, people as stubborn as Emerald did not always listen to common sense.

The evening meal was about to start. She lurked in the kitchen doorway, watching the entrance to the hall. The cooks were all men, mostly old. As long as she stayed out of their way, they did not seem to mind her or even notice her.

Intrepid had gone. Prime Marlon had tracked down the Brat and his guide in the hall and ordered Intrepid to run like a hare, bathe like a trout, and come back in clean clothes even faster.

"You may as well wait here," he had told Emerald. He smiled, but not unkindly. "I suggest you don't bother changing yet."

"No, sir." Wet clothes were a minor problem at the moment.

"Look at it this way, lad. In five years you'll be a deadly swordsman, probably living at court. If some drunken nobles come along and start taunting you, will you be able to control yourself? Or will you go mad and kill them?"

Was this how they rationalized sadism? "So it's a test?"

"Of course. If you can take it from these squirts, you can take it from anyone. If it goes too far, talk to Second." He did not explain how far was too far.

A bell tolled in the distance. Boys appeared as if by magic, trailing mud in through the front door and across to the hall—eager youngsters running ahead, dignified seniors strolling behind. Finally the knights came parading along the corridor with Grand Master in the lead. The infamous Doctor Skuldigger had enslaved people with loyalty spells, and Lord Roland worried that Silvercloak might do the same. Emerald was close enough to detect such evil, and she could not; nor had she done so earlier among the cooks and stablemen. It seemed the assassin had planted no accomplices in the school yet.

The kitchen staff went by her, pushing big carts. Marlon appeared again, bringing a dampish Intrepid and another senior—a sandy-haired, mild-seeming youth, hard to imagine as deadly with the sword he wore or even as capable of controlling the juniors.

"My name's Mountjoy," he told Emerald. "I'm Second. That means I'm kennel master." He smiled unhappily past her ear. "Unfortunately, hazing's traditional. There's not much I can do about it. Most of it's up to you." Still he did not look her in the eye. "Blades can't be forged from brittle metal, and if you can't stand the life here, then it's best for everyone to find out at once, before we start wasting time on you, right?"

"Oh, yes, sir," Emerald said sweetly. "I'd hate that."

He did not notice the bite in her voice. "Don't worry too much. Most of it's just talk, to frighten you. They don't do half the things they threaten. Try to stay very humble and never lose your temper. That's what they want to happen. Right, Intrepid?"

Intrepid nodded impatiently.

"Time to go," Marlon said. Empty carts were coming out for more.

At the far end of the hall, Grand Master saw the latecomers appear in the doorway. Beaming, he rose and clinked a goblet for silence. "Before we begin eating…" That won a laugh, for the beansprouts were already looking for seconds.

A lectern was wheeled over to him. Everyone rose and stood in silence as he opened the great book of the *Litany of Heroes*. He read out brief accounts of the two Sir Intrepids who had saved their wards. One had survived, one had not.

He closed the book and the audience sat down again in a shuffling of feet and creaking of benches.

As sounds of chewing resumed, Prime escorted the next Intrepid along the aisle, with Second and the new Brat following. They walked solemnly between tables full of leering sopranos, then less-crowded beansprouts' tables, with Servian conspicuous by his size and menacing stare. On they went, past the beardless and the fuzzies and a single table of seniors—only eight of those, not counting Marlon and Mountjoy. Again Emerald was alert for enchantment and found none.

The knights and masters seated on the far side of the high table watched the procession, Grand Master on his throne in the middle. When they arrived he rose again, smiling jovially.

"Who comes?"

"Grand Master, masters, honored knights"—Marlon turned sideways to include the boys in his reply—"and brother candidates in the Loyal and Ancient Order of the King's Blades, I have the honor to present Candidate... Intrepid!" Intrepid bowed to display the "SCUM" on his scalp and his wet half mane.

"Is he worthy, Prime?"

Prime turned full around to face the hall. "Is Intrepid worthy?"

Yes, he was. The hall roared approval. Boys cheered and chanted his name. They thumped tables. So Prime and Second lifted the new boy shoulder high and carried him the length of the hall to instal him with the sopranos, where he belonged. There he was mobbed, hugged, riotously accepted as one of the gang.

Ironhall had been doing this for centuries. If Emerald were the friendless, rejected boy she was pretending to be, he would be promising himself that if Intrepid could do it, he could—that he would earn such approval, too.

So what happened next? Why were Prime and Second running as they came back to take their seats? The hall stilled, waiting. She looked inquiringly at Grand Master, who had sat down to finish his dinner.

He chewed, swallowed, smiled. "You may go, Brat."

As she reached the seniors' table, the first crusts came curving through the air. *Roar!* Then vegetables. Then sausages. Those young demons were accurate! *Boos!* She reeled under the onslaught. There was only one door. Perforce, she began to run through the hail of missiles. Pandemonium became riot.

She made it past the fuzzies, but a beardless stuck out a foot and she pitched headlong. Cheers. Pitchers of water were tipped over her. She scrambled up and ran again. Everyone was on his feet and hurling. She was tripped again. How could a hundred boys make so much noise? She could hardly see through a mask of gravy. Then pewter beakers started coming, and they *hurt*. She doubled over, arms covering her head. A bench slid in front of her and she fell over it, landing heavily on the flagstones. *Big cheer!* The doors had been shut, of course. She wrestled one open in a final blizzard of food and tableware; she made her escape. Behind her, the booing turned to raucous laughter.

The fine new candidate had been accepted and the unspeakable Brat driven out.

Old men waiting outside with fresh supplies shook their heads at the waste of food and the mess they must clean up. One of them handed Emerald a cloth to wipe her face. "You're lucky we didn't feed them bones tonight," he mumbled.

The masters and knights left first, chatting among themselves, then the seniors, and so on down the ranks. The sopranos and beansprouts were last, but they came in a swarm like hornets. They divided into three hunting bands on a plan already agreed. One headed for the dorms, one for the bath house, and the third to search First and Main houses. That pack found the quarry limping along the corridor connecting those two buildings.

"Get him!"

"Fights tonight!"

Emerald turned and held up the brass token of inviolability. "I have to return this to Grand Master."

The only light at that point was a lantern behind them, so she saw them as anonymous dark shapes, but their eyes and teeth gleamed in the shadows.

"We can wait!"

"You cannot escape."

"Your doom is sealed."

None of them was tall enough to be Servian, but she knew now that even the small fry were dangerous—born warriors, faster than slingshots, many of them already felons or brutalized by spirits-knew what sort of ghastly home life. They hadn't even started on her yet, but her shins were bloody, she had wrenched one knee, bruised both elbows, and her back must be all over purple. She was uniformly splattered with garbage, as if she had rolled in a midden.

She was also madder than she had ever been in her life.

She hobbled away, ignoring the mindless mob at her heels, the shuffle of its footsteps, its eager breathing. She climbed stairs and all the treads squeaked as the pack followed. She turned into a dead-end corridor and her pursuers stopped as if facing wall-to-wall snakes.

This area was off-limits except on business. Two of the three doors stayed locked, Intrepid had said, and he did not know where they led, but the third was Grand Master's study.

Emerald marched in without knocking. The room was empty and dark, lit only by the flickers of the fire. Relieved, she leaned back against the door for a moment, struggling to calm her nerves.

Wart had brought her here through the unobtrusive door on the far side. That was how important people came unseen into Ironhall—by the so-called Royal Door in one of the corner towers. The room impressed her no more now than it had then: grim, shabby, and none too clean. One comfortable chair and an oak settle beside the fireplace, a few stools, a document chest, a table. The threadbare rug, the prints on the walls, a few ornaments...nothing matched anything else. Grand Master's taste was as erratic as the rest of him.

She was just lighting the last candle on the mantel when the man himself stomped in from the corridor and slammed that door behind him. He glared at her presumption.

"Well, Sister? Ready to admit defeat?"

"No. My task is far from finished."

He actually had the gall to smile! "Kindly remember in future that the Brat does not come in here without permission. I have no further need of his services this evening." He held out a hand. "The token, please. You may go."

"Don't be ridiculous." She sat down in his favorite chair, garbage and all.

He bristled. "You cannot have it both ways, Sister! Either you dress as a respectable woman and perform your duties openly or you stay in character. If you masquerade as the Brat, you must bear his burdens."

"You'd like that, wouldn't you?" She stared at him curiously. "You said I can't do it, so you will make certain I don't. Well, the Brat is not here. If you will just take a quick look out in the tower, you will see that he is not hiding out there either, so he must have run away across the moor. A pity the snow has melted so he left no tracks. Go and tell your rat pack the bad news."

"You do not give me orders!" he said shrilly.

"No." Her voice was rock steady. She had all night. "Your orders came from the King, remember? I already told Master of Rituals you want to see him. I may need to summon others. Do you really want the hyena cubs sitting on your doorstep all night? They will, you know."

Grand Master flounced around and charged out. She heard him shouting, and then an angry sound like the baying of hounds. When he returned, his face was pale with fury.

"Be warned, Sister! I will report your insolence to His Grace the moment he arrives."

"His Grace may not be arriving." She would humble this arrogant blusterer if it killed her. "My preliminary inspection has revealed some worrisome points. Unless I tender a favorable report the King will not come."

"Nonsense!"

"No. One word from me and the Guard will keep the King away. You know that! And Commander Bandit may billet White Sisters on Ironhall permanently."

Fortunately, knuckles rapped on the corridor door just then.

"Enter!"

Emerald had her back to it and did not see who had come. She heard a sigh.

"Sorry I'm late, Saxon. The wolves are really howling tonight...new Brat to taunt—seems they can't find him—talked to Prime...says Second's keeping an eye on things... What was it—"

Heading for the settle, Master of Rituals came around the chair and saw the missing Brat. He laughed. "By the burgomaster's belly button! That explains it!" Misunderstanding the reason for her presence, he squatted down on his heels and removed his glasses to peer closely at Emerald's battered shins. "This was when you fell over the bench, lad?"

He was a rumpled, vague man of about forty. That afternoon he had been lecturing bean-sprouts on the principles of enchantment. The door had been open, so she and Intrepid had paused to listen. She had been impressed by the way he held the boys' attention on a very dull topic.

He laid a cool hand on her swollen knee and frowned. He replaced his glasses to see Grand Master, who was leering at the situation. "Nothing serious enough for a healing. I can bandage—"

"Present me," she said angrily.

"Of course. Sir Lothaire...Sister Emerald."

"Sister?" Master of Rituals frowned. Then—"*Sister?*" He reared back in horror and fell flat on his back. His glasses flew off. "But tonight...you had to...they made you..."

"She insisted," the older man said sadly. "I warned her, of

course, but she saw it as her duty. Her courage is truly an inspiration."

"Is it really?" she snapped. "Please get up, Sir Lothaire. I am here on His Majesty's service, you understand. I need your assistance."

He scrambled to his feet and kissed the fingers she offered. "My lady, you have only to ask! Admit...a surprise...never dreamed..." His face was scarlet. Gentlemen were not supposed even to *see* a lady's knees.

"Do please sit." She waved him to the settle. "Sir Saxon, show him the Chancellor's letter."

Grand Master pouted and went to the document chest.

While Master of Rituals was reading the letter through for the third time, holding it at the end of his nose, Emerald found herself struggling to stay awake. It had been a very hard day and the fire was hot. Here she was safe. Release of tension was having its effect.

Grand Master, who had been sulking on a stool, suddenly beamed and said, "And what else can we do to assist you in your inquiries, Sister? You have only to ask."

She choked back a yawn while she considered asking him to jump off a high cliff. "I need to send an urgent letter to Lord Roland."

The smile soured into suspicion. "One of the carters could take it to Blackwater and give it to the hostler there. He can find someone to take it on to Holmgarth and put it on the coach."

"Would you be so kind as to send it under your seal? I did not bring my own, naturally."

That was better—he would be able to read it and see that she was not tattling about him. He smiled, sickly sweet. "Or I might possibly persuade one of our penniless knights to take it directly to Holmgarth—even Grandon itself, if you will guarantee the costs. They welcome any chance to visit court again."

"Very kind of you. I also need a safe place to sleep. This

Brat is going to be *exceedingly* good at hiding." Right here in front of his fire might be best of all.

Lothaire dropped the letter in his lap and began fumbling in pockets. "By the seven saving spirits! A remarkable document, eh, Saxon? Who's this Princess Vasar?"

He was accepting the situation much better than his superior had. But he must be clever. When Blades in the Guard were knighted and released from their binding, they might sink into poverty and vanish, or they might rise to great honors, as Sir Durendal had done. Or anything in between. Lothaire had entered the College of Conjury and become a sorcerer.

"No idea," Grand Master said. "Your glasses are on the floor by your foot."

"Oh...thank you...What did you want to see me about?"

"He didn't," Emerald said. "I did. Unless you know of anyone missing from the hall tonight, I am satisfied that no Ironhall resident has been bespelled, at least so far. But I cannot yet certify that the buildings are harmless. You keep conjurements in your laboratory, Sir Lothaire. I sensed them as I went by."

He blinked. "Enchanted bandages for first aid, until we can organize a healing. Nothing more."

"There was more."

"Oh?...nothing of any significance. Maybe the old books I brought from the College...."

He was lying, and that was a shock. Suddenly she was not sleepy.

"You will not mind if I examine them, as my duties require? The royal suite, Grand Master? I need to see in there. Upstairs in King Everard House, in the servants'—"

"The royal suite of course! But private quarters are private." Grand Master had forgotten he was trying to be helpful. "A girl disguised as a boy prying around in men's bedrooms? Think of the potential for scandal!"

"Then the King stays away."

"You cannot wander in those places without attracting

suspicion! The candidates never go into those areas! Especially the Brat."

"Tush, Saxon!" Master of Rituals said soothingly. "A White Sister need not enter a room to know if it contains magic. Right, Sister?"

"As long as the room is not too large and I am only concerned with really dangerous enchantment. I can sense that from outside the door. Tell me about the towers."

"Er, towers? Not much to tell, my lady." He removed his glasses to breathe on them. "The four on the bath house are fakes. The four on First House...all different. This one contains a stairwell, is all, and the turret room above is Saxon's bedroom. Right, Saxon? The Seniors' Tower is similar, but it has only one door. Nothing inside except a stair up to the turret. Nobody sane goes up *there* and I can't imagine anyone sane wanting to. Don't suppose it's been cleaned since my day. It had never been cleaned then.

"Mine...my tower?...The Bursar's office on the ground floor...my lab above it, and the turret's sometimes called the Observatory, for no reason. I keep junk in it. The fourth is called the Queen's Tower. Don't know why. Do you, Saxon?" He was lying again.

Grand Master said, "The ground floor room is Leader's office when the Guard's here. The room above is locked, and so is the turret room above that. They're said...they were the royal quarters before Main House was built."

"What's in there now?" Emerald asked.

Grand Master laughed. "I can't recall ever being in there. When I was elected I explored everywhere I could, but I could find no key to those rooms. The turret room windows are draped or shuttered. I have been meaning to break in, but I have never gotten around to it."

"There's sorcery in there."

Both men looked skeptical.

"Can't imagine how it got there." Lothaire was lying again.

"I sensed it as I went by with Intrepid," she insisted. "It's faint and I think not threatening, but I need to inspect it more closely."

"I shall have the door forced."

"Don't be hasty, Saxon," Lothaire said hastily.

"I have to find somewhere to put this Princess Vasar. Normally I'd put her in the royal suite, but it sounds as if she will be here at the same time as the King."

"Why not organize the sopranos to look for keys? They're turning the place upside down anyway hunting for the Brat.... I may have a bunch of 'em around—keys, I mean. In the lab somewhere? Somewhere." He was lying. She knew he was lying. He must know she knew. Whatever she had expected to find in Ironhall, it was not voluntary treason. "Sister, we cannot expose you to any more of this brutality. Saxon, I wish you'd get rid of that Servian brute...makes my flesh crawl. You need a refuge from the mob, my lady."

"I certainly do."

"How about the Observatory?...wonder if the rain's stopped?"

She needed sleep, but work must come first. "Would the middle of the night be a more private time for me to inspect some of these confidential places?"

"Not without an escort!" Lothaire said firmly. "Ghouls haunt the night hereabouts, especially when there's a new Brat around." He rose. "Come, Sister. Saxon will lend us a lantern, and I will show you some Ironhall secrets."

13

Secret Chamber

IT DID OCCUR TO EMERALD THAT SHE MIGHT BE crazy to go off into the night with a man she knew was lying. Yet Sir Lothaire's lies did not reek as much of death spirits as they would if he were luring her into danger. Whatever he was plotting could not be murder.

He led her out through the corner door to the stair, curving around and upward until it reached two doors. One must lead to Grand Master's bedroom. Her guide reached for the latch on the other.

"It's narrow out here, Sister. Stay close to the wall, please." He stepped out into moorland wind and a spray of mist. She followed, closing the door.

"Dark!" he said cheerfully. "Raining!" Even more unnecessary. "Wait a moment for our eyes...should have thought to borrow a cloak from Saxon for you."

"That's all right. Except I'm going to dribble soup all over your battlements."

He chuckled. "Keep away from the edge. The crenels are too low."

"Crenels?"

"The gaps you shoot through. The high bits you hide behind are called merlons. But even the crenels are supposed to be high enough to provide cover. These merlons are fakes—just pieces of wall. Any real archers out there could see all of you as you walked along the parapet...even your legs."

"And if I take a wrong step I walk right through and fall?"

"That sums it up. Stay inside the merlons."

She followed the sickly twinkle of his lantern. Once they were around the curve of the tower she no longer had its comforting stonework beside her, only lead-plated roof sloping down to ankle level. On her right was stone, slabs of masonry alternating with nothing, two stories of fresh air above the moor. She was glad that the overcast night was dark enough to hide the view.

"I take it the boys never come up here?"

"Never say 'never' in Ironhall." He spoke over his shoulder. "Seniors' Tower has no door out to the parapet, but a few maniacs have signed their names on the outside of it over the years."

Emerald shuddered. Earth people like her were rarely good with heights. If Wart were here, he would be running along the merlons and turning cartwheels.

Lothaire himself was another air type, probably air-chance. He was inquisitive, cheerful, and disorganized. He might still be a very fine swordsman if he didn't lose his glasses. She liked him and was inclined to trust him, in spite of his lies.

Soon she detected sorcery ahead and knew they were approaching the Observatory door. The lantern moved to the right and around the tower. A lock clattered.

Sir Lothaire had spoken truly when he told her he used the Observatory turret room to store junk. It was even more cluttered than the Records Office, with piles of boxes, books, barrels, pots, decaying bags, crumbling scrolls, all stinking to her of sorcery. The enchantments were so confused that she could not hope to identify individual spells. All eight elements were involved and yet death was the least noticeable. There was nothing deadly here.

"What is all this?"

"Hoping you could tell me, Sister. I brought some things from the College when I came...seems every Master of Rituals for centuries must have done the same. You think one day this place will just explode?"

"Or I will. I can't possibly stay here tonight."

"Oh, well...of course not," he mumbled. "You see no threat to His Majesty?"

What she could see mostly was dust. Nothing had been moved in this garbage heap for years. "None."

"Ah! And would you care to inspect my lab also?"

"If you don't mind."

"No, no...glad to be of—" Sir Lothaire disappeared through the floor.

In fact he went down a stair, but so steep and narrow as to be almost a ladder. Following, Emerald found herself in another hodgepodge dump of sorcerous junk, no tidier than the one upstairs and—curiously—almost as dusty. The healing magic racked her with waves of nausea, and she realized that she would never be able to tolerate a major healing.

"Something wrong, Sister?" Sir Lothaire inquired anxiously. He raised his lantern so his face was a gargoyle in the darkness.

"Too much spirituality, is all. I detect nothing that should alarm the Royal Guard."

He sighed, undoubtedly with relief. "Good, good.... see what I came for...around here somewhere..."

A box of keys, she decided. That had been his most resounding lie earlier.

"Ah, got it...have a confession to make, Sister. Prefer... of course—I mean, you must do your duty—if possible... prefer you not mention this to Grand Master...."

"I am here only to defend His Majesty, Sir Lothaire. Unless you are committing treason or a major felony, I shall not—"

"Not *major*. Minor, perhaps...a minor theft, technically. When I came here from the College...brought, um, this...."

It looked like an egg carved out of ice. It bore a powerful aura of motion, of rushing water, turbulent air. She had met that before somewhere…. Yes, on Master Nicely, the inquisitor.

"It's what the Dark Chamber calls a golden key." Even in the uncertain light, Lothaire was visibly blushing as he made this confession. "The College was trying to duplicate the enchantment. This was one of my final attempts…works quite well. Not as well as the originals…"

Emerald laughed as she saw the implication. "But quite adequate for Ironhall's ancient locks? And what does lurk in the Queen's Tower, Sir Lothaire?"

He sighed. "You'd better see for yourself. Can you remember the way from here?"

She flinched. "Can't we go along the parapet?" The wolf pack must have abandoned the hunt by now. Why risk rousing it?

"Not unless you want to try it in the dark. The Queen's Tower is visible from the yard, and I don't like showing lights there."

"You are not coming with me?"

He seemed puzzled by her reluctance. "I'll follow in a few minutes. I have to round up some candles. Here, take my token, just in case." He produced another lantern and lit it for her. "And the lantern…Even if there are people still wandering around, not everyone here is a baby hyena, Sister. Seniors and knights don't stoop to bullying children."

"I turn right. Down some steps. Left, right. Up stairs. Left. Right?"

"Yes. Well done. You go first. I'll follow. If you are unlucky enough to run into the cannibals, I'll chance by and conscript you to move books for me or something. That way they won't guess we're in cahoots." He beamed encouragingly. He enjoyed finding complicated answers to simple questions.

It wasn't far. She couldn't possibly be unlucky enough to run into Servian, could she?

Nevertheless, her mouth was dry as she peeked out the lab door and ascertained that the coast was clear, the corridor dark. Holding her lantern high, she hurried off.

* * * *

She arrived safely at the door she had passed with Intrepid.
It was still locked; the faint odor of magic still lingered. She
waited, looking back at the stairs. And waited, in steadily
rising panic. She had thought the Master of Rituals was
being honest with her, but perhaps in all that elemental
racket she had misjudged him.

Eventually light appeared in the stairwell. It grew brighter.
Only when it reached the top was she certain that Lothaire
was the one carrying it. He beamed cheerfully at her as he
approached, but she turned her face away, not wanting him
to see how relieved she felt. He touched the icy egg to the
keyhole. The lock clicked. They went in and closed the door.

He lit an extravagant number of candles so she could admire.

"These windows overlook the moor, you see...no one
will notice. Wall hangings...silk...artists from Gevily...
candlesticks must be gold—feel the weight of them!—
mother-of-pearl inlay on the spinet..."

The room was small but most gorgeously furnished, even
by palace standards. Its tapestries and carpets were exquisite.
The furniture was long out of style and the mosaic ceiling
even more so, but they were still beautiful and valuable, a
lost treasure.

"This is the salon," he said. "Through that door is the
tower room. That was the lady's dressing room, and her
bedroom was in the turret above. Can't show you those
tonight."

The suite had been shut up and forgotten for ages. The
ever-curious Lothaire had found it with his magic key. But
that was stolen property, so he had never told anyone about
his discovery until now. He welcomed the chance to show it
off and brag as if he owned it.

He had used it as if he owned it. His clutter was
everywhere. The elegant escritoire was littered with scrolls
and the carpet with discarded quills. The sorcery Emerald
had detected came from a pile of boxes, most of which were

still roped for transport. Rather than clean out his official quarters, he had moved his effects in here.

She perched carefully on a chair that looked as delicate as a spiderweb. "How could this have been forgotten?"

"After Main House was added, it wouldn't have been needed. And the key was inside! There's a key that fits the door lying right there in that drawer. All the others must have been lost. I suspect the last ruler to use it was Queen Estrith, a hundred years ago. Main House is older than that, but the gowns hanging upstairs are in the style of her time."

Estrith had been deposed and died in the Bastion. She had never come back for her gowns.

The sorcerer squirmed and added, "There are some papers dating from her reign...." Which he had read, of course.

Emerald grinned at him. "But tomorrow Grand Master's going to break down the door!"

He winced. "How can we stop him?"

"Easy! Do you really have old keys lying around your lab?"

"Sister, I have old *everything* lying around there."

"Then put the key from that drawer in a bunch of others and hand it to Grand Master! I won't tell, promise!"

Master of Rituals nodded sadly, looking around his secret chamber. "After I've tidied up here. I haven't used the tower rooms at all."

"I'll help you move in the morning." She had just condemned herself to several trips along the battlements. "Are there any blankets or covers upstairs?"

"Silk sheets, down-filled quilts!"

"No bats or rats?"

"Sister!" Master of Rituals protested. "We do not have rats in Ironhall! And no bats, unless you mean some of the old knights."

Emerald sighed happily. "So tonight the Brat will sleep in the Queen's bed!"

14

Walk into My Parlor

NIGHT HAD FALLEN ON GREYMERE PALACE. The flunkies and minions had gone. Few candles still burned in the offices of Chancery, and most of those were above the desk of the Chancellor himself. He was already late for an important dinner; Kate would be tapping her toe. He must go—as soon as he finished skimming through the late mail, brought by courier or coach from all parts of the realm.

The big antechamber, which by day was thronged with petitioners, was empty now, lit by a single candle. The figure that walked in front of that tiny flicker moved as softly as a cat, yet Durendal looked up.

"Leader!" He stood, as he always did to honor a fellow Blade. "Come and rest your bones, brother."

Blades guarding their wards could dispense with sleep—Bandit had likely not slept since he was appointed Commander—but they needed rest sometimes. His stride lacked its usual spring, and when he sank gratefully onto the chair beside the big desk, the candlelight showed the dust of the road on his livery.

Their friendship was too deep to need empty greetings.

For a moment they studied each other in silence. Duty and friendship could be awkward partners.

"I got your note," he said, "about Silvercloak being a woman. You believe it?" He had not ridden all the way in from Nocare to ask that.

"No, I don't. But I thought you should be advised. The inquisitors don't believe it either."

The Commander rubbed his dust-reddened eyes. "You asked me to let you know when Fat Man decides to go to Ironhall."

"And you rode two hours to tell me in person?"

No, he had ridden two hours to ask *why*.

Bandit shrugged. "He proposes to fly a hawk in the morning on the Meald Hills, and set off at noon. He will overnight at Bondhill and reach Ironhall before dark on the twenty-seventh, weather and chance permitting. Assuming the bindings proceed normally, he should start back on the twenty-ninth."

"The twenty-seventh will suit me very well."

Pause. "In what way, brother?" Bandit asked softly.

Durendal had chosen him to be his successor as Commander. Although he was an indifferent fencer by Blade standards, Bandit had turned out to be an excellent Leader—adored by his men and capable of handling the King as well as Ambrose could ever be handled. But he was a plodder, not a sprinter. He followed rules, not intuition. Whatever his loyalty to his friend and mentor, he alone was responsible for the King's safety. He would never bend on that.

"I am not trying to do your job for you, brother," Durendal said. "I hope you know me better than to think I would try."

Bandit smiled faintly. "I suspect you may be going to make it harder."

Kate would just have to wait. Durendal leaned back, crossed his ankles. "Easier, I hope. Do you recall when we had that meeting, the day Chef was killed? Young Stalwart—"

"Suggested that Silvercloak might strike at the King in

Ironhall. We all scoffed. You told him, in so many words, that he was a silly kid."

"I wasn't that hard on him, surely!"

"But you shut the meeting down right there!" Bandit raised his bushy eyebrows. "Could it be that you'd gotten what you wanted, Brother Durendal?"

"It could." A good plodder got to the right place in the end. "I admit I am merely playing a hunch, but a good hunch is better than a sword up your nose any day. Remember your Ironhall lessons?—the worst of all errors is underestimating your opponent. If he makes a mistake, of course you take advantage of it, but you never count on him blundering. A swordsman must always expect his opponent to make the best attack available to him. This Silvercloak is notorious for striking where and when he is least expected. He is a master of disguise, so that he has even been suspected of making himself invisible. I tried putting myself in his shoes. I asked myself where I would start. And always I came up with the same answer— Ironhall. When everyone at that meeting scoffed at Stalwart's idea, that merely convinced me that my hunch was worth playing."

"And he's a show-off."

"Well, he's young."

"I mean Silvercloak!" Bandit said. "I've read the Dark Chamber reports. He takes on impossible assignments and accomplishes them in showy ways. The Duke of Doemund, for instance—climbed into his coach and was driven to town with his armed escort all around him. He arrived dead, lying inside with his throat cut. Obviously there was sorcery involved, although no one knows how, but his killer went to a lot of trouble and expense and perhaps risk to do it that way. Silvercloak is a show-off! The King of Chivial's Blades are the world's finest bodyguards, so he'll kill the King right there in Ironhall, the Blades' headquarters...."

"I mean he'll try."

"You're right!" Durendal was intrigued. He had missed that point, perhaps because he was not without showmanship himself, whereas Bandit had none at all. Or were the Commander's Blade instincts sensing danger? To have Bandit believing in the Ironhall theory complicated things considerably. "Well done! I'm glad you didn't mention that at the meeting."

"I hadn't worked it out then. But the next day you 'borrowed' Brother Stalwart. Might I suppose he is now back in Ironhall?"

"You would be wrong. I have four reports from him, if you want to read them." While the boy had not said exactly how he spent his days, the Chancellor kept his letters locked in a box with some fragrant herbs. "Briefly, I have posted him on the western road. Look for him on the way and see if you spot him. I doubt that you will, but he will see you. If Silvercloak heads to Ironhall, good as he is, then my bet would be that he will never arrive. As of this morning he had not been sighted. I am much impressed by our baby Blade, brother. I left the details up to him and he has set his traplines beautifully."

"He is a sharp little dagger."

The Lord Chancellor groaned. "Don't you start that! So you now agree with the nipper that Ironhall is a possible danger site?" *Curses*!

Bandit shrugged. "It takes no genius to guess that the King will go there soon. And it is the *only* place he ever goes where we do not have White Sisters on duty. They can't stand the ambient sorcery."

"That's the ancient belief, but there are White Sisters who do not find Blade binding offensive. My own wife is one of them, I'm happy to say. It so happened that I knew of a certain White Sister who had visited the place briefly, without ill effects. That is why, three days ago, Grand Master admitted a boy who bears a curious resemblance to Sister Emerald."

Bandit jerked upright and made a choking noise. "You're joking! A female *Brat*?"

"I've had two reports from her. She has so far escaped detection."

"That can't last! I shudder to think what the rat pack might—"

"So do I, brother, so do I! But Saxon and Lothaire have protected her so far, and it is only a few more days. Already she certifies that there is no illegal sorcery in Ironhall—no bewitched inhabitants, no magic booby traps. She also says the Seniors' Tower needs dusting, but that's no surprise. Does this ease your burden, Leader?"

Bandit nodded. "Very much. Some of my men are certain to recognize her, but it won't matter then."

"Leave it up to her. If she wants to escape from Brathood, none of us will blame her. If she decides to stay under cover another day or so, then I doubt very much if anyone *will* recognize her."

"Does the King know about this?"

Durendal winced and shook his head. "He will roast me alive." If Kate didn't char him first, tonight, for keeping her waiting.

"Yes, it helps," Bandit said, mulling over the information. "It's one less worry."

Then now was a good time to extract a favor in return. "How many of the Guard will you be taking?"

Bandit frowned suspiciously. "Last time I took them all."

"That must slow you." Durendal knew only too well that a large party could never find enough remounts. Besides, the days were short now, roads bad, and there was no moonlight at the turn of the month. He noted that the Commander had not answered his question. Duty and friendship were on collision course.

"In view of the present tense situation," Bandit said deliberately, "I am tempted to send out a messenger requisitioning every remount in every posting house from Grandon to Blackwater."

"Fire and death, man! You would shut down the Great West Road!"

"Yes."

Collision. They stared at each other, each waiting for the next lunge. If Bandit carried out his threat, Silvercloak would have no means of reaching Ironhall before Ambrose left.

"You will block him or scare him away."

Bandit's eye flashed anger. "Are you suggesting, Your Excellency, that I *allow* this assassin to attack my ward in Ironhall?"

"To make such a suggestion would be treason."

"That is how I see it." Bandit's only concern was the immediate threat to the King; his nature and his binding were in agreement on that. Could he be made to see the wider possibilities? He leaned forward in his chair as if about to rise.

"What I wanted," Durendal admitted, "was to set this trap and then send half the Guard there, escorting a man who looks very much like His Grace."

The Commander smirked. "And Fat Man tore you in half?"

"To shreds." Ambrose had been adamant—to hide behind a double would make him seem a coward. It would demoralize the Guard. Durendal had rarely seen him more furious. "No, I certainly do not suggest you allow the killer to attack him, Leader! Not in Ironhall, not anywhere. But I *would* let the assassin start slithering in under the door. Then drop the portcullis on him. I do believe that this is our only chance to trap him. If you drive him away, he will simply choose another day, another place. Too much caution now merely increases the long-term danger."

Bandit's fault as a fencer was that he was too cautious. Durendal was a gambler. He weighed risks, but he was never averse to taking them when the odds seemed good. His flair had paid off for him many times over the years. Bandit certainly knew that, but could he bring himself to trust his former superior's judgment? Would his binding let him?

"So you have Stalwart watching the road. You have a White Sister in place. I approve of both those moves, my lord. I have always admired your dexterity. But to invite the killer in…" Bandit shivered. "I can't…. Convince me! What else? Have you more tricks up your sleeve?"

"I have you. I have the Royal Guard—maybe fifty or so, about what you usually take? Fifty of the world's best swordsmen alert to the danger? A White Sister to detect sorcery. Flames, brother, that should be enough!"

Bandit shook his head. "Sorry. Ironhall may not be impregnable, but it's not so pregnable that I'm going to leave the welcome mat out."

Durendal sighed. He had counted on Bandit cooperating just because he thought the whole idea ridiculous. Now he took it seriously, he would deliberately frighten the fish away from the net.

The spider had one last string to his web.

"There is also Princess Vasar of Lukirk."

Bandit said, "Who?"

15

Have Barrow, Will Shovel

YARD BOYS WERE THE LOWEST. THEY SLEPT IN the hayloft and ate scraps from the inn dining room, and the stinking clothes on their backs were the only pay they ever saw—rags far too skimpy for this unseasonably cold Tenthmoon. All their lives they had been starved of education and intelligent conversation. They had never strayed outside Holmgarth and never would. Their ambition, if they had one, was to become stablemen one day, earning hunger wages eked out by tips from rich travelers. Yet they had no curiosity about the shiny coaches and splendid horsemen who streamed through their squalid little world.

They found Stalwart frightening because he had a sword and a lute hidden away in the loft and could make music on the lute. He washed his hands every single night and he wrote letters that went off on the morning stage. He seemed more than human.

Like them, he rose from the hay before first light, shoveled and wheeled all day, and slept like a doorstep all night. His only visible difference was that he looked better fed and he wore a whistle on a string around his neck. He also took mental note of every traveler who entered the yard. But it was not until the fifth day of his yard torment that he saw anyone interesting going by, and even then it was not Silvercloak.

His daily reports held less meat than a roast sparrow. He mentioned seeing Lady Pillow's coach returning, with a single passenger. The same day he noticed Sir Mandeville, an Ironhall knight who often carried letters from Grand Master to Leader or the King and so earned a brief stay at court. Two days later he saw Sir Etienne, another Ironhall knight. If Emerald was at Ironhall, as Stalwart suspected, she would be sending in reports, just as he was.

Two days after that, Sir Etienne and Sir Mandeville returned together. They had known Stalwart for years, fenced with him scores of times, but neither recognized the stinking urchin with the barrow who walked past them as they stood waiting for horses. That was comforting...sort of....

They paid their respects to old Sir Tancred and gave him a private letter from Lord Roland. Toward evening, after they had left, the letter was handed to Sheriff Sherwin, who showed it to Stalwart. The part that mattered was very brief:

Pray inform my agent that his Peachyard friend suspects the person we seek may actually be a woman.

Peachyard was Emerald's family home, of course.

"You believe that, Pimple?" the fat man asked uneasily. "Still want us to hit him—or her— with quarterstaffs?"

"He didn't look like a woman to me," Stalwart said, and fortunately could add, "but I did warn you that he might disguise himself as a woman, didn't I?"

"You did."

"So remind your men. Man or woman, if in doubt, hit to hurt. We'll apologize later."

Mandeville and Etienne had also passed on the latest news from court. Grandon, they said, was agog over a mass trial of the sorcerers who had been arrested at Brandford. Testimony from Snake and his helpers was sending gasps of horror through the capital.

Interesting! Stalwart had been in on the Brandford raid. He had not been scheduled to testify, but he knew the trial had not been due to start for several weeks yet. The only person who could have changed that date was Lord Chancellor Roland.

It might mean nothing. Or it might mean that the Old Blades were being kept in the public eye so that Silvercloak would know he need not worry about them just now. One more piece of cheese in the trap.

On the afternoon of the twenty-sixth, a wagon came rumbling in. Stalwart noted first that it held a few wooden crates but could have carried a much greater load. Having been a driver in his time, briefly, he disapproved of such wasteful loading on a long-distance haul. A short haul would not require posting. Then he realized that the man on the bench was Inquisitor Nicely—sinister, squat little snoop. Stalwart had enough respect for inquisitors' powers of observation that he did not risk going close—indeed Nicely was already peering around as if sensing unfriendly eyes on him.

Instead, Stalwart wheeled his barrow over to a corner where Norton was talking with a couple of hands. Or listening to, more likely. Earthworms were chatterboxes compared to Norton.

"The wagon driver," Stalwart said.

Norton reached out a lanky arm. It came back holding a quarterstaff. There were staffs cached all over the yard.

"No, no, he's not the one! I'd like to know which road he takes out of town, though."

Norton shrugged, nodded, replaced the staff, and walked away.

He did speak, an hour or so later. He said, "West."

Stalwart said, "Thanks."

Was Master Nicely heading for Ironhall? Not certainly but probably. It was something to put in tomorrow's report, but not something likely to surprise Lord Roland. It might mean that things were about to happen at last.

16

The Invisible Brat

WHEN EMERALD AWOKE, SHE NEEDED A FEW moments to realize that she was back in Queen Estrith's bed in the turret room and that first light was showing gray beyond the windows. Her breath smoked, and yet the rest of her was cozy. On her first night in Ironhall the bedroom in the Queen's Tower had been squalid lodging—cobwebbed, deep in dust, and its bed not aired for a hundred years. Since then Grand Master had opened the suite and sent the servants in to clean, light fires, and make it worthy of the mysterious Princess Vasar. Knights and masters had been trooping through in small hordes ever since to admire this rediscovered treasure. The Brat had found herself safer lodgings in the royal suite and slept in the King's bed instead.

Last night she had been cut off from that refuge by a hunting pack of sopranos, so she had returned to Queen Estrith's hospitality. Which was a reminder that she had things to do before the carnivores awoke. Although she had found no illegal sorcery, she had a duty to keep looking.

She slithered out from the warm quilts, washed her face hastily in the bucket she had brought with her, and dressed warmly. Then she went out on the battlements to give her wash water to the moor.

Only the kitchen drudges would be awake yet. She was safe—there was light enough for her to see but not enough to make her conspicuous against the sky, no wind, and not enough frost to make the stones slippery.

She still hated heights. As a start, she made herself walk all the way around First House—past the Observatory with its stench of magic, past Grand Master's turret, and the Seniors' Tower. That one had no access to the parapet, but four names and years had been scratched in the stonework: "Despenser 95," "Eagle 119," "Aragon 282," and "Stalwart 365." In three centuries only four boys had found a way up. Or dared it, perhaps.

So she came back to the Queen's Tower and the task she had been putting off. The curtain wall began here, curving gently across to the bath house, with its bizarre battlements and turrets. The turrets showed no windows and had no access to the upper floor. She knew that because the infirmary, laundry, and linen rooms were directly below them and she had explored those thoroughly. Grand Master and Sir Lothaire insisted that the turrets were only dummies, but a conscientious White Sister always looked for herself.

Frightened her nerve would fail completely if she dallied longer, she set her teeth and walked out along the top of the curtain wall. The semi-darkness helped a little, but she must hurry before the light grew any brighter. It would need only one boy glancing out a window in West House and the sopranos would have a much better idea of where the Brat disappeared to at night.

The curtain wall parapet was *much* scarier than the walkway around First House. Instead of a sloping roof on her left, she had only a long drop to the paved quadrangle. On her right the fake merlons gave her a slight sense of security, but the drop on that side was much farther, down into the hollow they called the Quarry. Perhaps the low cliff she had seen from the coach had always been there and the builders had set their pretend castle along the brink for effect. Or perhaps they had quarried right up to the base of the wall. If she fell into the courtyard, she might just possibly escape with broken bones. Anyone falling through a crenel into that rocky pit would have no hope at all.

She stared straight ahead, trailing one hand along each merlon as long as possible, reaching out for the next as she crossed the gap. Her heart wasn't really in her mouth—it just felt that way. If she stopped she would freeze to the spot.

She lived. Knees shaky, head a little giddy, she came to the bath house. There was nowhere else to go. The battlements there were even more fraudulent than those on First House, with the fake merlons set directly against the gutters. There was no walkway behind them and none around the towers, either. She was close enough to the nearest turret to know that it contained no sorcery. Wart might be able to scramble over the roof to the others, but she was not Wart.

Relieved, she turned around and stalked back along the catwalk. Now she could honestly report that she had inspected every corner of Ironhall she had been able to reach.

The residents were divided on the subject of the current Brat, who had achieved something no other Brat had ever come close to. For four days now he had evaded the juniors' rat pack. He had been hassled a few times, but never seriously— never dunked in horse troughs, battered in fistfights, shaved bald, painted green, or made to turn somersaults until he was too giddy to stand. The majority view was the lad deserved credit for quick wits. The contrary opinion—which was held by all the sopranos and many others, including some of the old knights—was that those experiences were salutary and character building and the Brat was a sneaky coward for not submitting to tradition.

This Brat had unique advantages, of course. She carried tokens from both Grand Master and Master of Rituals, so when cornered she could always claim to be on business. More important, she also possessed a magic key. She did not enjoy carrying it around, because it made her feel as if she were in the middle of a tornado, but it would open any of the numerous locked doors in the school. This made vanishing fairly easy.

She did not escape completely. Crossing the courtyard at sunup, heading for the kitchens, Emerald heard the pitter-patter of overlarge feet behind her. A voice cried, "Brat!"

She turned to face five sopranos. As long as none of the older, meaner boys was present, she did not mind indulging them sometimes, especially in public places like this. Even Grand Master's sacred token might lose its power if it were brandished too often.

"Brat, where are you going?"

She knelt and bowed her head. "I was going in search of breakfast, O Most Mighty and Glorious Candidate Chad."

"Very well, then. You have our *pernishon* to proceed."

"Thank you for this kindness, Most Mighty and Glorious Candidate Chad."

She rose, took two steps....

"Brat, where are you going?"

Turn, kneel again. "I was going in search of breakfast, O Fearsome and Terrible Candidate Constant."

"That's *Most Fearsomest*! Ten somersaults for getting my name wrong."

She was quite sure she had not, but she performed the penance anyway. She promised herself that one day there would be retribution for all those bruises along her backbone.

After she had satisfied the Sinister, Uncanny Candidate Lestrange and the Fearful, Dangerous, Ferocious Candidate Travers, it was the turn of her former guide, Intrepid, who was showing pink stubble on the bald half of his scalp. She noted uneasily that some older boys had joined the group and one of them was Servian, sneering nastily over heads.

"I was going in search of breakfast, O Dauntless, Audacious, Presumptuous Candidate Intrepid."

"Then you must go on your hands and knees!" Intrepid said triumphantly. This suggestion was greeted with whoops of approval.

The long expanse of paving between her and Main House was gritty and cold, but it was too late to claim to be on business now. She set off. Her tormentors shouted a few insults at her, but they soon grew bored, as they always did when the Brat failed to fight back.

One said, "Come on! I'm starving!"

A deeper voice cried, "Stop!"

Emerald settled back on her heels hopefully. The newcomer was Prime Candidate Marlon.

"If you set the Brat a penance, Intrepid, then you must stay and make sure he performs it correctly. That goes for all of you who agreed with the punishment."

Groans.

Intrepid shrugged. "Awright! Brat, you can walk."

By the time Emerald was upright, the rat pack was heading for breakfast at full speed—all except Servian, who, tying a shoelace, lingering within earshot.

"Thank you, Prime," Emerald said.

Marlon smiled. "Is it true?"

"Is what true?" she asked warily.

"The story going around is that you're an illegitimate son of the King and that's why Grand Master is shielding you."

"Is he shielding me?"

"Somebody is and it must be him."

"Well, I am definitely not any relation to His Majesty."

"Son of a noble, though?"

She did not think she was anybody's son. "That's not the reason."

"Well, take care," Marlon said softly. "There are some who resent your success. If they can nab you at a good time and place, they may try some catch-up."

They both looked at Servian's retreating back.

Having established that Grand Master had no need of her services that morning, Emerald made herself useful helping Master of Archives decipher some ancient records. Her eyes were better than his and she wrote a fair hand. He was so impressed that he predicted she would be Master of Archives one day, after serving her ten years or so in the Guard. That prophecy seemed no more believable than her royal birth.

Around noon a revolting stench of magic suddenly became

evident in the record office. Emerald dropped her quill
and gabbled an apology as she fled out the door. Tracking
down anything so repulsive was an easy task, although a
highly unpleasant one. She went outside and saw a four-
horse wagon standing below the steps into Main House.
Something horrible had arrived in Ironhall.

The inevitable fencing lessons were under way all over
the yard, although the equally inevitable handful of juniors
had run over to gawk at the team. Grand Master himself
was conferring with the carter, an unmistakable squat, roly-
poly man. Emerald forced herself to walk closer and soon
detected his inquisitors' binding spell under the other magic.
Fish-eyed Master Nicely had come in person.

Would he know her? If he was here on the King's business,
then it would not matter whether he did or not. But why, if
he were, did the crates in his wagon contain something so
loathsome and deadly? A traitor, even an inquisitor traitor,
might give himself away when he discovered a White Sister
inspecting his behavior.

She went to stand at Grand Master's side, shivering
in the odious magic aura. She knew that spell. Once at
Oakendown she had been shown a sample of that sorcery,
or one very similar. Then it had been on a tooth as big as a
man's thumb—a tooth that had been dug out of the jaw of
one of the monsters that had ripped their way into Greymere
Palace on the Night of Dogs.

Grand Master was in a foaming temper. He clutched
a letter in both hands, kneading it as if about to rip it in
half. Emerald could not make out the seal on it, but she
would have bet her grandmother, if she still had one, that
she would recognize it when she did.

"...don't believe me," Nicely said, "then why not open the
noble lord's letter and see for yourself?"

"I resent your insolence and insubordinate attitude."
Grand Master, after all, was a Blade and must share all
Blades' feelings about the Dark Chamber. He swung his
scowl at Emerald like a saber. "Brat, go and tell Master
of Horse that we need four men to move furniture." Then

he noticed the gaping juniors and unleashed a roar that scattered them like chaff in the wind.

The Brat ran to the stable. She had abandoned her original shoes some days ago in favor of a smaller pair, looted from the wardrobe stores. No one had mentioned that her feet had shrunk. She returned in a few minutes with two stablemen and two of the younger kitchen hands. By then Grand Master was fuming in silence on the steps and Nicely had the tailgate down.

"This one and these two, if you would be so kind," he said prissily. "Will you lead the way, please, Sir Saxon?"

He still had not spared Emerald a glance, so she stuck to Grand Master's shadow as he crossed the entrance hall and headed up the great staircase to the royal suite.

"His real name is Nicely," she said quietly. "Senior Inquisitor Nicely. He has murderous sorcery in those boxes."

Her only answer was a scowl. By the time he unlocked the imposing main doors, though, Grand Master had made one of his lightning mood changes. He welcomed the inquisitor with a smarmy smile.

"This is the presence chamber, although His Grace rarely uses it as such." He gestured vaguely at the chair of state, the writing desk, and other furnishings. "That door leads to the robing room and bedchamber."

"And those have barred windows, I understand." Master Nicely prowled around, nodding his polished-ball head approvingly at the balcony and the large windows. "Yes, this will have to be the place. Ah, put it down there on the rug, men...gently, now!"

The four puffing porters were struggling under the first of the inquisitor's crates. It was large enough to hold two dead bodies, and the men's expressions suggested it was also heavy enough. Emerald's suspicions of what it held were enough to make spiders run up her back. And the other two boxes were almost as big.

"Brat! Go and put this in my study." Grand Master thrust the Chancellor's letter at her.

She said, "Yes, Grand Master," and departed. She had a

clear impression that he did not want Inquisitor Nicely to recognize her. She suspected he already had.

Grand Master could certainly have tucked the paper in his jerkin pocket. Emerald could therefore jump to the conclusion—if she chose—that what he really wanted was for her to read the letter.

She so chose.

The seal was not the Chancellor's, as she had expected, but the writing was. The message was very terse.

Honored Grand Master:
You are charged in the King's name that you give all necessary aid to the bearer of this missive, who travels as Master Cabinetmaker Nicely. He brings new furnishings for the royal suite, which need be installed in haste, as Princess Vasar of Lukirk follows betimes.

I have the honor to be, etc.,
Durendal, Knight

17

Contact

THAT DAY THE TRAFFIC IN HOLMGARTH WAS unusually heavy. The sun shone bright but gave no warmth; silver frost lingered in the shadows, and Stalwart's breath steamed as much as his barrow. All morning he trudged, paused to scoop, and then trudged on. Around and around and around. At intervals he wheeled his load over to the farm wagon. Up the ramp, tip, and run down again. All the time he must keep searching faces, studying everyone who came into the yard.

The Royal Guard rode in around noon. Suddenly the posting yard was full of blue uniforms, cat's-eye swords, and familiar laughter. Not all the Guard was there, of course, just an advance party of a dozen, about as many as the staff could handle at one time. Sir Herrick wore the officer's sash. There were senior guardsmen with him—men who had been escorting His Majesty to Ironhall for years, who had given Stalwart scores of fencing lessons there: Brock, Flint, and Fairtrue, one of the heroes of the Night of Dogs…. There was Raven, who had been Prime when Stalwart was the Brat, and youngsters who had been his friends until their binding only months ago: Fury, Charente, Hector….

Stalwart panicked. He turned his barrow and ran for the

stalls as fast as he could zigzag between horses and people and vehicles. He was doing this for his King, and there was no shame in it, and one day soon he would be on duty in the palace with those men, dressed as they were, strutting around. Then, perhaps, this would be an amusing memory. They could all laugh at how they had failed to see the Chancellor's spy serving his King with a shovel, right under their turned-up noses. But, oh!—what if they *didn't* fail to see him? What if he were recognized now? He had foreseen the problem, of course, but the true horror of it had not dawned on him until this moment, and he could not face it. Sweat streamed down his ribs.

He hid in an empty stall, cowering in a corner behind his barrow, until his heart stopped racing, his breath stopped sobbing, his stomach almost stopped churning. But the problem did not stop. Duty did not stop. *Coward! Poltroon!* He was running away, shirking. Silvercloak might be out there right now, this very minute, a wolf hiding among the guard dogs.

He must go back. Shivering and sick with apprehension, Sir Stalwart pushed his stinking barrow out into the yard again and returned to work. He had fought with naked blades against the King's enemies and it had taken less effort than that.

Most of the blue liveries had vanished into the inn. Herrick was chatting with fat Sherwin outside the office. Stalwart pushed his barrow right past them, almost under the Sheriff's beetling belly, and neither man flicked him a glance. After that he felt better. He watched faces, being careful not to make eye contact with Blades. He did not see Silvercloak, and he was almost surprised when Herrick shouted to mount and the Guard sprang into saddles. They trotted away, leading a couple of spare mounts.

Wart could breathe again.

"Nicely done, Pimple." Sherwin grinned through his beard to show he meant no harm.

"You did notice!"

"I did. He didn't. There's more on the way, o' course."

From one trip to the next, the Guard never repeated its procedures exactly. That day the King did not appear, although he was obviously in the neighborhood somewhere. No doubt the spare mounts were for him, for he must always have the freshest, in case of emergency. Later Bandit led in a second party, and Dominic a third. They changed horses and departed, never noticing their brother Blade dueling dunghills with his trusty shovel. Wart began to feel much better. If he could fool the entire Guard, then the joke would be on them.

He hoped his name would not get twisted into something like "Stall-worker."

The rest of the Guard bypassed Holmgarth and went on to the next posting house. To have taken every usable horse would have shut down the highway for other traffic, and they had come close enough. They had taken all the King's stock and all the best of the others.

As the sun touched the rooftops, Stalwart realized that Ambrose must be almost at Starkmoor by now. The immediate crisis was over, but the real game might be about to begin. If Silvercloak intended to ply his foul trade at Ironhall, he must follow close on the King's heels. He must come tonight or tomorrow at the latest.

The yard was chaotic. Coachmen and gentlemen travelers alike were screaming at the inferior quality of the stock being offered, arguing ten times as long as usual, driving the grooms to distraction, demanding to see five times as many choices, inspecting hooves, teeth, hocks in endless detail. They all had long leagues to go and the sun was setting. The inn was full. Tempers blazed. The yard boys were being worked twice as hard as usual, with far less space to do it in. One certain way to earn a beating was to foul a gentleman's cloak in passing.

Stalwart made a necessary trip to the wagon, ran his empty barrow back down the ramp, had a near miss with a horse—

"*Look out, you clumsy churl!*"

He spun around in dismay, knowing the voice. Two more

Blades were just dismounting, having ridden in while his back was turned.

It was Dragon, with Rufus beside him. Both in uniform. There were a hundred reasons why these two might be straggling behind the rest of the guard, and none of them mattered. Rufus had been next ahead of Stalwart in Ironhall, and Dragon next ahead of him. They had been bound the day Stalwart should have been bound. They were long-term friends. They knew him.

For an age they stared at him in disbelief, ignoring the grooms and horses and travelers milling close around. And he could do nothing but stare back, feeling his dung-spattered face burning brighter and brighter red. He needed to melt.

"Death and dirt!" Rufus said. "The lost sheep!"

"Lost rat, you mean. Looks like he sunk to about the right level."

"That's what happens to cowards who run away. Isn't it, *boy*?"

They had been friends, all three of them—once. But those days were gone. Blades could not be friends with a yard boy. They could not even admit to having been so wrong about him. He had run away rather than be Prime. Coward. Disgrace to Ironhall.

"Answer me, boy!" Rufus barked. His black beard bristled.

"You don't..." Don't what? Don't understand? Stalwart *couldn't* explain. He wasn't allowed to, by King's orders, and who would believe him anyway? "Yes, Sir Rufus," he croaked. "I am paying the price of my own weakness."

"You'd have done better to starve on the moor." Rufus was a decent enough man, easygoing or even lazy and a solid but unimaginative fencer. It would never occur to him to ask *why* his former friend had changed so suddenly and done something so shameful.

"You smeared my cloak, boy," Dragon growled. "That should cost some skin off your back. *Kneel when I speak to you!*"

Dragon was as large as Blades ever were. He enjoyed

throwing that weight around. As a soprano, he had always been hard on the Brat, including Wart in his time. But even an Ironhall Brat had more dignity than a coward who had sunk to being a yard boy. Stalwart threw away every last shred of self-respect and fell on his knees.

"Please, my lord, forgive my clumsiness. I swear I did not notice...."

Behind Dragon, the man bending to inspect a horse's feet wore a silver-gray cloak that seemed oddly familiar. He glanced up and his eyes met Stalwart's. Recognition was mutual and instantaneous—killer and carrot boy met again.

"Have him beaten if you want," Rufus said, "but have the hostler do it. We don't have time. And this trash isn't worth it."

"No, let's tell Sherwin to throw him out. I don't want to see this maggot crawling around here every time we have to come through Holmgarth."

"But then you'd have to admit to him that this dunghill was once one of ours, brother."

Neither Stalwart nor Silvercloak had been listening to that conversation. They recovered their respective wits at the same instant. The assassin sprang into the saddle and kicked in his spurs. Wart hauled the whistle out from the neck of his smock and blew as hard as he could.

Then it seemed as if every horse in the yard tried to go straight up in the sky, and several of the closer ones broke loose from their handlers. They bucked or reared. Dogs barked. Men screamed and cursed and backed into other men and horses. Hooves lashed out. Chaos.

"That one!" Wart howled. He grabbed his shovel—it was empty, unfortunately—but by then he'd lost sight of his quarry in the madhouse. "The gray cloak! Stop him!"

Rufus and Dragon were having troubles of their own avoiding flashing hooves, and they wouldn't have dirtied their hands trying to catch Stalwart anyway. He avoided them. Unfortunately, a horse swung into Dragon from behind and pitched him bodily into Stalwart's abandoned barrow. Rufus, trying to escape, slipped in something and sat down squelchily.

By the time Stalwart reached the gate, he knew he was too late. Sherwin was there, with six or seven grooms bearing quarterstaffs. They all looked glum or furious, or both.

"He's gone?" Stalwart asked.

"A whole fiery bunch have gone!" the Sheriff roared. "None of them paid. Four or five run-aways with them. And we have injuries."

Norton made a speech: "Didn't see the man you wanted."

"You sure?" Stalwart shouted. Could the killer be still hiding in the yard?

Norton nodded.

"Your boss going to pay for the injuries?" the Sheriff demanded, menacing as a thundercloud. "Men and horses both?"

"Yes, I'll sign the chit. How many of you saw the men who rode out of here?"

Several had, and they all insisted that no one answering to Silvercloak's description had left the yard.

"Then we've got him! Sheriff, hunt him down!"

Stalwart stood by the gate with a band of hefties while the yard was emptied. Dragon and Rufus may have seen him there, but they rode past without looking, too mad to speak. No new customers were admitted and the inn door was closed.

By the time the hunt finished, the first stars were watching from the wintry sky. Stalwart had long since given up hope. He had failed. Despite his bragging to Lord Roland, when Silvercloak came to Holmgarth, Stalwart had let him escape. Oh, he could find excuses. If he hadn't been on his knees the assassin would never have noticed him. If the yard had not been crowded far beyond its usual capacity...He could find excuses, but he could never use them. He had failed. No argument.

Failed!

He was shivering in his rags when Sherwin returned with his men. "Killed a few rats, is all," he said.

"Thanks, Sheriff. Thanks to all of you. It was my fault, none of yours. From now on, though, you can shovel your own stinking dung."

They chuckled.

"Three cheers for the Pimple!" someone said, and they cheered.

They meant well, so he had to laugh with them, and that hurt worse than anything. Then the posse dispersed to attend to its other duties.

"Sheriff, do you suppose your brother could find some soap and hot water for me? I'll sleep in the hay, but I must head back to Grandon in the morning."

"Grandon?" the fat man said thoughtfully. "Grandon? You saw your killer, didn't you?"

"Yes, but now he's been frightened away he..."

He is still the cleverest man I have ever met.

A man like that would have guessed right away that Stalwart had been posted in Holmgarth to watch for him heading toward Ironhall. With his plot exposed, he must now back off and try again another day, yes? That was what Stalwart had assumed, but suppose Silvercloak guessed that he would guess that way—that they all would? Suppose he just went on as if nothing had happened? Did the unexpected.

Stalwart studied the sly gleam in the Sheriff's eye.

"Or perhaps not."

Sherwin chuckled. "Worth a try?"

"Yes! Quickly! Hot water and soap and the freshest horse you have left. Send a note to Durendal in the morning, will you? Tell him what happened and say I've gone to warn Sir Bandit."

But he could not hope to reach Ironhall before the killer did.

18

Bait in the Trap

AS THE SUN TOUCHED THE WESTERN TORS, THE Guard was sighted on the Blackwater road. A scurry of activity swept through Ironhall, especially through the kitchens, because young swordsmen who had spent all day in the saddle were usually capable of eating their horses. The seniors bolted to their quarters to clean up. Emerald felt a great surge of relief that her ordeal was almost over. She took the news to Grand Master, and found him in his study, poring over account books.

"About time!" he responded sourly. "Wait out there until I need you. The Brat has ritual duties to perform. He summons the seniors who are to be bound, and tomorrow night he will present the candidates with their swords during the binding itself."

"I have no objection to herding seniors for you," she said cheerfully, "but the entire Guard will not get me inside the Forge, not tomorrow nor ever."

Evidently he had not thought of that problem, for he pouted. "When we have no Brat, the most junior soprano takes over. Intrepid? Wasn't that the name he took? Well, we can inform him later."

"You wish me to continue my masquerade?" She had

inspected Queen Estrith's long-abandoned gowns. Their style was so old-fashioned as to seem exotic, but they would be a reasonable fit. Parading into the hall on the King's arm was an amusing fantasy.

Grand Master attempted a smile, which never suited him. "Until I have spoken with His Grace, certainly. I assume he is aware of your presence here."

"And what of the inquisitor's presence? He is still working his foul deeds in the royal suite." She could catch whiffs of black magic even here, in First House.

"Another topic I shall discuss with His Majesty. Go."

She mockingly bobbed him a curtsey, which threw him off balance. "Be so kind, sir, as to inform Commander Bandit as soon as possible that I wish to see him." She turned her back on his outraged glare.

She settled on the bench in the corridor and prepared for a dull wait. The two doors opposite, she now knew, were of no interest, leading to pantries in which were stored dishes used only on the rare occasions when the entire Order assembled in Ironhall.

Commander Bandit came up the stairs and along the passage to her. He was dusty and muddy, but gave her his customary friendly smile. Having glanced around to make sure they were unobserved, he kissed her hand.

"I would not have known, Sister."

"That's not very complimentary, Commander."

He laughed. "I can't win, can I? If I say you are far too beautiful even to be mistaken for a boy, you would still take offense. That's also true, of course. Take your pick of insults."

"Who else knows?"

"No Blades but me. The King hasn't mentioned it. Who knows here?"

"Just Grand Master and Master of Rituals."

He shook his head in disbelief. "You are incredible, Sister! Not even a black eye! I hope the Blades will be less easily fooled—it's our job to be suspicious, you know. The password for tonight is, 'The stars are watching.' The rejoinder is, 'But they keep their secrets.' If you are challenged, that should keep you out of the dungeons."

"There aren't any dungeons!"

"There are stocks out in the courtyard. There are shackles just inside the Royal Door. And there are cellars with big, big locks."

"I'll remember the password!"

"And you give the school a clean bill of magical health?"

"I did until Nicely arrived!" she said angrily. "You do know that he's put some disgusting sorcery in the royal suite?"

"Yes. I just hope it stays there." Frowning, Bandit reached for the door handle.

"Did the Princess come?" she asked quickly.

He paused on the threshold and scrunched down his bushy brows in perplexity. "Princess Dierda? No. The King's marriage has been postponed until next spring."

"I mean Princess Vasar of Lukirk."

"Who?" Then he smiled. "She's already here."

Traditionally the King went to Grand Master by way of the Royal Door and they decided who was to be bound. The study was soundproof, so Emerald did not hear what was said.

Master Nicely came rolling along the corridor, escorted by Sir Raven and another Blade whose name she did not know. Raven remained outside and the other two went in. Briefly she heard the King booming away.

She expected Raven to join her on the bench, but he had been in the saddle all day and remained standing in front of the door. He did not glance twice at the Brat, although he had danced a gavotte with Sister Emerald less than two weeks ago.

Time passed.

Grand Master poked his head out, causing Raven to sidestep quickly. "Brat, inform Prime Candidate Marlon that I want to see him and the next five most-senior candidates in the flea room right away. Got that?"

"Total of six, sir. Yes, sir."

She collected a following even before leaving First House. It increased rapidly as she crossed the yard—lessons were over for the day but feeding time must wait upon the King's pleasure, no matter how loud the rumble of young bellies. Voices called out to her, demanding, "How many?" but she did not answer and no threats followed. This was tradition. The stars were indeed watching, as the password said, taking up their stations in the sea-dark sky. The night was already cold.

When she arrived at *Lion*, it seemed that half the school was at her back. She rapped. Mountjoy threw the door open, pulled her inside, and slammed it. Ten worried young men had been sitting around on beds. They stood as if frozen in the act of leaping to their feet.

"How many?" Marlon demanded.

"Including your honored self, Prime—six."

Marlon nodded. Four other faces broke into grins of worried relief. Five fell. Grand Master always sent for those who were to be bound plus the one who would become Prime, which in this case was Standish.

Emerald followed them as they marched off along the corridor, past the whispers and curious eyes, downstairs, across the yard to First House. Only she knew that one man was missing. The current Prime leading this parade ought to be Wart. Under the charter, he should be the next man bound. The King was not playing by the rules.

Yes, Wart had been enrolled in the Guard, but he could not go armed into the King's presence. He would never be a proper Blade until he had been bound. She wondered where he was and what he could be doing that was more important than guarding his ward, right here in Ironhall this night.

19

Lonesome Road

STARS SHONE GOLD ON INDIGO AS STALWART rode out of Holmgarth, following the Great West Road. Although the livery stable was out of fresh mounts, Sherwin had done him proud by loaning him a horse of his own, a chestnut mare named Yikes.

"Call her that 'cos she's a tad skittish," he explained. "A Blade can handle her. She's got stamina like you never saw. *An' I wan' her back!*"

"You shall have her back, Sheriff," Stalwart promised. "You hold the best security I can give." He meant his lute, which he loved almost as much as *Sleight*. "And I shall tell the Chancellor how helpful you have been."

So he shot out of the yard, letting his nervy horse run off her excess energy for the first league or so. He had a long way to go and no moon before dawn. But with a good mount, a dark lantern, his rapier at his side, gold in his pouch, all he needed was fair chance. Those and a lot of endurance would bring him to Ironhall before daybreak.

Failure was still a sour taste in his mouth. He had come so close! He could not even understand what he had done wrong. Silvercloak had ridden out in the stampede, obviously, but why had Norton and the other hands not seen him go?

He had not been disguised when Stalwart saw him—at least he had been wearing the same face as he had in Quirk Row, which was the face the men had been told to look out for. Could even a magical disguise be changed so swiftly?

It was something to think about in the night.

The posting house at Beaslow was dark and closed. Knowing she had done her fair share, Yikes nickered hopefully. She could scent other horses and sweet hay. Normally a Blade would bang on the doors and shutters until he got service, but there was small chance of finding a better mount in Beaslow after the Guard had passed through. Moreover, Stalwart lacked a binding scar. Several times since he joined the Old Blades he had been challenged to justify his cat's-eye sword. Always he had got by with some bluster, sometimes flaunting a flashy document or his White Star. Tonight he had neither of those with him. A hostler hauled out of bed at this hour might well insist on the letter of the law.

"Sorry, Your Highness," he said. "We have a long way to go yet." He rode on by, into the dark and cold. But Yikes could not carry him all the way to Ironhall.

20

Princess Vasar

"BROTHERS, CANDIDATES," GRAND MASTER declaimed. "Before our customary reading from the *Litany*, I have His Grace's permission to make an important announcement."

He had been relegated to a stool, like the other masters. The King occupied the throne, overflowing it, making it look much smaller than usual. Ironhall swarmed with Blades. Some were eating at the seniors' table; others stood guard along the walls. There were even Blades in the kitchen, tasting the royal food and escorting it every step of the way to the table. Master Nicely was nowhere in sight, still tending his own vile business elsewhere.

Emerald stood in the doorway, studying the gathering. A wise Brat ate early and left early, and it was almost time for her to disappear. Hazing was officially frowned on before bindings, because the Brat ought to be left in his right mind for the ritual, but she did not trust the likes of Servian and his henchmen to observe such rules.

"It is not only His Majesty who honors us tonight but also many companions in our Order—as you may have noticed." Grand Master's attempts at humor rarely won smiles, let alone laughter. "They are welcome, but they are dangerous.

If they were not dangerous, Ironhall would not have done its duty by them. In normal times we tolerate a certain amount of illegal activity in the hallways after lights-out. Recently it has been less productive than usual, I understand." That small witicism did raise some sniggers. "However, there must be none of that during our guests' stay. None whatsoever! If you go a-roaming tonight, you will be risking a lot more than a few days' stable duty. Every corridor and stair will be patrolled. The Blades see much better in the dark than you do, but they are authorized to run you through first and question you after...."

Even at the far end of the hall, Emerald could tell that the King was displeased. There had been none of the usual boisterous royal laughter.

"Brat?"

She jumped halfway to the ceiling. She would have sworn any oath that no man in boots could have approached her undetected over the paving stones. She spun around angrily, and found herself nose-to-nose with Sir Fury, who was certainly not the largest of the Blades but might well be the cutest.

He said, "Sorry! Wonderful reflexes! You can be proud of those, boy. Glad you're not armed!"

Ironhall humor, no doubt. Emerald just blushed scarlet, and he fortunately misunderstood. "Leader wants to see you, lad. Come."

She had danced only one gavotte with Raven. But with young Sir Fury she had danced a multitude of gavottes—also minuets, courantes, and quadrilles—on several evenings. Sir Fury had expressed serious interest in Sister Emerald. And here he had failed to recognize her! He would never forgive her when the truth came out.

She walked beside him in silence, knowing that some people recognized voices more readily than faces. As they passed the great stair, she glanced up and saw four Blades guarding the door to the royal suite. Others were patrolling the hallways.

Halfway along the corridor to First House, she realized that Fury was stealing glances at her.

"Do you by any chance have a sister, Brat?"

"No, sir."

"Fury's my name. Cousins, then? There's a girl at court who looks very like you."

"I'm sorry for her."

Fury sighed. "Don't be. She's gorgeous!"

Emerald felt her face warming up again. "Then are you certain she looks like me, Sir Fury?"

"There's a strong resemblance. I'm desperately in love with her, and I think she likes me but can't bring herself to say so. She's very shy, you see."

Emerald probably turned purple about then, but apparently he did not notice. Shy? *She?*

The guardroom was full of Blades—snacking, dicing, talking, or sharpening swords. Some were doing several of those things at the same time. A few were changing their clothes. They took no notice as the Brat was escorted through and ushered into Leader's room, the lowermost chamber of the Queen's Tower. It was circular, of course, sparsely furnished but well cluttered with masculine junk—swords, fencing masks, boots, rope, axes, horse tack, lanterns, and document chests. Commanders came to Ironhall and were gone again in a couple of days, following their king. For centuries, none of them had found time to tidy up.

Bandit had been reading papers under a candelabra. When the door had been safely closed, he stood up and offered her a stool. He looked tired and beset, but he managed his usual smile. "Why are you grinning?"

"Because the last time I parted from Sir Fury, he was extremely eager to kiss me."

The Commander cleared his throat loudly and sat down. "Understandable, but let's not make this any more complicated than we have to. I assume you're not crazy enough to sleep in the sopranos' dorm. Where can I find you tonight if I need you?"

"*Falcon*'s empty just now. I have a key." *Falcon* was an overflow dorm for seniors.

Bandit nodded. "Tell the guards downstairs if you sense anything untoward. Did you hear Grand Master's announcement?"

"Some. I assume it was about Nicely's pets?"

"He was told not to mention them specifically, but we want as few candidates eaten as possible."

"They're the same as the monsters on the Night of Dogs?"

Bandit grimaced. "They're copies. Nicely claims these are more controllable, but I don't put much stock in that. He's going to loose two of them to roam the moor and leave the largest inside the royal suite. That suite is easily recognized, you see—it has the only balcony in the school, it has the royal coat of arms in the windows and over the door at the top of the big stair. Lord Chancellor Roland is most anxious for Silvercloak to drop in and be torn limb from limb."

"By a dog? He killed Demise and Chefney."

"Sister, we worked in *teams* on those brutes! The only man who managed to kill one single-handed was Durendal, and his was one of the smallest. Worry more over how we get out of here if Nicely can't put the horrors back to sleep and nail them up in their crates. Spirits! That thing in the suite is the size of a pony."

"So the King sleeps in the Queen's Tower?"

"State secret." Bandit's smile said she had guessed correctly.

"And Princess Vasar of Lukirk is the dog?"

"It's a code for all three dogs." He rubbed his eyes wearily. "I wish I never let Durendal talk me into this! You know, Sister, if you include the seniors and the knights, we must have close to a hundred able swordsmen in Ironhall tonight, not to mention three monsters. And there's only one man out there in the dark! So why do I feel besieged?"

He was an honest man doing his best, and she felt angry at Lord Roland for adding to his burdens. Yet the situation was not really Roland's doing. At least he had seen the danger and taken precautions.

"Could you have stopped the King coming to Ironhall?"

"Probably. But he would soon have found himself a new Leader."

"Does he know I'm the Brat?"

Bandit shrugged. "Not from me. From Roland maybe. The King knows only what the King admits to knowing, Sister. He's in a monumentally foul temper, but that may just be from finding Nicely here and having to sleep in a strange bed—and the very idea that there could be royal quarters like the Queen's Tower existing unknown in Ironhall all this time did *not* improve his mood! White Sisters and inquisitors are not things he associates with Ironhall. He doesn't want to be bothered with those here. He looks on his Ironhall excursions as recreation. He hates to think his Blades are not capable of protecting him."

"I can't be Brat at the binding."

"No, we'll let you off that. Ambrose is very sensitive to scandal, too. A woman in Ironhall sets his teeth on edge."

"Does Master Nicely know I'm here?"

"Not from me," Bandit said sharply. He might enjoy deceiving the inquisitor or perhaps did not trust him— Blades trusted no one except one another.

"I'll stay the Brat for now," she agreed. "But then you owe me a favor."

"Name it."

"You did tell one man who the Brat really is, didn't you?"

Bandit nodded sheepishly. "Had to warn him when I sent him to fetch you. Didn't want him letting any cats out of bags."

"Give me your solemn promise that you will not tell him you told me you'd told him!"

"Er...I promise."

Oh, did young Fury have something coming to him!

21

The Way into My Parlor

NOT A DOG BARKED IN BLACKWATER. THE hamlet lay like a corpse under the stars, with only a rare bat squeak to show life. Yikes was footsore and far too weary to attempt the climb onto Starkmoor.

Stalwart thundered on the hostler's door with the hilt of his sword. "Longberry!" he yelled. "Osbert Longberry! In the King's name!"

Osbert must sleep soundly. He was not in Sherwin's class for thinking—not the fleetest steed in the meadow, Snake said—but he was painstaking and honest.

"Know you," said a growl from an upper window. "You're Sir Stalwart."

"You have wonderful eyesight!"

"Knew your voice. Gave me a silver groat, you did."

"I did. I'll give you a gold crown tonight."

Osbert cackled but stayed at the window. "In a hurry to catch up with the King, likely? Called me by name, he did. 'Good chance to you, Master Longberry,' he says. Always remembers me, His Majesty does, spirits bless 'im."

So much for Bandit's efforts at security!

"And I ride on his service. But tell me, did another man come this way tonight, after the King and the Blades?"

"Well, old Will up the valley, and farmer—"

"A stranger?"

"Oh, a stranger…darkish fellow, hooked nose? All alone. Very jumpy sort, peering everywhere?"

"That sounds like him," Stalwart said. "How about a horse?" Or dawn would find him frozen to death on this doorstep.

"Nothing left. Need their sleep, horses do. Came a long way."

"*Two* gold crowns?" Bribery might not work on Osbert; he loved horses much more than money.

"Well there's Lumpkin," he said reluctantly.

"What's wrong with Lumpkin?"

"Nothing. Big strong gelding. Just some folks think he's got a hard trot."

"Lumpkin will do fine. He'll keep me awake. *Now, please, Master Longberry!*"

So Yikes found her dry stall, with oats and a good rubdown to come—Osbert would not skimp. He solemnly swore he would keep the mare just for Stalwart, not trade her away. He saddled up Lumpkin, who was indeed a tower of muscle. And a very hard ride.

Stalwart paid the two crowns and set off up the moor trail, feeling as if he were being bounced on a picket fence.

The night was cryptically still, a huge icy silence broken only by the steady clop of his horse's hooves. Stars filled the sky to bursting. It was long after midnight before he saw the black bulk of Ironhall rise against them.

His lantern's feeble glow writhed over the trail ahead. So far as he was aware—which was not very far—the Guard never patrolled outside the walls. He hoped his light would be noticed, because to sneak up on the Royal Guard was an excellent way of becoming very dead. Not that he was far off dead now. Cold and a sense of failure had sunk deep into his bones. All the long hours of clop…clop…clop…Not to mention the pounding from Lumpkin—

Panic! The gelding tossed up his head and screamed a

whinny, then jittered sideways, catching his rider by surprise. It was the first spark of personality he'd shown.

"Easy, fellow, easy! *Lumpkin*! Nothing to be scared of." Stalwart wrestled him under control, although he remained skittish. "What spooked you, lad?" Then an owl soared in silence overhead and he laughed. "Never seen an owl before?"

He had decided to bypass the gate. The Royal Door would be less public. It would certainly be guarded, but the mere fact that he knew enough to go to it should allay some suspicion.

He veered off onto the almost invisible path that led around the back of Main House. Candlelight glowed in the King's windows, with the royal heraldry in them as blazon stains of red and blue. Candidates were never allowed inside the royal suite, but there was a balcony outside the presence chamber. Anywhere a squirrel could go, the younger Stalwart had gone. He had peered in those windows—had even taken a peek in the window of the next room, clinging to the bars with his feet dangling. What a crazy kid he had been!

The lights meant that there were Blades in there, standing watch outside the King's bedroom. In fact they would be sprawled on the floor, playing dice. No matter. Either Bandit or Dreadnought would be in charge. Stalwart could flip a few pebbles up at the door and introduce himself. But then he might break one of the King's windows or waken the big man himself, and His Grace could be very ungraceful when he wanted to be. Better stick to the original plan.

The tower, when he reached it, was dark. He had expected to see light in the windows beside the Royal Door. Surprisingly, there was a glow of candles visible up in Grand Master's study, so either the old sourpuss had not yet gone to bed or the Guard had taken it over.

He groaned as he slid from the saddle. Never had he been more pleased to end a journey. He tied the reins to the rail and patted the gelding's neck. "Well done, big fellow. I'll beg some oats for—"

Again Lumpkin whinnied in alarm, jerking at his tether, stamping feet. "Whoa, there!" Stalwart laughed. "Easy! You're too big to be an owl's supper."

Leaving the lantern to comfort the animal, he hobbled over to the door. There *were* chinks of light showing above and below it, so the windows had been draped. He hammered on the planks and then hopefully tried a tug on the latch string, and felt movement. A gentle push at the door made it creak open a finger width. This seemed suspicious, if not downright hair-raising. Normally this postern was left unlocked for the use of secret visitors, but tonight it should be barred, surely?

"Friend!" he said. "Stalwart of the Royal Guard. I bring an urgent report for Commander Bandit or Sir Dreadnought."

No reply.

Thinking, *Here goes*! he put a foot against the door and pushed. It was stiffer than he expected. He pushed harder and suddenly it flew wide. He stumbled off balance.

He had been so long in the dark that even candles could dazzle him for a moment. A moment was long enough. Hands jerked him forward. He was tripped and slammed facedown on the floor. The door thundered shut behind him, a bolt thudded home.

A sword point pricked his back, right above his heart.

"One twitch and you're dead," Dragon said. An unseen hand slid *Sleight* from her scabbard and took her away.

"I recall a candidate called Stalwart," a deep voice remarked. "Didn't know he'd been bound."

"He wasn't." That was Panther. "He was next behind us three."

Rufus: "Should have been Prime—"

"—but he ran away," Dragon finished.

"*Wha-a-at?*" scoffed the unidentified man. "You're telling me *Prime* ran away? Nonsense! I'd have heard about that."

"He never was Prime." Panther was a decent guy, with more brains than either Dragon or Rufus. "He disappeared before we were bound. He was always lippy, so we thought he must've sassed Grand Master once too often, but the old man swore he hadn't puked him. He just puked himself."

"Di'n't wanna tell anyone this," Dragon muttered. "But we saw him today, Rufe an' me. He was shoveling horse stuffing in the posting yard at Holmgarth. Dressed in rags, stinking, an' filthy an'—"

"Isn't it about time," yelled a voice from the floor, "that somebody asked me for my side of the story? I came here with a very urgent message for Leader, and you are treating me like...like..." Like Silvercloak would be treated. "You may not believe this, *brothers*, but I'm as much a member of the Royal Guard as any one of you." They had better believe it, or he was in trouble!

"That's a genuine cat's-eye sword," said the deep voice. "Lovely rapier. Name of *Sleight*. That familiar?"

Two men grunted, meaning no.

Panther said, "Does sound like what Wart might name a sword. And he'd no use for sabers."

"Well, let him sit up. Remember what Leader said. He may not be who he looks like. At the least sign of trouble, strike."

Moving very gingerly, Stalwart rolled over and sat up. He crossed his legs. He could see two swords pointed at him and guessed that there were two more at his back. The deep voice belonged to Sir Fitzroy, one of the senior guardsmen. He would undoubtedly have been knighted and released by now had it not been for the Monster War. He wore the sash, of course. No one would trust any of those other baboons with responsibility.

Like the Seniors' Tower, this one was a hollow drum, with a spiral staircase winding up the wall, complete with marble bannister. Rusty iron shackles in the walls suggested that horses had once been kept there, or it had been used as a punishment cell. It was off-limits to candidates, but anytime Stalwart had peeked in, it had been empty. It had been empty when he came through with Emerald. Tonight some stools and candles had been added, plus a rug so the watchers could roll dice, the Blades' invariable antidote for boredom.

"You look like I remember," Fitzroy said. "Explain."

"Watch him, brother," Rufus growled. "He's nimbler than a cricket."

"I know. I remember the last time I tried him on rapiers."

Stalwart ignored that. "The day these three and Orvil were accepted for binding, Leader took me aside and offered me a special enlistment into the Guard before I was bound."

"That's nonsense."

"The King—*Fat Man!*—approved it. They needed someone to track down some sorcerers, to help Snake. Which I did. Which I have continued to do. And today I was on a special posting for Durendal. I'd have hoped that old friends might have given me the benefit of a little doubt." He glared up at Rufus. If he had the grace to blush, which he probably did not, his massive black beard hid it.

"It's illegal to wear a sword like that without a binding scar," Fitzroy said. "Show it."

"I told you, my binding was postponed! And if you think Silvercloak could disguise himself to look this much like me, wouldn't he be able to fake a little sword scar?"

"If he thought of it."

"Silver who?" Dragon said.

Fitzroy looked even less trustful now. "That's the man we're watching for, but not many people were told his name."

"Oh, this is ridiculous!" Stalwart said. "Fetch Leader! Or Dreadnought. Or Grand Master! Or Master of Archives! Any of them will vouch for me. Or the King. I've played lute duets with him, burn you!" He should guard his tongue—why not tell them about his White Star and end the conversation completely?

Fitzroy said, "You three knew Stalwart. Is this him?"

Rufus and Dragon made uncertain noises.

Panther said, "Yes. And I never did believe he'd run away. I thought Grand Master was lying."

"We'll take him upstairs. Search him."

"Up!" Rufus said, nudging the prisoner with a toe. "Should tie his hands?"

Fitzroy hesitated. Then—"No. I won't risk binding a brother Blade."

Nevertheless, they made Stalwart remove his cloak. They searched him and took away his scabbard and baldric.

Were he not so tired and discouraged, he would have been spitting fire. As it was, he fumed. "I can understand your having doubts about me, Sir Fitzroy, but these dogs will kneel when they apologize to me. Or I will make them kneel." Dueling was a serious offense in the Guard, but it happened.

Fitzroy, granted, was looking unhappy. "You know we must do our duty. Up you go. Panther, Dragon, stay here. You will not open that door if the King himself orders it, understand?"

The stair was narrow. Fitzroy went first, the prisoner second, and Rufus followed with drawn sword.

It occurred about then to Stalwart that the only other time he had come up these stairs, some two months ago, he had been less than tactful in his encounter with Grand Master. He had done his best to humiliate the old blackguard. He had succeeded very well. Chance, as they said, was a great leveler....

Fitzroy knocked and pushed open the door. Grand Master and Master Inquisitor Nicely were lounging on either side of the dying fire. A chess set on the table revealed how they had spent their evening. The candles had burned down to stumps; the air reeked of tallow, wood smoke, and wine.

"Pardon the intrusion, Grand Master," Fitzroy said. "Sir Rufus, cover that other door. Gentlemen, this person claims to be a companion in the Order, although he admits he has no binding scar. He was carrying this rapier, which certainly looks authentic." He laid *Sleight* on the table. "He says you can vouch for him."

"He does, does he?" Grand Master leaned back in his chair. "He was a candidate here, certainly...Stalwart, I think. That right, boy? 'Stalwart' was what you called yourself?"

The glint of spite in his eyes sent Stalwart's temper flaming skyward.

"*Sir* Stalwart! You know I was admitted without binding!"

"That is forbidden under the charter."

"The King ordered it! You know that! You know I came back here later, bringing a royal warrant, wearing royal honors!"

Grand Master reached for the decanter. "More wine, Master Nicely?"

"He's lying?" Fitzroy demanded.

"It certainly is not a very *believable* story, is it? Improbable, I mean. I suppose an unorthodox enlistment would be possible if His Majesty issued a special edict, but I have never seen such a document. I don't know how the boy got hold of this sword, either." He took up *Sleight* to peer at her hilt and inscription. "It looks genuine enough." Nothing he had said was an actual lie.

"Wait!" Stalwart howled before anyone else could speak. He was almost mad enough to throw himself at the detestable old phony's throat. "Master Inquisitor Nicely! You know me and who I am! You know what I've been doing these last three months!"

The inquisitor's unreal eyes stared at him without expression. "Sir Fitzroy, I have never seen that boy in my life before."

Fitzroy's hand grabbed the scruff of Stalwart's neck. "Thank you, gentlemen. Sorry to have disturbed—"

"What are you going to do with him?" Grand Master inquired with a yawn.

"Shackle him to the wall downstairs. Even if he is a coward and turncoat, we can hardly throw him out on the moor—not tonight. And if he is the assassin we're expecting, he'll do no harm there."

Rufus was at the far side of the room. *Sleight* was back on the table with her hilt toward Stalwart. He stamped hard on Fitzroy's instep, which released the grip on his neck, grabbed up his precious rapier, and spun around. Fitzroy had his sword out already, but he was no match for Stalwart.

Grand Master and Nicely and Rufus all drew and leaped forward and ended in a hopeless tangle with the table. Four or five flickering parries and *Sleight* stabbed into Fitzroy's forearm. He yelped.

"Sorry!" Stalwart shouted, slamming the door. He plunged down the stairs. Panther and Dragon heard the racket and ran to intercept him at the bottom. Sword in hand, Panther swung around the newel post to face the threat charging down, but Stalwart jumped up on the bannister and came racing down that, leaning into the curve. Before Panther could spit him, he leaped off. Dragon had just time to turn toward him and not enough to raise his sword before Stalwart's boots came down on his shoulders. He collapsed with a scream. Stalwart's bounce took him almost to the door; he swung around to fend off Panther's attack. He wished it were Rufus, not the only one of the three who had believed his story.

He had always respected Panther's fencing, but that was before Chef and Demise had made him over. No time for subtlety. Rufus and Fitzroy were hurtling down the stair to help. Panther cried out as *Sleight* ripped his ear.

Stalwart slid the bolt and pulled the door.

"Sorry!" he said again, vanishing out into the dark.

22

Rats, of Various Sorts

EMERALD WAKENED VIOLENTLY, DREAMING SHE was choking, buried alive. She sat up, bewildered and gasping for air. She was in *Falcon*, the dormitory. It was large and dark, smelling stale and chill, unused. A froth of stars shone through the windows opposite, and starlight glimmered spookily on beds arrayed along both walls. A tiny chink of light showed from the dark lantern she had set on the chair beside her bed, left lit in case of emergency.

Sorcery! That was what had disturbed her. Earth elementals...death elementals...close. Very close! Not Silvercloak's personal sorcery but something else—earthy, dark, detestable. There was fire in it, too, which seemed wrong. It was over...there?...no, more that way.... *There!*

It came from those eyes...two tiny eyes peering in a window.... She slapped open the lantern shutter. The room blazed impossibly bright after the dark, and the eyes vanished. They had not been peering in at her. They were inside the dorm. A rat leaped from sill to bed, from bed to floor, and streaked along the room in a skitter of tiny claws. It vanished under the door.

Ugh! Nasty, filthy vermin! But *sorcerous* vermin? The stink of enchantment had gone when it did. Master of

Rituals claimed that there were no rats in Ironhall. Death and earth would certainly be right for rats, but why *fire*? Incendiary rats? Fire included heat, light, vision.... Spying? Could a sorcerer send rats, real or conjured, to spy for him?

Hunt down the King, perhaps?

Emerald threw off the covers and leaped out of bed.

In the few moments it took her to dress, she almost lost her nerve. She would be challenged by armed guards, hair-trigger-ready to strike at imagined assassins. Even when she reached Bandit, would he believe her? Silly, flighty girls see rats and imagine sorcery all the time, of course. This was *not* imaginary! There had been a vile little sorcery right here in the room with her. Her duty was clear.

Ironhall was under attack! No time to waste.

She paused at the door to take stock: warm cloak, lantern, and Sir Lothaire's magic key— which she preferred to carry, when she must carry it, dangling in the toe of a sock. She slipped out the door as quietly as squeaky hinges would allow.

Her feet made little hushing noises on the boards as she hurried along the corridor, then downstairs, lantern light dancing ahead of her, shadows leaping away in panic. Under her breath she kept repeating the password, *The stars are watching*. The hallway was dark, with no signs of Blades. Of course most of the Guard would be staying close to the King, in First House. There would be only a few patrolling the whole complex of West and King Everard houses.

Right or left?

"At last!" A man stepped out of the shadows to her left. She whipped the beam of her lantern around. A scream died as her throat seemed to close up altogether.

It was Servian.

Why? What in the world was he doing here in the middle of the night? Had he been lying in wait, hoping to catch the elusive Brat? Sleeping in corners? How many nights?

"Stay away from me!" she squeaked, backing. "You heard what Grand Master said!"

He smiled, strolling after her, blowing on his hands. In the tricky light he looked enormous, a giant. "But you didn't? We have waited too long to begin your education, Brat. We have many lessons to get through tonight. Take his lantern."

Before she realized that there was someone behind her, arms reached around and snatched the lantern away. She squawked and jumped free. There were two of them— Castelaine and Wilde, of course, Servian's favorite cronies. She was trapped. Where was the Guard?

Servian chuckled and advanced purposefully. "You knocked me down in the mud, Brat. We'll start by explaining the folly of that."

She did not see the blow coming, did not even realize he intended to hit her. Blue and red fire and terrible pain exploded in her left eye. She reeled back in shock, almost fell. She had never guessed how hard a man could punch.

"Fists up, Brat!" Wilde said. "You're in a fight. The first of several. Defend yourself."

"What's he got in his hand?" asked Castelaine, who had the lantern.

Through the thundering pain came the thought that, whatever happened, she must not let these hooligans get their hands on Lothaire's magic key. She cowered away, arms up to defend her head. Servian's second punch slammed into her back, sending her sprawling headlong against a door.

Which was not properly latched. She stumbled through it, and in a flash of inspiration slammed it shut and hit the lock with the magic key. For a moment nothing happened— some of these doors had not been locked in generations. The ancient tumblers clicked.

Servian jiggled the latch and shouted angrily. Fists hammered on the wood.

"What's happening?" Intrepid squealed, sitting up. Other trebles echoed him.

"It's the Brat!" Lestrange shouted.

Ironhall was under attack, and Emerald had locked herself in *Rabbit* with sixteen sopranos.

23

Stalwart Comes in from the Cold

FITZROY AND HIS MEN SLAMMED THE DOOR AND slid the bolt and did not come out to look for the escaped prisoner. Stalwart felt trapped in a nightmare, like a fly in hot soup. Why had Nicely and Grand Master denied him? He had the rest of the night to wonder that, and he was not going to come up with an answer.

So here he was, shut out on a freezing night with no cloak—and no lantern. He found the ancient hitching rail snapped in two and Lumpkin gone. Spooked, pulled loose, and fled? Spooked by what? What had Fitzroy meant about not throwing Stalwart out on the moor *tonight* especially? What haunted the dark besides owls? The lantern was a battered ruin, kicked by the gelding in his struggles. He hoped it had managed to make a getaway and was not lying dead at the bottom of the Quarry by now. Or being eaten somewhere by something.

Tucking his hands under his arms, he retraced his path around to the balcony and the lights of the royal suite. Fitzroy would certainly send a report to Leader about him, but he was not inclined to wait for the results of that. He wanted to be *inside* as soon as possible. Either Bandit or Dreadnought would be on duty in the royal suite. He scrabbled up some rocks and stepped back to aim. Not at the windows themselves, but at the door.

The door was open.

Silence up there. Candles burning bright and ghostly smoke trailing from the chimneys above. Yet the door stood open on a freezing night like this? It had not been open when he went by the last time. All the little hairs on the back of Stalwart's neck started to dance.

There was only one tree on Starkmoor, it was said. Ages ago someone had planted a seed or dropped an apple core under the royal balcony. In that sheltered, sunny nook, it had prospered enough to send up a very spindly sapling. It was still so puny that the Guard had not gotten around to chopping it down, although three years ago it had been strong enough to support Stalwart the Human Squirrel. He had grown faster than it had, but at the moment he had no choice.

With *Sleight* tucked through his belt, he started up. The sapling bent. It creaked pathetically. In the darkness he fumbled, scratched his face, lost his temper, but eventually was able to grab hold of the balcony rail and haul himself over. He felt better then, although he knew that monsters could climb, too.

"Starkmoor!" he said loudly, the rallying cry of the Order. As he stepped in, he went to rap on the door, but his knuckles never reached it. Whether he first noticed the stench or the ugly sucking noises didn't matter. Something was alive in there.

Only just alive. There was blood everywhere. Furniture had been scattered askew and if the candles had been set in candlesticks instead of chandeliers, half Ironhall would be in flames by now. And the smell...He had heard many stories of the Night of Dogs, of how the monsters had climbed the walls, ripped out iron bars with their teeth, and of how they had to be hacked into pieces to kill them. They stank as they died.

The one on the floor was as big as a horse, and it was not

quite dead. It had trashed the room in its death throes. It was still writhing, kicking, making horrible gurgling sounds as it tried to breathe. Something had ripped out its throat.

Something or someone? Silvercloak? Nothing human, certainly. Had the killer somehow set one monster against another?

Stalwart just stared as he struggled to make sense of this. All Ironhall had been dragged into his nightmare. The hellhound could not stand. Its head was bent backward so that the huge hole in its neck seemed like a gaping mouth, yet it sensed it had company and began beating its legs faster, trying to reach him, making little progress but hurling a chair aside. Where was the Guard? Why had no one heard this struggle and come to investigate?

If Silvercloak had sent the monster against the King, then it should have been chopped up by the Blades. If the Blades had set it out as a trap for Silvercloak, then how had he managed to dispose of it so easily? That did seem more likely, though. That would explain why there were inquisitors in Ironhall and no Blades in this room. When Master Nicely had mentioned dogs, Lord Roland had squelched him as fast as he had squelched Stalwart.

Where there was one deadly booby trap, there might be more. The moor now seemed much less dangerous than the royal suite.

Stalwart gagged. "Nice doggy!" he mumbled, and rushed out to the fresh air.

He descended the tree at a cost of two fingernails, a painfully scraped shin, and three branches. Now what? He peered around at the night apprehensively. A rapier would be as useless as wet string against one of those monsters.

The need to inform Bandit that Silvercloak might be on his way had passed. The present need was to save Stalwart from whatever was haunting the moor. If the royal suite had been booby-trapped, anywhere might be booby-trapped, including the gate. He knew a way into Ironhall that no one else did, though. As a soprano, in his Human Squirrel days, he had climbed to the fake battlements and hung a suitable memento up there for everyone to see. Grand Master had given him two weeks' stable duties for that.

At the far side of the Quarry, where the curtain wall met the bath house, there was a narrow gap between the wall and the curve of the corner tower. He had worked his way up that crevice, feet against one side, back against the other. He was older and larger now. He was cold and weary. It was dark, and frost might make the stonework slippery.

But he was very highly motivated.

He stumbled off through the night, waving his rapier before him like a blind man's cane. Every footfall sounded like a drumbeat. He fought a temptation to walk backward, watching for glowing eyes following him. The monsters might just as easily be waiting up ahead anyway.

He must go more carefully now, for there was no path. Ahead lay the Quarry, which was close to impassable even in daylight. He should be safe if he kept very close to the wall, although he would have to fight through thorn bushes and climb over rocks. There were places where the ledge was very narrow.

He spun around, heart pounding. "Who's there?"

Silence.

Imagination? He had thought he had heard something.

He went on again, moving as fast as he could over the rough ground. He ought to be due for some *good* luck soon, surely?

24

The Action Heats Up

FIRE WAS AN EVER-PRESENT DANGER. NO candidates, even seniors, were allowed to have light in their rooms after lights-out, and this rule was strictly applied.

Slavish observance of rules was not what landed one in Ironhall. Out came flint and steel and tinder. Sparks flew, and in moments a dozen candle flames brightened the dorm. Behind the door, Servian had fallen silent. Either a Blade patrol had chanced along, or he was hoping the Brat would jump back into the frying pan again.

Emerald struggled to adjust to both the absurdity of the situation and the sickening throb in her face. The pack converged on her. Some, like Intrepid, were mere boys. Others were taller than she—notably Tremayne, the stumblebum swordsman who shaved. Some of them seemed amazingly unaware of how cold the room was.

"Who did your eye?" Chad inquired.

"Servian. Now listen, all of you. Listen *deep*! I am not the Brat you think. Get dressed, all of you. I need your help. There's—"

"There's no help here!" Jacques shouted, raising a laugh.

"*Quiet!*" she barked. "You get dressed. And you,

Conradin. You're indecent. You want to know why Grand Master has been shielding me?"

"He's not here now!"

"Catch-up time!"

"I'm not a boy. I'm a woman." She gave the stunned silence no chance to erupt in hilarity and disbelief. "Not only that, I am a White Sister. My name is Emerald, and I was sent here by Durendal himself, Lord Roland, because there is sorcery...."

There was sorcery! Again she detected the reek of earth and death. The rat had followed her, or there were more of them around. It was behind her, in the corridor. It hurried by and was gone, but the brief contact made her hesitate and broke her tenuous control over the mob. Voices erupted in raucous and predictable demands that she prove her claim. She had no intention of doing so in the way they suggested.

She shouted them down. She could shout louder than they could because they did not want Blades or anyone else coming to investigate a riot. "Listen and I'll prove it. Constant! Why were you put here, in Ironhall? What did you do?"

He scowled. "Stole a horse."

"That's true. Conradin! Why were you put here?"

"My mom died. No one wanted me."

"You're lying. I'm a White Sister and I can tell when people lie to me. Tremayne?"

"Stepfather," Tremayne growled in a voice very far from soprano. "He hit my mom and I larruped him with a spade."

"Good for you! That's true. Chad?"

True, false, false, true...The trivial party trick caught their attention and won their belief. Even before she had asked all of them, the sorcery was back. "There!" she shouted. "Under that bed! There's a rat!"

Chaos. She was certain that beds would burst into flames as boys with candles went after the rat. The tumult ended with one dead rat and two boys sucking rat bites. They were all convinced now.

"Get dressed! There's sorcery around. Sorcerers are

attacking the King, and I have to report to Commander Bandit."

"But Grand Master said—" Jacques began.

"I'll handle Grand Master. And don't worry about the Blades—I know the password. But that idiot Servian is out there, and I need your protection. I need an escort. Hurry! I must report to Sir Bandit. The King will thank you, I promise you."

Her eye was so swollen that she could barely see out of it, but she could ignore the pain now. By the time she had turned her back to hide her magic key and then managed to unlock the door—for a few horrible moments she thought it was not going to work—her army was ready. She led it out into the corridor.

Servian and his henchmen had disappeared, but another dozen sopranos and beansprouts had emerged to find out what all the noise was about. With much yelling of explanations, the tide rolled along the hallway, gathering strength. Someone began beating the fire gong. Beardless and fuzzies came running down the stair in varying shades of undress.

At the outer door—now that they were not needed— were Blades: Sir Raven, Sir Dorret, and another man she did not know. They stared in disbelief at the approaching riot. Dorret wore the sash.

"The stars are watching!" she told him.

He peered at her face. "What happened to your— *what* did you say?"

"The password, you idiot. You want the rejoinder, too? 'But they keep their secrets.' I am Sister Emerald and I must see Commander Bandit immediately."

"You can't go out there, lad, er, miss, I mean Sister. Fire and death! *What is going on?*"

"Sorcery. Ironhall is under attack. And I must go out there. Have the inquisitor's dogs climbed over the gate? If they have, you must deal with them for me. *Open that door,* guardsman!"

"This Brat shows promise," said an anonymous voice from the mob.

If Master Nicely's dogs had escaped whatever control he was using on them, a messenger trying to cross the courtyard might never arrive. The Blades could not just open the door and let Emerald go alone. With the King's safety invoked, their bindings overruled any lesser duty to guard dormitories, so they all went with her. So did her army, some of them barefoot and half naked. They raced over the frozen paving under the icy stars, and no monsters came ravening out of the dark.

Fists hammered on the doors of First House. A spy hole was opened, password demanded, and given. Deputy Commander Dreadnought himself admitted the visitors and was almost bowled over by the shivering tide that poured in after them.

Fortunately Fury was there in the confusion. He shied like a horse when Emerald came into the light.

"*Who did that to your eye?*"

"Tell you later. Bandit, quickly!"

"This way." He grabbed her arm and pulled her free of the mob. Satisfied that a dead rat was being waved under Dreadnought's nose while at least a dozen voices shouted explanations at him, Emerald ran upstairs with Fury.

There had to be more cloak-and-dagger word passing before they were admitted to the queen's quarters. Then Fury went straight across to the inner door and tapped softly.

The exquisite little salon seemed a very odd place to find half a dozen swordsmen. The reek of their binding spell would have made Emerald's head spin had it not been spinning so hard already. There was other, more sinister sorcery present as well.

The Blades' attitude annoyed her. They clustered around her, glowering suspiciously and fingering sword hilts. She knew only one of them by name, and obviously none of them recognized her. She was not your average White Sister, floating like a swan through the court, simpering at gentlemen's flattery.

"Why, Sir Fairtrue!" she trilled, offering fingers to be kissed. "How delightful to meet you here! Won't you present your friends?"

Her fun was spoiled right away by Bandit, who came striding out from the dressing room with Fury at his heels.

"Rats," she said. "Enchanted rats. They're in West House and they're here, too. Not pure conjurations, because the sopranos killed one, so real rats bespelled somehow. I think they may be spies. They're hunting for the King."

Bandit pulled a face. "I was hoping we'd got our man. Someone triggered our trap in the royal suite. I'm told it sounded like quite a fight. We haven't investigated yet."

"Proceed on the assumption that Silvercloak won." Suddenly she felt very tired. The assassin seemed to be bypassing Ambrose's defenses with terrifying ease.

"Certainly. So he's using *rats* to find His Majesty?"

"They've found him. They're here, very close—several of them, I think. And they may do more than just spy. Rats can climb walls or carry small objects. I'm afraid they could be used to ferry magic around."

Eight Blades exchanged grim glances. Swords were not the best weapon against rats. Slingshots or terriers were what they needed now.

"You think Silvercloak could send a...a poisoned rat against the King without even coming into Ironhall himself?"

"I don't know. Assume the worst."

The Commander squared his shoulders. "I'm going to wake Fat Man. Sir Fairtrue, inform Sir Dreadnought. I want Master Nicely and Master of Rituals here immediately. Sister, I'll need you to sniff out...inspect the turret room. Come with me, please."

He headed back to the dressing room.

"Just a moment." Bandit hurried up the cramped little stair. Sounds of royal snoring overhead suddenly ended.

Emerald waited. The magical stench of rat was stronger in the tower, away from the Blades. She fancied she could even smell real rat, a whiff of sewers, and hear furtive rustling in the shadows. A massive book lay open beside the candelabra and the chair where Bandit had been keeping vigil outside the King's door. To take her mind off the rats, she wandered across and snooped. It was a treatise on common law. Everyone to his own taste.

He came down again. "Give him a minute."

She nodded. How did one fight magical rats? Oakendown had never mentioned such things, but Silvercloak seemed to have a million personal tricks up his sleeve. The Sisters could detect sorcery, but rarely was there any defense against it.

"I have had more bad news," Bandit said grimly. "You want to hear it or wait until we know for sure?"

"Can this night get any worse?"

"A lot worse."

"Tell me."

"Wart. Seems he came to the Royal Door. He was unable to convince my men that he was genuine. They tried to chain him up. He ran off into the moor."

The night could certainly get colder. *Wart!* She shivered convulsively. "But Nicely's dogs...What do you mean, 'unable to convince your men'? He had his cat's-eye sword with him? They know him!"

"Perhaps he wasn't genuine. He was one disarmed prisoner against four Blades, one knight, and an inquisitor, but he wounded two Blades slightly, broke both Sir Dragon's collarbones so he'll need a healing, and then escaped. Doesn't that sound like sorcery?"

"It sounds like Wart."

"Perhaps it does," Bandit admitted with a wan smile. "I'm not sure where he's been these last few days, but he certainly wasn't supposed to come here. I'll investigate properly in the morning. It may have been another Silvercloak trick."

"I hope so!" she said furiously. "It had better be!" *Wart, Wart, driven out on the moor to be hunted down by monsters?*

"Follow, please." Bandit went back up the ladder to the bedchamber.

Queen Estrith, if she had designed the room, had been very fond of frilly lace and silver ribbons. The window drapes, bed curtains, and upholstery all featured faded pink rosebuds. This decor did not suit the awesome presence of King Ambrose, who was sitting on the edge of the bed glaring, still not fully awake and clearly in a mood to chop off heads at random. He wore a woolen nightcap pulled down over his ears and a white linen nightgown that would have made a substantial tent. To prepare for his visitor he had swathed himself in a voluminous velvet cloak of royal blue and stuffed his feet in boat-sized slippers.

"Sister Emerald!" he growled.

Emerald bowed.

"What happened to your eye?"

"Naught of moment, sire. They're here," she told Bandit. "There's sorcery in this room, sire. Black magic. It's carried by rats."

Even Ambrose's harshest critics—he did not lack critics—never accused him of cowardice. The cunning, piggy eyes narrowed a little. Extra chins bulged out behind his fringe of beard. The fat lips pouted. But he did not flinch at this dread news.

"It would seem, Sister Emerald, that we are once again placed in your debt in dramatic circumstances. Pray take thought to what reward we may bestow on you and do not skimp in your request. We shall discuss this later."

He seemed to have no doubt that there would be a later. "Well, Commander? The Lord Chancellor's strategy has successfully drawn the wolf to the fold. What do you propose now?"

Bandit's voice was much harsher than usual. "Sire, I am going to strip this room down to bare walls and put a dozen swords around you until the emergency is passed. By your leave—" He spun around and ran down the stair, shouting.

"Let us begin!" the King said, heaving himself upright. "I

cannot stand this impsy-wimpsy furniture. Open that door, Sister. I intend to enjoy this."

Emerald hastened to obey, and then had to back out to make way for a rosewood commode wrapped in the King's great arms. He went to the battlements and let go. Sounds of demolition came a long moment later. As an antique that piece had been worth a fortune. Fortunately he had dropped it on the moor side, not into the courtyard where it might have brained someone.

"Good riddance!" the big man huffed. "Want to try a chair or two, Sister? I think I'll enjoy the loveseat next. Hideous thing! Should be good for—"

The turret room exploded. Caught on the threshold, Ambrose recoiled from the blast of heat, throwing up his arms to shield his face. Flames and smoke poured out the windows and door, and up into the sky. Emerald was out of the direct line of fire, but the accompanying wave of sorcery was stunning. She screamed and stepped back. She might well have fallen to her death had the King's meaty paw not grabbed her wrist.

He tried to go around the tower toward the Observatory, but flames blasting from the window blocked the walkway.

"I think we shall proceed in this direction," he growled, doing so and towing her behind him. He marched out onto the curtain wall.

She looked back in dismay. The whole tower had become an inferno, sending flames leaping high into the night. Golden light illuminated all of Ironhall and a billowing cloud overhead; even the snowy tors in the distance glowed amber. The Queen's Tower must collapse very shortly and the rest of First House would follow. Without the King's childish decision to trash furniture, both he and Emerald would be mere cinders by now.

Was that true? There was more to that sorcery than just an incendiary spell.

Ambrose had a very complex personality, but the experts at Oakendown were satisfied that his dominant elements were earth and chance. "A human landslide," they called him. Like Emerald, therefore, he must dislike heights, but he showed no signs of nervousness as he plodded purposefully along that narrow catwalk toward the bath house. It was a tight fit—his right elbow brushed the merlons and his left overhung the drop to the courtyard.

They were far enough from the tower now that distance had weakened the maddening scream of magic in her head. "Sire, stop! Your Grace, there is no way out at that end!"

The King halted and turned to scowl at her. He seemed to have taken no damage from the explosion, although she had seen him bathed in flame in the doorway. "You are sure?"

"Yes, sire. The turrets are dummies. There is no walkway behind the merlons." The idea of Ambrose running up and down pitched roofs like a cat was not tenable. It hashed the mind.

"That fire is behaving oddly," he rumbled, staring past her at the inferno. "It is not making as much noise as it should. Why has that turret not collapsed yet?"

"Because the fire is not real. It's illusion!"

"It felt real."

"But it isn't."

"So we walked into a trap? Our opponent maneuvered us into doing exactly what he wanted?"

She did not need to answer. A man strolled casually out through the wall of flames and proceeded along the top of the curtain wall towards them. He carried a sword, flicking it up and down as if to limber his wrist. Firelight glinted on his silvery cloak.

25

Rampage on the Ramparts

"**I**F THAT FIRE IS SORCEROUS," KING AMBROSE muttered, "then the Blades' bindings will resist it. We must play for time until they find a way through. Meanwhile, there is no need for suicidal heroics." Backing into a crenel, he grasped Emerald's arm and effortlessly moved her past him, then emerged between her and the assassin. She did not resist, for he was right—she would do no good being a human shield. Besides, even cats would not try wrestling on this catwalk.

Although she was trying not to look down, she knew that the courtyard was full of spectators, with more spilling out of every doorway. Horrified faces were staring up at the spectacle so brightly lit by the inferno.

"Good evening, King!" the assassin called cheerfully. He was still sauntering slowly toward them, as if he were enjoying himself too much to hurry. "Or morning in exactitude. Chilly for the time of year, I comprehend."

"Commander Bandit warned me you were a show-off." Ambrose was quietly backing away, keeping the distance between them constant and forcing Emerald to retreat toward the bath house.

"The wise physician trumpets his cures and buries his

mistakes in silence. I bury my successes, but not without public demonstration."

"Then you did not arrange this meeting for the purpose of negotiation?"

"Whatever to negotiate?" Silvercloak conveyed surprise, although his face was shadowed and indistinct against the fire.

"Release of your fellow conspirators, perhaps?"

He laughed. His voice was high-pitched for a man, yet Emerald had trouble imagining any woman displaying that sort of uncaring homicidal arrogance. Although he had no accent, he used an odd choice of words, which was typical of persons who had been conjured to speak a foreign tongue.

"After your inquisitors have completed with them? What purpose are they for, then? Likewise, they were unvalued to me anyway. They paid. I kill. I collect."

Something bounced off his cloak. He ignored it. Men and boys in the courtyard were throwing things at him— books, pots, bottles, tools—with no apparent effect except a few yells of pain from below, as the debris bounced back on the crowd. Younger boys were racing back and forth to the buildings, fetching ammunition. Pliers struck a merlon and clattered down on the walkway, joining a candlestick and a hairbrush. Unfortunately Ironhall taught no courses in archery.

"You must survive to collect," the King growled, continuing to ease back. "You really think you can get away from here alive?"

"Oh, yes! Did you ever appraise I could get in?"

"No. I'm very impressed. Shall we talk about a king's ransom? Would you like to be my Grand Inquisitor? A peerage, plus ten times what the Skuldigger gang paid you."

Silvercloak chuckled and shook his head. "I must contemplate my professional reputation. An honest crook stays bought. Kings rarely do."

Ambrose stopped moving and folded his arms. He had reached roughly the middle of the curtain wall and seemingly decided to retreat no farther. "I compliment you on your ethics. You will allow my companion to leave in peace, though?"

"Alas! My condolences to the boy, but he may seek to interfere with my departure."

"But this is no boy—"

"Excuse me," said a voice near Emerald's ankle. "Move the King back a pace or two, will you?"

She did not quite leap to her death in shock, but obviously the stress had driven her insane. That could not really be that familiar face down there peering up at her.

"Of course," she mumbled, and poked a well-upholstered royal loin. "Move back three steps, sire. Right away."

Ambrose did not stop lecturing the assassin on the moral depravity of killing innocent women, but he did resume his deliberate backing up. As soon as he had cleared the crenel, Wart scrambled up on the catwalk, rose to his feet facing Silvercloak, and drew his rapier.

The spectators' cheers echoed off the buildings and from the distant hills. From knights to sopranos, they screamed with joy. He was recognized, and shouts of "Wart! Wart!" spread through the crowd. Perhaps sharp eyes even made out the gleam of the cat's-eye on *Sleight*'s pommel.

They were seeing the King's salvation. Emerald saw a friend about to die. They did not know about Chefney and Demise. Even the great Durendal had admitted he had never fenced like Silvercloak.

Of course he could not swarm up stone walls like a human ant, either. How had Wart managed this miraculous arrival?

"Bless my celebrated eyebrows!" the assassin said. "What have we here? Last week you were a carrot boy. Yesterday you collected animal excretion. And today you're a swordsman. What are you really?"

"I'm a swordsman," Wart said. "But you aren't."

"Back," Ambrose grunted. "Must give him room." He renewed his retreat, driving Emerald behind him.

Wart said quietly, "No. Stay there for now, please."

"I manage in humble fashion." Silvercloak swished his rapier up and down a few times. He was left-handed after all, although Emerald thought he had been carrying the sword in his right hand earlier. Perhaps he was ambidextrous. He resumed his slow approach.

"No." Wart did some swishing of his own. He stepped forward two paces and halted. "You killed Chefney and Demise. They were friends of mine, so I dedicate your death to their memory." He raised his sword in a brief salute and went back to guard. "That made us all think of you as a swordsman, but we were wrong. You're not. You are only a sorcerer."

"Only? I never saw a sorcerer kneel in the dung of a stable yard."

"Nor yet a Blade. It was a regrettable expedient." Pompous talk was not Wart's style, so what was he up to? Was he playing Ambrose's game, dragging it out until the Blades could come? Even if the duel was a foregone conclusion, he could reasonably hope to delay Silvercloak a few seconds. That might be long enough to save his King if the Guard was on its way. The illusory fire in the tower was faltering, shooting green and even purple flames at times. It had stopped making any sound at all.

Silvercloak halted his approach when he was close enough to launch an attack. The barrage of missiles had stopped.

Wart had his left side to the merlons and his sword arm clear. That should be the better position on this parapet, but the advantage canceled out because Silvercloak was left-handed. Being left-handed was itself an advantage, Emerald knew. Right-handed swordsmen found few chances to practice against southpaws, while southpaws could always find right-handers.

"I worked it out on the ride here," Wart said. "It's pretty obvious now. The door in Quirk Row was the first clue, of course. And at Holmgarth I had a score of men in that yard looking for you. I had described you exactly. I gave them the signal that you were there, and some of them were watching the gate. Yet you rode right past them."

For the first time Emerald thought the assassin hesitated,

as if re-appraising his opponent. "I have a very unremarkable face."

"Very. And the dog tonight—that was the clincher. You fence as a southpaw—usually. Tell you what, *messer* Argènteo," Wart said brightly, "why don't you drop that cloak of yours and we'll make an honest fight of this?"

The assassin's laugh sounded a trifle forced. "I think not. If you have gotten that far, young man, then you are smarter than you look, but you also know that your case is hopeless. Why die so young?"

"I won't die. I will avenge my friends. Come on, then, killer! Two hundred thousand ducats await if you can get past me: Stalwart of the Blades. I say you can't."

Silvercloak did not move.

This time it was Wart who laughed. He raised his voice in a shout to the audience below—and certainly no one in the Guard could play to a gallery better than he could, with his minstrel background. "Brothers! There's a horse down in the Quarry. It's in some sort of trance and there may be warding spells on it, but that's how this Blade-killer intends to escape. If you hurry—"

Silvercloak leaped and lunged, a fast appel. Wart parried without riposting. He parried the next stroke, too, not moving his feet. And the next. The swords flickered and clinked with no apparent result. Then stillness. The contestants stood frozen in place, the tips of their rapiers just touching, eyes locked.

No blood had been shed, but the spectators whooped and cheered. The experts clearly thought Wart had shown the better form. The juniors were almost hysterical with excitement.

"That the best you can do, *messer*? That wasn't how you treated Sir Demise and Sir Chefney! The fire behind you is turning a most sickly color. I think the Blades will be here soon."

When the killer made no answer, Wart raised his voice again, never taking his eyes off Silvercloak.

"Your Majesty! If I may presume, sire. There is a cord tied around the merlon behind me. It holds up a rope ladder, which this man expects to be his escape route. If you would be so gracious as to—"

Silvercloak lunged again, his rapier a blur of firelight. Steel rattled against steel.

Someone—it must have been Wart, although it did not sound like him—screamed piercingly. It was certainly Wart who pitched headlong through the crenel and went hurtling down to the jagged rocks of the Quarry, far below.

26

Finale

A S A SKILLED TUMBLER, HE TWISTED AROUND
IN the air. He landed on his feet with hardly more jolt
than from jumping off a stool. By luck or magic, he had
found a tiny patch of turf between two vicious rocky teeth.

He had guessed right.

Someone had to die after that fall. Although it was
not he, the mental shock was considerable. He needed a
minute to catch his breath, and several minutes before his
heart stopped woodpeckering his ribs. It was easy enough
for a rank amateur to spin fancy theories about the way
Silvercloak's sorcery worked when all the experts in the
kingdom were stumped. Gambling his life on such wild
notions had been rank insanity. But it had been necessary,
and it was going to change a lot of things.

The horse was still there, a few rocks over, saddled
and frozen in place, waiting for a rider who now would
never come. Master of Rituals might know how to de-spell
it. Meanwhile, the night was still cold and the light from
the blazing tower was dwindling fast. Stalwart slid *Sleight*
through his belt and began picking his way over to the rope
ladder. He had some scores to settle: Rufus, Grand Master,
Nicely....

As he stepped on the first rung, the fire overhead went out. Good chance and bad chance always evened out in the end, they said. Had that blaze in the tower started a few minutes later than it had, he would have been past the ladder, fighting his way toward the bath house end of the wall. As it was, the first thing he had seen in the sudden glare had been the horse. Guessing why it was there, he had looked for a ladder and found one. As he neared the top, he had heard the King's voice.

And now, again, he heard voices. Torches flared against the sky, silhouetting heads peering over the edge. He did not want people trying to climb down while he was climbing up.

"If you're looking for my body," he yelled, "I'm bringing it as fast as I can."

"How about this one, then?" Dreadnought asked, thrusting another jerkin at him. "I've known ants with fatter waists."

"Lazy creatures, ants. Sit around getting fat." It was not easy for Stalwart to try on livery while Leader himself was toweling his hair for him. They were in the bath house. Fitzroy was kneeling at his feet, cleaning his boots; Fairtrue was polishing *Sleight*. A dozen of the most senior members of the Guard were falling all over themselves in a mad rush to make the hero presentable. They had chosen Hawkney and Charente as the nearest to Stalwart's size, and stripped them.

The King was waiting.

"What—*ouch!*—does Silvercloak really look like?" Stalwart asked as someone combed his hair.

"A bag of broken bones," Bandit said. "He dropped dead at Fat Man's feet when you disappeared. Before that—plump, swarthy, fortyish. Mustache. Nothing like you described."

"Of course not."

"I think that'll have to do until he grows up," Dreadnought said. "Here, Brother Wart, I'll loan you this." He pinned his diamond star on Stalwart's jerkin and then saluted. "Ready to go on duty, guardsman?"

* * * *

It was a dream. It had to be. The King never held court in Ironhall! Yet there he was at the far end of the hall, sitting on the throne in splendor, under the glittering sky of swords. Tables and stools had been removed. A dozen blue-liveried guardsmen flanked him on either side. Everyone else was standing along the walls—knights, masters, more Blades, candidates, servants; and they were all screaming their lungs out as the hero marched in at the head of his honor guard.

Any minute now he was going to wake up.

But he might as well enjoy it while it lasted.

Ambrose was even smiling, although he notoriously resented anyone else being cheered in his presence. He lacked the crown and robes he wore on state occasions, but he did have a few fancy jeweled orders spread about his person. He was imposing enough. He would do.

And now he was rising! Kings never stood to honor anyone except ambassadors. This could *not* be real. Twenty paces...fifteen...ten...

"Guard, halt!" Bandit barked.

Stalwart stopped and drew *Sleight*.

"*What are you doing?*" roared the King. The hall cringed into mousey silence.

"Er...Sire, he is not bound." Even Bandit sounded disconcerted. "Tonight, after—"

"Bound? Bound? Why does he need binding?"

"Um, loyalty, sire...?"

"*Loyalty?*" Ambrose bellowed, even louder. "The man throws himself off a cliff for me and you question his *loyalty*? We allow Lord Roland to come armed into our presence and now we extend that same distinction to Sir Stalwart. Give the man back his sword!"

Still dreaming then, Stalwart made formal approach to the throne: three bows, kiss royal fingers....

"Good!" said the King, sitting down again. "Now, Sir Stalwart, stand here at our side and tell us exactly what you did and how you knew to do it." His little amber eyes regarded Stalwart suspiciously.

The hall hushed, every ear craning to hear.

"It was his cloak, sire. I mean, the dog made it obvious. It had its throat ripped out. And the door in Quirk Row. I pushed it and instead of thumping him it thumped me, only harder. And he looked much like me. To me, I mean. He looked different to everyone...never threatening to anyone, because he was always familiar. He fenced southpaw. And better—I mean his silver cloak *reflected* everything, but stronger." Stalwart was not doing a good job of this explanation. "He was a hopeless fencer. I could have killed him on the first riposte—but that's what Chefney and Demise tried. I'd have died. I had to make *him* attack *me*... Your Grace?"

"And then kill you?"

"Er...yes. And he wouldn't, because he knew what would happen. So I let him drive me off the edge. He didn't mean to, I mean...."

The hall buzzed.

The King frowned. "But he could kill people when he wanted to! Not all his victims died from trying to kill him, surely. So how could you know that his cloak would work for you?"

"I, er...I did sort of gamble on that, Your Majesty. I assumed he could switch the magic off somehow but he wouldn't dare do that when he was fencing with an expert."

"Mm?" said the King, as if he needed to think. "Stand back a moment, Sir Stalwart. When you arrived we were questioning...Sister Emerald?"

The dream grew stranger, for there was Em curtseying in a fantastic ball gown of green silk, all ruffles and pleats, with a long train. The effect was not improved by her magnificent multicolored shiner.

"We were about to inquire, Sister, who was responsible for that eye?"

"It was a misunderstanding, sire."

"*Answer!*"

Emerald jumped, sending ripples along her train. "Candidate Servian, Your Grace."

"Who?" the King said incredulously. He scowled around to locate Grand Master. "Where is this boy?"

Grand Master shuffled forward, looking flustered. "Candidate Servian!" he shouted shrilly at the hall. "A promising fencer with sabers, Your Grace, although I have been keeping an eye on...Servian?"

No response.

"He is sometimes inclined to...*Servian!*"

Silence.

"Candidate Servian is indisposed, sire." Sir Fury advanced a pace and saluted. He had a split lip and a bruise on his cheek.

"Indisposed?" growled the King. "Show me your hands."

With obvious reluctance, Fury displayed two hands swollen and battered as if he had punched his way through the curtain wall. If Candidate Servian had done that damage by beating on them with his face, Stalwart decided, then Candidate Servian must be very indisposed indeed. Which was long overdue. A hint of a cheer rippled through the sopranos and was hastily hushed.

"You indisposed him?"

"A lesson in manners, sire." Fury tried to return the royal glare defiantly, but that was never easy.

His Majesty growled. "On what grounds, guardsman, do you take it upon yourself—"

"Because I asked him to!" Emerald said.

Fury looked surprised and then extremely pleased, in quick succession.

Emerald avoided his eye and blushed. Which was strange, because Stalwart had never thought of her as being shy.

The King said, "Umph!" suspiciously. He waved Fury away. "We shall take this matter under advisement. Meanwhile, we instructed you earlier, Sister, to consider what reward we might bestow on you for your outstanding service. Have you decided?"

"I beg leave to defer to Your Majesty's renowned

generosity. Well, there is one small matter. Last night some of the candidates assisted me. If Your Grace would spare a moment to acknowledge—"

Not willingly. Normally the King ignored candidates lower than the seniors ready to be bound. Only Ironhall's finished product interested him, not the raw material. He shrugged his consent with a poor grace and scowled as the sixteen wide-eyed residents of *Rabbit* shuffled forward and lined up in awed silence to be presented.

"Candidate Tremayne," Emerald said. Tremayne advanced a pace and bowed awkwardly.

"Candidate Conradin..." And so on. "And lastly, sire, Candidate Intrepid."

Intrepid stepped forward. "That means, 'without fear!'" he explained.

"Obviously," the King retorted.

The brief break had allowed him to reach a decision or two, though. "Stalwart?"

"Sire?" Wart came forward.

"We are also curious to know just how you came to be at the bottom of that ladder." Ambrose already had a fair idea, clearly. His piggy little eyes glinted wickedly. "Begin when our Lord Chancellor assigned you another of those special duties you have been performing so admirably these last few months."

Oh, royal favor was heady stuff!

And when the tale was told—

"Strange!" said His Majesty. "You mean that when you arrived at Ironhall Grand Master failed to recognize you?"

Payback time. Looking across to the far side of the throne, Stalwart admired Sir Saxon's appalled expression and the way his face was turning green, like a tree in springtime. He also sensed that the spectators were holding their breath, that everyone was waiting to hear his answer, not least of all the King. Grand Master's fate was in his hands. He wished Snake were there to advise him. He wondered what the entire Loyal and Ancient Order would say if its youngest, most junior member, trashed its Grand Master. That didn't feel like a wise move. He glanced at Emerald. Very slightly, she shook her head, which confirmed what he was thinking.

Sigh!

"Oh, no, sire. He merely declined to confirm my story. That was his duty, since he had never been officially advised of my position. I should not have expected him to do anything else."

All Ironhall released its breath.

"And Inquisitor Nicely?" asked the King, still watching the witness intently.

Saving Grand Master's hide was bad enough. No Blade should be expected to side with an inquisitor! "I confess that his denial surprised me."

"Master Nicely?" the King rumbled.

Nicely came forward and bowed, but his glassy eyes failed to register any satisfying dread. "I was merely following the Commander's instructions, sire. He informed us of Your Grace's wish that Sir Stalwart remain incognito."

Ambrose grunted and peered inquiringly at Stalwart again.

Fortunately, Wart had heard Snake tell many tales of the King's little tricks. He was offering revenge, yes—Stalwart could exterminate Nicely if he wanted—but he was also testing his new favorite's judgment and how far he could be trusted. No one could ever succeed at court without large quantities of tact.

To have an inquisitor by the throat and not squeeze? Was there no justice? *Sigh!*

"I recall hearing Leader tell him that, sire," Stalwart said. "I accept his explanation."

The King nodded, pursing his blubbery lips. "But Sir Fitzroy, Sir Rufus, Sir Panther, and Sir Dragon—those men over there in bandages and slings? They threw you out to be eaten by monsters."

Having forgiven an inquisitor, Wart could do no less for brother Blades. "With respect, not so, sire. They could hardly accept my story after Grand Master and the inquisitor failed to support it. I was the one who decided to leave. I am sorry I hurt them."

The sopranos started a snigger, then the hall erupted in laughter and applause. Even the King smiled approval.

"I hope you will restrain that temper in future, Sir Stalwart. Our Guard is presently shorthanded and cannot afford such casualties every time you take offense."

"I will try my best, sire."

"Grand Master? If we accept his promise to behave, will you write his exploits into the *Litany*?"

"Indeed, I will, Your Grace! It will give me the utmost pleasure."

Stalwart hadn't thought of that. He gaped as the hall cheered him yet again. Few Blades ever made that honor roll, and even fewer of them lived to know it.

Then the King rose, and the hall fell silent. "Remove that star."

"Sire?" Puzzled, Stalwart unpinned Dreadnought's badge, wondering if the King could possibly know one from the other. They all looked the same to him. Then he saw Bandit and Dreadnought frantically gesturing at him....

Hastily Stalwart dropped to his knees.

"We give you this one instead." Ambrose took the eight-pointed order from his cloak. He raised his voice to stir jingling echoes from the sky of swords overhead. "Know all ye here present, that we, Ambrose, King of Chivial and Nostrimia, Prince of Nythia, do hereby raise our trusty and well-beloved Stalwart, member of the Order of the White Star, to the rank of companion in the said—" Renewed cheering drowned out the rest.

The King chuckled. The only person in Ironhall not making a noise was Stalwart himself. He was speechless. *Companion* in the White Star? Like Roland? He was going to be hobnobbing with the Chancellor, royal dukes....

About to pin the badge on Stalwart's chest, Ambrose paused, as if having second thoughts. "You do realize," he muttered, almost inaudible under the tumult, "that this probably makes you the premier commoner in the land? I'll have to ask the heralds, but I do believe you'll even out-rank the Speaker of the House."

"Your Majesty is being very generous," Stalwart said hoarsely.

The piggy little eyes twinkled. "Well, I couldn't be generous if I were dead. There!" And, as Stalwart was about to rise—"One other thing."

"Sire?"

"We promise to stop making jokes about the King's Daggers."

Aftermath

SERVIAN, HAVING BEEN OFFICIALLY EXPELLED, was last seen begging a carter to give him a ride into Torwell, where he could hope to find work in the lead mines.

The assassin's horse recovered from its trance, and when Ambrose left Ironhall a couple of days later, Stalwart rode it down to Blackwater. Lumpkin was there, having found his own way home safely—although he never let anyone ride him on Starkmoor again. Stalwart rode Yikes from Blackwater to Holmgarth, where she was reunited with Sheriff Sherwin.

Wart persuaded Sherwin to show Emerald his magic whistle, but Emerald said she couldn't find any magic on it, which was very strange, because it would still alarm dogs and horses, and yet it made no noise at all.

The hard part of that whole journey back to Grandon was being a royal favorite, expected to remain in close attendance on the King. Stalwart would have much preferred to ride beside Emerald, but most of the Royal Guard had that very same idea. Sir Fury was there first, though, glaring murder at any other man who came close. Since Sister Emerald did not seem to mind, he was allowed to get away with this...for the time being, anyway....

About the Author

Dave Duncan, born in Scotland in 1933, is a Canadian citizen. He received his diploma from Dundee High School and got his college education at the University of Saint Andrews. He moved to Canada in 1955, where he still lives with his wife. He has three grown children and four grandchildren. He spent thirty years as a petroleum geologist. He has had dozens of fantasy and science fiction novels published, among them *A Rose-Red City, Magic Casement,* and *The Reaver Road,* as well as a highly praised historical novel, *Daughter of Troy,* published, for commercial reasons, under the pseudonym Sarah B. Franklin. He also published the Longdirk series of novels, *Demon Sword, Demon Knight,* and *Demon Rider,* under the name Ken Hood.

In the fall of 2007, Duncan's 2006 novel, *Children of Chaos,* published by Tor Books, was nominated for both the Prix Aurora Award and the Endeavour Award. In May 2013, Duncan, a 1989 founding member of SFCanada, was honored by election as a lifetime member by his fellow writers, editors, and academics. His website is www.daveduncan.com.

OPEN ROAD
INTEGRATED MEDIA

Open Road Integrated Media is a digital publisher and multimedia content company. Open Road creates connections between authors and their audiences by marketing its ebooks through a new proprietary online platform, which uses premium video content and social media.

CPSIA information can be obtained
at www.ICGtesting.com
Printed in the USA
BVHW071054040320
574060BV00003B/296